PENGUIN  CLASSIC

FAUST, PART II

JOHANN WOLFGANG VON GOETHE was born in Frankfurt am Main in 1749. He studied in Leipzig, where he showed interest in the occult, and in Strasbourg, where Herder introduced him to Shakespeare's works and to folk poetry. He produced some essays and lyrical verse, and at twenty-four published *Götz von Berlichingen*, a play which brought him national fame and established him in the current *Sturm und Drang* movement. *Werther*, a tragic romance, was an even greater success. Goethe began work on *Faust*, and *Egmont*, another tragedy, before being invited to join the government at Weimar. His interest in the classical world led him to leave suddenly for Italy in 1786, and the *Italian Journey* recounts his travels there. *Iphigenie auf Tauris* and *Torquato Tasso*, classical dramas, were begun at this time. Returning to Weimar, Goethe started the second part of *Faust*, encouraged by Schiller. During this late period he finished the series of *Wilhelm Meister* books and wrote many other works, including *The West-Eastern Divan* and *Elective Affinities*. He also directed the State Theatre and worked on scientific theories in evolutionary botany, anatomy and colour. Goethe was married in 1806. He finished *Faust* before he died in 1832.

DAVID CONSTANTINE was born in 1944 in Salford, Lancashire. He read modern languages at Wadham College, Oxford; he wrote a D.Phil. there on the poetry of Friedrich Hölderlin. From 1969 to 1981 he was Lecturer then Senior Lecturer in German at the University of Durham, and from 1981 to 2000 was Fellow in German at the Queen's College, Oxford. He is now visiting Professor in the School of English, University of Liverpool. From January to May 2004 he was Distinguished Visiting Professor in the Department of German, University of Rutgers, New Jersey. He lives in Oxford, working as a freelance writer and translator. He has published half a dozen volumes of poetry, most recently *Collected Poems*, all with Bloodaxe Books. He is a translator of Hölderlin, Goethe, Kleist and Brecht. He was the literary editor of *Oxford Magazine* and is now joint editor (with Helen Constantine) of *Modern Poetry in Translation*.

A. S. BYATT was born in 1936 and educated in York and at Newnham College, Cambridge, of which she is now an Honorary Fellow. She taught English at University College London from 1972 to 1983. She appears regularly on radio and television, and writes academic articles and literary journalism both in England and abroad. Her fiction includes *The Shadow of the Sun*; *The Game*; *The Virgin in the Garden*; *Still Life*; *Sugar and Other Stories*; *Possession*, winner of the 1990 Booker Prize and the 1990 *Irish Times*/Aer Lingus International Fiction Prize; the novella *Angels and Insects*; *The Matisse Stories*; *The Djinn in the Nightingale's Eye*, a collection of fairy stories; *Babel Tower*; *Elementals: Stories of Fire and Ice*; *The Biographer's Tale*; *A Whistling Woman* and *The Little Black Book of Stories*. Her work has been translated into 28 languages. Her critical work includes *Degrees of Freedom: The Early Novels of Iris Murdoch*, *Unruly Times* (on Wordsworth and Coleridge) and, with the psychoanalyst Ignês Sodré, *Imagining Characters: Six Conversations About Women Writers*. *Passions of the Mind*, a collection of critical essays, appeared in 1991; a new collection, *On Histories and Stories*, appeared in 2000; *Portraits in Fiction*, a study of the relationship between painting and the novel, and (ed.) *Selected Essays, Poems and Other Writings*, by George Eliot, in 2001. She was appointed DBE in 1999.

JOHANN WOLFGANG VON GOETHE

Faust
The Second Part of the Tragedy

Translated with an Introduction and Notes by
DAVID CONSTANTINE
with a Preface by A. S. BYATT

PENGUIN BOOKS

PENGUIN CLASSICS

Published by the Penguin Group
Penguin Books Ltd, 80 Strand, London WC2R ORL, England
Penguin Group (USA) Inc., 375 Hudson Street, New York, New York 10014, USA
Penguin Group (Canada), 90 Eglinton Avenue East, Suite 700, Toronto, Ontario, Canada M4P 2Y3
(a division of Pearson Penguin Canada Inc.)
Penguin Ireland, 25 St Stephen's Green, Dublin 2, Ireland
(a division of Penguin Books Ltd)
Penguin Group (Australia), 250 Camberwell Road, Camberwell, Victoria 3124, Australia
(a division of Pearson Australia Group Pty Ltd)
Penguin Books India Pvt Ltd, 11 Community Centre, Panchsheel Park, New Delhi – 110 017, India
Penguin Group (NZ), 67 Apollo Drive, Rosedale, North Shore 0632, New Zealand
(a division of Pearson New Zealand Ltd)
Penguin Books (South Africa) (Pty) Ltd, 24 Sturdee Avenue, Rosebank, Johannesburg 2196, South Africa

Penguin Books Ltd, Registered Offices: 80 Strand, London WC2R ORL, England

www.penguin.com

First published 1832
This translation first published in Penguin Classics 2009

024

Translation and editorial material copyright © David Constantine, 2005, 2009
Preface copyright © A. S. Byatt, 2005, 2009
All rights reserved

The moral right of the translator has been asserted

Set in 10.25/12.25 pt PostScript Adobe Sabon
Typeset by Rowland Phototypesetting Ltd, Bury St Edmunds, Suffolk
Printed and bound in Great Britain by Clays Ltd, Elcograf S.p.A.

ISBN: 978-0-140-44902-0

www.greenpenguin.co.uk

Contents

Contents

PART ONE

Preface

Faust is one of the magnetic figures in Western culture. We use his fate to plot our thoughts about human nature and destiny, along with Don Juan, Hamlet, Don Quixote, Peer Gynt, Captain Ahab, Wagner's Wotan, Balzac's Vautrin and Ulysses. These are all male figures who are what Marlowe called 'overweeners'. They are clever and passionate, their intellects are restless, they want too much (whatever that is). They resist apparent order – the two 'good' men in the list, Quixote and Hamlet, see more things in heaven and earth than the common man, and are destroyed partly by their own imaginations. Most of the rest make pacts with dubious or evil forces, from Satan to modern capitalism, and are corrupted and destroyed. They ally themselves with tricksters, manipulators and demons. They take on aspects of each other's tales – Faust mixes with Don Juan; Peer Gynt is trickster, entrepreneur and fool; Vautrin is Satan, Faust and Mephistopheles.

Faust and Mephistopheles are also part of a string of paired characters – master and servant, wise man and fool, man and demon – whose dialogue represents (in part) the struggle in one mind between scepticism and idealism, self-seeking and altruism, honour and cynicism. Falstaff is Prince Henry's comic demon, descended from the Vice in the mystery plays. Diderot's amoral Jacques le Fataliste is both a servant and the voice of nihilism. Kafka brilliantly reversed the relationship by writing a parable in which Don Quixote is Sancho Panza's demon, who is deflected from destroying the 'free and responsible' Sancho by a diet of chivalric fantasy, leading to a comic madness which 'harmed nobody'. In literary dialogues between man and devil, from Marlowe to Thomas Mann and Mikhail Bulgakov, the devil has the best lines, and most of the human wit. This goes deeper than the simple dramatization of seductive charms, designed to defraud and betray. Dramatized devils represent human scepticism that moralists and idealists dare not admit. They also represent the terror of death, annihilation and inhuman eternity, which they understand better than their prey. When these two force-fields are combined, there are new possibilities both of horror and bitter comedy. In Adelbert von Chamisso's *An Attempt* (1804), a Faust published after Goethe's *Faust. A Fragment*, the evil spirit induces despair in his Faust with the Kantian idea that we cannot know reality. The Faust story comes from a Christian world in which the Lord forbade the eating of the Tree of Knowledge of Good and Evil, and the Devil takes the souls of those who sin through the intellect or the senses. It is still potent in a world where human beings have become afraid, both of what human ingenuity can achieve, and of the limited ability of human mind and moral orders to control those achievements responsibly.

Goethe's *Faust* came after a vast number of popular and literary Fausts, and in turn gave rise to a whole new literature of poetry and drama.[1] Marlowe's Faust, though written by an atheist, derives its power and terror from the reality of the eternal damnation, which tortures both man and witty demon, against which the drama is played out. The Faust figure goes back to the conjuring magus who really tried to control spirits, and to times when men and women were burned for witchcraft and blasphemy. The religious Faust comes from a world in which Luther saw the devil and threw his inkpot at him. Goethe first met Faust, as a child, in the puppet plays, 'which resounded and hummed within me in many tonal variations'.[2] The puppet plays combine slapstick farce with magical illusions and conjuring in both senses. It is not insignificant that one of the greatest puppeteers, Georg Geisselbrecht, at the beginning of the nineteenth century, finally gave up playing Faust, out of some fear of the conjuration of devils and the opening of the Pit. He feared for his own soul.[3]

Goethe's *Faust* begins by using this Nordic and medieval

Gothic material, with its Germanic background of dusty study, church and university, the essential nature of which, as all critics have observed, is at odds with his own anti-Christian, rational, optimistic world-view. In what becomes *Faust, Part I*, he introduces the tragic story of Gretchen, which is not part of the older versions. He also – at the end of *Part II* – saves Faust, tricking Mephistopheles of the fulfilment of his pact, or wager, through the intervention of some seductive boy cherubs. A saved Faust deprives the original tale of much of its energy and power. *Part II* represents, as Schiller said, a story which 'runs, and must run, into the crass and the shapeless'.[4] In this giddy phantasmagoria Faust and Mephisto make paper money for emperors, attend a classical Walpurgis Night, call up a phantom Helen of Troy, and then bring her back in solid flesh from Hades to bear Faust's child, Euphorion, doomed and Byronic. Faust wins battles and rolls back the sea to make new land. At the age of one hundred, blinded and accompanied by Care, he finally asks the fleeting moment to stay, but is carried away by a heavenly choir. *Part II* represents the other side, not only of Goethe, but of German art and thought – a dialogue with ancient classicism and non-Christian mythologies.

Schiller wrote that 'We can never lose sight of the contradictory double nature of humankind and the failed endeavour to unite the divine and the physical in the human being',[5] and saw the work as a philosophical poem. If anything holds the whole of the two parts of *Faust* together it is the power and *diversity* of the poetry, the range of forms used, from medieval ballad to classical trimeter. That is one paradox. The other is that it is held together by Goethe himself – it is not an autobiography, but is one of those great works of literature into which a writer has been able to combine his ranging preoccupations and understanding as he worked. Karl Eibl's brilliant book on *Faust* has the splendid title *Das Monumentale Ich* – 'The Monumental "I"'. But the work isn't self-regarding or an apologia for the self. It is a man thinking and making images in extraordinary language. It is the work of a thinker interested in government and theatre, astrology and alchemy, geology, morphology, colour forms, charlatanism, sex of all kinds, and the stuff of life, mind and culture. Goethe is amazing. Faust himself, in Goethe's version, is frequently both tedious and curiously non-existent, the puppet of the plot, of the God of the prologue, of Mephistopheles and of Goethe himself.

A. C. Bradley remarked that after Hamlet Shakespeare never again attempted to make an intelligent tragic hero. Hamlet is a thinker who cannot bring himself to act. His utterance of his inner life in his soliloquies is the intense point of his drama, which is so long because it nevertheless does contain action and tragedy. Shakespeare's other tragic heroes are soldiers and men of action, trapped by events and other people and their own weaknesses. Faust's traditional sin is 'curiosity' – the desire for knowledge, including the knowledge of good and evil, Adam's sin. The Faust story is the tale of the damnation of thinking men. It is an irony that Goethe's thinking Faust thinks best at the beginning, when he rewrites the opening of the Gospel of St John – 'In the beginning was the Word', as 'In the beginning was the Deed' (1224, 1237), for this Faust does very little except talk, and the action of the drama (apart from Gretchen's tragedy) is not dramatic. It is diffuse and symbolic. It is a commonplace of dramatic criticism that the Romantic poets wrote bad plays because the kind of things they wanted to say were best conveyed in monologues, or dramatic monologues – the true conflict was between parts of an argument, or a world-view, or a psychic tension. It is, so to speak, theatre in the head. Wordsworth and Coleridge, Tennyson and Browning wrote plays in which people described their feelings, rather than acting and being acted upon. *Faust* is drama in the head in the sense that it appeals most to one reader, staging its scenes and savouring its words inside his or her own head. There have been triumphant stage productions, but it is a daunting project. Nevertheless, it does not resemble British Romantic verse drama, because its author was interested in, and involved with, theatres. He was Director of the Weimar Court Theatre, and the theatrical, earthly Prelude to *Faust* displays a comic wisdom about the conflicting priorities of poet, director, comic actor and audience.

In Goethe's novel *Wilhelm Meister's Theatrical Mission* (an

early version of *Wilhelm Meister's Apprentice Years*), Wilhelm
Meister sets out to use the theatre as a means of moral and
social cultivation, possibly as a way to give the Germans a
unified cultural life. There is room on the stage for those whose
days are normally spent getting and spending to present them-
selves as thinking and passionate beings – to 'appear' and to
'be'.[6] *Faust* had some of its origins in Goethe's interest in the
staged illusions of Mozart's *Magic Flute*. The young Goethe
was interested in puppets and marionettes. Part of the peculiar
quality of the form of the two parts of *Faust* is the way they
transmogrify and shape-shift, operating at all levels, from the
magic lantern and conjuring trick (Mephistopheles in Auer-
bach's tavern, Mephistopheles conjuring up the forms of Helen
and Paris as a court entertainment, the phantasmagoria, both
verbal and visual, of both Walpurgis Nights) to the tortured
inner debate of Faust's first speeches, the dramatic directness
of Gretchen and her world, and the cosmological anxieties and
yearnings of the bottled homunculus made by Wagner in
Part II. The work isn't psychic allegory partly because it is so
much about illusion and showmanship.

I agree with those critics, including David Constantine in his
Introduction to *Part I*, who see *Faust* as not ultimately unified
or coherent as a work. It flies apart, it pulls apart, it starts too
many flights, and does not end them, or cohere. But one of the
ways in which to think about the kind of unity it does have is
to think about the women in it, Gretchen in *Part I* and Helen
in *Part II*, and the patterns of language and action in which
they are constructed. Their opposition is a kind of unity. And
they are both part of an idea of the female, *das Ewig-Weibliche*,
which underlies the work, representing both human origins and
the object of desire.

Helen of Troy, phantom or revenant, is a more ancient and
more essential figure from the old Faust legend than the late-
comer, Gretchen. She is the beautiful human body as power –
'Is this the face that launched a thousand ships/ And burned
the topless towers of Ilium?' She is Platonic Beauty, desired
alongside wisdom and knowledge. She is, as the object of
bodily, sexual desire, the ultimate attainment, to die for, to lose

one's soul for. In Greek mythology she is given to Paris by
Aphrodite, in reward for the Apple of Discord. In Greek legend
and myth she already shows a propensity to appear as a wraith,
or a simulacrum – according to one version the 'real' Helen
spent the long years of the Trojan War in Egypt, whilst Paris
slept with an eidolon, a puppet. In the old Faust legends and
plays she sometimes gives Faust a son, Justus Faustus. She is
the perfect Face Faust sees in the Witch's Kitchen, for whose
sake he is rejuvenated by magic. In *Part II* of Goethe's *Faust*
she is conjured twice, once for the Emperor, and once when
Mephistopheles, disguised as Phorcyas, a female Fate in the
form of a hag with one eye and one fang, brings her and her
chorus of handmaids back from the underworld to be rescued
by Faust and to join him in a medieval German castle. The first
conjuring, for the Emperor, is Mephistophelean trickery – the
figures disappear when desired and touched. The second brings
with it Greek tragedy – Helen, confused and distraught, sup-
poses she is returning to Menelaus' house, where she is to
prepare for her own sacrifice. Faust 'rescues' her with magic.
As a woman this Helen is wonderfully human and real, a
beautiful woman and a princess, aware of the unsought effects
of her excess of beauty. She bears Faust a son, Euphorion, who
hubristically tries to fly like Phaethon and destroys himself – at
which point she again becomes a wraith and returns to Hades,
leaving only her clothing. The Greek tragedy is gripping; Faust's
(successful) attempts to teach her to speak medieval rhyming
verse are funny and moving; Euphorion is ludicrous and dra-
matically bathetic, and the whole episode is a thorough attempt
to see and hear the classical world that is vanished – which ends
in a sense of its vanishing.

The Gretchen of *Part I*, on the contrary, is a Christian charac-
ter in a Christian story, taking place in a world where salvation
and damnation are real, more real than human acts. It is not a
love story. Faust's inclination for the innocent girl is casual and
lustful. She is seduced by jewels and fine manners and a kiss.
Her innocent fault leads to the death of her mother and brother,
and to her brother's curse. It leads also to infanticide, and
condemnation by cruel human law to a theatrical execution.

The events are terrible, but the power of Goethe's rendering is in the simplicity of the language. Gretchen would not be Gretchen without the songs she sings, the rhythms she thinks in, and the quite different rhythms of the Church Faust causes her to doubt and disobey. Her first wonderful song, 'There was a king in Thule' (2759), combines the idea of some Nordic extreme with the powerfully simple idea of a love longer and deeper than life, with the 'holy' golden goblet hurled into the water. It is the essence of the ballad and of the values that went with it. The shuttling, hurrying repetitive rhythm of 'Meine Ruh ist hin'[7] both reinforces and destabilizes the world of poetic simplicity. And the sinful Gretchen, in the scene before the Mater Dolorosa and in the cathedral with the Evil Spirit, faces the full blast of the Christian terror that never catches up with this Faust. She sees the Queen of Heaven with a sword in her heart, contemplating her dead Son. In the cathedral she is taunted by the Evil Spirit with the image of the gaping grave and the flames of hell, to the terrible music of the Dies Irae, the Day of Wrath, a measured apocalyptic vision that drowns her small voice and her consciousness. What follows for Gretchen is child murder and madness. She is the human opposite of the Virgin Mary with her dead Son, though she asks to be buried with her slaughtered child on her breast, and Goethe has made it clear that she is naturally motherly, with her tales of caring for her little sister who died. Goethe in Italy rejected the suffering visions of painted martyrdoms. Gretchen lives and dies in a world that believes in them.

The two Walpurgis Nights are tours de force of wild rhythms, orchestrated appearances and disappearances of real, unreal, imagined and shape-shifting creatures, human, inhuman and the two combined. Both at one level represent the flux of chaos out of which forms come to be – and both have their own sexual atmosphere, one derived from medieval witchcraft and wickedness, one from serene classical voluptuousness – which makes Mephistopheles, a creature of the Christian cosmos, socially and morally anxious. Goethe at one point intended to end the Witches' Sabbath with the sexual embrace of witches and goat-formed Satan. The classical Walpurgis Night is inhabited by sphinxes, sirens and many other innocent, earthy and watery creatures, including the wise centaur, Chiron. The dramatic placing of the scene on the Brocken in the Harz Mountains in *Faust, Part I* is crucial to our feeling for the play. It comes between the killing of Valentine and the discovery of Gretchen's crime and fate, and is the one place in the drama where we feel that Faust is carried away and truly tempted by the forces of darkness – most of all by their speed and rush and variety.

At the end of his time on the Brocken Faust sees a pale, heavy-footed child who resembles Gretchen. Mephistopheles makes busy efforts to distract him, telling him that what he sees is 'a magic image, an idol, not alive' (4190) – something, he adds angrily, that will turn men to stone, like the Medusa. Faust continues to stare at the dead eyes, the breast, and finally the red ribbon – no wider than a knifeblade – round her neck (like the ribbons flaunted by the aristos in the French Terror). Mephisto continues to hector – 'Fool easily misled, that is the magic art' (4199). This vision of a damned ghost of the not-yet dead is the nearest Goethe's Faust comes either to damnation or repentance. It does also bear some resemblance to the eidolon of Helen, the vanishing wraith. Between this scene and the dramatic horror of Gretchen's dungeon comes a very theatrical Intermezzo, a dream of the Golden Wedding of Oberon and Titania, including a stage manager, a dancing master, Puck, Ariel and a Will-o'-the-Wisp. Unreal stuff, formal unreal stuff, which has an odd effect on our apprehension of the unreal stuff of ghosts, spectres, apparitions and Medusas. 'Glamour' in English is a word for fairy illusion covering a bleak reality. Goethe understands glamour. It is Ariel who leads the choir of spirits who soothe Faust's consciousness at the opening of *Part II* after the tragedy.

Gretchen kills Faust's child. His child by Helen destroys his life with her, by overweening. I think there is a third child, the magical homunculus made of fire and earth in a flask by Wagner, Faust's servant (though he was earlier projected to be made by Faust himself). The homunculus, who does not issue from the union of man and woman, is wise and funny, and

vanishes when he breaks his glass and is dissolved in the sea
surrounding the chariot of the beautiful Galatea – thus joining
earth and fire to air and water. I think the homunculus is in
part a theatrical image for the work of art itself – not a Black
Art, not a deception, but a forming of something human in
miniature which holds together for a time and then is reab-
sorbed into the primeval flux. His death is a birth, whereas
Gretchen's child, and Helen's, are born to die. The fact that
Faust does not make the delightful homunculus adds to our
sense that he doesn't do anything, is only acted upon. Wagner
made the little creature with Faust's original materials and in
his old study.

    Helen, Gretchen, the witches of the kitchen and the Brocken
come together in the concept of the Eternal Female, who
appears as the Mater Gloriosa at the end of *Part II*, amongst a
singing choir of angels, anchorites and repentant women sin-
ners, including one '*formerly called* GRETCHEN' (12069) who
pleads for Faust. Nobody much likes this scene, which hovers
on the rim of the absurd. The best we can do is to connect it to
the earlier mysterious scene where Faust has to travel under
the earth to the Mothers in order to find the key which will
help him release Helen. Faust is terrified of the idea, of the
word itself. Mephistopheles describes them deep down (or high
up, it is all the same), making and unmaking the images of all
creatures. 'They will not see you, they see only forms' (6290).
The final Chorus Mysticus in *Part II* tells us that all that passes
is only a semblance, that what is incomplete here becomes
actual, that what cannot be described is here enacted – as the
Eternal Female draws us onwards. Women, the female, give
birth to forms from formlessness, they make shadows – includ-
ing the shadows and actors of Prospero's speech, who vanish
into thin air – into real acts and real things. This in turn takes
us back to Faust questioning the nature of reality and illusion
in his study at the beginning of *Part I*.

What do modern readers – especially non-Germans – make of
Faust today? It has always been a difficult play for the English
– though it was popular amongst American transcendentalists.

Even those who responded to Gretchen's tragedy in *Part I* have been baffled and sometimes repelled by the exuberance, shocking shifts of tone, learned references and Protean ungraspability of *Part II*. Nobody much likes Faust himself, and very few think his belief in 'striving' ought to have been sufficient to save him. Goethe's failure to punish him for the death of Gretchen – indeed his failure to punish him for any-thing – leaves readers with a primitive dissatisfaction, to put it mildly.

Two fairly recent accounts of *Faust* today are illuminating in different ways, and seem at first sight to be contradic-tory. Harold Bloom, in *The Western Canon*, calls Faust 'the most grotesque and unassimilable of major Western poems in dramatic form'. He asks, 'What makes so strange a poem permanent and universal?', and answers himself that it is the 'mythopoeic' counterpoint of *Faust, Part II* which he compares to, and sets above, Blake's Prophetic Books, and includes in his canon. At the beginning of his provocative and exciting essay he says that 'Of all the strongest Western writers, Goethe now seems the least available to our sensibility.' He goes on to make the wise point that, 'though he stands at the true beginning of imaginative literature in German, Goethe is, from a Western perspective, an end rather than a beginning.'[8] He sees a direct line from Homer to Goethe; literature changes with the advent of the modern world. In some sense Goethe's power sums up both the classical and the Christian traditions before the French Revolution. He is not part of our world.

Franco Moretti, on the other hand, sees *Faust* as part of a new genre which he calls 'Modern Epic', a category containing indisputably great and important books which neverthe-less have rebarbative and difficult aspects, are hard to read and describe, and are sometimes incomplete, put together by *bricoleurs* (as described by Claude Lévi-Strauss). These works include *Moby-Dick*, *Ulysses*, Ezra Pound's *Cantos*, Gabriel García Márquez's *One Hundred Years of Solitude*. They are books with pantechnicon forms, that grow by accretion or collecting. Goethe, Moretti maintains, began by choosing Faust as a tragic hero, and went on to realize that Mephistopheles was the principal character in a new, ironic, protean form. Bloom's version and Moretti's are not mutually exclusive – they both recognize something dynamic and unachieved and excessive in the text. For an Anglo-Saxon reader to have any real sense of what the work is, it must be translated into *good* poetry. This is one of the most daunting challenges to any translator, and David Constantine has met it with the requisite energy and plainness, subtlety, lyricism and wit.

Man and demon continued their conversation after Goethe. German poets and playwrights produced many more Fausts. The operas by Charles Gounod, Arrigo Boito and Hector Berlioz were followed by *Faust, a Rock Opera*. Goethe's *Faust* was the beginning of Russian interest in the story, and was translated by, among others, Boris Pasternak. I think of two Russian texts when I think of the afterlife of *Faust* – the terrifying and brilliant dialogue between Ivan Karamazov and the Devil in *The Brothers Karamazov*, and Mikhail Bulgakov's phantasmagoric and furiously energetic masterpiece, *The Master and Margarita* (finished in 1938).

In Bulgakov's novel, Voland (one of the names of the Faustian Mephisto) and accompanying demons and black cat rampage through Moscow, in scenes that include an infernal ball and a theatrical conjuring with paper money and vanishing goods. Margarita (Gretchen, Margarethe) becomes a witch and, among other acts, prays for the remission of the punishment of a child-murdering girl. The epigraph to the novel is Mephisto's self-description from *Faust*:

FAUST
So then, who are you?
MEPHISTO
                                          A part of the power who
Wills evil always but always works the good.

Thus Voland suggests that the existence of Evil is an inescapable part of the existence of Good. 'What would your good do if evil did not exist, and what would the earth look like if shadows disappeared from it?'

The devil who visits Ivan Karamazov also quotes Goethe. Ivan is a Faust figure in that he is intellectually arrogant and questions both the divine and the human order. He believes and doesn't believe that his devil is a part of himself, a hallucination split off and visible. The devil appears as a sordid and vulgar 'lackey' or 'flunkey', and is both ingratiating and morally riddling. 'But, dear Lord, I don't claim to be your equal in intellect. Mephistopheles, when he appeared to Faust, introduced himself as one who desired evil but did only good. Well, that's as he pleases, but I'm quite the opposite. I'm perhaps the only man in the universe who loves truth and sincerely desires good.'[9] This devil desires to save Ivan's soul in order to claim it, and mocks Ivan's idea that humanity will be innocent and blessed once the idea of God is destroyed. Ivan is the author of the story of the Grand Inquisitor, and his devil further mocks him by claiming that his art – his iconoclastic passionate stories – is the devil's own work. This devil is the continuing presence of the religious sense – however equivocal and tricksy – in the consciousness of a rational atheist.

The German Faust is re-embodied in Thomas Mann's great and witty and appalling *Doctor Faustus* (1947). This is, as Erich Heller observed, in one sense an 'unwriting' of Goethe's Faust.[10] It is the story of another curious overweener, Adrian Leverkühn ('to live audaciously'), whose pact with the devil makes him able to compose great music, but condemns him to die, like Nietzsche who is one of his models, in a syphilitic disintegration and mindlessness. Leverkühn also resembles Ivan Karamazov, and holds a long dialogue which is a parody of Ivan's with that other sleazy, casuistical devil. This devil has the quality, reminiscent of Dante's Lucifer, of creating an absolutely icy atmosphere around him. He is freezing to resist the flames, he says. Leverkühn's story is more a parody of the *Faustbuch* (first published in 1587) than of Goethe, and ends with his collapse into madness before a gathering of friends, where he announces to them that he is eternally damned. The music he writes is both German and Faustian, moving from lyrics through the oratorio for puppets, based on the *Gesta Romanorum*, and the 'Apocalypse with Figures', based on

Dürer's woodcuts of the Last Judgement, to his final triumph, 'The Lamentation of Dr Faustus'. The narrator of the 'biography', Serenus Zeitblom, a liberal humanist, begins his tale on 27 May 1943 (the day Thomas Mann began to write the novel) and records the fall of the corrupt and 'Satanic' Nazi empire in comments interpolated through his account of the collapse of Leverkühn in the First World War. In this novel, Germany is Faust, and is inviting damnation. 'Our "thousand-year" history, refuted, reduced *ad absurdum*, weighed in the balance and found unblest, turns out to be a road leading nowhere, or rather into despair, an unexampled bankruptcy, a *descensus Averno* lighted by the dance of roaring flames.'[11] (Both empire and the historical bankruptcy with its heaps of meaningless paper money are facts which recall the fictions of *Faust*.)

Goethe's Faust is saved because of his energy and striving. Mann's Faust is damned, though there is a shiver of equivocation – he can say, like the Faust of the *Faustbuch*, 'I die a good and a bad Christian.' Zeitblom can see a hope for his Germany, as 'clung round by demons, a hand over one eye, with the other staring into horrors, down she flings from despair to despair.'[12] The *descensus Averno* is from Aeneas' descent to the Underworld in Virgil's *Aeneid* – from where he returns living, as does Dante from the *Inferno*. Mann uses Dante's invocation to his Muse[13] as an epigraph to his novel, and this too is a glimmer of hope. The Faust story, a tale of a compromise with the forces of destruction and mockery in pursuit of knowledge, of art, of wisdom, is still a story to conjure with.

A. S. Byatt

NOTES

1   See David Constantine's Introduction to *Part I* for some historical details.
2   Goethe, *Poetry and Truth*, Part II, Book 10.
3   Elizabeth M. Butler, *The Fortunes of Faust* (Pennsylvania University Press, 1952; reprinted Sutton Press, 1998).

4   See The Writing of *Faust*, Schiller to Goethe, 23 June 1797.
5   Ibid.
6   T. J. Reed, *Goethe* (Oxford University Press, 1984).
7   'I have no peace', see 'Gretchen's Room', 3374.
8   Harold Bloom, *The Western Canon* (Papermac, 1995), chapter 9.
9   Dostoevsky, *The Brothers Karamazov*, chapter 9.
10   Erich Heller, *The Ironic German* (Secker and Warburg, 1958), chapter 7.
11   Thomas Mann, *Doctor Faustus*, chapter 43.
12   Ibid., final paragraph.
13   Dante, *Inferno*, Canto 2, lines 1–9.

Chronology

1749 *28 August*, Goethe born into a well-to-do family in Frankfurt am Main.

1752–65 Goethe privately educated; he has tutors in French, Hebrew, Italian, English. His early reading: the poetry of Klopstock, Homer in translation, the Bible, French classical dramatists.

1755 Lisbon Earthquake.

1756–63 Seven Years War.

1765–8 At the University of Leipzig reads Law and a good deal else; friendships and love affairs (Käthchen Schönkopf); many poems in rococo style, his first comedies. First readings of Shakespeare.

1768 *8 June*, Winckelmann, historian and enthusiastic apologist of Classical art, murdered in Trieste. *August 1768– March 1770*, Goethe mostly at home in Frankfurt, often ill. Interest in alchemy; association with Pietists.

1770–71 Student in Strasbourg; in love with Friederike Brion; friendship with Herder, who directed him to folksongs and ballads. Reading Shakespeare, Ossian, Homer. The breakthrough into his own poetic voice. In Frankfurt and Wetzlar. The first version of *Götz von Berlichingen*, a drama in 'Shakespearian' style, written in six weeks. Some legal, more literary activity. He writes the first poems of his *Sturm und Drang*.

1771 *14 January*, execution of Susanna Brandt for infanticide.

1772–5 (possibly even earlier) First phase of work on *Faust*.

1774 He writes and publishes his epistolary novel *Werther*. *Götz* staged in Berlin. Vast success of *Werther*.

1775 In love with Lili Schönemann; engagement to her. Journey to Switzerland. His drama *Egmont* begun. Invited to Weimar, to enter the service of Duke Karl August. Breaks off his engagement. *November*, arrives in Weimar and meets Charlotte von Stein.

1776 American Declaration of Independence. Herder moves to Weimar. Goethe becomes a servant of the State. Interest in the silver mines in Ilmenau; beginnings of his geological studies.

1776–86 Increasingly engaged in duties of the State (ennobled 1782); journeys on business and for pleasure to the Harz Mountains, Berlin, Switzerland; involvement with Charlotte von Stein. Work for the Weimar Court Theatre; scientific studies. Many poems, work on the novel *Wilhelm Meister*, the plays *Iphigenie auf Tauris* and *Tasso*. Things unfinished, frustration and a feeling of confinement.

1786 *September*, flight to Italy. *29 October*, arrives in Rome.

1786–8 In Italy: Rome, Naples, Sicily, Rome. Lives among artists; studies to become one. The making of his classicism. *Iphigenie* recast in verse; *Egmont* finished; further work on *Tasso* and *Faust*.

1788–90 Second phase of work on *Faust*.

1788 *18 June*, back in Weimar. Released from most of his State duties. *12 July*, begins living with Christiane Vulpius. *September*, the first of the *Roman Elegies*, which, in classical style, celebrate love and Rome; work on *Tasso*.

1789 French Revolution. *Tasso* completed. *25 December*, birth of a son, August, their only surviving child.

1790 *March–June*, second Italian journey (Venice) a disappointment. Publication of *Faust. A Fragment*.

1791 Becomes Director of the Weimar Court Theatre. Tom Paine, *Rights of Man*.

1792 Goethe at the Battle of Valmy, with Duke Karl August, on the side of the Prussians against the Revolutionary armies of France.

1793 *21 January*, execution of Louis XVI. *May–July*, Goethe again with Karl August and the Prussians, at the Siege of Mainz.

1794 Beginning of friendship and correspondence with Schiller.

1795 *Roman Elegies* published; they give offence.

1796 The verse epic *Hermann und Dorothea*, the novel *Wilhelm Meister's Apprentice Years*.

1797 Ballads, with Schiller. In Switzerland again.

1797–1801 Most of the third phase of work on *Faust, Part I*; some notes for *Faust, Part II*.

1798–9 Poems in classical metres (including the unfinished epic *Achilleis*).

1799 Schiller moves to Weimar.

1800–1805 Poems; a great deal of scientific work.

1805 Death of Schiller. Goethe ill, withdrawn, depressed.

1806 *April, Faust, Part I* finished. *14 October*, Battle of Jena, defeat of the Prussians; French troops in Weimar. *19 October*, Goethe marries Christiane Vulpius.

1807–9 Relationship with Minna Herzlieb. The novel *Elective Affinities*; work on *Wilhelm Meister's Years of Travel*, which is the continuation of the *Apprentice Years*; begins work on the autobiography, *Poetry and Truth*. Received by Napoleon; awarded the Cross of the Legion of Honour.

1808 *Faust, Part I* published.

1812 Goethe meets Beethoven. The French retreat from Moscow.

1814–19 Relationship with Marianne von Willemer. Poems of the *West-Eastern Divan*, an abundant collection.

1815 Battle of Waterloo.

1816 *6 June*, death of Christiane. Prose drafts for *Faust, Part II*.

1816–17 Publication of the *Italian Journey*, from notes, diaries and letters of 1786–8.

1821 *Wilhelm Meister's Years of Travel* published.

1821–9 Greek War of Liberation.

1823–4 In love with Ulrike von Levetzow. *Trilogy of Passion*. From *1823*, conversations with Johann Peter Eckermann, who will publish them after Goethe's death.

1824 Death of Byron.

1825–31 Continues work on *Faust, Part II*.

1827 Part of Act One and the whole of Act Three of *Faust, Part II* published.

1830 Revolution in France; the July Monarchy. *28 October*, death of August von Goethe in Rome.

1832 *22 March*, death of Goethe. *Faust, Part II* published in *December*.

Introduction

One striking factor in the genesis of *Faust, Part II* was Goethe's willingness, indeed his eagerness, to involve other people in discussions of the work as it progressed. He asked their advice, he needed responses. He read his text aloud in company, or had it read to him. This vast classic, hard to grasp, off-putting to many in its uncompromising idiosyncrasy, advanced towards completion through long afternoons and evenings in sociable and domestic intimacy. Of course, the writer writes in a lone-liness like that surrounding the Mothers to whom Faust descends; but Goethe, surfacing, wanted the company and the opinions of young and old among colleagues, friends and his own family. He needed them to witness and encourage the work proceeding. And he had to hear what the voices in his head really sounded like, in their endlessly varying tones and rhythms, when he or another reader uttered them off the page. Those little gatherings at the house in Weimar, the talk, the readings, as well as the letters to absent attentive friends, they lend the work a local sensuous presence, before it goes into print, becomes a book and travels down the generations in many tongues all over the world.

Goethe took more than thirty years (early 1770s–1806) to write the first part of his *Faust*. The writing of *Part II* was not quite so drawn-out. Sketches for it go back to 1797 and 1800, and a prose narrative to 1816, but substantially *Faust, Part II* was written in the last six or seven years of Goethe's life, in periods of concentrated and determined work. Still, it is a characteristi-cally disjointed composition. Goethe did what he could or what

he felt like doing in no particular order and also at some exter-
nal prompting – when urged by Johann Peter Eckermann, for
example, as he had been, in the writing of *Part I*, by Schiller;
or to meet a deadline for publication in the *Ausgabe letzter
Hand* (1827). He left gaps, in Acts One and Five, for example,
for infilling later; he wrote Act Four in its entirety last. As with
Part I, this manner of composition militates against unity in
the completed work; which is not to say that *Part II* wants such
unity only because of how it was composed.

Part II*, begun in earnest after a gap of nineteen years, is at
the outset very definitely *dis*-connected from *Part I* by the
Heilschlaf, the healing sleep of forgetting, which Goethe grants
his hero. Remorse would be backward-looking. Thus liberated,
Faust is removed into 'the greater world'. Goethe says several
times that such a move, after forgetting, was necessary. That is
a fact of concept and execution, whatever we may think of it.

Of course, there are also connections between the two parts.
Faust and Mephistopheles continue as chief characters. In Act
Two, they (Faust in a coma) return to Faust's study; Mephisto
has a second interview with the now-graduated student and
attends the now-eminent Wagner in the creation of Homuncu-
lus. The 'Classical Walpurgis Night' is a counterpart to that on
the Brocken. The opening of Act Four is a return to the sphere
of Gretchen (Faust sees her shape, a reminder of her, in cloud).
In Act Five, at Faust's death, comes an abrupt revival of the
wager, its wording, the question of his damnation or salvation,
and in the final scene Gretchen intercedes for him. There are
other more or less important links: the prefiguring of Helen in
Part I in the 'Witch's Kitchen' (2429 ff.); flight through the air
by magic cloak or carpet (or barrel or balloon); Faust's regrets
that he is bound to Mephisto and necromancy (3241–6;
11403–7).

This peculiar mixture of connections and radical disconnec-
tions makes for a whole which is, as Goethe often said, a
composition of incommensurables.

Faust himself is absent from *Part II* for quite long periods in
Acts One, Two and Three. For much of Act Four he is an
observer, scarcely a mover, of the action. In the latter half of

Act Five he is present only as a corpse or a soul. Altogether he is less a unified character than a figure around which the action forms, the agent of a variety of crystallizations, of both plot and poetic argument. And he does not even need to be present at the further development of things of which he was agent or occasion.

Much in *Faust, Part II* is so debatable, so variously discussable, that one cannot possibly, in my view, sustain a whole view, a unified feeling, towards the action and its hero. Such things as the *Heilschlaf*, the distinction between a Little World and a Greater World, the question of Faust's salvation, are bound to sow division in opinions. And Goethe's irony continually fissures the work, unsettling any reader who might want it to make coherent moral sense.

Goethe himself commented on the peculiar character of *Faust, Part II* (see particularly pp. lxvii, lxx, lxxii). It is a play of *episodes*, not organic development. It is a montage of scenes, which is to say of images, that illuminate, qualify and even contradict one another. Scarcely a linear progression at all. Oddly enough, given their very different views and purposes, Brecht's notes on the differences between Aristotelian and Epic theatre are helpful in reading *Part II*. Brecht located himself in a dramatic tradition that passed from the English Elizabethans into German *Sturm und Drang* (Storm and Stress) and through Georg Büchner into the twentieth century. That, in Brecht's reading, was a theatre of ballad-like leaps and gaps, scenes like discrete stanzas, each asking to be read in itself, then in montage with those before and after, the audience attending closely scene by scene, making connections, but not anxiously looking ahead for an outcome. Such theatre eschews the consequential linear drive to a conclusion. The scenes are set up in montage, in a sort of lingering coexistence, illuminating one another. Goethe's own *Urfaust* and Büchner's *Woyzeck*, both unfinished, are supreme examples of this mode. And *Faust, Part II*, in its extraordinary heterogeneity, its sudden and bizarre shifts and juxtapositionings, is closer to that tradition than to the chief alternative, the so-called Aristotelian.

Brecht called his theatre 'epic', meaning narrative, so joining two of the three genres (we shall come to the third, the lyric, in a moment). Events in Brecht's theatre are very often narrated, not acted; or narrated and commented on while they are being acted. So also in *Faust, Part II*. The Herald narrates and comments on the masque and its ending in conflagration; he and the courtiers narrate and comment on the appearance of the ghosts of Helen and Paris (which is an action on a stage); Homunculus narrates Faust's vision of Leda among the swans; Helen recounts her meeting with Phorcyas, who later narrates the antics of Euphorion; onlookers, chiefly Faust and Mephistopheles, narrate the battle between the armies of the two emperors; Lynceus narrates the burning of the grove. And there is besides a good deal of direct telling to other characters and the audience of past events: Chiron to Faust (7365 ff.), Helen to the audience and the Chorus (8488 ff.), Mephisto to Faust (10075 ff. and 10242 ff.). Much of the play is presented through narration and commentary. Or – another Brechtian-Epic technique – Mephisto stages a play within the play (Helen and Paris at the end of Act One, Helen and Faust in Act Three), which offers that action in a distancing frame for more or less ironic commentary.

The medium of *Faust, Part II*, as of almost all of *Part I*, is verse. For Goethe, as for many other dramatists, verse is that through which the action of the play proceeds and reflections on the action are articulated. But striking in Goethe is the variety of verse-forms having these functions. They are iambic pentameters (blank verse), the commonest dramatic verse-medium in English since the Elizabethans and in German throughout the *Goethezeit* (Goethe's lifetime) and beyond; rhyming *Knittelvers* and madrigal verse (rough iambic lines of varying length), as used in *Part I*, connecting back to the fifteenth century and thus to the period of the Faust story itself; alexandrines (six-feet rhyming couplets), a form Goethe himself used seriously as a young man but in *Faust, Part II*, harking back to Baroque pomp and sententiousness and sideways to a rather played-out tradition in French, his use is largely ironic. *Knittelvers*, madrigal verse and blank verse are a good dramatic medium: plot can be moved forward and reflected upon in rhythms quite close to those of real speech but with enough stylization to signal the otherness of poetic drama. Apart from them – as appropriate, beginning in Act Two, very present in Act Three and lingering briefly into Act Four – Goethe writes unrhyming iambic trimeters, the chief medium of classical drama. In fact the main distinction in the verse of the play, and a concrete gesture of one of its greatest concerns, is between the blank or rhyming verse of the Moderns and the unrhyming iambic trimeters, trochaic tetrameters and choral verses of the Ancients. This is most beautifully staged in Act Three, in Helen's learning how to rhyme.

So much for those verse-forms through which the action is moved along. But just as striking in *Faust, Part II* are the numerous and extensive passages which are not dramatic at all, but lyrical. The lyric is far less suited to the narrating and furthering of action than are blank verse or classical trimeters. Indeed, in essence it contradicts the dramatic genre. *Faust, Part II* is remarkable as a play, a dramatic work, for being continually contradicted by its lyricism. Shelley's lyrical dramas have a similar dynamism. Though Goethe was often rude about the German Romantics, he is of course, in a European context, himself an arch-Romantic, and *Faust, Part II* is in many respects the realization of the idea of a Romantic work as Friedrich Schlegel expounded it in his famous *Fragment 116* in 1798. Goethe thoroughly mixes the genres: epic (narration), dramatic (passages and scenes which by action and dialogue advance the plot) and lyric (song, choruses, the elision into opera). The work qualifies as Romantic, in Schlegel's sense, in other ways too, notably in its mixing of action and reflection, high serious-ness and scurrility, its ceaseless growing and open-ended end-ing, its pervasive irony. But to keep to the most obvious: in *Part II* the three genres, lyric, epic and dramatic, coexist as restlessly as wind, currents and tide in a rocky sea. And in this work called a tragedy and presented as a play, the dramatic genre does not even preponderate.

*

Keats said that poetry 'should surprise by a fine excess'. Excess is inherent in all poetic language. It is that in it which does more than tell a story, present an argument, deliver instructions. It is poetry's defining characteristic – as it moves into autonomy and away from serving any extra-poetic end. This will be felt in all verse; even in verse having a dramatic or an epic purpose, poetic language can be felt exceeding that purpose; but in the lyric the excess is very comprehensive. The lyric genre in *Faust, Part II* is, as I have said, strongly present throughout and for long stretches actually dominates. And the excess it surprises us with is not always fine; often, indeed, it is almost gross. By that I mean that again and again, out of the lasting abundance of his lyric gift, Goethe writes verses far exceeding the particular topic, context or any dramatic need of plot or mood: in the masque in Act One, for example, the celebrations of the sea in Act Two and of the earth in Act Three and in the extraordinary choruses and lyrics of the Finale. He continually does more than is necessary; he enlarges, floats, dignifies topics which of themselves may be trivial or silly; but that is the power, and the risk, of all poetic language. There is a very great deal of self-delighting play in the verse of *Faust, Part II*. It is as pointless wishing the author would move on, advance the plot, as it is wishing that Bach would hurry through the words of a chorale and not linger, elongate or repeat. If you are not enjoying it, you might glance at the composer's text and note with dismay that he still has far to go. Readers will feel some *longueurs* in *Faust* to be very long indeed if what they really want is to know what happens next. As well be impatient to know what happens next in much opera and most ballet. Goethe's play, like classical opera and ballet and certain seventeenth-century plays designed to amuse a king, delights in interludes and intermezzos.

Again and again in *Faust, Part II* spoken theatre moves out into other modes: into allegorical masque in Act One, vast cantata and cinematic revel in Act Two, opera or operetta in Act Three, oratorio in Act Five. There are fantastical effects: the uprising of a small mountain in Act Two, the routing of the army by fire and flood in Act Four. There is dance, and music-making on a variety of instruments; solo and choral song, that may be frivolous, sublime, ecstatic or bawdy. *Part II* in its totality is Schlegel's 'progressive universal poetry', musically and ironically realized in a mixing of the genres. A phantasmagoria, as Goethe said.

Much in Goethe's procedure may be offputting to a modern reader. But *Faust, Part II* was hardly more congenial to contemporary taste in the year of its publication, 1832, nine months after Goethe's death. The late 1790s might have liked it better (the Romantic theorists, at least), but in many respects – in the modes of masque, allegory, oratorio – Goethe was closer to the theatrical expectations of the seventeenth or early eighteenth century. For all that, for all its uncompromising and at times archaic strangeness, his *Part II* was in many ways troublingly topical at its first appearance, and in some ways it is so still.

Certain of Goethe's most serious concerns swim, as we might say, in the sea of *Part II* or drift through its almost Finnegan dreaming and surface here or there into shape and clarity and sink again. When they appear, like Proteus (a patron figure of the work), they will hold still in one shape or another, if we grasp them.

First, surfacing into beautiful clarity in Act Three, at the heart of the play, is the relationship of Modernity with Antiquity, of Romanticism and the modern world with the classical past. The hold the Ancients had on the European Moderns, from the Renaissance till well into the nineteenth century, may be hard to understand nowadays. The twentieth century broke the old uniqueness of the classical past, relativizing it in an opened-up world of many other cultural possibilities. But if that particular struggle and dialectic of Greece and Europe is no longer quite so compelling, the ground of it, which is the making of self-identity, should be. Nothing is, except in relation to something else. We are what we are in a continuous intercourse and struggle with what we are not. Most obviously, in our efforts to know ourselves *now*, we cannot do without the past. So Faust's rhyming with Helen, their brief union, their short-lived child, should turn in the mind as images of desires made

palpable at the very limits of individual identity. Restlessly
Faust stretches the scope of the self, into dealings with others,
themselves likewise extending.

The recovery of the classical past may sound like an academic
matter – academic in the worst sense, remote from how people
live. But in Goethe's day, admittedly concerning only the happy
few, a physical recovery of beautiful things – temples, statues,
vases, wall-paintings, terracottas – was underway in Rome and
in the old Greek territories of Southern Italy, in Pompeii and
Herculaneum, Paestum, and in Sicily. Goethe visited these sites
in 1786–8 and met men, notably Sir William Hamilton, the
British Ambassador to the Court of Naples, who were great
amateurs and collectors. In Weimar he kept up with the
scholarly researches and debates on classical matters and had
around him in his house memorials of his happy time in Italy.
And he read the travellers, men who had gone further than he
had, into the homelands of Ancient Greece, Athens, Delphi,
Olympia, the Archipelago, the wonderful ruined cities on the
coast of Asia Minor. But more importantly, and very typically,
Goethe turned his reading and his scholarly sightseeing into the
practice of his life and art. Better than anyone except Hölderlin,
he brought the sites, the metres and the forms of classical verse
and drama into German – recovered them, in that sense, for
present living use, in his own vernacular, expressing his unique
self, enriching his country's language. He is a thorough embodi-
ment of the productive struggle between tradition and the indi-
vidual talent. Instinctively, he knew what he needed; with
appetite he took it, reshaping it and himself in doing so.

In Naples Goethe met not only Sir William Hamilton but
the new arrival in his household, Emma. And he watched her
perform. In an entertainment of Hamilton's devising, wearing
dresses like those the dancers of Herculaneum and Pompeii had
worn, she struck poses her audience would recognize, from the
statuary, paintings, reliefs and drama of the Ancient World,
passing from one into the next with the quickness of the slippy
nymph Thetis. So Hamilton, as her impresario, brought the
classical past to life, in her fluid acting. Goethe saw that,
admired Hamilton as a man who knew how to enjoy life, and,

back home in Weimar, followed his example, taking Christiane
Vulpius to live with him, and re-creating his *erotica romana*
with her in person and in the hexameters and pentameters of
his *Roman Elegies*. For Goethe, the determined heathen, bring-
ing the classical past to life meant living it, living happily. Eros,
the life force, was the way.

Act Three of *Faust, Part II* takes place in Sparta, first at
Menelaus' palace, then, somewhere to the north of that, in
Faust's castle. Locating the action there was a particularly
happy strategy and Goethe more than once and very justifiably
congratulated himself on it. For on the one terrain, Ancient
Lacedaemon, he could encompass, as he said, three millennia
of Greek history, from the fall of Troy to the War of Indepen-
dence. In very satisfying fashion, he could bring Helen to Faust
by a large step in time and a small step in space. Mistra, until
long after Goethe's day believed to be the site of Ancient Sparta,
had been since the passing of the Greek and the Roman empires,
restlessly overlaid by invaders, settlers, new invaders. Castles
such as Faust's were indeed built close to Menelaus' palace.
The mist that dissolves the first scene of Act Three dissolves
time too, so that Faust and Helen can meet, Lynceus can speak
for the barbarian invader, but Phorcyas warns them that venge-
ful Menelaus is still approaching. At 9573 comes a further
extension, into Goethe's own day, into the life of Byron, his
involvement in the war for the independence of Greece and his
death. But the scene and the act end with a lasting incorporation
of the Ancient into the Present, as Helen's young women enter
Nature as nymphs. All this under the sardonic eye of Phorcyas–
Mephistopheles, alter ego of Goethe himself, the ironic maker.
Poetically the whole act, in its unities of time and action in
suspended time, is deeply satisfying.

The Greeks' unsuccessful insurrection of 1770 and the long
and complicated war of 1821–9 were understood by many,
both Greeks and European Philhellenes, as attempts to re-
cover the classical past *in situ*, in the places themselves. The
Greeks' barbarous behaviour at Mistra in the spring of 1770
was particularly painful to Western Philhellenes because of its

discrepancy (in their minds at least) with the reputation of
Ancient Sparta, on whose ruins the town was thought to lie.
Byron's involvement in Greek politics was very often presented,
by others even more than by himself, in the tones and rhetoric
of antique heroics. He was *costumed* for the part. Goethe,
fascinated by him, but watching him on the public stage with
very mixed feelings, saw something impure (*etwas Unreines*)
in his enterprise. Byron's turning to politics and violence to
recover an ideal that Goethe thought a matter of individual
appropriation and living, disturbed him; he thought it suspect.
So the large question of the recovery of the classical past, which
Act Three of *Faust, Part II* (but not just Act Three) is intensely
about, contains within it another pressing question: that of
poetry and politics. What are the writer's peculiar responsibili-
ties towards his times?

Goethe's age – actually called by many the *Goethezeit* – was
the age of revolution, war, the violent making and breaking of
nation states. Our modernity starts then. Goethe saw it with
his own eyes at Valmy and Mainz in 1792 and 1793, and again
in Jena and Weimar, after the Prussian defeat, in 1806. He
began *Faust* as America parted violently from England, and he
was finishing it as France passed through another revolution
into the bourgeois July Monarchy. Really, he lived all his long
life in the midst of the making of modern Europe and the
Western world. And though at times, in the *West-Eastern Divan*
(1814–19), for example, he would insist on the poet's indepen-
dence of world events (like Hafiz, the Persian poet, singing
while Tamburlaine rampaged), in fact, in the epic and dramatic
genres (more suited to it than the lyric) he did frequently address
the times. More or less obliquely, he treated questions of rule
and government, reform, revolution and war, indeed the whole
urgent business of the improvement of civil society through
actions by the individual, by classes and by the institutions of
the state.

Faust, Part II is laced with such concerns, and that is the
chief sense of Goethe's assertion that *Part I* moves in 'the small
world' and *Part II* 'in the great'. Not that Faust's crimes in the
first part matter less than in the second; only that they are more

public in the second, they enlarge on the subject of the wrong use of power.

The discussion between the Neptunist Thales and the Vulcanist Anaxagoras in Act Two, which Faust and Mephistopheles continue in Act Four, is of course primarily a geological and cosmological matter. But, very typically, Goethe wanted wholeness and unity in his thinking, and his own Neptunism matches his gradualist views in politics. His dislike of Vesuvius is of a piece with his hatred of violent political change. It suited Goethe to sort his thinking like that, but there is no absolute value in doing so. Sir William Hamilton, in his study of the natural sciences, was enthusiastically on the side of the Vulcanists, he believed all seismic activity would prove in the end productive; but in his politics, as Britain's ambassador in Naples, he was at least as gradualist and conservative as Goethe. Comparisons between the French Revolution and Vesuvius (at that time more active than it had been since AD 79) were commonplace; but whereas Hamilton resisted the analogy, Goethe accepted it.

Though Goethe strongly disapproved of the French Revolution, he was nonetheless critical of the corruption, foolishness, injustice and misrule that preceded it. He touches on the failings of the *ancien régime* in the first part of *Faust* (in the 'Witch's Kitchen', for example) and addresses them at length in the second. Much of Act One deals with a state on the verge of collapse. It might recall the Holy Roman Empire under Maximilian I in the sixteenth century, but the nearer reality is pre-revolutionary France, where the temporary solution, paper money, was tried and failed. In Act Four, again set in the days of one or another of the Holy Roman Emperors, Goethe had the Restoration – Europe after the defeat of Napoleon (whom he admired) – clearly in mind. Mephistopheles and Faust, colleagues in black magic, aid the Emperor with banknotes in Act One and with unearthly forces in Act Four; which suggests something rotten in the state, before the Revolution and after the Restoration. The whole rigmarole of the reconstitution of the Empire, the pompous rhetoric (the parodistic alexandrines), are a sardonic mark of it. Faust, in league with the devil, takes his cut, the new lands from the sea; which leaves the Emperor, restored to his temporal possessions, having to buy off the Church, restored to its full rapaciousness. In his actions against Philemon and Baucis, Faust, thoroughly guilty in his own person, also typifies the dealings of predatory states and churches, seeking, like the devil, whom they may devour. Sometimes glancingly, sometimes in great depth and breadth, and in a variety of tones and modes, Goethe in *Faust, Part II* treats the facts and events of the world he lived in and also the forces at play in them. His play is politically interesting in those two senses: it is concerned with a particular and very important period of European history and with the dispiritingly perennial workings of power.

Political satire is one strand and aspect of *Faust, Part II*, but only one. Likewise the recovery of the classical past: important, but neither the whole thing nor the key to the whole thing. There is no such key, the work systematically and consequentially resists being reduced to any one driving concern or idea. Nor do its parts add up to a coherent (all-inclusive) whole. It is a heterogeneous entity, a montage of incommensurables, irreducible. And yet from the 'Prologue in Heaven' at the start of *Part I* to the Chorus Mysticus closing *Part II* a structure remains more or less intact whose implication seems to be that this play, this tragedy, is concerned from first to last with the salvation or damnation of its hero, Faust. We have to look critically at that implication.

Damnation was to Goethe a detestable idea and he never had the least intention of damning his character Faust. We shall return to the question of striving – whether that in itself could ever be thought redemptive – but we can say here and now that Goethe, born into the Enlightenment and a passionate believer in the autonomy of the self, would never send a man to Hell who, appearing in the Renaissance, desired more than the rules of the day allowed. So in the Faust legend Goethe took on something whose essential idea – wanting more than is permitted and being damned for it – was deeply antipathetic to him. His relationship with the subject was bound to be discordant.

Whenever that crux is approached – in the 'Prologue in Heaven', in 'Faust's Study (II)', at Faust's death, in the lifting of his soul towards heaven – Goethe's self-assertion against it is palpable, in irony, scurrility, nonchalant evasion. Elsewhere, for most of the course of his play, he asserts himself by blithely ignoring and exceeding the premises of the material he started with.

That relationship of contraries (in Blake's sense, 'Without Contraries is no progression') is highly characteristic of Goethe in his dealings with subjects he took up for epic and dramatic treatment. Much in Christianity was anathema to him, but for all his love and admiration of the Ancient World there too, in important matters, he revolted. He planned and began an epic poem, *Achilleis*, on the death of Achilles, a work to fill the gap between Homer's *Iliad* and *Odyssey*; but could not find his own way around the premise of that world, implacable Fate. Not at home there, human autonomy being so reduced, and not finding a way of asserting himself persuasively against the ethos of the time and place, he abandoned the attempt. In an earlier encounter, with the story of Iphigenia, he was more successful, asserted himself thoroughly and completed a five-act drama, *Iphigenia in Tauris*, which is, as Schiller observed, 'astonishingly modern and un-Greek'. In that material Goethe was most appalled by the deeply tragic view that Fate will work itself out very bloodily down the generations of an accursed family. He wrote against that idea, his Iphigenia breaks the curse by a brave and humane act of faith which is then recipro- cated by Thoas, a very enlightened 'barbarian'; not at all in the style of Euripides. The same quarrel, of modern poet with traditional story, can be felt in *Faust*. It is a productive quarrel; out of it comes progression.

Goethe's treatment of material whose ethic and ethos are repugnant to him is not a simple case of thesis, antithesis and synthesis. It is more mixed and subtle than that. For, of course, in the material, the old story, there is much that attracts him, or why take it up at all? And even where he must revolt, there too it is the revolt of a poet doing what a poet must do: assert himself against something in which, by poetic sympathy, by entering into another identity, he has made himself complicit. This is most obvious in 'Peaks and Ravines'. The Paters Ecstaticus, Profundus and Seraphicus may be absurd, but they are not just absurd. Goethe enters their identity, then lives the part into his own self and voice. Compare the finale of *Faust, Part II* with Brecht's parody of it (and of Schiller) in the bitter finale of his *Saint Joan of the Stockyards* and this dynamism of complicity and revolt will be apparent – by the difference. Brecht damns his Meat Kings unequivocally; or he makes them damn themselves, in verse that should remind the guilty bourgeoisie of the Weimar Classics they think they own. He adopts their voice only to show them how riddled with bad faith they are.

Goethe is famous or notorious for ending his works equivocally. After *Werther* (and the unfinished *Urfaust*) his great novels and plays end in unanswered questions, irreconcilables and irony. His *Iphigenia*, for example, leaves the good King Thoas to face the consequences of being good. (We might say that Brecht *began* his *Good Woman of Setzuan* precisely where Goethe, in *Iphigenia*, left off.) *Tasso*, *Wilhelm Meister*, *Elective Affinities* all refuse, as they end, to be reduced to any one clear understanding of the outcome; and the last of them anticipates *Faust, Part II* in its incongruities and irony.

Goethe then is a writer who takes up subjects in which he makes himself complicit but against which he must revolt, and who, most characteristically, ends his works with questions not with answers. In epic and dramatic forms his deepest loyalty is to the lyric, whose very nature is to go out into other identities, to entertain them as possibilities, never to foreclose. Those perennial factors, the writer's characteristics, and also the peculiar manner of composition – disjointedly, over many years – have to be borne in mind when we read *Faust*. We must read appropriately; we mustn't ask, as readers, for the wrong things, for things this particular writer had no interest in supplying.

All that by way of premise to some brief discussion of what seems to be – but may not actually be – the play's chief concern: the damnation or salvation of its hero, Faust.

To repeat, Goethe never had any intention of damning Faust. Neither in Heaven, between the Lord and Mephistopheles, nor on earth, between Mephistopheles and Faust, is there a binding pact (twenty-four years of fun and damnation at the end of it). There is a wager whose terms, especially in the latter case, are so imprecise they might be endlessly quibbled over by all the angels, devils and scholars in the universe. Faust dying in the delusion that his massive ego is even then being further enlarged by more land-reclamation, utters words (11581–2) that do indeed hark back to the words he wagered he would never utter, but still so conditionally that it is by no means clear whether Mephistopheles has won or not. And the strength of Mephisto's case is not even tested; right or wrong, he is scandalously distracted, and the soul he thinks his is filched off heavenwards. So Faust is saved – whatever that means. The angels (at 11936–7) say they *can* save a human who has never ceased striving; striving *may*, as far as they are concerned, be redemptive; but what clinches it is Gretchen's intercession, her forgiving love, her plea for him. Lines 11938–41 (especially in German) are remarkably bouncy, like a train riding over the points, not quite derailing, steaming ahead, the crux is got over, what a relief!

That may be the ethic of this play's heaven, but it is certainly not the last word on the subject. So much throughout the two parts of the tragedy gainsays the idea that striving alone could ever, of itself, be redemptive. We could more easily swallow the proposition that Faust is saved *despite* his striving, through love, through grace, through intercession, undeservedly. For in truth, he is *very* undeserving. He ends *Part I* as the more or less direct killer of Gretchen's brother, mother, baby and herself. In *Part II* he reinvigorates the economy of a corrupt *ancien régime* with paper money; and with more black magic he helps hold it together against revolt. Monarch then of nearly all he surveys, he gains the last bit he still wants by murdering Philemon and Baucis and their brave and grateful visitor. His regrets, for their killing, for still being in thrall to Mephistopheles, are brief and slight. He dies as he has lived, an egomaniac. He is about as undeserving as they come.

It was always Goethe's intention that the scope of the play should be enlarged in *Part II*. But after the Gretchen tragedy, uncompromising in *Urfaust* (punishment, and no suggestion that she is 'saved'), and still desolating in the finished *Part I*, he saw that his hero, so burdened with crime and suffering, would not be fit for the 'greater world' of *Part II*. Hence the *Heilschlaf*, the healing sleep of forgetting. Without this stratagem, Goethe felt, there could be no *Part II*, since remorse is backward-looking and Faust is bound (damned, one might say) to strive ever onwards and upwards. But with it, all customary notions of deserts and accountability are set aside. The second part opens on a world in which, so long as we keep the framework of Faust's wager and judgement in mind, striving becomes his morality and will weigh in his favour with the powers that will judge him. I repeat my opinion that striving is, of itself, neither moral nor immoral, but, as Faust practises it, is, again and again, indistinguishable from criminal selfishness. There used to be apologists, but surely can't be any left, of the view that great men operating in the great world are licensed to behave as their daemon dictates; that is, according to a morality other than, even superior to, that which the rest of us live by. Philemon and Baucis then, obstructing a great man's vision, can be removed. As so often, Mephistopheles tells the truth: it's the old old story, from Naboth's vineyard to the present day, a rich man wants to build a golf course, a powerful state an air base, just where you, the poor, the powerless, happen to be living. Eviction, clearances, land-grab, and thugs to do it for the man who says I want this done. *Part II* opens with an undeserved forgetting and comes towards its conclusion (salvation!) via another murder.

It is natural to want to make some moral sense of a literary work, and Goethe's *Faust*, which at least began in – took up a story about – questions of judgement of human behaviour, is bound to make us wonder about just deserts. My own view, strengthened by the years of close reading that translating it entailed, is that *Faust* is the tragedy of a man living badly, a man who lives in a hell of his own making here on earth.

He harms himself and others and dies without remorse in his delusions.

But that would be a very inadequate reading of the whole play. Much of *Part II* (which is nearly twice as long as *Part I*) could not be fitted into it. As I said, the original framework erected in the 'Prologue in Heaven' is still, just about, standing in the choruses nearly 12,000 lines later; but really the roof was blown off it along the way. *Part II* is less a continuation of *Part I* than an explosion of its premises and structure; and by worrying too much over Faust's deserts, we shall greatly lessen our reading of the whole. (See Goethe's own comment, p. lxviii.)

It is striking how often and for how long Faust is absent from or only tangential to the action of *Part II*. He wakes in the opening scene to deliver a determined speech; speaks next as Plutus, 900 lines later; absents himself in search of the Mothers at 6304; returns at 6420; is knocked unconscious at 6563 and dreams through another 500 lines till he wakes in Greece. Then having appeared briefly with the Sphinxes, Chiron and Manto, he vanishes (at 7494), missing the glorious Festival of the Sea (though perhaps his tiny alter ego Homunculus stands in for him) and does not reappear till 9181, in his castle near Sparta. He is lifted into the air as Helen vanishes, leaving Mephistopheles, who has, so to speak, staged a play in which Faust was a character, to close the act in an ironic light. He is present for much of Act Four, but largely as an onlooker, while Mephistopheles recruits auxiliaries and conducts the battle. The act concludes without Faust, though his evil involvement is mentioned. In Act Five, having got Philemon, Baucis and their guest murdered, he soon dies and the rest of the play, though concerning him, proceeds first over his dead body, then with 'what is immortal' of him. All in all, he spends much time prone, sleeping, dreaming, absent (undergound), tangential and dead. Strange hero! Is he really what the play is all about?

I return to Keats's view that poetry 'should surprise by a fine excess'. *Faust*, a lyrical drama, or one vast poem, is in that sense excessive, it 'o'erflows the measure', it continually exceeds what would be necessary to answer the demands of the traditional story of its hero. The reason – or, better, the unstoppable impetus – for that excess lies, of course, in Faust himself, in the headlong urge to enjoy more and more of life which attracted Goethe to him more than sixty years before he wrote 'Finis' on the work he made of him. He knew they were kith and kin. Goethe wrote in all three genres: epic, dramatic and lyric; he wrote essays, biography, autobiography, reams of letters; he was a scientist, a privy counsellor, a theatre director, and much besides. But first and foremost, through and through, he was a poet, a lyric poet of colossal genius and energy. He and Faust are kith and kin because the Faustian drive, as he understood it, is the drive of the lyric poem to enter all of life, endlessly to extend experience beyond the merely biographical, to partake of past, present and future time, to counter death by ceaseless and lasting creation. And cannily, not dying young, surviving sane into old age, Goethe lived like that, hungry, ruthless, wanting more and more. His epitaph should be what he wrote to Zelter on 23 February 1831 after the death of his hapless son, August, in Rome: 'Over the graves then, onwards!' He was eighty-one and still had *Faust* to finish.

So *Faust*, as colossal poem, vastly exceeds its hero and the story's traditional interest in transgression and punishment. Capacious (baggy) though the structure is, still it feels at times as though it is bursting at the seams. In the already interminable masque in Act One there are places where Goethe would, had he got round to it, have expanded further. Having finished the whole work and sealed it in July 1831, the following January he opened it up again, read aloud from it to his bereaved daughter-in-law Ottilie, made a few changes, felt 'a new impetus' to expand where he had been 'too laconic'. What Goethe had said of Hafiz, 'dass du nicht enden kannst, das macht dich gross' (what makes you great is that you cannot end), applies in the highest degree to himself. In a letter to Humboldt on the subject of *Faust*, five days before his death, he wrote, 'the best thing I can do is further heighten, if possible, all that I am and have remained and *cohobate* my own peculiarities.' Alchemist, still brewing.

The 'Classical Walpurgis Night', so abundant in creatures already partaking of more than one species (horse and man, bird and woman, horse and fish etc.), moves like a fiction of Proteus himself, Old Man of the Sea, the archetypal shape-shifter. Indeed, much of the play has his instability and inventiveness. Faust appears as Plutus; the Emperor as Pan; the Boy Charioteer comes again as Euphorion; Mephistopheles is Fool, Astrologer, Zoilo-Thersites, Skinflint (formerly Mrs Avaritia), Faust (in the re-encounter with his former student), Phorcyas. These embodiments and connections are not idle, and readers who have a mind to can sort them out. But they shouldn't be fixed, they should be allowed to float, crystallize and dissolve, like images in dreams. Faust dreams and Homunculus tells us the images. Much of the play feels like that: the telling of images. And plays within plays: the masque, the conjuring up of Paris and Helen, all of Act Three, and so much prompted and directed by Mephisto.

The levels of time slip as easily as do the levels – air, earth and underworld – of the universe. Helen steps from the fall of Troy, through a crusader castle, to the fall of Missolonghi. She is summoned up from Hades, vanishes into thin air. Her women go into the rocks, trees, streams and the vintage. Homunculus shatters and comes into being in the sea. Faust goes down to the Mothers with a key from Mephistopheles; down again into Hades, conducted by Manto; flies to Greece on a cloak, flies back in a cloud, and is carried (bodiless) towards Gretchen by angels. The whole play is unstable, expands into boundlessness, but is held in place – strictly, on the boards of a stage – in verse, by rhyme and by metre, by one man dreaming and writing it, over sixty years.

Faust overrides the traditional story's chief moral concern, transgression and punishment, but does not thereby reduce that concern to unimportance. It and others – good and bad government, for example – are vitally present but have to struggle for a hearing and will continually be relativized by the *excess* of the whole poem. That is what is meant by calling *Faust, Part II*, even more than *Part I*, incommensurable (Goethe's word). Contradictory and irreconcilable things are vigorously going on in it, the whole serves them all but will give nothing – except the excess itself – primacy.

Early British readers (and translators) of the first part of Goethe's *Faust* were shocked by what they felt to be the blasphemous levity of the 'Prologue in Heaven'. The second part increases in levity, blasphemous or not, the nearer it gets to the joining up of that Prologue with the long-postponed 'Finis'. We have Mephisto's almost demented preparations to seize Faust's soul, not sure which hole it might exit from; then his being distracted by the come-hither choirboys. Next, the levitating Pater Ecstaticus and his colleague Seraphicus, who ingests the blessed infants dead before christening: not so scurrilous, but grotesque, comical, in ways that quarrel with but do not annihilate poignancy, passion, elevation. Bursting as it is with heterogeneous subjects, *Faust, Part II*, necessarily, accommodates all registers and tones. Access to the Mothers is through the floor of a notably shallow imperial court. Faust intrudes his deadly seriousness into the foolish audience for whose light entertainment he has summoned up the potent ghosts. High pathos, tenderness and grief have to live with mawkishness and clowning in the opera or operetta of Faust's union with Helen and the birth, deeds and death of Euphorion, their bouncy child. Examples of such mixing are legion, in every act. They are a continual reminder that nothing in this strange work, however demanding or engaging, will be given sole primacy, but all things must struggle productively in a context that will relativize and often flatly contradict them. It makes *Faust*, in a positive sense, quite peculiarly offensive. Christians, pagans, Hellenists, humanist-moralists, those who want poetry pure, those who want it *engagée*, Romantics and Enlightenment Rationalists will all by turns be gratified and insulted.

The atmosphere of planet *Faust* is largely ironic. Irony, at least as Goethe practises it, is remarkably sustaining. It holds possibilities in suspension, without killing them off. They continue, the mind entertains them. As I have said, Mephisto is the prompter and stager of much of the play-within-a-play of *Faust*, and though early on (1338) he characterized himself as 'the spirit of always saying no', he does not in practice work as the annihilator of possibilities. Goethe being his author (and very much at home in him), Mephisto powerfully contributes to the ironic atmosphere in which the entertaining possibilities thrive. He is at least as important as Faust but, unhappy in Greece, for example, has to shift as Faust himself does among the other contenders for our attention. Goethe's irony is benign, in the sense that incommensurable things can live in it. He is in *Faust* par excellence Keats's 'chameleon poet' and as such is bound to shock 'the virtuous philosopher' who might wish him more often to be ironic as Swift is in 'A Modest Proposal', or Shelley in 'The Masque of Anarchy' or Brecht in *Saint Joan* – theirs (on those occasions) being an irony which makes very clear what its practitioner hates. Fortunately, the Republic of Letters is indeed a republic and Goethe, though very eminent, is not king. There is room in it for the savagely ironic, who know exactly what and whom they hate; also for Hölderlin, outraged and wholly unironic.

Life exceeds art and always will. The best works of art demonstrate and revel in that obvious truth. *Faust* is one of them. The excess I have spoken of is that of life itself, hurrying through the form and rhythms of a poem, manifesting itself in all its variety with ruthless force, and passing on. A great poem will always leave you with the sense of life exceeding it and passing on, like pentecost, blowing through the rooms. That force, that excess, cannot be relativized and ironized because it subsumes all possibilities and their relations in it. A name for it, the most comprehensive perhaps, is Eros. Eros as the life force, the opponent of Thanatos, inclusive of all things that aid and further and celebrate life, chief among them, for Goethe and for many poets, being sexual love. Why else should this vast poem, so thoroughly heterogeneous, finish as it does, in the further beckoning of 'das Ewig-Weibliche' (Eternal Woman)? Goethe was always more or less in love. His loves and their poems are abundant. He might be remembered for 'Over the graves then, onwards!' but also as the seventy-four-year-old widower and privy counsellor who stood on a public street in the fashionable spa of Marienbad weeping at leaving the nineteen-year-old Ulrike von Levetzow, whom he seriously wished to marry. The erotic is only one strain in *Faust*; but powerful, perhaps the most powerful.

Love and sex, coarse, passionate, comical, tender, obscene, ecstatic and grotesque, pervade *Faust* thoroughly. The play opens in the agreeably sensuous setting of pastoral, there is an erotic lilt in the verses sung to the man still suffering the effects of catastrophic love. In the masque there are flower girls and gardeners, fisherboys and birdstalkers flirting cheerfully; and a mother desperate to offload her daughter. The Furies, attractive young women, promise discord, betrayal and vengeance in love and marriage. Their verses are a good example of a drastic shift in tone. Mephisto-Skinflint provides the obscene, kneading gold into a phallus. Then enter fauns, a satyr, gnomes, giants (like Green Men), nymphs and Pan. When paper money refloats the Empire, much of it, with Mephisto's sardonic commentary, goes on sex. The women at court want Mephisto's help in sex; Faust entertains them and the gentlemen with sex-stars Paris and Helen, and falls – *coup de foudre!* – in love with her. Thereafter he is haunted, Homunculus sees his dreams of 'lovely women in the nude', and he stumbles and gallops through the classical Walpurgis Night as a man possessed, leaving Mephisto among the sphinxes, sirens, lamiae. The Festival of the Sea – Galatea riding in as a new Aphrodite on a shell, the Dorides with their shipwrecked sailor boys – is a joyous celebration of love and the elements ('Eros is sovereign! Of all, the beginning!'), prefiguring similar upsurges in the finales of Acts Three and Five. Much of Act Three plays under the sign of Eros. Helen, praised by Lynceus in the extravagant language of courtly love, lives in this play as she does in Sappho's verses, driven by the god, and a centre of calamity in a world of smitten, abandoned, violent and vengeful men. She suffers under what Yeats calls 'burdensome beauty'. Her women revere her, knowing that her beauty is her fate. They are notably clear-sighted (9385–9400) about the relative powers of women and men. But Faust and Helen, as he shows her the ways of rhyming, enjoy an interlude of tenderness and equality and withdraw for a while into the highly eroticized landscape of Arcadia. Their child, Euphorion, has an ungentle (and unsuccessful) way with women and would have been, like Lord Byron, perhaps 'mad, bad and dangerous to know' had he not crashed like Icarus. Act Four opens with cloud-shapes of lovely women, but moves then to its sad conclusion through brutal war and politics, the erotic being kept alive by the ungentle Lootfast and Grabber, by Mephisto's grandseigneurial fantasies and by the undines, the 'watery girls', he conjures to the battlefield. In Act Five Faust eradicates the very image of conjugal love, Philemon and Baucis. In Ovid they are granted their wish, to die together, becoming companionable trees in a grove. Faust's agents incinerate them and the grove. Mephisto, for his part, provides whores for thugs; then lusts after the encouraging angels, as he did after the lamiae, and is discomfited. But his exit by no means signals the exiting of Eros from the play. On the contrary, there the crescendo of love begins.

Many religions, including Christianity, have a mystical strain in them, the imagery of which is sexual. The intensest human union is offered as an image, an imagining, of what union with a godhead would be like. The mind and the senses are excited to outbid that offering and to reach, in hyperbole, towards the unsayable. There are two great traditions of such writing in German, in the medieval period and in the Baroque, and for both the Song of Songs, interpreted (and so authorized) by Bernard of Clairvaux as expressing the longing of the soul (Psyche) for union with the bridegroom Christ, was a rich fund. Goethe practises that mixing in the finale of his *Faust*; but he does it as he had done fifteen years earlier, drawing then on the Persian tradition, in many of the poems of his *West-Eastern Divan* – so thorough a mixing that there is no possibility of separation, so that it cannot be said that the one (the erotic) merely 'stands for' the other (the spiritual). Not without precedent, he eroticizes and feminizes certain elements in Christian belief and iconography; but entirely in his own fashion, for his own ends, to serve his own very peculiar version of the old Faust legend's outcome. The Pater Ecstaticus, the levitator, himself very high, is outbidden by the Doctor Marianus, in the highest and purest cell, who (11989) shifts the verse decisively towards praise of the feminine, in fact towards the final extolling of Eternal Woman, in his adoration of Mary and her chorus of female penitents. This is not just 11,000 lines away from the Old Gentleman in the 'Prologue in Heaven', it is quite a different order of life. And God's son appears here as the recipient of the love of women: Mary Magdalene anointing his feet, drying them in her hair; the Samaritan woman, as prodigal with her men as the Wife of Bath, giving him cooling water at the well. Then Mary the Egyptian, the sailors' prostitute en route to the Holy Land, and Gretchen, who loved Faust, cluster with them around an indulgent Virgin in a composite image as charged with sex as it is with loving forgiveness. For this is poetry, not dogma. The sweetness of the women's ministering and sinning is not just recalled – it *revives* in the present tense of poetry, it is there again, incarnate. 'Heavens, it was good, oh it was sweet', as Gretchen said (3586), before the man betrayed her. Poetry does that, makes present and palpable; so that in an image of the forgiveness of sins, the love which can forgive is of one flesh with the love that transgressingly gave. The Doctor Marianus trusts the Virgin to understand very well indeed what sexual attraction is like (12020–31); and the Chorus Mysticus, as he prostrates himself, shift in their last two lines (but still within the same sentence, after only a semicolon, all of a piece) back from the Beyond into our continuingly being bidden – which is to say, attracted, beckoned – by Eternal Woman. Goethe at the end of his life, sealing up *Faust* to trouble the world after his death, saluted what had driven him his long life long, the love of women, Eros the life force, the heart and soul of his verse, still beckoning. The poem imagines the crossing over into the zone of the Virgin, the angels and the saints and martyrs of love, but does so, as it must, in the present tense, this side of death, in present rhyme and rhythm. And in those lines, to the very last, is the beckoning of Eros, the quickening, in which the whole play of life began.

Translator's Note

Translating *Faust, Part II* differs only in degree from translating *Part I*. There is a great deal more of it (7499 lines to 4612) and its tones, voices and verse-forms are vastly more various. Still, the undertaking is in essence, in the nature of the difficulties and in the certainty of falling short, much the same. So I shall refer readers interested in such matters, which of course extend beyond the translating of this particular text, to the equivalent note introducing *Part I*.

In my present Introduction I have tried to describe the peculiar nature of *Faust, Part II* under the rubric of Keats's remark that poetry 'should surprise by a fine excess'. Such excess was of course already obvious in *Part I*, in much of the 'Walpurgis Night', especially the Intermezzo, for example. There and elsewhere the lyric mode dominates, ousting the dramatic. And it does so even more exuberantly and for longer periods in *Part II*. Coleridge, in 1814, negotiating a contract to translate *Part I*, said very definitely to the intended publisher John Murray that 'a large proportion of the work cannot be rendered in blank verse, but must be in wild *lyric* meters'. Goethe himself employs blank verse scarcely at all in *Part I*, but Coleridge understood that form as the natural one for drama in English, as the one best suited to a production if the play were to be staged; but he understood also that an adequate translation would have to be true to the play's important lyric mode. In the event, despite claiming to have worked six hours a day for a month at the project, he delivered nothing to Murray; and in the version he did for Thomas Boosey and Sons in 1821 (only about half of Goethe's play and serving to expand on and fill out the gaps between Moritz Retzsch's famous illustrations), he wrote prose and blank verse and only occasionally attempted to match Goethe's lyric passages 'in wild *lyric* meters' of his own. Coleridge's fraught dealings with Goethe's *Faust* are of great interest (see *Faustus: From the German of Goethe* (Oxford, 2007)), but I mention them here chiefly to point up again the mixing of lyric and dramatic in the work, especially in *Part II*; and also to cite Coleridge's opting for blank verse as a wrong choice at the outset, only one degree better than opting for prose. He understood that the lyric needed translating lyrically, but in practice disregarded that insight almost totally. Blank verse flattens the *Knittelvers* and madrigal verses of the German *Part I*, and saps the lyric passages of most of their vitality. Coleridge's procedure, based on a very unadventurous sense of what might work on stage, fails *Part I* and would grievously attenuate the peculiar power of *Part II*. Faced with the 'excess' of *Part II*, I felt confirmed in my view that I must strive to match the German, keeping close to its forms, conveying all their variety, and, whilst never taking my eye off the lexical sense of the text itself, seek in the resources of my own language for the autonomy to which poetry naturally aspires. That is the paradox at the heart of the endeavour to translate poetry. The translator is the servant of the foreign poem; but truly to serve that poem, to bring across as much of its vitality as possible, he or she must write *poetry*, whose inalienable ambition is autonomy.

The text of Goethe's *Faust* is agreed and not problematic. I used the Hamburg edition, edited by Erich Trunz (1963), for my translation of *Part II* as for *Part I*. I have numbered my lines to match the German. The lines themselves, their actual content, may not always correspond exactly, but they will always be close enough to the German for a quotation to be found or a comparison of German and English to be made.

I have been greatly helped in my thinking about *Faust, Part II*, and so in my translation, Introduction and Notes, by Ulrich Gaier's *Erläuterungen und Dokumente* (Reclam Nr. 16022, Stuttgart 2004), and by the notes and other material Erich

Trunz includes in his German edition and David Luke, Walter Arndt (and Cyrus Hamlin) and John Williams include in theirs.

I worked at *Part II* just as I did at *Part I*; that is, I translated it entirely and revised it frequently without consulting anyone else's version. Then, when I felt sure my English had at least the autonomy of my own voice, I assembled some respected predecessors and checked my translated lines against theirs. So I am indebted to them – Philip Wayne, Walter Arndt, David Luke and John Williams – for help along the way to becoming more exact. After that, I had my translation read by Sasha Dugdale and Charlie Louth and read it aloud, not all at once, to my wife Helen. For their close reading and attentive listening, much thanks. Indeed, I must thank all my family and quite a few of my friends, who these last few years have had to hear rather a lot about Faust, the not very likeable man, and *Faust*, the extraordinary poem. I thank also Monica Schmoller, copy-editor extraordinary, and, first and last, Hilary Laurie, who in July 2000 wondered would I like to translate *Faust* for Penguin Classics and who, from when I began till the finish, has been my loyal editor.

An extract from this translation first appeared in *The Liberal*, summer 2008.

The Writing of *Faust, Part II*

A manuscript probably dating from 1797–1800:

> Ideal striving to enter by deed and feeling into all of Nature.
> Spirit manifesting itself in the world and in deeds.
> Quarrel of form and formlessness.
> Formless content preferable to empty form.
> Content entails form; and where there is form, there must be
>   content.
> To widen, rather than reconcile, these contradictions.
> Lucid cold striving for knowledge   Wagner.
> Inchoate warm striving for knowledge   Student.
> ~~Life-Deeds   Ways of Being~~.
> The person's pleasure in life seen from without *Part I*
>   inchoate passion.
> Pleasure in doing, directed outwards *Part II*. And *conscious*
>   enjoyment. Beauty.
> Pleasure in creating from within. Epilogue in chaos on the way
>   to hell.

These cryptic and not wholly legible jottings (from the period of Schiller's close involvement in the *Faust* project) mostly concern *Part I* but do also give some indication of the scope and intentions of *Part II*.

Sulpiz Boisserée's diary, 3 August 1815:

> *Faust*, the first part, closed with Gretchen's death, now, by a
> rebound, he has to begin again, and that is very difficult, he says,

the painter has a different hand now and a different brush, what
he can produce now won't fit with what he did before. – I replied,
he shouldn't entertain such doubts, one man can put himself in
another's place, all the more so the master into his earlier works.
– Goethe: 'I freely concede it, and indeed much is already done.'
– I asked about the end. – Goethe: 'I shan't tell you, *musn't* tell
you, but it is done and very well done too, with grandeur, from
my best period.' – I imagine the Devil is proved wrong. – Goethe:
'At the outset, Faust sets the Devil one condition, and everything
follows from that.'

Boisserée (1783–1854), from Cologne, was a wealthy historian
and collector of German art. Goethe saw a good deal of him
when travelling in the Rhineland during the summer and
autumn of 1815 and began to share his enthusiasms.

Sketch of the content of *Part II*, 1816:

At the beginning of the second part Faust is discovered sleeping.
Choirs of spirits are hovering all around him, with visible symbols
and pleasant songs presenting to him the joys of honour, fame,
power and rule. They clothe their offers, which are in fact ironic,
in seductive words and melodies. He wakes, feels himself forti-
fied, all his earlier dependence on sensuality and passion has
vanished. The spirit, purified and fresh, striving for the highest.

Mephistopheles enters and gives him an amusing and excit-
ing description of the parliament in Augsburg, summoned by
Emperor Maximilian, all the while pretending that everything is
taking place in the square below their window, where Faust,
however, can see nothing. Finally, Mephistopheles claims to see
the Emperor at a window in the city hall talking to a prince, and
assures Faust that they are asking after him, his whereabouts,
whether he might be fetched to court. Faust is persuaded, and
his cloak speeds up the journey. They land in Augsburg near
a secluded hall, Mephistopheles goes off to reconnoitre. Faust
meanwhile falls back into his former abstruse speculations and
demands on himself; and when Mephisto returns Faust sets the
strange condition that he must not enter the hall but must remain

on the threshold, and, further, that in the Emperor's presence
there shall be no magic or trickery. Mephistopheles agrees. We
are transported into a great hall where the Emperor, just risen
from table, steps to the window with one of his princes and
confesses that he wishes he had Faust's cloak so that he could go
hunting in the Tyrol and be back for the session of parliament
next day. Faust is announced and graciously received. The
Emperor's questions all have to do with earthly obstacles and
how they might be removed by magic. Faust's answers point
towards higher demands and higher means. The Emperor does
not understand him, still less does the courtier. The conversation
loses all direction, falters, Faust becomes embarrassed, looks
round for Mephistopheles who at once steps behind him and
answers in his name. Now the conversation picks up, others
approach and everyone is happy with their strange guest. The
Emperor demands apparitions and is promised them. Faust with-
draws to make his preparations. Then Mephistopheles assumes
Faust's shape to entertain the ladies, and in the end is thought a
quite exceptionally estimable man, since he cures a wart on a
hand by lightly touching it and a corn with a good kick of his
disguised hoof, and a blonde young woman even allows his sharp,
thin fingers to dab at her pretty little face when her mirror swiftly
assures her that one after another her freckles are vanishing.
Evening arrives, a magic theatre sets itself up. The figure of Helen
appears. The comments of the ladies on this paragon of beauty
lighten a scene which is otherwise terrifying. Then Paris appears.
He is treated by the men as Helen was by the women. Mephisto-
pheles, still impersonating Faust, agrees with both parties and
the scene becomes very cheerful.

There is no agreement what the third apparition shall be; the
summoned spirits grow restless; several of importance appear at
the same time. Strange dealings ensue, till finally the theatre and
the phantoms vanish together. The real Faust, lit by three lamps,
is lying at the back, unconscious. Mephistopheles makes him-
self scarce, his doubling-up suspected, the business leaves all
uneasy.

Mephistopheles, coming upon Faust again, finds him in a very
passionate state. He has fallen in love with Helen and now

demands that the conjurer fetch her and deliver her into his arms. But there are difficulties. Helen belongs to Orcus and, though the magic arts may lure her out, she cannot be held. Faust insists, Mephistopheles undertakes it. Faust's infinite longing for the – now recognized – highest beauty. An old castle, whose owner is fighting in Palestine but whose steward is a magician, will become the dwelling place of the new Paris. Helen appears, restored into her body by a magic ring. She believes she has just returned from Troy and arrived in Sparta. Everywhere feels lonely, she longs for company, especially male company, which all her life she could never do without. Faust enters and, as a German knight, looks very strange indeed alongside her, the heroic figure from the ancient world. She finds him repellent, but he knows how to ingratiate himself; little by little she is won over and he becomes the successor of many a hero and demigod. A son is born of this union who, no sooner arrived, dances, sings and fences with the air. Now, it is important to know that the castle is surrounded by a magic fence and only within this fence can these half-realities survive. The growing child gives his mother much joy. He may do whatever he pleases, except cross a certain stream. But one day, a holiday, he hears music on the other side and sees the people and soldiers dancing. He crosses over the line, joins them, there is a quarrel, he wounds many but is in the end killed by a sacred sword. The steward-magician recovers the body. The mother is inconsolable and wringing her hands in despair she, Helen, slips the ring from her finger and falls into Faust's arms, but all he embraces is her empty clothing. Mother and son have vanished. Mephistopheles, who in the guise of an old housekeeper has witnessed everything, seeks to console his friend and induce in him the desire for possessions. The owner of the castle has died in Palestine, monks want to take his property, they utter benedictions and break the circle of enchantment. Mephistopheles advises violence and provides Faust with three henchmen, by name Thug, Grabber and Tightfist. Faust thinks himself well enough armed now and dismisses Mephistopheles and the steward, wages war against the monks, avenges the death of his son and wins a great deal of land. Meanwhile he has aged, and what further befalls him will be revealed when we at some future date

collect and arrange the fragments or rather the already separately
written passages of this second part and in that way salvage
something that will be of interest to readers.

Goethe dictated this sketch in 1816 for inclusion in *Poetry and
Truth*, at that time thinking he would never complete *Faust*.
The ideas it contains may go back as far as the 1770s. In the
end it was not published; rather, Johann Peter Eckermann (see
p. lvii below) used it to encourage Goethe to take up the whole
second part of the drama again, which he did, greatly altering,
expanding and exceeding his sketch.

Goethe's diary, 11 June 1818:

> Marlowe's *Doctor Faustus*.

Letter to Karl Ernst Schubarth, 3 November 1820:

> I was moved by your conjectures about the second part of *Faust*
> and its resolution. You were entirely right in your feeling that we
> should draw closer and closer to the Ideal and open fully within
> it at the last; but my handling of this had to go its own way: and
> there are still many splendid, real and fantastic errors on earth
> in which the poor human being might lose himself, and in nobler,
> worthier and higher ways than in the commonplace first part. –
> And these our friend Faust was indeed to struggle through. In
> my youthful solitude I might have trusted my instincts to manage
> this, but in the bright daylight of the world it would look like a
> scurrilous satire. – Your feeling was right about the outcome
> also. Mephistopheles must only half-win his bet, and if Faust
> half-loses then the old Lord's right to pardon at once comes into
> play, and the whole thing ends very happily. – You have so keenly
> rekindled my thinking on the thing that now I have a mind to
> write it, just to please you.

Schubarth (1796–1861), a literary critic, published a book on
Goethe in 1812, visited him 24–28 September 1820 and inter-
ested himself greatly in the continuation of *Faust*.

Goethe's diary, 1825:

> 25 February. Reflected, for myself, on the year 1775, especially
> *Faust.* – 26 February. Thought about *Faust* and wrote something.
> – 27 February. Reflected on *Faust*. Took out my older efforts to
> continue it. Put a few things in order. – 28 February. Some work
> on *Faust*. – 2 March. *Faust*, put a few things in order. [Almost
> daily notes of this kind till 5 April.]

Goethe's diary, 1826:

> 12 March. In the evening Dr Eckermann. Read him things from
> the new *Faust*. – 13 March. Gave more thought to *Faust* ...
> Went into the lower garden. More thoughts on the same. –
> 14 March. Continued with *Faust* ... In the evening Professor
> Riemer ... Also spoke about the versification of *Faust*. [Almost
> daily entries of this kind, especially about 'Helena', until July. By
> then Goethe had finished Act Three.] – 8 July. Professor Zelter
> read 'Helena' ... Professor Zelter stayed and read out the
> beginning of 'Helena' to me. – 10 July. In the evening Professor
> Zelter read out more of 'Helena'. – 11 July. Zelter read out the
> rest of 'Helena'. – 16 July. Dr Eckermann read the whole of
> 'Helena'.

Johann Peter Eckermann (1792–1854), like Schubarth the
author of a book on Goethe, became his companion and unpaid
secretary from 1823 until he died. Eckermann's *Conversations
with Goethe in the Last Years of his Life* were published in
1837 and 1848. Friedrich Wilhelm Riemer (1774–1845), tutor,
schoolteacher and librarian in Weimar, was an editor of
Goethe's letters and, with Eckermann, of his *Complete Works*
(the *Ausgabe letzter Hand*). Karl Friedrich Zelter (1758–1832),
a composer of vocal music, was a close friend of Goethe's from
1795.

Having finished Act Three Goethe decided to include it in his
Complete Works, then being published; and, since the last his
readers had seen of *Faust* was *Part I*, in 1808, he thought he

must indicate how and where in the whole work the Helen episode belonged. In fact this sketch, dictated on 10 June 1826, was never published, and is interesting chiefly because it shows what Goethe had still not thought of at that time: the Mothers and Galatea, for example.

First sketch of an advertisement for '*Helena*', June 1826:

> '*Helena*, a Classical-Romantic Phantasmagoria, an Intermezzo for *Faust*.'
>
> Following the old puppet play, itself based on the older tale of Faust, I too intended in the second part of my tragedy to show Faust in his arrogant over-boldness desiring to hold in his arms the most beautiful woman in all of history, Helen of Greece. This could be achieved neither through the company on the Blocksberg, nor through the hideous Enyo [one of the three Graeae], related as she is to northern witches and vampires, but – in the way that everything in the second part occurs on a higher and nobler level – was to be sought for directly in the ravines of Thessaly among the daimonic Sibyls who, by strange negotiations, finally got Persephone to allow Helen to return to reality, on condition that the site of her enjoying her life again should not be anywhere but on the real ground of Sparta, and further, no less important, that for all else, including the winning of her love, only human means should be employed; though to make a beginning some involvement of the fantastic might be permitted.
>
> The play begins then outside the palace of Menelaus in Sparta, where Helen, accompanied by a chorus of Trojan women, has just come ashore, as she makes clear in her opening lines:
>
>> Greatly admired and censured greatly Helena
>> I come from the sea, this minute set ashore . . .
>
> But it would not be right to divulge more of the action and substance of the piece.
>
> From the first conception there was never any doubt that this intermezzo should be a part of the whole, and from time to time I gave thought to how it might be developed and carried through.

And though I can give hardly any account of that now I will point out that in my correspondence with Schiller, in 1800, the work is mentioned as being seriously in hand; and I do remember very well that, urged by my friend, I did from time to time go on with it and that, like much else that I had undertaken earlier, things were recalled out of the distant past.

And now that a complete publication of my works is under way, this manuscript has been brought forth again out of safe-keeping and, with renewed enthusiasm, the intermezzo has been finished, and with such sustained care that it may stand alone and for itself and be communicated to the public in Volume 4 of the new edition under the rubric 'Dramatic Works'.

From a letter to Wilhelm von Humboldt, 22 October 1826:

I have spent the whole summer at home and, without any inter-ruptions, have pushed ahead with the edition of my works. I wonder, my dear friend, do you still remember a Helena drama that was to appear in the second part of *Faust*? From Schiller's letters at the beginning of the century I see that I showed him the start of it and that he loyally urged me to go on. It is one of my oldest conceptions, based on the puppet-play tradition, that Faust obliges Mephistopheles to fetch Helen to his bed. At intervals I did more to it but only in the fullness of time could it be com-pleted, for now it lasts fully three thousand years, from the fall of Troy to the fall of Missolonghi. This can then, in a higher sense, be understood as a unity of time; the unities of place and action are here likewise in the usual sense very exactly observed. It is presented under the title 'Helena. Classical-Romantic Phan-tasmagoria. Intermezzo for *Faust*.'

Admittedly, that tells you very little, but enough, I hope, to quicken your interest in the first instalment of my works, which I have a mind to offer to the public at Easter.

Humboldt (1767–1835), noted for his work in philology and education, was a chief representative of German humanism, a major correspondent of both Goethe and Schiller, and elder brother of the famous traveller Alexander Humboldt.

In December 1826 Goethe dictated another and much longer introduction to '*Helena*', 'Antecedents', he called it. Again, for his own benefit rather than anyone else's, this was a matter of clarifying and detailing how his *Faust* could get from the end of *Part I* to Act Three of *Part II*. The long sketch, again never published, was in many respects disregarded and in other respects triumphantly superseded in the execution completed in 1830. The sketch is worth having, to show how Goethe surpassed it. '*Helena*' was published in Volume 4 of Goethe's works in April 1827.

Goethe's diary, 1826–7:

> 8 November. Because of '*Helena*' took out the scheme for the second part of *Faust* again ... Meyer read the beginning of '*Helena*'. – 10 November. Continued the scheme for the second part of *Faust*. – 21 November. Did some editing of '*Helena*'. – 15 December. Dictated antecedents for *Faust* to John. – 16 December. Dictated an introduction to '*Helena*' to John. – 17 December. Finished the scheme for the antecedents to '*Helena*'. – 18 December. Last part of the introduction to '*Helena*'. – 20 December. Schuchardt copying the antecedents to '*Helena*'. – 21 December. Antecedents for '*Helena*' completed. In the evening Dr Eckermann, I gave him the introduction to '*Helena*' to read and discussed it with him. – 22 December. Professor Riemer. Went over the antecedents to '*Helena*' with him. – 28 December. Herr von Humboldt ... read '*Helena*' and made various observations on it. Thereafter he read the antecedents and was also of the opinion that for now they should not be published. – 25 January. '*Helena*' parcelled up.

Hans Heinrich Meyer (1760–1832) was a Swiss painter whom Goethe met in Rome; they became close friends. From 1807 he was director of the Weimar School of Art. Johann August Friedrich John (1794–1854) was Goethe's secretary from 1814 to 1829. Johann Christian Schuchardt (1799–1870) became one of Goethe's three secretaries in February 1825.

Second sketch of an advertisement for '*Helena*', December 1826:

Faust, on the level to which new treatments of the old and crude folk tale have lifted him, is a man impatient and uneasy in the general constraints of earthly life, who thinks the possession of the highest knowledge and the enjoyment of the finest goods quite inadequate to even the slightest satisfaction of his longings, so that his spirit, going out in all directions, returns ever more unhappy.

This disposition is so close to the modern that several eminent thinkers have felt driven to address the questions it raises. My own efforts were applauded; some excellent men pondered and commented on my text, which I gratefully acknowledged. At the same time I was surprised that those who undertook a continuation and completion of my fragment did not hit upon the very obvious consideration, that in any treatment of a second part it would be necessary to lift oneself out of the previous miserable sphere entirely, and conduct such a man as Faust into higher regions and through worthier circumstances.

My own beginnings in this direction lay quietly in my mind, and from time to time I did feel impelled to work them up; which I kept secret from one and all, being always hopeful that I might be able to bring the work to its desired conclusion. But now I must not hold back any longer, and on the occasion of the publication of all my literary endeavours must have no more secrets; but rather I feel myself obliged gradually to make public all my efforts, even the fragments.

Accordingly I decided that the above-mentioned dramatic piece, which is not too long, is complete in itself and belongs in the second part of *Faust*, should be included forthwith in the next instalment of my works.

But in order that the great gulf between the miserable ending of the first part, which is already known, and the entry of a heroic woman of Antiquity should in some degree be bridged, I trust that an account of what has preceded her entry will be kindly received and will be thought, for the time being, to be adequate.

The old legend tells us (and the puppet play shows us) that

Faust in his domineering pride orders Mephistopheles to get him possession of the beautiful Helen of Greece, and that Mephisto, somewhat reluctantly, obliges. I was duty-bound not to omit this very significant matter from my own treatment of the story; and the following notes may serve, for the time being, to explain how I handled it and what introduction to it I thought proper.

On the occasion of a large festivity at the court of the German Emperor, Faust and Mephistopheles are ordered to stage a conjuration of spirits; reluctantly, under pressure, they summon up the phantoms of Helen and Paris, as commanded. Paris enters, the women are ecstatic; in vain the men strive to cool their enthusiasm by finding fault with him. Helen enters, the men are beside themselves. The women, examining her closely, making fun of her heroically solid feet and her ivory-coloured complexion, very probably painted, and more by speaking ill of her, for which, it must be said, her true history gives them grounds, cast a contemptible slant upon her splendid person. Faust, carried away by the Sublimely-Beautiful, is foolhardy enough to try to push aside Paris as he leans to embrace her. A clap of thunder throws Faust to the ground, the apparitions vanish, the festivities end in tumult.

Faust, summoned back into life from the toils of a long and heavy sleep (during which his dreams have been visible to the audience in every detail), steps forward in an exalted state and, penetrated through and through by the supreme vision he has had, vehemently insists on possessing her, through Mephistopheles. He, not liking to admit that he has no influence in the Hades of the Ancient World and that he is not even welcome there, does what he has done successfully before: he keeps his master moving in all directions. This occasions very many and various things that require attention; and finally, to soothe his master's growing impatience, Mephisto persuades him, as it were on the way to their goal, to visit Doctor Wagner, now appointed Professor, and they find him in his laboratory exultant that a chemical manikin has just come into being.

At once this creature smashes the shining retort and steps forth from his confinement in it as an agile and well-shaped little dwarf.

The recipe for his mystical creation is hinted at; he demonstrates his qualities and abilities, and in particular he is shown to contain within him a general historical calendar of the world, so that at any moment he is able to say what, since the creation of Adam, at the same conjunction of sun, earth, moon and the planets, has occurred among human beings. And, in proof, he announces that the present night coincides precisely with the hour of the preparations for the Battle of Pharsalus when neither Caesar nor Pompey could sleep. This is disputed by Mephistopheles who, citing the Benedictines, claims the event, so momentous in the history of the world, took place not then but several days later. They object that the Devil has no right to adduce monks as his authorities; but since he obstinately insists on that right, their quarrel over chronology would have run on without ever being decided, had not the chemical manikin given a further proof of his profound historical-mythical talent and observed that at the same point in time the classical Walpurgis Night Festival took place and since the beginnings of the mythical world had always been held in Thessaly and that, because there is a fundamental connection between the epochs of world history, the festival was really the cause of the Pharsalian disaster. All four decide to journey there and Wagner, despite the hurry, remembers to take a clean phial with him so that, with luck, he may gather the necessary elements for a tiny chemical female as they go. He puts the glass in his left breast-pocket, the chemical manikin in his right, and they entrust themselves to the magic travelling cloak. Dazed by the arrow-like velocity of their conveyance and by the endless flurry of geographical and historical observations on the places they flit across issuing from the mouth of the pocketed manikin, they cannot think clearly until, by the light of the clear though waning moon, they land on the plain of Thessaly. Here on the heath their first encounter is with Erichtho, greedily breathing in the smell of mould that clings ineradicably to these fields. Erichthonius [son of Hephaestus and Gaia, became King of Athens] joins her, their close family relationship, unknown to the Ancient World, being proved by etymology; but since this wondrous child is no great walker she is unfortunately obliged to carry him, and when he then conceives a strange passion for the chemical manikin, she must carry him too, on her other arm, Mephistopheles commenting mercilessly the while.

Faust has entered into conversation with a Sphinx squatting on her hindquarters. Their to and fro of extremely abstruse questions and equally enigmatic answers might go on for ever. A Gryphon, one of the gold-hoarders, squatting and listening nearby, has his say too, but quite without clarifying anything. A colossal ant, also a scraper of gold, joins them and further confuses the talk.

The rational mind thus despairing among contraries, now it is the turn of the senses to doubt themselves. Empusa enters, wearing an ass's head in honour of the festival; and, by continually changing her shape, though she cannot bring the other decided figures to change theirs, she does arouse their constant impatience.

Now appear countless multiples of Sphinxes, Gryphons and ants, evolving, as it seems, out of themselves. And there is besides a swarming and running to and fro of all the monsters of antiquity, the chimarae, tragelaphs and other whimsical hybrids, and among them innumerable many-headed snakes. Harpies flutter and dip like bats and circle unsteadily; the serpent Python itself appears in plural form, and the Stymphalian raptors, with webbed feet and sharp beaks, whirr past as fast as arrows one after the other. But suddenly a formation of Sirens, singing and making music, hovers over all like a cloud. They dive into the Peneus and bathe there with a din of soughing and whistling, then rise up among the trees along the river, singing most beautifully. More important still, however, there comes an apology from the Nereids and Tritons who, despite the proximity of the sea, are prevented by their physiology from taking part in the festival. But then in the most pressing manner they invite the whole company to come and enjoy themselves among the manifold waters, bays, islands and coastlines in the vicinity. Some of the multitude follow this tempting invitation and dash towards the sea.

Our travellers, however, grown more or less accustomed to such ghostly activity, pay little attention to the busy noise of it all around them. The chemical manikin, creeping over the earth, plucks up from the humus a mass of phosphorizing atoms, some of which emit a blue fire, others crimson. Conscientiously he collects them in Wagner's phial, whilst doubting that a small chemical female will ever be made of them. But when Wagner, wishing to examine them more closely, shakes the phial hard, the massed cohorts of Pompey and Caesar appear in a bid, perhaps, violently to appropriate the components of their individualities, for their legitimate resurrection. They come close to seizing these physicalities, in which no trace of spirit remains, but the four winds, that throughout this night never cease blowing one against the other, protect the new owner, and the ghosts are obliged to hear from all sides that the ingredients of their Roman greatness have long since dispersed as dust to the four quarters and have been taken up into and used in millions of further stages of creation.

The uproar continues unabated, though for a while perhaps not quite so angrily, when all attention is directed towards the centre of the extensive plain. At that point comes the first quaking of the earth; it bulges, and a mountain chain forms upwards to Scotusa [town in Thessaly between Larissa and Pherae] and downwards to the Peneus, whose course it even threatens to block. The head and shoulders of Enceladus [one of the giants who rebelled against Olympus] break forth; and thus, creeping hither under the sea and the land, he also celebrates the important hour. Flames lick up fleetingly from a number of cracks. Philosophers of science, Thales and Anaxagoras, present, as you would expect, on this occasion, quarrel violently over the phenomenon, the former ascribing everything to water and wetness, the latter seeing molten and melting masses everywhere. Their solo-perorations join the general chorus of noise, both citing Homer, both calling past and present as their witnesses. In waves of didactic smugness Thales adduces spring tides and deluges, in vain. Anaxagoras, wild as the element that rules him, speaks a more passionate language, foretells a rain of stones, which does indeed then at once fall from the moon. The crowd laud him as a demigod and his opponent is obliged to retreat to the shore.

Even before the ravines and peaks of the mountains have consolidated themselves, Pygmies swarm forth from gaping crevices on all sides, take possession of the upper arms and the shoulders of the uprisen and still stooping giant and use them as a place to dance and riot on. Countless hosts of cranes meanwhile hover screeching around the head and hair, as though these were impenetrable woodlands, and announce an entertaining tournament, before the general festivities come to an end.

So all this and as much besides as a mind may imagine, and all happening simultaneously, just as it comes. Mephistopheles meanwhile has made the acquaintance of Enyo [one of the Phorcyides], whose grandiose ugliness discomposes him and startles him almost into uttering discourteous and insulting remarks. But he pulls himself together and, thinking of her high ancestry and of the influence she may have, he seeks her favour. He reaches an understanding with her and enters into an agreement whose overt terms do not amount to very much, the covert however being all the more remarkable and far-reaching. Faust for his part has approached Chiron who, as a dweller in the nearby mountains, is making his usual tour. Faust's earnestly pedagogical conversation with this most ancient of tutors is, if not quite interrupted, at the very least mithered by a company of Lamiae moving constantly between him and Chiron. Attractiveness of every kind, blonde, brunette, tall, petite, delicate or strong in build, all speaking or singing, striding or dancing, hastening or gesticulating, so that had Faust not taken into himself already the very highest image of beauty, he must necessarily have been seduced. Chiron meanwhile, old and unshakeable, desires to enlighten his new and thoughtful acquaintance as to the maxims according to which he educated his illustrious heroes; and speaks then of the Argonauts, one by one, and finally of Achilles. But when the teacher comes to the results of his efforts, he has little joy; for those heroes lived and behaved as though he had never taught them.

When Chiron learns of Faust's desire and intention, it delights him after all that he has once again met a man who wants the impossible, that being a quality he always approved of in his pupils. He at once offers this modern hero help and guidance,

bears him on his broad back to and fro over the fords and gravel
of the Peneus, passing Larissa on their right, and only pointing
out to his rider one place or another where Perseus, the unhappy
King of Macedonia, fleeing in terror, paused a few moments to
draw breath. So they make their way down to the foot of
Olympus, where they encounter a long procession of Sibyls, far
more than twelve in number. Chiron describes the first going by
as old acquaintances of his, and commends his protégé to the
thoughtful and sagacious daughter of Tiresias, Manto.

She reveals to him that the way down to Orcus will very
soon open, against the hour when on that former occasion the
mountain was obliged to gape, to allow so many great souls to
descend. This is indeed what happens, and favoured by that
moment of the horoscope, in silence they all make their descent.
Suddenly Manto covers her charge in her veil, pushing him away
from the path towards the walls of rock, so that he fears he may
suffocate and expire. Soon uncovering him, she explains why she
took the precaution: the head of the Gorgon, larger and wider
with every passing century, had come up out of the gulf towards
them. Proserpina [another name for Persephone] tries to keep the
head away from the festival on the plain because the ghosts and
monsters assembled there would be thrown into a panic by its
appearance and would disperse. Manto herself, gifted though she
is, would not dare to look upon it. Had Faust seen it, on the spot
he would have been annihilated so that thereafter in the whole
universe, body and soul, nothing of him would ever again be
found. Finally they arrive at the dwelling and court of Proserpina,
immeasurable in extent and densely crowded with all manner of
spectral shapes. The opportunities for incident here are infinite;
until Faust is presented as a second Orpheus and kindly received,
his request, however, is thought to be somewhat strange. Manto's
speech on his behalf must carry weight. She draws first on the
power of precedent, recalling in detail the favours shown to
Protesilaus, Alcestis and Eurydice. Why, Helen herself once had
permission to return to life, to be joined with her early love,
Achilles! But the further course and flow of Manto's speech we
must not divulge, and least of all its peroration, after which,
moved to tears, the Queen says yes, and directs the petitioners to

the three Judges in whose brazen memory everything lodges that
in the waters of Lethe rolling before their feet has seemed to
vanish.

Here it is revealed that Helen's previous return to life was
allowed on condition that she would dwell and remain within
the confines of the island of Leuce [in the western Black Sea].
Similarly, now she will return to the land of Sparta and there,
truly alive, will appear in a simulacrum of Menelaus' house, it
then being left to her new suitor to work upon her volatile spirit
and receptive disposition and win her favours if he can.

And at this point the advertised intermezzo begins, sufficiently
connected with the course of the main plot, but, for reasons
which will be communicated later, now offered in isolation.

Of course, this brief sketch ought to have been given to the
public executed and adorned by all the arts of poetry and rhetoric;
but, just as it is now, it may serve provisionally to present the
antecedents which, prefacing the advertised '*Helena*, a Classical-
Romantic Phantasmagoria, an Intermezzo for *Faust*', need to be
known and thoroughly reflected upon.

Goethe in conversation with Eckermann, 6 May 1827:

And really what strange people the Germans are! With all the
deep thoughts and the deep ideas they look for everywhere and
put in everywhere, they make their lives much harder than need
be. Why won't they risk it for once and give themselves up to
impressions or let themselves be amused or moved or up-
lifted . . . ? But they come and ask me what *idea* I was trying to
embody in my *Faust*! As though I knew or could tell them! That
the Devil loses the wager and that a human being forever striving
upwards out of grievous errors towards something better, is
redeemable, that is, admittedly, a good and effective thought that
explains quite a lot, but it is not an idea that the whole thing or
every scene in particular is based on . . . Altogether, it was not in
my nature as a poet to strive for the embodiment of something
abstract. I felt impressions in me, they were impressions of a
sensuous, lively, attractive and manifold kind . . . and as a poet

all I had to do was give these images and impressions a rounded
artistic shape and form.

Goethe took up *Faust* again, referring to it as his 'main
business', 'main purpose' or 'main work'. He was connecting
the Helena episode with the play before and after it.

Goethe's diary, 1827:

> 18 May. I applied myself to the main business, very satisfactorily.
> – 21 May. Discussed 'Helena'. Then things having to do with the
> second part of *Faust*. – 22 May. Had some thoughts about the
> second part of *Faust*. Also sketched things out. – 24 May. I
> thought about the second part of *Faust* and ordered those parts
> of it that are already written. – 27 May. I worked at the scheme
> of *Faust* to connect with what is already done.

Goethe in a letter to Zelter, 24 May 1827:

> But now let me confess to you in secret that with the help and
> encouragement of kindly spirits I have gone back to *Faust* and,
> more precisely, to the moment when, stepping down from the
> antique cloud, he again encounters his evil genius. Don't tell
> anyone. But I tell you in confidence that I think I shall be able to
> proceed from this point and fill out the gap between it and the
> ending, which was finished long ago.

Goethe in conversation with Eckermann (discussing 'Helena'),
5 July 1827:

> My earlier ideas for the ending were quite different. I had thought
> it out in various ways, one of them really very satisfactory . . .
> Then the times brought me the business of Lord Byron and
> Missolonghi [Byron died here in 1824] and I gladly dropped
> everything else for that. But you may have noticed that in the
> threnody the Chorus falls quite out of character. Previously they
> had been consistently antique in style or at least had always

spoken as young women. But in the threnody they suddenly become serious and highly reflective and utter things they have never thought of and never would have thought of.

Goethe's diary, 1827–8:

28 July. Some work at the main business. – 29 July. Applied myself to the main business. – 30 July. Felt unwell when I woke and was mostly idle all day, but did something at least towards my main purpose. – 1 August. Advanced the main business. – 4 August. Pushed on with the main business. [Frequent brief entries of this kind, of which the following are among the more interesting.] – 27 September. Night and early morning busy filling in some gaps in my chief work. – 13 October. Continued with my main business. Read the Throne-Room scene to Zelter. – 23 November. Sorted out some things in the carnival. – 26 November. Towards evening showed Dr Eckermann things from the second part of *Faust* and discussed them with him. – 30 December. Some work on the main business. – 1 January. Faust's third scene completed. Transition to the fourth. – 2 January. Professor Riemer. Went through the carnival with him. – 15 January. Got closer to the end of work on *Faust* by slotting some things in … Evening Professor Riemer, went through drafts with him. Then the end of the carnival in the second part of *Faust*. – 18 January. Went through the *Faust* scenes again.

Goethe in a letter to Karl Jakob Ludwig Iken (touching on his characteristic poetic practice and so suggesting how *Faust* might be read), 23 September 1827:

And with reference to other obscure passages in earlier and later poems I might observe the following: since much in our experience cannot be roundly and directly communicated I long ago adopted a technique of juxtaposing images so that by their interplay and mirrorings, my more secret meanings would be revealed to the attentive reader.

Iken (1789–1841), from Bremen, was an Orientalist and Philhellenist.

In conversation with Eckermann, 1 October 1827:

> In the Emperor I tried to present a ruler supremely well qualified to lose his empire, as indeed later he does. He gives no thought to the good of the empire and of his subjects; he thinks only of himself and of some new amusement every day. And there Mephisto is truly in his element.

Karl August, Goethe's patron and friend for more than half a century, died in June 1828. By grief and the funeral ceremonies Goethe was halted in his work on *Faust*. He withdrew to nearby Dornburg, to recover himself.

Goethe in a letter to Zelter, from Dornburg, 27 July 1828:

> My very real hope of sending you the continuation of *Faust* at Michaelmas has been thwarted by these events. If the thing, in its continuation . . . does not force the reader to venture beyond himself, then it is worthless. So far, I think, any thoughtful and intelligent reader already has enough to do if he wishes to master everything I've smuggled into it . . . The beginning of the second act is a success – I can say that in all modesty . . . Now I have to conclude Act One, every detail of which I have already thought out.

Conversations with Eckermann, 1829–30:

6 December. *Goethe speaks of the difficulty of completing a poetic work fifty years after its first conception; and says of the Baccalaureus that he personifies the arrogance of youth.*
16 December. *Discussing the relationship of Mephistopheles and Homunculus, he says that Mephisto has a part in Homunculus' creation and that Homunculus is like him in clarity of intellect but superior in his disposition towards beauty. Faust's dream of Leda prefigures the Helena scenes.*

20 December. *There is some discussion of whether* Part II *could ever be staged. How will the masque and Homunculus be managed? The effect on an audience:*

> 'The audience,' Goethe said, 'are no concern of mine. The main thing is that it is written. People must do their best with it and make whatever use of it they can.' – Next we spoke about the Boy Charioteer. 'It will not have escaped you that Plutus is Faust and Mephistopheles is Avarice, in disguise. But who is the Boy Charioteer?' – I hesitated and did not know the answer. – 'Euphorion!' said Goethe. – 'But how can he,' I asked, 'appear here in the carnival when he isn't born until Act Three?' – 'Euphorion,' Goethe replied, 'is not a human but only an allegorical being. He is the personification of Poetry, which is not bound to any time or place or person. The selfsame spirit whom it pleases later to be Euphorion appears here as the Boy Charioteer, and in that he resembles ghosts who are present everywhere and may at any moment make an appearance.'

27 December. *Goethe reads the scene 'A Pleasure-Garden' (the effects of the creation of paper money) aloud to Eckermann.*
30 December. *Goethe reads Eckermann the first part of 'Dark Gallery' and the whole of 'Ceremonial Hall'.*
3 January. *They discuss the new French translation of* Faust, Part I *by Gérard de Nerval. Goethe adds:*

> Really, *Faust* is quite incommensurable and all efforts to present it to the rational mind are vain. Also, you need to remember that the first part arose from quite a dark condition of human individuality. But that very darkness teases people and they wear themselves out over it as they do over all insoluble problems.

Between December 1829 and April 1830 Goethe finished Act One and most of Act Two. A few specimen entries follow from among the very many chronicling the work. Goethe's word for it in his diary is *Poetisches*, 'poetic business'.

Goethe's diary, 1829–30:

2 December. Corrected scenes in *Faust*. – 7 December. Poetic business. – 8 December. Carried on with yesterday's work. Poetic business. – 10 December. Poetic business ... – 30 December. Poetic business. Put some drafts in order. – 1 January. Poetic business, editing and writing up. – 3 January. Got on with the poetic business ... Afterwards on my own. Looked more closely at some poetic matters. – 5 January. Poetic business, drafting and writing up. – 6 January. Got on with the poetic business, drafting, writing up, fitting things in, rounding off. – 31 January. Poetic business, more begun. – 23 February. Some poetic business, writing up. Bound various things, looked at what comes next and thought about it ... In the evening thought about the further plans. – 24 February. Wrote up the drafts from yesterday evening. Partial new scheme. – 6 March. Poetic business, drafting, writing up. Rewrote the scheme ... Carried on with the main business. – 18 March. Poetic business, editing. – 22 March. Poetic business, drafting and writing up. Got on with second fair copy. Thought through what still needs doing for the whole thing. – 18 April. Dr Eckermann. Went over the Classical Walpurgis Night. – 27 April. Talked about the continuation of *Faust*.

In conversation with Eckermann, 1830:
10 January. *Goethe reads Eckermann 'Dark Gallery' and with reference to the Mothers said:*

All I can divulge is this. I discovered in Plutarch that in Greek Antiquity the Mothers were spoken of as divinities. That is all I owe to tradition, the rest is my own invention. I'll give you the manuscript to take home, study it carefully and see what you make of it.

24 January. Faust is with Chiron now and I have high hopes of the scene. If I am diligent and keep at it I can finish the Walpurgis Night in a couple of months. Now I shan't let myself be distracted from *Faust* again. For wouldn't that be a fine thing if I lived to finish it! And I might: the fifth act is as good as done and the fourth in due course will almost write itself.

The last great period of work on *Faust* was 2 December 1830–
22 July 1831. There are almost daily entries, of which a small
selection follows.

Goethe's diary, 1830–31:

2 December. In the night thought about *Faust* and made some
progress. – 3 December. After 1 I was awake for a few hours.
Thought about various things [in *Faust*] and made some progress.
– 4 December. Some work on *Faust*. – 12 December. Some
work on *Faust*. At noon Dr Eckermann, he brought back the
manuscript of *Faust*. Discussed what was new to him in it and
approved what I have just done. He took the Classical Walpurgis
Night away with him. – 15 December. More work on *Faust*. –
12 February. Addressed my main work in good spirits and with
success. – 20 February. John finished binding the first three acts
of *Faust* in manuscript. The fair copy needed bringing together
from various places. – 9 April. Philemon and Baucis and related
matters, very engaging. – 7 May. Went on with poetic business.
– 14 May. Early, poetic business. – 7 June. At noon, Dr Ecker-
mann. I gave him the fifth act of *Faust* to take away. – 26 June.
Continued with my main purpose. – 1 July. More at my main
purpose. By myself, getting on with my chief business. – 11 July.
Continued with my main purpose. – 19 July. Progress in my main
business. John wrote up what I had done. – 20 July. Continued
with my chief business. – 21 July. Concluded my chief business.
– 22 July. Chief business brought to a successful conclusion. Final
writing up. All the fair copy bound in with the rest.

In conversation with Eckermann, 1831:

17 February. Now *Faust* won't let me alone, every day I think
about it and more and more occurs to me. Today I had the whole
manuscript of the second part bound so that I can have it before
my eyes as a physical shape. I put blank sheets in where the
missing fourth act belongs and without doubt the finished parts
tempt and incite me to do what still needs doing. There is more

virtue in such physical things than you might think. The mind
wants helping along by all manner of tricks ... The first part is
almost wholly subjective. It all sprang from a more hampered
and more passionate individual and that half-darkness may itself
be agreeable to people. But in the second part almost nothing is
subjective. Its world is higher, broader, brighter, more dispassion-
ate. And no one will know what to make of it who has not lived
and seen a few things.

6 June. My Philemon and Baucis have nothing to do with the
famous classical couple and the story attaching to them. I only
gave mine those names to enhance the characters. They are simi-
lar people and similar circumstances and so the names have a
good effect ... I think of Faust, as he appears in the fifth act, as
exactly one hundred years old and I'm not sure it wouldn't be a
good idea to say so quite explicitly ... And you will concede that
the conclusion, with the soul ascending to salvation, was very
difficult to do and that among such suprasensual and scarcely-to-
be-guessed-at matters I might easily have lost myself in vagueness
had I not given my poetic intentions a beneficent limit, shape and
solidity in the sharply delineated figures and ideas of the Christian
Church.

In the following weeks Goethe finished the missing fourth act
so that in August the whole second part lay before him bound
and complete. Achieving this end, towards which he had striven
for so long, made Goethe extremely happy.

Henceforth I can view the rest of my life as a pure gift and it does
not matter now what else, if anything, I might do.

Goethe in a letter to Heinrich Meyer (telling him that he has
finally completed the second part of *Faust*, which he had
resumed work on in earnest a good four years before), 20 July
1831:

And I hope I have succeeded in expunging all the differences
between earlier work and later.

I knew a long time ago what I wanted, and indeed also how I wanted it, and carried it around within me as a secret fairytale, only bringing to paper the individual parts that from time to time particularly appealed to me. This second part could not be allowed to be as fragmentary as the first. The rational mind has a right to be satisfied by it, as will have been apparent from the scenes already published ['Helena']. I admit, it needed great determination to work the whole thing together so that it could withstand the scrutiny of an educated intelligence. So I resolved in myself that it should be done before my birthday. And so it was. Now it lies before me in its entirety and only a few small details want correcting. So I seal it up and may it increase the specific gravity of the further volumes of my works, whatever they may be. And if it still contains problems, since – as in the whole history of the world and the human race – the solving of one problem always at once presents us with another wanting solving, surely it will nonetheless please any reader alert to gesture, hint and quiet suggestion. Such a reader will find even more than I myself was able to give.

Goethe in a letter to Sulpiz Boisserée, 24 November 1831:

Sealing up my finished *Faust*, I did have some misgivings. For of course it occurred to me that I was thereby preventing my dearest and very like-minded friends from enjoying at once the few hours of fun these seriously meant jests might give them, and from learning what for so many years had knocked around in my head and my heart till it took this shape and form. Even as the poet wishing to hide his light under a bushel, I felt dejected, for I was depriving myself of an immediate and close response. But I take consolation from the fact that those I particularly care about are all younger than I am and that what I have made and stored up for them they will in due course enjoy, in memory of me.

In January 1832 Goethe unsealed *Faust*, perhaps made slight alterations, and certainly read aloud from it to his widowed daughter-in-law, Ottilie, and to Eckermann.

Goethe's diary, 1832:

8 January. Towards evening . . . Ottilie. She had read what has
been published of the second part of *Faust* and given it much
thought. We talked about it all again and then I read more in
manuscript. – 9 January. In the evening Ottilie. I read her the
end of the first act of *Faust*. – 12 January. Afterwards Ottilie and
Eckermann. I read more of the second part of *Faust*. – 13 January.
Later Ottilie. We read more *Faust*. – 14 January. In the evening
Ottilie. The end of the Classical Walpurgis Night. – 15 January.
At one o'clock Ottilie for a reading. The beginning of the fourth
act . . . [In the evening] we read more *Faust*. – 16 January. Later
Ottilie, I read her more *Faust*. – 17 January. Improved a few
things I had noted in *Faust*. – 18 January. Rewrote a few things.
– 20 January. Later Ottilie, I read her the beginning of the fifth
act. – 24 January. *Faust*, a new impetus – for a larger realiz-
ation of the main motifs which, in order to finish, I treated too
laconically. – 27 January. At one o'clock Ottilie. Read her *Faust*.
– 29 January. In the evening Ottilie. Read her the rest of
Faust.

Goethe in a letter to Wilhelm von Humboldt, 17 March 1832:

More than sixty years ago in my youthful way I had the concep-
tion of *Faust* from the outset clearly there before me, though not
its whole order in any detail. My purpose remained with me, as
a quiet companion, and I worked up sections of it, individually,
only when they happened to interest me. This meant that in
Part II there were gaps that needed an equal interest to fill them
and there arose then the great difficulty of achieving by intention
and force of character what should really be left to the voluntary
workings of Nature. But had I not managed it, after a lifetime's
active thinking about it, that would have been a poor show. I am
not at all fearful now that older parts will be able to be distin-
guished from the newer, the later from the earlier, but will leave
that to the kind understanding of my future readers.

Without question, I should be infinitely glad to dedicate and
communicate these very serious jests to my dear, far-flung and

gratefully acknowledged friends during my lifetime, and to hear
their response. But really the age we live in is so absurd and
confused I am convinced that my honest and very lengthy efforts
over this strange construction would be poorly rewarded and
that it would be driven ashore and lie there wrecked and in
pieces and fast be covered over by the debris of the daily tides.
Confusion rules, in thought and in the deeds that come from it,
and the best thing I can do is further heighten, if possible, all that
I am and have remained and *cohobate* my own peculiarities.

Goethe died on 22 March.

Faust, Part II Act by Act:
Composition and Synopsis

ACT ONE

A Pleasant Place (4613–4727)

Goethe wrote the first part of this scene (4613–78) in the summer of 1827, having already written the remainder in the spring of 1826. The scene, set in the *locus amoenus* (pleasant place) of pastoral verse, serves not so much to connect with the ending of *Part I* as to break with it. Faust is shown restless, unable to sleep for remorse. Ariel and the elves, with music and singing, give him a healing sleep through the four watches of the night. They allow him to forget what he has done. Remorse would hold him back. Thus *Part II* opens as it will continue and end: by setting aside all usual notions of accountability and deserts. Goethe himself, in conversation with Eckermann (probably summer 1827), commented very clearly on the function of this scene:

> Considering the horrors that, at the end of Act Two [that is, at the end of *Part I*], had descended upon Gretchen and their necessarily devastating aftermath upon the whole soul of Faust, I had no other recourse than to paralyse my hero utterly, consider him annihilated, in order then to kindle a new life out of this apparent death. For this I was obliged to seek the assistance of those beneficent and powerful spirits we are accustomed to think of in the form and character of elves. It is all compassion and deepest pity. There is no sitting in judgement and no asking whether he deserves it or not, as might be the case if they were human judges.

So Faust wakes refreshed and eager to carry on striving. He can't outstare the sun but, turning to the rainbowed waterfall, he is determined to have all he wants of life's 'flung-off colours' (4727).

The scene serves as a prologue. Then the main action of Act One follows in six locations at a late-medieval or Renaissance imperial court which in his prose synopsis of 1816 (see The Writing of *Faust*) Goethe specified as that of Maximilian I. But in the finished scenes the setting is more allegorical than historical and alludes very pointedly to conditions in France before the Revolution.

Throne-Room in the Imperial Palace (4728–5064)

The scene was written in the summer of 1827. The Emperor's officers tell him how bad things are. Mephistopheles, usurping the place of the Court Fool (and prompting the Court Astrologer), guides the Emperor towards ruin by persuading him that he has no reason to worry about money, there is abundant wealth buried in the earth and it all belongs to him.

Spacious Hall with Adjoining Rooms (5065–5986)

This long scene was written in the autumn and winter of 1827. It consists of an extensive carnival masque involving a great many traditional and allegorical figures. With the arrival of the Boy Charioteer, driving Plutus and Skinflint (5520), there is some allegorical furtherance of the plot. The Charioteer, as Goethe explained to Eckermann, who had not understood (see The Writing of *Faust*), is the Spirit of Poetry and prefigures Euphorion–Byron in Act Three. Plutus, God of Riches, is Faust in disguise; he will make the Emperor rich by dubious means with the help of Mephisto, here appearing as Avaritia (Skin-and-Bone, Skinflint). These are the obvious connections; but the sense of this scene will not serve to interpret the rest of the play. Goethe works through configurations of images which may illuminate one another but cannot be read as a developing and consistent argument. Of interest here, for example, is the relationship between Poetry and Wealth, the poet and his patron, as it might be Goethe himself and Karl August of Weimar. That interest is not present in the Faust–Helen–Euphorion nexus in Act Three. Gold might support poetry but Mephisto (as Avaritia–Skinflint) demonstrates its usefulness for the purposes of lechery (5767–96). The Emperor then, entering as Pan (5801) and peering too avidly into the spring of molten gold, causes a conflagration, which may be a symbolic warning to rulers to handle wealth carefully.

A Pleasure-Garden (5987–6172)

Lines 5987–6036 were written early in 1828, the rest in late 1829. Goethe published Act One as far as 6036 in Volume 12 of his *Complete Works* (the so-called *Ausgabe letzter Hand*) in April 1827. He resumed work at 6037 in the autumn of 1829. The Emperor thanks Faust and Mephisto for their fiery entertainment. He then learns that he has authorized them to introduce a paper currency guaranteed by the riches buried in the ground. His officers easily persuade him that this is an excellent thing. The Empire is awash with money; business is booming. Having done his work, Mephisto allows the Fool back in.

Dark Gallery (6173–6306)

In this scene and the two following, all written late in 1829, Goethe treats an episode of the traditional Faust story: the conjuring up of Helen and Paris. But the Mothers, the keepers of the tripod necessary for the conjuration, are Goethe's own invention out of some suggestive details in Plutarch.

Brightly Lit Rooms (6307–76)

Chamberlain and Marshal grow impatient for the promised conjuration. Courtiers pester Mephisto for spells and advice.

Twilit Ceremonial Hall (6377–6565)

The Emperor and his court assemble for the conjuration. Mephisto signals his involvement by again prompting the Astrologer. The courtiers comment frivolously and conventionally on Paris and Helen. Faust, however, is carried away by Helen's beauty and, despite Mephisto's appeals to hold back, he intervenes in the spectacle he has himself summoned up. By the ensuing explosion he is knocked unconscious and remains in that state until he lands in Greece (7056).

ACT TWO

A Cramped and High-Vaulted Gothic Room (6566–6818)

This and the following scene were written late in 1829. Unconscious, carried by Mephisto, Faust is returned to the oppressive study in which they made their wager. Mephisto sends word to Wagner, formerly Faust's assistant, now an eminence in the learned world, and amuses himself in the meantime by receiving again the young man, now a very arrogant graduate, whom he had misled, in Faust's role, at the start of his studies (*Part I*, 1868–2050).

A Laboratory (6819–7004)

Mephisto intrudes on Wagner just as his efforts to create life by alchemy are finally about to succeed. So he is present at and seems even to have aided this outcome. Goethe's idea of Homunculus, the manikin in a flask, developed considerably between the synopsis of Act Two he wrote in 1826 (see The Writing of *Faust*) and the act as he wrote it three years later. Homunculus himself wants 'to come into being', and in that sense is akin to Faust in his striving and longing for Helen. Homunculus can see and articulate Faust's dreaming of Helen's conception (6903–20); he proposes the trip to Greece, by which

Faust might be 'cured' (since conjuring up Helen into modernity proved wrong and disastrous); and he, Faust and Mephisto at once set off for the Classical Walpurgis Night, leaving the now redundant Wagner behind.

Classical Walpurgis Night (7005–8487)

Goethe wrote this long and astonishingly various scene between January and June 1830 with finishing touches in December. Editors and translators divide the scene into four parts or five. Following the Hamburg edition, in my translation and in this synopsis I opt for five.

Pharsalian Fields (7005–79)

Goethe invents a Classical Walpurgis Night as an ironic counterpart to the northern sabbath presented in *Part I*. He sets it in the night of the anniversary of the Battle of Pharsalus, 9 August. Erichtho, the hideous witch, reflects on the battle and the spectres gathering again; but when she sees Homunculus, Mephisto and Faust approaching through the night sky she absents herself. Her verse – classical trimeters – is a first sign of the joining of ancient and modern that will culminate in Faust's marriage with Helen in Act Three. The three travellers land. Each having a particular interest, they will go their separate ways: Homunculus seeking 'to come into being', Mephisto after Thessalian witches; Faust, reviving immediately, thinking only of Helen.

On the Upper Peneus (7080–7248)

Mephisto is not at home in the classical world; and though he will in the end find an important function in the shape of Phorcyas (8012 ff. and throughout Act Three) for most of the time he wanders haphazardly and at a disadvantage. Here with the Gryphons, giant ants, Arimaspians and Sphinxes he cannot feel comfortable. The Sirens' singing cannot touch him. In this pre-Christian context his existence is shrunken and deficient. Faust on the other hand, joining the company (7181), feels, rather like Goethe arriving in Italy, that he is connecting (or indeed reconnecting) his life to what matters. He disregards Mephisto, hearkens to the Sphinxes' advice, and goes looking for Chiron. Mephisto then, further disconcerted by the monstrous Stymphalides and the heads of the Lernean Worm, is sent off somewhat fearfully on a chase of his own, after the Lamiae, who, the Sphinx suggests, might suit his tastes.

On the Lower Peneus (7249–7494)

The river, among its waters and nymphs, has been woken by a tremor of the earthquake that will strike in the next scene. Faust, in a waking dream (dreaming and remembering), sees again the vision of Leda and the swan (the conception of Helen) that Homunculus watched him enjoying in the laboratory. Peneus and Sparta's river Eurotas easily double up. The tremors that first the nymphs then Faust hear and feel are not the earthquake but Chiron the centaur, arriving. Faust recognizes him, grasps him and is borne away by him. Again, things he has heard, read and dreamed about here become present and palpable. As he questions Chiron about the Argonauts, he gets closer and closer to Helen; and is excited beyond measure when he learns that she rode where he rides, on the centaur's back. Chiron, a healer, thinks he needs healing and conveys him, via the battlefield of Pydna, to Manto, daughter of Asclepius. But she only encourages him in his longing for the impossible and, in a doubling of his descent to the Mothers, she will conduct him down to the underworld where Helen is, among the other dead. We don't see Faust again till halfway through Act Three.

On the Upper Peneus, as before (7495–8033)

The earthquake, sensed at 7254–6, arrives now in the person of Seismos. He disturbs the river, heaves up a new mountain and boasts of his part in the making of the earth. Gryphons and ants at once take an interest in the gold brought to light by this upheaval. Then come the Pygmies. They colonize the new territory, and oblige its inhabitants, the Emmets and the Dactyls, to forge them weapons – with which they massacre a colony of herons for their plumes. Cranes, witnesses once of the murder of Ibycus, observe this evil-doing also and promise to avenge it.

Mephisto is further disconcerted by the seismic activity. In the Harz, where he is at home, there has been none for quite some time. But he continues to pursue the Lamiae, who lead him on. Empusa intrudes, claiming kinship with Mephisto. When he reverts to the Lamiae and seizes them, one after the other they disappoint him.

An Oread, calling from an ancient mountain, speaks snootily of the upstart hill just made by Seismos. This is another contribution, after Seismos' own, to the debate about to be staged at length by Thales and Anaxagoras, the 'philosophical pair' whom Homunculus, now crossing Mephisto's path, has taken up with to learn 'How best to come to life' (7836, 7831). Mephisto doubts if they will help and leaves them to it.

Anaxagoras points to what Seismos has just done as proof that fire with its accompanying violence is the chief shaper of the earth. Thales, like the Oread, belittles the achievement by setting it against the slow working out of Nature's great purposes. Goethe was a geologist and knew very well what shaping force volcanic activity has; he had also met in Naples and read the works of the eminent vulcanologist Sir William Hamilton; still, by inclination he was a Neptunist, siding here with Thales, in part because he could sort that cosmological view with his very gradualist views in politics. (Hamilton, as gradualist as Goethe in politics, was nonetheless a passionate Vulcanist in his science.) Anaxagoras draws their attention to the swarming life of the new mountain. Conveniently for Thales, the cranes arrive and massacre the murderous Pygmies. Goethe, no friend of revolutions and famously appalled by Vesuvius, distributed his conviction that violence begets violence into the speeches of, for example, Mephisto (6956–63) and Erichtho (7012 ff.), and exemplifies it in the violence of Seismos, Pygmies and cranes here. The episode ends yet more violently when a meteorite, which Anaxagoras, in his ecstasy, believes he has summoned down, falls from the moon and strikes the new mountain, 'squashing and slaying friend and foe' (7941).

Mephisto meanwhile, stumbling around rather dolefully and getting no sympathy from a Dryad, encounters the Phorcides, who are a vision of grotesque ugliness in a land celebrated for its cult of form and beauty. He inveigles his way into their confidence, claiming a kinship he was chary of acknowledging with Empusa, and, in a third impersonation (after playing the Fool and prompting the Astrologer), he borrows the shape of one of them and as Phorcyas he will conduct and comment on much of the action of Act Three.

Rocky Coves on the Aegean Sea (8034–8487)

This scene – Anaxagoras has dropped out, Thales has become Homunculus' only mentor – is a triumphant celebration of the Neptunist view that life originates in water. It is a festival of the sea at whose culmination Homunculus smashes his encasing glass and comes into life.

The scene opens under the high moon with exchanges in music and song between the Sirens and the Nereids and Tritons. The undertow of the Sirens' singing is of course wreck and drowning, as exemplified in the young sailors later. Abruptly the Nereids and Tritons depart for Samothrace, to fetch the Cabiri. This will prove to the Sirens, in the Alice-in-Wonderland world of Goethe's Classical Walpurgis Night, that they 'are more than fish' (8063).

Thales brings Homunculus to Nereus, father of the Nereids, Old Man of the Sea, for advice on how to come to life. But Nereus, rather like Chiron, is tired of giving advice to humans who in the end do as they please. He is besides awaiting the arrival of his beloved daughter Galatea and doesn't want to be pestered and annoyed. He directs them to Proteus.

The Sirens, from their vantage point, announce the return of the Nereids and Tritons. They come bearing three of the Cabiri on a giant tortoise shell. The Sirens laud them and the Nereids' achievement in fetching them. Homunculus and Thales comment more sceptically. That mixing of tones – other exchanges also (8194–9) are notably matter-of-fact – is characteristic of the whole scene, or, for that matter, of the whole play.

Proteus, the greatest shape-shifter among the many in Faust, usually does his utmost to avoid giving prophecies or advice; but Homunculus intrigues him and he does not hesitate to recommend the sea as the best possible place in which to come to life. Homunculus willingly goes with him and Thales to observe the approaching masque.

After the Cabiri from Samothrace now come the Telchines from Rhodes. They, like the Dactyls, are famous for their handiwork. But it is chiefly remarkable here that Goethe brings to his festival these primitive and obscure figures from the Eastern Aegean (the Psylli and Marsi, supposed to be from Cyprus, follow) to celebrate the triumph of Galatea, a new Aphrodite. This is not the classical pantheon of Athens but an odder mythology of Goethe's own devising. The Mothers, Proteus, the numerous mixed-forms (Sirens, Sphinxes, Chiron, Tritons, the Telchines themselves) are a bizarre but curiously kindred troupe.

Proteus counters the Telchines' boasting about their works on land with further praise of the sea. He transforms himself into a dolphin (a fish-mammal) and, rather as Chiron did Faust, carries off Homunculus, with Thales' blessing, into the myriad life of the sea.

Again the Sirens act as heralds. Galatea is appoaching, riding Aphrodite's scallop shell with an entourage of Psylli and Marsi riding sea-beasts. The Dorides on dolphins bring their human lovers, the shipwrecked sailors, before Nereus, asking of him what he cannot give: lastingness, the escape from change and death. The sea is the locus of eternal change, of life dying and reviving. Nereus cannot even halt the swift passage of his own beloved daughter. Their eyes meet and she is borne away.

Thales raises an ecstatic hymn of praise to water, to the sea from which water rises and to which it returns. Homunculus is persuaded and, to come into life, he smashes his glass against Galatea's shell. His light (his fire) enters the water, and this consummation (which is his beginning) is celebrated as an act of love and, adding the sea-caves and the mild air to the sea and the fire, as a union of all four elements.

ACT THREE

Probably in 1800 Goethe wrote a version of the first 269 lines of Act Three in iambic trimeters. This may be 'the start' he remembers showing to Schiller (see The Writing of *Faust*, letter to Humboldt, 22 October 1826). In the prose sketch of Acts Two, Three and Four (1816) Goethe summarized the story of Faust's liaison with Helen; he gave further brief trails in the two sketches he dictated in 1826 (see The Writing of *Faust*). But, apart from the beginnings at the turn of the century, there were two main phases in the composition of the act itself: February–April 1825 and March–June 1826. Act Three was published separately as '*Helena*, an Intermezzo for *Faust*' in Volume 4 of Goethe's *Complete Works* in April 1827.

Outside the Palace of Menelaus in Sparta (8488–9126)

Helen, returning from Troy with a Chorus of captured Trojan women, arrives in Sparta at the palace of her husband Menelaus, from where she had absconded with Paris (or been abducted by him), so starting the war that has now ended in the sacking of Troy and her recovery. In classical style and verse she recounts her arrival and shares with the Chorus her feelings at being home, among them the fear that she may be the sacrifice Menelaus intends to make.

Helen enters the palace – and soon comes out again, having encountered not the expected housekeeper but the hideous Phorcyas, who herself then emerges into the daylight and trades insults with the Chorus. Helen too comes under Phorcyas' critical commentary. Worse, Phorcyas confirms what Helen feared: that Menelaus has murderous intentions; she even begins the grisly preparations for them to be carried out. Finally, as Menelaus approaches, Helen agrees to save herself and the women by accepting Phorcyas' suggestion that they seek the protection of the foreigner who has established himself north of Sparta. The scene dissolves, eliding into the next.

The Inner Courtyard of a Castle (9127–10038)

The shift is small in space but large in time. Goethe was glad of the unity that the real history of that region of Greece allowed his play (see Introduction, p. xxxiii). Sparta was layered by invaders, including the medieval brigands and crusaders from the north, among whom Goethe's Faust fits pretty well.

The castle is as astonishing to the newcomers as Phorcyas had made it sound (9017–43). After elaborate preparations Faust enters and lays the life of his watchman Lynceus, who has failed to announce her coming, into Helen's hands. Lynceus pleads that her beauty blinded him and he is pardoned. Then follows an extravagant praising of Helen in Petrarchan or *Minnesang* style, Lynceus (one barbarian invader among thousands) offering her the treasure he has collected. The meeting of classical and modern – each side has so far kept to its characteristic verse-forms – begins to be a union when Faust teaches Helen the art of rhyming. Their affectionate exchanges are interrupted by Phorcyas, warning of the approach of Menelaus. Faust marshals his troops, making a roll-call of the hordes from the north and east and allotting them their territories. They are all to serve and protect Helen, now Queen of Sparta, while she and Faust remove themselves into the idyll of nearby Arcadia.

The scene shifts (9574) and Phorcyas describes the magical seclusion into which Faust and Helen have withdrawn. More extraordinary still are the antics of their leaping child. Vanishing down a deep fissure in the rocks, he reappears and shows himself off (perilously) as the Spirit of Poetry. The Chorus comment that he is not nearly so extraordinary as Hermes. Then follows a rather grotesque operetta in which Faust and Helen, anxious parents, watch the ever wilder behaviour of Euphorion, their uncontrollable son. His career culminates, high up on a rock, in the aspiration to join in the fighting for the independence of Greece. He flings himself into the air, crashes to earth, and, dying, looks familiar: the audience are intended to recognize him as Lord Byron. The Chorus sing a dirge for him, and end the interlude. Helen vanishes, leaving her clothing in the arms of Faust, who is himself then carried off in the cloud into which the clothes have dissolved. The interlude ends for Panthalis and the Chorus too. She exits to Hades, after Helen, her queen. The young women of the Chorus continue on earth as atoms of elemental life and Act Three finishes, as Act Two did, in a celebration of life, here in the Dionysiac revels of the vintage. Mephistopheles, emerging out of the costume of Phorcyas, has, in a sense, staged this play within the play of *Faust*, so that one view at least of Faust's union with Helen, modernity's union with antiquity, must necessarily be ironic.

ACT FOUR

Goethe barely touched on this act in his long narrative draft of 1816; he may have written its opening monologue in May 1827; but he did not work at it steadily, to fill in the play's remaining gap, until February and then July 1831. Act Four was thus the last part of *Faust* to be written, in the year before Goethe's death.

High Mountains (10039–10344)

Faust, borne roughly north-west by the cloud formed of Helen's clothing, steps out on a high bare mountain, and in iambic trimeters, his lingering connection with the classical world, he says goodbye to beauty such as Helen's and recalls, without naming her, his first love, Gretchen, into whose sphere he has now returned. Mephisto steps down from his seven-league boots, a conveyance more suited to northern fairytale, and the two resume the discussion (conducted by Thales and Anaxagoras in Act Three) about the origins of the earth, Mephisto as an infernal Vulcanist, Faust as a gradualist. Faust now, prompted by Mephisto, announces his new ambition, formed during his flight. It is to reclaim a large tract of land from the invading sea. Mephisto suggests they help their old friend the Emperor, now in deep trouble, and ask for coastal terrain, for Faust to work on, as their reward. He summons up three violent fighters as allies, thus binding Faust further into magic and wrongdoing.

On the Foothills (10345–10782)

The Emperor surveys his position. His scouts bring him no news of help but rather of the gathering strength of his opponent, whom he then challenges to single combat. Faust, arriving, argues against this course and when the Emperor's challenge is contemptuously refused, offers the services of his Three Mighty Men. Pretending to come as agent for the grateful Necromancer of Norcia, he and Mephisto make the Emperor, who accepts the help, complicit in black magic, just as they did in Act One, when they gave him paper money. The battle goes badly and is only won when Mephisto conjures up undines, gnomes and old suits of armour to fight on the Emperor's side.

The Anti-Emperor's Tent (10783–11042)

First into the tent, as promised, are Grabber and Lootfast (10525 ff.). Goethe's view of war is notably realistic. Act Four altogether is scathing in its verdict on the wars and politics of revolution and restoration as Goethe had witnessed them close up for half his life. The men of the bodyguard admit their uneasiness about the victory they have won. Then the Emperor, in a scene deriving from Charles IV's Golden Bull of 1356 but alluding to the Congress of Vienna in 1815, carves up the Empire among his Elector-Princes. The Archbishop, conveniently doubling as Lord Chancellor, deplores the involvement of Faust and the Devil in their affairs, puts the fear of God (or the Pope) into the Emperor and secures large advantages for the church he heads. All this business of church and state is conducted in rhyming alexandrines, a verse-form which in Corneille and Racine had real stateliness and grace and which even in the German Baroque at least had such pretensions. But in 1831, for the subject matter of Act Four, its effect is parodistic and satirical.

ACT FIVE

Open Country (11043–11142)

This scene and the next two – that is, the whole of the Philemon and Baucis episode – were written April–May 1831, the rest of the act by then having already been completed. The Traveller returns to the house of Philemon and Baucis, who, years before, saved him and tended him after shipwreck. He finds them still alive but the terrain greatly changed by Faust's work against the sea. Baucis expresses her grave misgivings about this achievement and about Faust's designs on their little property.

A Palace (11143–11287)

Lynceus, the sharp-eyed watchman from Act Three, announces the arrival of more booty, got by piracy, for Faust. But Faust cannot enjoy his possessions, however they accumulate. He covets the land still belonging to Philemon and Baucis. The one small patch he does not own irritates him unbearably. He wants them out of the way: Mephistopheles and the Three Mighty Men will oblige him.

Deep in the Night (11288–11383)

Lynceus, used to being delighted by all he sees, must suddenly witness the destruction by fire of the old couple's house as well as the chapel and the lime grove. Faust sees it too, with brief and slight regret. Mephistopheles, returning with the thugs, recounts the murders of Philemon, Baucis and the Traveller. Faust blames them, his agents, for acting beyond his orders.

Midnight (11384–11510)

This and the two scenes following were perhaps drafted and worked on as early as 1800–1801. All three were completed in March 1825.

Four ghostly female figures materialize out of the smoke. Three of them, Want, Debt and Need, cannot touch Faust, because of his wealth. But the fourth, Care, enters and characterizes herself as the anxiety that undermines all decisive thought and action. Naturally, Faust wants nothing to do with her; he is as determined as ever to carry on regardless. Even when she blinds him, he has an inner vision of further work and summons the labourers to accomplish it.

In the Palace's Great Forecourt (11511–11603)

The labourers who arrive, with Mephistopheles as their gangmaster, are the grotesque lemurs, and their work is not the draining of a marsh but the digging of Faust's grave. To Mephisto's sardonic accompaniment, Faust imagines a free and vigorous people enjoying their risky lives on land reclaimed from the sea. His massive ego finds its correlative in this future colonization; and forefeeling the satisfaction of it, he utters words that Mephisto claims give him victory in their all-but-forgotten wager.

Entombment (11604–11843)

Mephistopheles, anxious to get his hands on Faust's departing soul, summons a good number of devils to watch around the corpse with him. The scene is grotesque in its action and gestures, thoroughly ironic in tone. Marlowe, the atheist, was much more serious. Here the devils are soon routed by angels strewing fiery rose petals. Mephisto, as susceptible to their pretty-boy attractions as he was to the lascivious Lamiae in Act Two, is distracted and Faust's soul is filched off to heaven.

Peaks and Ravines (11844–12111)

This final scene was probably written in December 1830, perhaps added to in 1831. The setting is, roughly, that of the Pisan Frescoes (see note to line 11844) depicting, among other things, anchorites in the Theban desert. Goethe adopted this Christian

iconography for its long tradition of seriousness, and operated
in it entirely to suit his own very peculiar poetic character and
purposes. Most striking is his feminization of the religious
ethos. Mary, distinctive though she is, belongs with Galatea
and Helen. Gretchen appears among other Penitent Women,
but neither her nor their sexuality is denied (the verse asserts
it). She intercedes for her lover, Faust. Few now would think
his striving alone redemptive. In fact, the entire vexed question
of salvation or damnation feels rather swept aside in the ecstatic
adoration, like that in the finale of Act Two, with which this
act and the whole 'tragedy' concludes. The ironies in this scene
are chiefly those of juxtaposition with other parts of the play.
In the veins of the verse itself courses the thorough seriousness
of a man near to death expressing and praising the love that
has driven him all his life.

Further Reading

English translations of *Faust*, arranged chronologically

Samuel Taylor Coleridge (Oxford, 2007), about half of *Part I*, first published 1821; this volume also contains versions of *Part I* by John Anster and Francis Leveson-Gower.

John Anster (*Part I*, 1835; Oxford World's Classics, 1907, reprinted with Marlowe's *Doctor Faustus*).

Anna Swanwick, in Bohn's Standard Library (*Part I*, 1850; *Part II*, 1879).

Theodore Martin (*Part I*, London, 1865; *Part II*, New York, 1886); revised by W. H. Bruford and reissued in Everyman's Library (London, 1954).

Bayard Taylor (London and Boston, *Part I*, 1871; *Part II*, 1876).

Philip Wayne, Penguin Books (*Part I*, 1949; *Part II*, 1959).

Louis MacNeice and E. L. Stahl, Faber (1951; reissued 1965), both parts, abridged.

Barker Fairley (Toronto, 1970), a prose version of both parts.

Walter Arndt (New York, 1976; reissued 2001), both parts.

Randall Jarrell (*Part I*, 1976; reissued by Penguin, 2001).

Stuart Atkins (Cambridge, Mass., 1984; Princeton, 1994), both parts.

David Luke, Oxford World's Classics (*Part I*, 1987; reissued 1998; *Part II*, 1994).

John R. Williams, Wordsworth Classics (Ware, 2007), *Part I*, *Part II* and *Urfaust*.

Books in English on Goethe's *Faust*

Butler, E. M., *The Fortunes of Faust* (Cambridge University Press, 1952; 1979).

Fairley, Barker, *Goethe's Faust: Six Essays* (Oxford University Press, 1953; 1965).

Gearey, John, *Goethe's Faust: The Making of Part One* (New Haven, Conn., 1981).

Mason, Eudo C., *Goethe's Faust: Its Genesis and Purport* (University of California Press, Berkeley, 1967).

Williams, John R., *Goethe's Faust* (Allen & Unwin, London, 1987).

Books in English on Goethe and his age

Boyle, Nicholas, *Goethe: The Poet and the Age*, vol. I: 1749–1790, vol. II: 1790–1803 (Oxford University Press, 1991, 2000).

Bruford, W. H., *Germany in the Eighteenth Century* (Cambridge University Press, 1935; 1952).

—, *Culture and Society in Classical Weimar, 1775–1806* (Cambridge University Press, 1962).

Fairley, Barker, *A Study of Goethe* (Oxford University Press, 1947).

Friedenthal, Richard, *Goethe: His Life and Times* (Weidenfeld and Nicolson, London, 1965).

Gray, R. D., *Goethe: A Critical Introduction* (Cambridge University Press, 1967).

Lewes, G. H., *The Life and Works of Goethe* (London, 1855; reissued in Everyman's Library, 1949).

Lukács, Georg, *Goethe and his Age* (Merlin Press, London, 1968).

Reed, T. J., *The Classical Centre: Goethe and Weimar 1775–1832* (Oxford University Press, 1984).

—, *Goethe* (Past Masters Series, Oxford University Press, 1984).

Williams, John R., *The Life of Goethe: A Critical Biography* (Blackwell's, Oxford, 1998).

FAUST, PART II

FAUST, PART II

THE SECOND PART
OF THE TRAGEDY
IN FIVE ACTS

ACT ONE

A Pleasant Place

[FAUST *bedded on a flowery greensward, fatigued, restless, seeking sleep. Twilight. A ring of spirits, graceful little figures, hovering and quick.*]

ARIEL [*song, accompanied by Aeolian harps*]
When the springtime showers of blossom
Over all things float and fall,
When the fields' green benediction
Shines on the earthborn, one and all,
Spirits large in kindness, quickly
The elves come helping where they can.
Be he holy, be he wicked,
They grieve for the unhappy man.   4620
About his head hovering in an airy round,
Do now the good deeds of your generous kind,
Quieten the savage trouble he is in,
Extract the scalding barbs of blame, delete
The sum of horror of his life to date.
There are four watches in the passing night.
Fill them all kindly now. First lay
His head down on a cool pillow,
Then bathe him in a Lethe dew, allow
His limbs, stiffened in cramps, to loosen,   4630
And sleep him strengthening towards the day.

Spirits, do what is right and sweet.
Return him to the holy light.

CHORUS [*solo, duet or many, by turns and in unison*]

When a mildness freights the breezes
Round the bordered sward of green
Scented breathings, veils and haze
Fetch the evening gloaming down.
Sweetest peace, come *sotto voce*,
Hush the heart with lullabies,
4640   Show this weary man your mercy,
Shutter up his seeing eyes.

Night has sunken down already,
Star connects with holy star,
Light and sparkle, large and tiny,
Glittering near and shining far;
Glittering mirrored in the lake here,
Shining night on clear skies,
While the ruling moon's full splendour
Seals the bliss of deep repose.

4650   Quenched already are the hours,
Joy and pain have fled away;
Feel already how your powers
Mend and trust the breaking day.
Combes are greening, hills are swelling
Bushily with grateful shade;
Towards the scythe the slinky billowing
Silver waves of harvest ride.

See, your listed wishes, they all
Beckon in that radiance!
4660   What encumbers you is trivial.
Sleep's a husk – fling it hence!
Dare to now! The many bend
This and that way, hesitant,
But the lords, who understand,
Seize the chance, get all they want.

[*A tremendous noise announces the approach of the sun.*]

ARIEL

    Hark now! Hear the storming Hours!
    Dinning in the spirits' ears,
    See another day has broken.
    Gates of rock creak rattling open
    And the noisy daylight rolls   4670
    Out on Phoebus' jangling wheels.
    Now the lifted trumpets blaring
    Strike the sight, astound the hearing!
    Things unheard of, things past bearing!
    Slip away to flower crowns,
    Deeper, deeper, under stones
    Under greenery shut tight
    Your ears against the deafening light.

FAUST

  Life's pulses beat again freshly alive
  Kindly to welcome the dawning in the air.   4680
  Earth, you endured this night too, you revive
  And at my feet in quickened life respire,
  Already with pleasures you environ me
  And start and stir the willing of my power
  Ever to strive to live life at the acme.
  The world lies open in a dawning light,
  Life's thousand voices sing from tree to tree,
  The lengths of valley are mistily replete,
  But the sky's brightness sinking deep
  Among the wettening trees, they sprout   4690
  In the scented gulph, the deep place of their sleep,
  And the flowering leafing grounds release
  Through pearly water all the colours they keep –
  I am the midpoint of a paradise.

  Look up! – Of the most solemn hour
  Already the giant summits give advice.
  To them, before it bends our way down here,
  The first enjoyment of eternal light's allowed.
  Now on the steeped green meadows a sheer

4700 New brightness and new clarity are bestowed
And lowering towards us, step by step, come down.
The light enters! – Enters like a blinding blade,
I turn away, my eyes pierced through with pain.

But so it is: trusting our hopeful longings
We fight our way to the highest, we are shown
The doors of satisfaction wide as wings:
And from that everlasting ground leaps out
Excess of flame. Poor astonished things!
We desired to light the torch of life – and meet
4710 An overwhelming sea of fire. Such fire!
Is it love? Is it hate? Turn and turn about
In pain and joy we writhe in the hot glare,
Monstrous. Then down to earth. We look
Through childish fingers at the hard to bear.

So let the sun keep at my back.
With waxing ecstasy I watch the flume
Of water roaring through the cleft of rock,
From leap to leap see how it splits its stream,
And how the split streams further multiply,
4720 Spume flinging skywards, spume on whizzing spume,
But then, how fine, sprung from this hurly-burly,
Arcs a bright bow of change and lastingness
Now clearly drawn, now fading airily,
Broadcasting all around it shivers of quickness.
That is the image for this striving life of ours.
Think more of that and grasp with more exactness:
We have life only in its flung-off colours.

Throne-Room in the Imperial Palace

[*State Council awaiting the arrival of the* EMPEROR. *Trumpets. All manner of courtiers, splendidly dressed, make their entrance. The* EMPEROR *seats himself, the* ASTROLOGER *standing on his right.*]

EMPEROR

My loyal friends, you are welcome here
Gathered together from near and far –
I have the wise man next to me   4730
But not the Fool. Where is he?

JUNKER

A pace or two behind your train
There on the stairs his legs gave way.
His Lardship was stretchered from the scene.
Dead or drunk? Who shall say?

SECOND JUNKER

At once with strange celerity
Another pushed to take his place
Dolled up most amusingly
But so grotesque all stop and stare.
The guards prevent his entering here,   4740
They cross their halberds at the door.
But see! The bold Fool shows his face.

MEPHISTO [*kneeling at the throne*]

What's always cursed and kindly greeted?
Always desired, always refused?
And always hotly advocated?
And roughly scolded and accused?
Whom may you never bid appear?
Whose name do all hear with delight?
What nears the steps and throne of power?
What banished itself from your sight?   4750

EMPEROR

Spare me further words at present.
No riddles, please. Those gentlemen there,
Riddling riddles is their affair.

Solve some of theirs, I'd be content.
My old Fool, I'm afraid, has gone beyond.
You take his place and sit on my left hand.
          [MEPHISTOPHELES *climbs up and stands on the* EM-
          PEROR's *left*.]

MURMURINGS IN THE CROWD
A new Fool – A new affliction –
Where's this one from? – Who let him in? –
The old one fell – He quit the scene –
4760   We had the fat – And now the lean.

EMPEROR
My loyal friends, I say again
Welcome here from near and far!
You assemble under a lucky star,
Above us health and happiness are written.
But tell me then why in these days
When we put off our cares and woes
And mummer up for festivities
And wanted only cheerful things
We pain ourselves with councillings?
4770   But since we have no option, in your view,
And here we are, what must be done, let's do.

CHANCELLOR
The highest virtue, like an aureole,
Circles an emperor's head. He is its sole
True competent executor:
Justice, that all men love and long for,
Demand and cannot do without, to him
The people turn to grant it them.
But oh what good is a reasonable mind,
Hands that are willing, a heart that's kind
4780   If fever runs in rage throughout the state
And evils further evils propagate?
Whoever looks below from this high room
Into the wide realm, he thinks it a bad dream
Where one deformity couples with another
And illegality is the law
In a whole world of rampant error.

This man steals cattle, that a wife,
Cup, cross and lamp from the Lord's Table
And boasts about it and lives his life
Hale, hearty and untouchable.   4790
And claimants crowd the halls of justice,
The Judge, in splendour, cushions his seat,
Meanwhile rebellious turmoil waxes
Horribly into savage spate.
They thrive in crime and ignominy
Who have the guiltiest for friends;
The courts find none but those guilty
Whom innocence alone defends.
So the world hacks itself to pieces,
Annihilates all ought and should.   4800
How shall we in the midst of this
Direct our steps towards the good?
The well-intentioned man will lean
At last to those who keep him sweet;
And in the end the Judge will join
The criminals he cannot beat.
I've painted black but wish I might
Blanket the picture with thick night.
    [*He pauses.*]
We can no longer temporize.
When all are done by as they do   4810
Among the thieves the Crown falls too.
ARMY CHIEF
What madness raves in these wild days!
Kill and be killed on every hand,
The soldiery beyond command.
The citizen behind his walls,
The baron in his craggy lair
Withhold their help. Their common care
Is to outlive us in all that falls.
The mercenary is malcontent,
Loud in the mouth demands his pay,   4820
And if we settled our account
There and then he'd run away.

Stop people doing as they please
Is poking in a hornets' nest.
The realm they owe protection lies
Plucked and plundered, laid to waste.
They have the freedom to run riot,
Half the world's already lost,
There are still kings in the Empire but
4830   None thinks it is his business in the least.

TREASURER

What good are our alliances?
The subsidies they promised us
Like piped water never arrive.
And, Sir, in all of your wide lands
The properties are in whose hands?
Wherever you look new owners live
And want no ties or duties doing so.
We are spectators while they play.
We have given so many rights away
4840   There's nothing left that we have any right to.
Nor are the so-called parties now
A thing to be relied upon.
They frown on you or smile on you,
In the end their love and hate are one.
Whether they're Ghibelline or Guelph,
They hide away, they take their ease.
Who helps his neighbour nowadays?
Each man's interest is himself.
All barricade our passage to their gold,
4850   All scrape and save and have and hold,
And leave the imperial cupboard bare.

MARSHAL

I too see nothing but calamity.
Daily we vow economy
And every day devour more.
Daily some new distress is mine.
True, there's no shortage in the kitchens,
Wild boar and deer and hares and chickens
And guinea-fowl and ducks and geese

And cash and kind on rent and lease
They still come in, we can't complain.   4860
But what's the good of it? We're short of wine.
Our cellars that in former days
The best vineyards and vintages stacked high
Our indefatigable lords of booze
Have drunk quite dry.
The Town Council itself must broach its barrels.
In bowlfuls and bumperfuls
Under the table the tipple flows.
Who pays the wages and settles the bills?
The Jew won't let me off a jot,   4870
He sets me dates that must be met,
We're eaten up for years ahead.
We kill the pig before he's fat,
We pawn the mattress off the bed,
We've already eaten our daily bread.

EMPEROR [*thinks for a while, then to* MEPHISTOPHELES]
What further ill, Fool, can you add to that?

MEPHISTO
I? None. I see such glory all around
Of you and yours. And must not faith abound
Where Majesty commands? Who dares say no
Where ready power disperses every foe   4880
And goodwill, strengthened by good sense,
Is there and many-sided diligence?
What then towards disaster could combine
Or towards the dark, where such stars shine?

MURMURINGS
The man's a rogue – He knows the way –
Arrives with lies – And hopes to stay –
I know – What's at the back of this –
What next? – Some little scheme of his –

MEPHISTO
On earth there's lack of something everywhere,
This thing or that, and money's lacking here.   4890
The wise, who know it does not grow on trees,
Will root the deepest up however deep it lies.

In wall footings and mountain veins
There's nugget gold and gold coins.
And who'll deliver it? He will who bends
Mind and Nature under his commands.

CHANCELLOR

Nature and Mind! You offend our Christian ears.
Talk like that puts you in mortal peril.
We burn atheists alive for such ideas.
4900   Nature is sin, Mind is the Devil,
They nurture Doubt who is their ill-
Favoured and ill-begotten cross-between.
Don't give us them! – Only two family lines
Come down from the Emperor's old domains
And worthily they prop his throne:
The men of the Cross, the men of the Sword,
They stand fast, let it blow however hard,
And pocket Church and State in recompense.
In the muddled heads of low plebians
4910   Arises a resistance:
These are the heretics and the magicians,
And they corrupt us, town and country,
And now with insolent levity
You'd slip them into this noble society.
You keep corrupt companions,
They are the fool's near relations.

MEPHISTO

There speaks the learned gentleman!
What you can't touch is way beyond your ken,
What you can't grasp with hands wholly eludes you,
4920   What you can't calculate you think cannot be true,
What you can't weigh you say it has no weight,
What you don't mint you won't let circulate.

EMPEROR

This will not mend our sad predicament.
Have you a mind to sermon us through Lent?
I've heard enough of the endless how and when.
We're short of money. Good: get money then.

MEPHISTO

I will, a surplus too, you have my word.
Easy enough, but easy things are hard.
It's there already. The whole art
Is getting at it. Who knows where to start?   4930
Only consider: in those terrible times
When foreign tides submerged your native homes
How one man and another *à contre coeur*
Hid his best-loved possessions here and there.
It was so in the days of mighty Rome
And yesterday and still today the same
And all lies in the quiet ground deep down.
The ground's the Emperor's: let him have his own.

TREASURER

For a fool he speaks with some insight.
That is indeed the Emperor's ancient right.   4940

CHANCELLOR

Those are the golden coils of Satan.
By good and lawful means it can't be done.

MARSHAL

If he brings welcome benefits to court
Being a little wrong won't hurt.

ARMY CHIEF

The Fool's no fool. He says good things will come
To all. And soldiers never ask where from.

MEPHISTO

But if you think yourselves lied to by me
Ask this man here and his astrology.
He knows the hour, the house, the wheeling way.
So tell us what the heavens have to say.   4950

MURMURINGS

Two rogues – Already eye to eye –
Fool and fantasist – Raised high –
The old old story – Again and again –
Fool prompts Sage – Line by line –

ASTROLOGER [MEPHISTOPHELES *prompting him*]

The Sun is gold without impurity,

Mercury goes between for love and money,
All of you lie under Lady Venus' sway,
Early and late sweetly she looks your way.
Chaste Luna's moody humours switch and flit,
4960   Mars strikes or not, his power is still a threat.
But Jupiter has the brightest sheen of all.
Saturn is big, but seen remote and small,
For him, the metal, our esteem's not great:
Worth very little, though a heavy weight.
But Luna coupling nicely up with Sol,
Silver with gold, the prospect then is cheerful
And each will see whatever thing he likes –
Halls, gardens, apple breasts and rosy cheeks –
Procured him by a learned man
4970   Who can do things none of our number can.

EMPEROR

I hear him double. Nonetheless
His words still want persuasiveness.

MURMURINGS

They waste our time – A joke, a game –
Prophetical – Alchemical –
So often said – And never did –
Where he arrived – There he deceived –

MEPHISTO

See how they stand and stare and doubt
The treasure-trove will ever be found.
One raves we need a mandrake root,
4980   Another the Black Hound.
But let them snigger and condemn
Magic all they please,
One day the plodded ground will tickle them
However thick their shoes.
Of nature, sovereign and unending,
All have felt the secret throes
And living signs subtly ascending
Towards the light by veins and flues.
When limbs are tingled through and through
4990   And eeriness surrounds the spot

With pick and spade fall to, fall to!
There's golden music underfoot.

MURMURINGS

A leaden weight is in my feet –
Cramps in my arms – The pangs of gout –
As though a crab had my big toe –
All my spine is paining so –
These indications surely prove
Vast reserves of treasure-trove.

EMPEROR

No more evasions and excuses.
To prove the bubbles you have blown   5000
Show us the lovely buried places.
My sword and sceptre I lay down,
With these imperial hands of mine
I'll do the work if it's truth you tell
And if it's lies send you to hell.

MEPHISTO

I think I could find my own way there . . .
But let me turn your minds once more
To all that lies awaiting claim.
The peasant furrowing his field
Lifts with the clod a pot of gold;   5010
Or scratching daub walls for saltpetre bloom
His worn hand strikes in joy and dread
Gold in a golden roll instead.
What vaults there are to burglarize!
Along what cracks and tunnelled ways
The treasure-minded man must squeeze
Into the nether parishes.
In spacious cellars hollowed long ago
He sees before him, row on row,
Golden tankards, plates and dishes   5020
And ruby goblets line the shelf
And should he wish to serve himself
There's liquid still from the ancient days
But – if you'll believe a man who knows –
Long since the staves have rotted through

And all the wine's barrelled in tartar now.
The essences of such fine wines
Not only gold and precious stones
Are wrapped around in night and gloom.
5030   The wise man will not cease from searching here.
Daylight knowledge is small beer,
In darkness mysteries are at home.

EMPEROR
I leave dark things to you. What good are they?
All things of worth must see the light of day.
Who knows a rogue at dead of night for sure?
Night muddies the true colour of the creature.
Those pots down there, full of a golden weight,
Harness your plough and work them to the light.

MEPHISTO
Fall to yourself, take pick and spade,
5040   A peasant work will prove your worth
And all the golden calves you need
Will surface from the clinging earth.
Then with delight and with no more ado
Adorn yourself and your beloved too.
The gemstone's colouring and brilliancy
Enhance alike beauty and majesty.

EMPEROR
Why make me wait? Give it me now! At once!

ASTROLOGER [as above, prompted by MEPHISTOPHELES]
Sir, curb a while your hot desire with patience.
First let us have our cheerful pleasure-play.
5050   Distracted, we shall only go astray.
First in good state we must be conscience-cleaned,
Earn what's below by what's above the ground.
Who wants good things must first himself be good;
Who wants to enjoy, let him first calm his blood;
Who asks for wine must have ripe grapes to press;
Hoping for miracles, grow in faith no less.

EMPEROR
So let us pass the time in jollity,
How welcome then Ash Wednesday will be.

Whatever else, more merrily still we shall
Celebrate meanwhile our wild carnival.   5060

[Trumpets. They exit.]

MEPHISTO

The fools discern no link between
Happiness and earning it.
They might own the philosopher's stone
And yet of all philosophy – not one bit.

Spacious Hall with Adjoining Rooms

[Adorned and decorated for the masque.]

HERALD

Forget the air you breathe's the breath
Of German folly, sin and death.
A cheerful treat awaits you now.
Campaigning as the Romans did
Your Lord has climbed through Alpine snow
And won a cheerful realm below   5070
For your delight and his own good.
Your Emperor at Peter's Stool
First begged and got the right to rule
And when he went to fetch himself the crown
He brought us back the cap that fits the Fool.
Now all of us are born again
And every travelled worldly man
Covers his head and ears and is glad.
It gives him the appearance of the mad
And he acts wise in it the best he can.   5080
Already I see them crowding hither
Staggering apart and cosying together,
One shoving choir upon another choir.
Hither or hence, but boldly either way!
The world today like yesterday
With all its multifarious idiocy
Is one big fool and nothing more.

FLOWER GIRLS [*singing, accompanied by mandolins*]
        All to please you we have passed
        The night in donning finery.
5090   Florence is our city. Now
        We visit princely Germany.

        Though the curls of our brown hair
        With many cheerful flowers are dressed
        Little bits and bobs of silk
        Assist the naturals in the cast.

        For we reckon it a thing
        Deserving only praise from you:
        Manufactured flowers of ours
        Will bloom as brightly all year through.

5100   We have paid a fair regard
        To coloured snips in every style.
        You may mock this part or that
        And yet be taken by the whole.

        Are we not a pretty sight?
        At once the garden and the salon.
        What is Nature, what is Art
        Are closest kith and kin in woman.

HERALD
        Let us view the abundant baskets
        You carry on your heads and those
5110   Brightly buoyant on your arms.
        What he likes best let each man choose
        Speedily so that a garden
        In paths and bowers may arise!
        Here the sellers are as great
        A pull as is their merchandise.

FLOWER GIRLS
        In this cheerful marketplace
        All your trading must be fair.
        Short and sweet say what you're selling

So the buyer knows for sure.

SPRIG OF OLIVES

    Flowers never excite my envy,   5120
    I avoid controversy,
    My nature won't allow it me.
    Am I not a country's good
    And the certain guarantee
    And sign of peace on every stead?
    May I have the luck to crown
    Today the brows of someone fine.

WREATH OF GOLDEN CORN

    Ceres comes for your adornment,
    Her gifts will suit you sweetly well.
    Let your ornamenting marry   5130
    Useful and Desirable.

FANTASTICAL WREATH

    Brilliant blooms, resembling mallow,
    A mossy flowering, wondrous.
    Not the usual thing that Nature
    Creates herself. But Fashion does.

FANTASTICAL BOUQUET

    Theophrastus would not dare
    Utter you the name I bear.
    Though not all will like me, still
    One or other of you will.
    I would bind myself to girls   5140
    Who will wind me in their curls,
    Who will boldly follow where
    The heart leads, and have me there.

ROSEBUDS [*a challenge*]

    Fantasies, however gay,
    Let their fashion have its day
    Taking shapes more wondrous strange
    Than anything in Nature's range.
    Let through copious curls be seen
    Bells of gold on stems of green.
    We keep hidden. He will wish   5150
    For nothing more, who finds us fresh.

When the signs of summer quicken,
When the buds of roses redden
Why abide in joyless wanting?
All this promising and granting
Will command in Flora's pleasaunce
Sight and sense and heart at once.
[*Under leafy walks the* FLOWER GIRLS *set up pretty arrangements of their wares.*]

GARDENERS [*singing, accompanied by theorbos*]
    Flowers, by all means, watch them growing,
    See them prettily wreathe your hair.
5160   Fruits have more in mind than flirting,
    Present taste is their affair.

    So if sunburned faces offer
    Cherries, plums and peaches: buy!
    Tongue and palate will deliver
    Better judgement than the eye.

    Come then, feast with taste and pleasure
    On all the ripe and ready fruit.
    Roses are fit meat for poems;
    Apples: for the mouth to eat.

5170   Let us complement your wealth
    Of young florescence, two by two.
    And we'll raise abundant ripeness
    Neighbourly alongside you.

    Under merry garlandings
    In bowers that we decorate
    All may there be found together:
    Bud and leaf and flower and fruit.
[*Both choirs, singing in turn and accompanied by guitars and theorbos, continue to set up ever higher arrangements of their wares and to offer them for sale. Enter* MOTHER *and* DAUGHTER.]

MOTHER

> Girl, the day you saw the light
> I thought what a bride you'd be,
> Your little face, the sweetest sight,   5180
> And pretty little body.
> There and then I saw you smile
> Your way with Money down the aisle,
> A little wife already.
>
> Alas, so many years have gone
> Down the wind and did no good.
> All the merry tribe of men
> That ever courted you have fled.
> Neatly footsied it with this one,
> Gave that one a nice come-on,   5190
> Him the nod and him a prod.
>
> Parties, parties every week,
> The man and you would never click.
> Murder, forfeits, hide and seek,
> No game ever did the trick.
> Every simpleton and sap
> Is out today. In your fly-trap
> Girl, surely one will stick.

[*The* DAUGHTER's *friends, all young and pretty, join her.
They engage in confidential chatter. Enter* FISHERMEN
and BIRDCATCHERS, *with nets, rods, limed sticks and
other equipment. They mix with the pretty girls. Attempts
among them from one side and another to win over, seize,
escape, keep hold give rise to some very pleasant
exchanges.*]

WOODCUTTERS [*entering with uncouth haste and noise*]

> Make way for us!
> Give us elbow room!   5200
> We chop trees down,
> They crack, they fall,
> When we hump and haul

We are dangerous
But it must be said
In praise of us
Without us bruisers
On their land
How would the well-bred
5210   For all their wit
Have any foothold?
You must understand:
You'd die of cold
If we didn't sweat.

PUNCHINELLOS [*awkward, almost puerile*]
You're the nincompoops,
You were born to stoop
And we're the bright ones
Who never bore burdens.
For our caps and bells
5220   And motley frills
Weigh very little
And always idle
We caper about
On slippered feet
Self-satisfied
Through the market crowd
And we stand and gawk
And cackle and squawk
And by these appeals
5230   Like mating eels
Through crush and smother
We find one another
And jig together
And rave and whether
You love us or not
We care not a jot.

PARASITES [*lasciviously flattering*]
You tree-toting men
And your kith and kin

The charcoalers, oh
We're beholden to you!   5240
For all the bowing,
The yessing, kow-towing
And tortuous phrases,
The floating two faces
That warm you or chill
Whichever you will,
What good is it all?
Even if from the skies
Enormous supplies
Of fire were to fall   5250
Still we need stacks
Of logs and charcoal
To grill by the fieldful
The herds and the flocks.
A frying and fizzling,
A seething and sizzling:
The dishlicker who
Would lick spittle for you
He senses a cutlet,
He sniffs out a trout,   5260
It moves him to eat
Wherever he's let.

DRUNK [*oblivious*]

Friends with all the world today!
Feel myself so frank and free!
Singing cheerful! OBJ!
Who do I say thanks to? Me.
So I'm drinking, drinking, drinking,
Chinking glasses, clinking, clinking.
You at the back there, raise a glass!
Clink and drink will do for us!   5270

Bawling wife, beside herself,
Mocked this motley coat of mine
(The coat on which I pride myself)

Called me Rags, the Panto Clown!
But I'm drinking, drinking, drinking,
Chinking glasses, clinking, clinking.
Panto Ragbags, raise a glass!
Clink and drink will do for us.

Don't tell me I should not be here:
5280   Where I am I'm at my ease.
Mine host tight? His wife is freer
And the barmaid can't refuse.
Always drinking, drinking, drinking,
You and me now, clinking, clinking,
Each to each now, raise a glass!
Seems like more is best for us.

How and where I take my pleasure
Let me take it, let me be.
Where I'm lying, let me lie there.
5290   Standing is too much for me.

CHORUS
One and all now, drinking, drinking,
Raise your glasses, clinking, clinking!
But sit tight a while because
Under the table does for us.

[*The* HERALD *announces various poets: of nature, the
court, chivalry – the tender and the enthusiastic. In the
press of competitors of all kinds none will allow any other
to perform. One creeps by, with these few words:*]

SATIRIST
I tell you this, as a poet
Nothing would please me more
Than being allowed to utter
What nobody wants to hear.

[*The Poets of the Night and the Graveyard beg to be
excused. They are engaged in a most interesting conver-
sation with a freshly risen vampire, from which encounter
a new strain of poetry may perhaps develop. The* HERALD

has to leave them to it, and in the meantime summons up
figures from Greek mythology who, even in modern dress,
have all their old character and appeal.]

THE GRACES
AGLAIA

> Grace is what we bring to living.
> Put grace also into giving.

HEGEMONE

> Grace also into receiving.
> Sweet to reach what you were craving.

EUPHROSYNE

> And when quiet days contain you
> Graceful be your thanking too.

5300

THE FATES
ATROPOS

> I, the eldest, on this occasion
> Am asked to be the one to spin.
> Life's a very weighty matter
> But the thread of it is thin.
>
> Here to make it sleek and even
> I sought out the finest flax
> And my clever fingers smooth it
> Soft and workable as wax.
>
> If, however, dancing, prancing,
> You do not know when to stop,
> Bear in mind this thread has limits
> And be careful: it might snap.

5310

CLOTHO

> At this present time, be easy,
> The shears are in my custody.
> For not all were happy with
> The conduct of the old lady.

5320

First she trails her idle tissues
Lingeringly in the light,
Then she drags the hope of winnings,
Snipped, into eternal night.

I myself a hundred times
Erred under the sway of youth
But I toe the line today:
See, the shears are in their sheath.

I am glad of my restriction,
5330   Show the world a smiling front.
You, allowed these hours of licence,
Revel to your hearts' content.

LACHESIS
I remain the regulator,
Level-headed of the three.
Spools and bobbins, ever lively,
Never run away with me.

Threads arriving, threads a-winding,
All I guide the track they must,
Never let one jump the circuit,
5340   All will wind as I insist.

Doubtful would the world survive
Any flightiness of mine!
Tell the time in hours and years
Till the weaver takes the skein.

HERALD
These coming now you'll scarcely recognize
However well you're travelled in the old books.
The doers of so much ill, judged by their looks,
Are guests you'd welcome in with glad surprise.

They are the Furies, no one will believe us,
5350   Young, shapely, amiable and well-inclined.
Have anything to do with them, you'll find
These turtle-doves wound as the serpent does.

Two-faced they are, but won't on this occasion
(Where every fool boasts of his every blot)
Announce themselves as Marys-Without-Spot:
They admit they are the bane of town and nation.

THE FURIES
ALECTO

You're bound to trust in us, do what you will,
For we are young and pretty and make eyes.
If one of you is fonder than is wise
We'll tickle him behind the ears until   5360

He'll listen when we tell him tête-à-tête
That she likes more than one man at a time,
Soft in the head, crook-backed she is and lame
And as his bride-to-be not worth a lot.

And we beset that bride-to-be as well:
Her man himself, a little while ago,
Spoke ill of her to some Miss So-and-So.
They may make up, but something rankles still.

MEGAERA

Frivolities! For once they are joined together
I step in. I can convert love's good   5370
On the swing of a mood to gall and wormwood.
Time and humanity, unsteady as the weather!

Once in his arms holding the wished-for fast
He longs for something yet more wished-for than
That highest happiness become quotidian,
Flees from the sun, the fool, to warm the frost.

With all of this I know what I must do
And introduce Asmodeus, the ever faithful,
Who strews bad karma when the time is favourable
And so I ruin humans two by two.   5380

TISIPHONE

> I whet knives, I mix poison
> Worse than words, to hurt the traitor.
> Love another, sooner or later
> You will lie with Perdition.
>
> All that's sweetest you will trade for
> Sourest in an equal measure.
> There's no haggling your debt lower,
> What you did, that will be paid for.
>
> Beg forgiveness? Save your breath.

5390
> I appeal to walls of rock:
> 'Revenge! Revenge!' they answer back.
> The one you left her for is – Death.

HERALD

> Step to one side a while, if you don't mind.
> Our next arrival is not of your kind.
> A mountain shoulders forward. See his slopes
> Magnificently hung with coloured drapes,
> The serpent trunk, the long teeth in his head:
> He is a riddle I will help you read.
> A *petite* woman riding on his neck

5400
> Steers him exactly with a little stick.
> Around the other, upright and austere,
> A radiance shines that is too bright to bear.
> He has a noble woman either side,
> One gladdens us, the other makes us afraid,
> One feels at liberty, the other longs to be.
> Let each speak her identity.

FEAR

> Smoky lamps and lights and torches
> Glimmer through the muddled feast.
> In among these lying faces

5410
> Chains of magic hold me fast.

How your laughter – laughable –
How your grinning worries me;
All the night that I inhabit
Heaves with black hostility.

Where a friend was, there a foe is,
Now the mask falls from his face.
See, my would-be murderer
Creeps, discovered, from this place.

Down the four winds, oh how gladly,
Far abroad I might have fled.   5420
But from there my ruin threatens,
Holds me here in gloom and dread.

HOPE

Greetings to you, sisters. Though you
Yesterday and still today
Have enjoyed the masking play
This I know for sure: tomorrow
All of you will show your faces.
And although by torchlight no one
Feels especially at ease
Come the free and cheerful days   5430
We shall walk through pleasant places
Now together, now alone
Doing wholly as we please
Deeds, or nothing, as we choose,
Ours will be a carefree living,
Never wanting, always having.
We are welcomed everywhere,
Enter with an easy mind:
For the best is, here or there,
Surely waiting to be found.   5440

WISDOM

Fear and Hope, two of the greatest
Enemies of humankind,
I hold off from mixing with you.
You are safe now. They are chained.

See, I steer the live colossus
Tower-bearing, step by step.
Nothing ruffles him, he climbs
Mountain paths without mishap.

High upon the battlements
5450   Rides the goddess with the wide
Speedy wings and spies the winnings
To be had on every side.

Flings around in every quarter
Brilliantly her light and glory:
Goddess of all activities,
And her name is Victory.

ZOILO-THERSITES
Have I not timed my arrival well?
I could badmouth you one and all
But I address particularly
5460   Her Highness Lady Victory.
Because of those white wings of hers
She gives herself an eagle's airs
As though wherever she looked the land
And folk were under her command.
But I'm the Anti-Champion
When deeds of derring-do are done.
Raise up the low, abase the high,
Make crooked straight, make straight awry,
No other state of affairs will suit
5470   And only then do I feel right.

HERALD
You'll feel my sacred rod salute
You, toe-rag, with a masterstroke.
Wriggle and writhe now all you like!
But look! That shape of double pygmy
Conglobates disgustingly,
The wondrous blob becomes an egg
And swells up bigger and too big
And pops, and twins fall out of it,

Sister viper, sister bat,
First sister through the dust exits,   5480
Black second to the ceiling flits.
They hurry to meet in the open air,
I should not like to join them there.

MURMURINGS

Quick! The dancing has begun –
No. I'd rather I were gone –
Oh the brood of ghosts and ghouls
Wrapping us in feeling coils! –
Felt it whizzing through my hair –
Felt my foot become aware –
Seems that none of us is harmed –   5490
All however are alarmed –
Now our revelry is ended –
Which the beastly things intended.

HERALD

Since the herald's job was made
Mine at every masquerade
On your threshold I have stood
Sentry so no bad thing should
Creep upon you in your play,
Never wavered or gave way.
But through every window now   5500
Chilly draughts of spirits blow
And I don't have what it takes
To free you all of spells and spooks.
From that dubious dwarf has sprung
All this multitudinous throng.
I should do what heralds do
And explain these shapes to you.
But how to elucidate
What I cannot understand?
Help me, will you! Give me insight.   5510
See that splendid chariot float
Through the crowd, a four-in-hand
Carrying onward but without
Any parting of the assembly,

Nowhere do I see a mêlée.
Coloured glitterings at a distance,
Wandering stars' bright luminance
As in a magic lantern show.
Steeds that like a tempest blow
5520   Near. Make way! I tremble!

BOY CHARIOTEER
                                        Whoa!
Horses, fold your wings and feel
The bridle's reasserted rule.
Curb yourselves, being curbed by me.
When I inspire you, then ride free:
Let us give these rooms their due!
How they widen, look around you,
Circles of admiration.
Herald, acting in your function
Before we vanish from your sight
5530   Name us, say how we appear.
We are allegories, you are
Duty-bound to get us right.

HERALD
I can't put a name to you,
Might perhaps describe you though.

CHARIOTEER
Try.

HERALD
        I will say, first of all,
You are young and beautiful.
You are a boy, half grown, but very likely
Women imagine you full-grown already.
I seem to see you courting, fit
5540   And eager to seduce them, born to it.

CHARIOTEER
Flattering, I'm sure. Go on
And find the riddle's sweet solution.

HERALD
Black lightning of the eyes, curls black as night
Enlivened brightly by a band of jewels,

And such a pretty costume ripples
Hemmed with crimson, glittering with baubles,
Down from your shoulders to your feet
You might be censured for your girlishness
But that for good or ill
Among the girls already you impress: 5550
They'd teach you how to count and spell.

CHARIOTEER

And this magnificent shape riding
High in the chariot in splendour?

HERALD

He seems to me a rich and giving king.
Happy the man who has his favour!
What further thing could that man strive to get?
Whatever lacks, those eyes will spy for it
And the pure joy he has in giving
Exceeds the happiness of having.

CHARIOTEER

You may not rest there. You must fashion   5560
The exactest possible description.

HERALD

Is dignity describable?
Healthy moon-countenance, ample
Lips and mouth, the cheeks in bloom
Below the turban's crown!
A rich contentment folds him in a gown.
Beyond words, such a bearing! I seem
To know him as a Lord of Power.

CHARIOTEER

His name is Plutus, God of Wealth, come here
In his magnificence, to answer   5570
The high Emperor's hot desire.

HERALD

Speak now of your own identity.

CHARIOTEER

I am the careless gift of Poetry,
The Poet whose self-perfection is
The careless giving away of what's most his.

Immeasurable wealth is mine as well,
I rate myself God Plutus' equal,
His feasts I animate and ornament
And deal his guests whatever he might want.

HERALD

5580   Boasting becomes you. But now will you
Show us what clever things you can do?

CHARIOTEER

I snap my fingers. Before your eyes
Around the chariot light plays!
A loop of pearls leaps in the air,
   [*on all sides continually snapping his fingers*]
There's gold to fit at the neck or the ear
And flawless combs and little crowns
And rings set with priceless stones
And now and then I might donate
Flames, to see what they ignite.

HERALD

5590   How the people snatch and grab!
Shall we lose the giver in the mob?
He summons up jewels as though in a dream
And hands are grabbing throughout the room.
But now there comes another turn:
Our friends, for all their efforts, earn
Poor reward. What the giver gave
Behold it flutter up and leave!
The string of pearls dissolves, disbands,
And beetles tickle in the hands.

5600   Who flings them off him feels them still
Humming round his numb skull.
Others, instead of solidities,
Snatch hold of wicked butterflies.
The rogue, to promise gold and only
Deliver what glitters goldenly!

CHARIOTEER

I note you do well at announcing masks
But fathoming the hearts within these husks
Is not the business of a court MC.

It wants a sharper sight, to see.
But I'm not one for quarrelling. And so,   5610
Master, I'll address myself to you.
        [*Turning to* PLUTUS]
Have you not trusted me to ride
The four-in-hand, the wind-bride?
Do I not steer as you direct me?
Arrive where you had wished to be?
And say did I not boldly go
Winged and win the palm for you?
However often I fought your fight
Always the lots fell right.
To the cunning of my hand and brain you owe   5620
The threaded laurels on your brow.

PLUTUS

If you need good report from me I give it
Gladly: you are spirit of my spirit.
In all you do as I would do,
You are the richer of us two
And higher than any other crown of mine
In thanks to you I rate the sprig of green.
        [*To the crowd*]
I give you all my authorized
Beloved Son, in whom I am well pleased.

CHARIOTEER [*to the crowd*]

See all around my hand sends forth   5630
Among you gifts of greatest worth.
My little spray of flame alights
On one or other of your pates
And flits from yours to your neighbour's
And bides on his or quits for hers
And rarely, flowering, enjoys
A brief and brilliant rapid blaze.
Many, before they realize,
The flame goes dim in them and dies.

COARSE VOICES OF WOMEN

        Him up there on the chariot   5640
        He is a fraud, be sure of that,

The clown back there, hunkering down,
Hungry, thirsty, skin and bone
Never saw the like. There's not an inch
Enough of him to feel the pinch.

SKIN-AND-BONE

Hands off me, filthy female crew!
I never could do right by you.
When women looked after hearth and home
Mrs Avaritia was my name.
5650   Then the house stood in a goodly state,
Much coming in, nowt going out.
Strongbox and safe were my passion then:
Are you telling me that was a sin?
But the women latterly have left
The old accustomed ways of thrift
And like all bad debtors they
Have far more wants than cash to pay.
The husband has a lot to bear,
Wherever he looks, debts everywhere,
5660   What comes her way she spends it on
Her body or her fancyman
And eats better, drinks even more,
With all the idlers courting her.
So I love money better and best:
I'm *Mister* Skinflint, *Mister* Tightfist.

LEADER OF THE WOMEN

Let him skin his dragons, he's one of them.
It's lies and trickery when all's said and done.
He's only here to incite the men,
Trouble enough without any of him.

WOMEN EN MASSE

5670   There's nothing to him. Box his ears!
Who does the old gibbet think he is
With a face like that come threatening us?
His dragons are only paper tigers.
At him! We'll have his guts for garters!

HERALD

By this staff of mine, you'll keep the peace!

But I hardly need to interfere.
Look where the monsters in a trice
Bestir themselves and clear a space
And spread their double pairs of wings
With furious scaly shudderings   5680
And open wide and puff fire.
They rout the crowd, the place is clean.
   [PLUTUS *descends from the chariot.*]
Now he descends, how regally.
He signals. Now the dragons are busy
Carrying down the chariot chest
That holds the gold and Mr Tightfist.
They set their burden at Plutus' feet.
Prodigious deed! Prodigious sight!

PLUTUS [*to the* BOY CHARIOTEER]
Now you are rid of the overburdening weight,
Return where you are free and clear and bright!   5690
Here's not your zone. All's chequered here,
A muddled, mad, besetting caricature.
Go where you view sweet clarity open-eyed
And own yourself, in your sole self confide,
And only the beautiful and the good give pleasure,
Return to solitude! – Make your world there.

CHARIOTEER
I am the worthy go-between and love
You as the closest kith and kin I have.
Where you are, riches are; so too do all
Feel gloriously lucky where I dwell.   5700
Except life contradicts and they incline
More your way one day and the next more mine.
Those serving you can take it easy, true;
Whereas my followers have much to do.
I cannot do my deeds in secrecy,
Soon as I breathe, that very breath betrays me.
As you wish me so I wish you good luck.
Farewell. Soft-summon me and I'll be back.
                        [*Exits as he entered.*]

PLUTUS

    The time has come to set the treasure free.
5710   I smite the chest locks with the Herald's rod.
    They open! There in brazen cauldrons see
    How it proceeds and seethes with golden blood:
    Crowns, chains and rings all going, going, gone,
    So it seems, in meltdown to oblivion.

SHOUTS HERE AND THERE IN THE CROWD

    Look there! The riches welling up
    Filling the chest to the very top –
    Out of the melt of golden vessels
    A mint of golden rouleaus spirals –
    And ducats stamped with a sovereign crest
5720   Jump for joy like the heart in my breast –
    And I see what I most desire
    Rolling around on the ground here –
    It is offered you, it is yours to use,
    So get rich quick, on your hands and knees –
    The rest of us, by force of fist,
    Will take possession of the chest.

HERALD

    You ruffians! You fools! These are
    Masked amusements, nothing more.
    Tonight you've coveted enough.
5730   Would we dole gold and precious stuff
    To such as you? Toy money is
    The most you'll get from pageantries.
    What dolts you are! A clever show
    At once seems solid truth to you.
    And what a truth! You batten on
    Every dumb delusion.
    Costume Plutus, hero of our play,
    Kindly drive this tribe away.

PLUTUS

    Your rod's the thing. I'll borrow it
5740   A little while, if you'll permit,
    And quickly dip it in frothing fire:
    Now, masks, watch out! Beware! Beware!

It flashes and bangs and sparks fly off,
Behold my incandescent staff!
Now whomsoever comes too near
Mercilessly I singe and sear.
Shall I begin my walk-about?

SHOUTS [*with pushing and shoving*]

Alas, we're done for – Turn about
And run for it – But we must stay
Forward until the rear gives way –   5750
Sparks in my face! – I fear the thwack
Of his redhot rod across my back –
The tide of masks is strong – They keep
Us fronted here. There's no escape –
Give way behind, you mindless herd! –
How shall I fly? Am I a bird?

PLUTUS

The ring that pressed us has retreated
And none, I think, incinerated.
The crowd yield
And quit the field.   5760
Order restored, I draw a line
That signals it and can't be seen.

HERALD

A famous victory! For such shrewd
Force you have my gratitude.

PLUTUS

Steady, friend! We'll likely get
Varieties of trouble yet.

SKINFLINT

With your permission, Sir, who won't
Look on this circle with delight?
When there's a treat to gawp at or to eat
It's always women who are at the front.   5770
My person is not wholly knackered yet,
A lovely woman still looks good to me.
Therefore today, when I can do it free,
I will a-wooing go. Why not?
But since when there are crowds of people

Not every word in every ear is audible
I'll cannily, in hopes I'll get somewhere,
By miming what I want make myself clear.
Hands, feet and gestures will not be enough,
5780   I need a joke, a trick, some funny stuff.
I'll mould the gold there like wet clay
For you can bend that metal every which way.

HERALD

What's he about, the bony fool?
A hunger artist with a smile?
He's kneading all the gold to dough,
It softens in his hands. But though
He plumps and squeezes as he likes
It's still unshapeliness he makes.
And now the women: he turns to them,
5790   They scream and shout, want none of him,
Conduct themselves disgustingly
And he, the old devil, thrustingly.
I fear his entertainment is
A series of indecencies.
I have to act. Give me my staff.
It is my duty to chase him off.

PLUTUS

Little does he know what threatens from without!
Let him continue tomfooling about.
There won't be room for it much longer.
5800   The law is strong, necessity is stronger.

TUMULT AND SINGING

The wild army is on the move
From mountain top and combe and grove
They march unstoppably on
To celebrate their Great God Pan.
For they know things no others know
And crowd the ring that's empty now.

PLUTUS

I know you well and your Great Pan.
The step you take together is a bold one.

Things that not everybody knows, I do
And open this small circle as I'm bound to.   5810
May a good ending travel with them,
The very strangest things can happen,
They do not know their story's outcome,
They have not made provision.

A WILD SINGING

A flimsy show! A posh parade!
But now the rough and raw brigade
In leaps and bounds, alive and keen
Come thumping on the scene.

FAUNS

Fauns in droves
They wear the oak's   5820
Wreathing leaves
In their curly hair
And through that tousled cover pokes
A delicately pointed ear.
The wide face, the snub nose:
Women are not put off by these.
The loveliest, should a faun extend
His paw to dance, will give her hand.

SATYR

Now from behind the Satyr jigs
On goat feet and scrawny legs.   5830
He wants them thin and sinewy.
On mountains, like the chamois, he
Looks about him merrily
And high on freedom's breezes then
Laughs at child and wife and man
Who snug in the valley's smoke and stew
Imagine they are living too
Whereas of course up there the clean
Unspoilt world is his alone.

GNOMES

The little trotty gang appears   5840
Single file, never in pairs

But rapidly, in suits of moss
And carrying lanterns, they criss-cross
Like ants of light, a million,
While each looks after Number One.
They bustle in a busy pother
To and fro, hither and thither.

Good fairies' kith and kin, renowned
Physicians of the stony ground,
5850   We fleece the lofty mountain chains,
We bleed their superabundant veins,
In quantities we blast and hack
The metals out. So wish us luck.
We have the good of man in mind,
We are his friends, he should be kind.
And yet we mine the gold for use
By men who thieve and who seduce
And will not leave them short of steel
Who do their murdering wholesale.
5860   Forget those three, God's other do's
And don'ts you will forget likewise.
For none of this are we to blame.
We live with it. You do the same.

GIANTS

And these are called the wild men,
In the Harz they're known to everyone.
Nature-naked, full of vim,
And giant-sized the lot of them,
In their right hand a bole of pine
And twigs and leaves around them twine
5870   A rude skirt, a gross hoop:
Oh, they might bodyguard the Pope!

CHORUS OF NYMPHS [surround the GREAT GOD PAN]

And he is here!
We see the One
And All appear
In Great Pan.

Encircle him in joy, entrance
His spirit in your ring of dance.
For he is serious but good
And gladdened when the world is glad.
He can wake and watch throughout   5880
The blue daylight however bright
But babbling water, mild breeze
May induce his eyes to close
And when he sleeps at mid-day no
Leaf will stir on any bough,
Only the healthful plants respire
Sweetly on the quiet air.
Even the lively nymphs must keep
The peace and where they stand they sleep.
But if into the empty space   5890
Suddenly he hurls his voice
Like bangs of lightning, roaring sea,
Then all the mind's advisers flee,
The army's hold on courage breaks,
The hero facing fire shakes.
So honour be paid where honour is owed
And hail the leader we have followed.

DEPUTATION OF GNOMES [*to* GREAT PAN]
While the stock of glittering riches
Threads through splits in rock and shows
Only the diviner's hazel   5900
All its labyrinthine ways

We in vaulted holes in darkness
House in troglodytic style
While above, in airy daylight,
You distribute treasure-dole.

Now nearby we have discovered
A phenomenon, a spring
That bids fair to give with comfort
A hitherto elusive thing.

5910   What it promises, accomplish!
        Be the guardian of it!
        From a treasure in your keeping
        All the world will benefit.

PLUTUS [*to the* HERALD]

  It is required we make our minds steadfast
  And equably let happen here what must.
  Show now the strength you have already shown.
  The worst is imminent and will not be
  Believed by our world or posterity:
  Faithfully in your record set it down.

HERALD [*taking hold of the staff which* PLUTUS *has retained
      in his hand*]

5920   Gently the little people bring
  Great Pan to the fire-spring.
  It boils up out of the depths and then
  Back it sinks down the shaft again,
  The black mouth gapes open
  And retches up more hot ferment.
  Great Pan stands there, content.
  The wondrous thing gives him delight,
  A pearly foam flies left and right.
  Why must he go so near and stoop
5930   Over the beast, to know how deep?
  And now his beard has fallen in!
  Whose, I wonder, is that smooth chin?
  A hand obscures our vision.
  And now a very great mishap:
  The beard ignites and flutters up
  And lights the wreath and leafy chain.
  Our pleasure ends in burning pain.
  To douse and damp the people run
  But fire fastens on everyone.
5940   They beat and flap but only arouse
  A greater fury in the blaze.
  Caught in the element of flames
  A tangled masquerade consumes.

But what is this? What do I hear?
A word that's mouthed from ear to ear.
This night will live for evermore
Remembering the grief it bore.
The coming day will open on
News welcome to no one.
But everywhere I hear them cry   5950
'The *Emperor* suffers this agony!'
I wish some other thing were true!
The Emperor burns and all his crew!
Curse them for getting him to lace
Himself in resinous greenery
And roar and riot to this place
Of general catastrophe!
Youth, oh Youth can you not confine
Your pleasure to the golden mean?
And Majesty, not affiance   5960
Absolute power to common sense?

The foliage goes up in flames
That tongue and tickle and lick the beams
And pannelling above our heads.
A total conflagration spreads,
This is more grief than we can bear.
But how shall rescue come? From where?
One night! Under tomorrow's sky
Ashed the imperial wealth will lie.

PLUTUS
Terror's tenancy is done.   5970
Now let help be ushered on!
Seize the staff of power! Strike!
Make the boards boom and quake.
O roomy ranging air ingest
All you can of cool and wet.
Heavy streamers, breaths of mist
Come and hover here and blanket
This uproar of flames.
Clot the sky with ruffled nimbus,

5980   Soughing, mizzling, fine as sea-fret,
        Damping, dousing, succour us
        You powers of soothing, powers of moistening
        Turn this fire's idle games
        To a show of sheet lightning.
        Threatened by bad spirits we need
        Active magic on our side.

A Pleasure-Garden

[*A sunny morning, early.* EMPEROR, COURTIERS. FAUST,
MEPHISTOPHELES, *dressed respectably, conventionally,
not ostentatiously, both kneeling.*]

FAUST
    Do you forgive us, Sir, our tricks with flames?
EMPEROR [*motioning them to rise*]
    I should be glad of many more such games.
    I saw myself rapt to a zone of fire
5990   And I was Pluto, so it seemed, before
    The rock-floor of the night ablaze
    Like coke. Up deep wells rose
    Thousands of whirling flames that built,
    By interflickering, one vault
    Of tongues, higher and higher, and became
    An ever-shaping, ever-unshaping dome.
    I saw the long processions of the peoples
    Approach from a far perimeter down aisles
    Of interlacing fires, to the hub, to pay
6000   Me homage in the customary way.
    I recognized some of my courtiers
    And seemed the Prince of a thousand salamanders.
MEPHISTO
    And so you are! For every element
    Gives Majesty its absolute acknowledgement.
    You have made a trial of fire's obedience,
    Now leap in the ocean's greatest turbulence.

No sooner shall you tread its pearly ground
There'll be a splendid working all around
And you will see the waves, light-green, agile
And crimson-hemmed, swell to the loveliest domicile   6010
Round you, the midpoint. Wherever you go
At every stride palaces will go too,
The very walls delight in their own living,
In their quick teeming, their contrapuntal striving.
Sea-monsters pelt against this new mild light
But none will be let in. They congregate.
Here dragons play, in gawdy golden mail.
A shark gapes: you laugh into his smile.
Centre of your court's delight, never before
Were you so thronged about as here.   6020
Nor must you do without the sweetest thing of all:
Curious Nereids approach that hall
Of splendour and eternal freshness,
The youngest shy and lascivious as fishes,
The older shrewd. Soon Thetis hears of this
And offers hand and mouth to the second Peleus.
Taking your seat then in the Olympian *quartier* –

EMPEROR

Spare me the airy mansions for today,
Sooner than wished we shall ascend that throne.

MEPHISTO

And the earth, my sovereign, you already own.   6030

EMPEROR

You seem a character from the Arabian Nights
Sent here among us by the kindly Fates.
If you're as fruitful as Scheherazade
You will have highest favour, on my word.
Stand by for those occasions – they will be
Many – when the daylight world disgusts me.

MARSHAL [*hurrying on*]

O Majesty, I never thought that I
Should ever be the announcer of such joy
As this I bring you now that throws
Me, the announcer, into ecstasies: 6040

One reckoning and another paid,
The vulturous creditors pacified,
Hell's torturers have all left me in peace,
Heaven itself can't be a happier place.

ARMY CHIEF [*hurrying on after him*]
We pay them on the instalment plan!
All forces sworn to serve again!
The ranks are fit for fun. Once more
To work go publican and whore.

EMPEROR
You breathe again! The wrinkled brow
6050   Of worry is smooth and cheerful now!
How speedy now are your entrances!

TREASURER [*entering*]
And why? Ask these whose work it is.

FAUST
The Chancellor should speak. Lend him your ears.

CHANCELLOR [*approaching slowly*]
Happiness enough in my declining years.
Behold the fateful paper. Hear me tell
How it has made all things well.
      [*He reads*]
'To whom it may concern: Whoever owns
This note is owed a thousand crowns.
For its sure guarantee and certain bond
6060   Untold wealth's buried in the imperial land.
Provision enough! So without more ado
Let this wealth you can pocket serve in lieu.'

EMPEROR
I smell a crime, a monstrous deceit.
Who forged my name? Has this gross counterfeit
Been perpetrated without retribution?

TREASURER
Think back only last night. You were the one
Who signed. You stood as Great God Pan.
The Chancellor addressed you, as our spokesman:
'Allow yourself this pleasure at our festival,
6070   With the stroke of a pen be saviour of your people.'

You signed. Magicians spawned
Your name in thousands before day dawned.
And that some good should come to everyone
We stamped the complete series there and then:
Tens, Thirties, Fifties, Hundreds, fit for service.
How gladdened were the populace by this!
A lusty life teems in your town that wore
The cast of moribundity before.
Your name, always a blessing, was never so
Amicably viewed as it is now.   6080
The alphabet's redundant. All will be
By this sole sign redeemed sufficiently.

EMPEROR

My people take this as good gold, you say?
And the army and the court for their full pay?
Scarcely believable, but I must let it stand.

MARSHAL

It can't be reined in now. Throughout the land
The fleet things whisked away at lightning speed,
The welcoming exchanges open wide,
They honour – at a profit, to be sure –
Every note with gold and silver there.   6090
And so to butcher, baker, publican,
Half the world's one thought is tucking in,
The other half shows off new buttons and bows.
The draper cuts the cloth, the tailor sews,
Toasts fizz in tap-rooms to the Emperor,
And boiling, roasting, plate-rattling galore.

MEPHISTO

Lone strollers on the terraces soon note
Some lovely woman fabulously kitted out.
Behind the peacock-feather fan she spies
For men who have these paper promises.   6100
They reach the sum of love, the best of it,
Much faster than by rhetoric or wit.
Who uses purses now? Too cumbersome.
A banknote fits so snugly in the bosom
And couples nicely with a love-note there,

The priest will bed one in the Book of Common Prayer,
The soldier all the faster can stand to,
A lighter belt being easier to undo.
Your Majesty, forgive me if I seem
6110   To debase the workings of this noble scheme.

FAUST

Treasure in superabundance lies
Deep in the ground throughout your territories
Frozen, unused. Thought's farthest reaches
Come nowhere near the measure of such riches.
Imagination, however high it flies,
Falls short, however hard it tries.
But spirits fit to see deeply invest
In what is boundless a boundless trust.

MEPHISTO

Paper like this in place of pearls and gold
6120   Is handy. You know what your hands hold.
No need to haggle or swap coin before
You lose your mind in loving or liquor.
Should you want metal, the exchange will do a deal;
Or if not, you must dig a while.
You auction off a torque or precious pot,
This paper then, amortized on the spot,
Shames the doubter who had dared to mock.
Accustomed now, we don't want the old way back.
Throughout the imperial lands henceforth there'll be
6130   Jewellery, gold and paper in plenty.

EMPEROR

We owe the wellbeing of our realm to you
And for such service like reward is due.
All the Empire's underworld be in your care,
Be priests and keepers of the treasure there.
You know the well-kept and abundant hoard
And none shall dig for it without your word.
My Treasure Masters, be united here,
Fulfil with joy the duties of your cure
In which the worlds above and below the ground
6140   In happy unison are joined.

TREASURER

> There'll be between us not the least dissent.
> The magician for a colleague! Excellent!

[Exit with FAUST.]

EMPEROR

> My courtiers now, some gift for each of you,
> And let each say what use he'll put it to.

PAGE [*receiving his gift*]

> I'll have a merry time enjoying things.

ANOTHER PAGE [*doing the same*]

> I'll buy my sweetheart necklaces and rings.

CHAMBERLAIN [*accepting a gift*]

> The wine I drink now will be twice as nice.

ANOTHER CHAMBERLAIN [*doing the same*]

> A happy moment for my frisky dice!

BANNERET [*thoughtfully*]

> I'll pay off all I owe on all I own.

ANOTHER BANNERET [*likewise*]

> I'll lay this wealth to other wealth laid down.   6150

EMPEROR

> I had hoped for zest and force to do new deeds
> But knowing you, we know you from all sides.
> I see very well: whatever riches pour
> On you, you'll be the things you always were.

FOOL [*arriving*]

> Remember me, Sir, in your giving vein.

EMPEROR

> Alive again, you'll drink my gifts again.

FOOL

> These magic leaves, I don't quite understand . . .

EMPEROR

> By you they will be put to no good end.

FOOL

> Now more are falling. What am I to do?

EMPEROR

> Collect them up. Why not? They fell to you.   6160

[Exit.]

FOOL
So I've five thousand crowns in my possession?

MEPHISTO
O sponge, o keg on legs, I see you've risen.

FOOL
I often have. But this is the best yet.

MEPHISTO
And you rejoice so much it makes you sweat.

FOOL
Tell me, is this worth money or is it not?

MEPHISTO
Enough to please your gullet and your gut.

FOOL
And buy me land and livestock and a home?

MEPHISTO
Indeed. You tender it and good things come.

FOOL
And mansion, forest, hunting, fishing?

MEPHISTO
                                       Yes.
6170   You will do well among our best noblesse.

FOOL
I'll make my bed on real estate tonight.

                                         [Exit.]

MEPHISTO *[alone]*
A very canny fool beyond a doubt.

Dark Gallery

[FAUST, MEPHISTOPHELES.]

MEPHISTO
Why drag me down these dismal galleries?
Is there not fun enough inside
And chance of jokes and gainful lies
In the thick of court amid the motley crowd?

FAUST

> Don't speak of that. Like an old shoe
> What mirth I had long since you wore it through.
> But now you hurry to and fro
> So as not to give me yes or no.   6180
> But I must act and entertain,
> Am plagued by Marshal and by Chamberlain.
> The Emperor wishes to set eyes upon
> The male and the female paragon
> Paris and Helena at once
> Before him in a clear appearance.
> To work, and quick. I cannot break my word.

MEPHISTO

> Reckless to promise that, absurd.

FAUST

> You never wondered, friend, did you
> Where your arts might lead us to?   6190
> First we make him rich and then
> It's our job to amuse the man.

MEPHISTO

> And all must promptly fit your wish!
> We stand before a steeper step,
> You trespass into deeply alien regions
> And further raise the debt of your transgressions,
> Think you can summon Helen up
> As easily as paper ghosts of cash.
> For sex with witches, shapes of air
> And changeling dwarves – I'm at your service, Sir!   6200
> But devil-sweethearts, amiable enough,
> Are not exactly demigoddess stuff.

FAUST

> The same old tale! You never lead
> Anywhere but into uncertainty.
> You are the one who obstacles the road
> And wants, for clearing it, another fee.
> A little mumbling will do fine,
> You'll fetch her faster than it takes to tell.

MEPHISTO
    The heathen folk are no concern of mine
6210   They domicile in their own hell.
    But there's a way.
FAUST
                 Tell it without delay.
MEPHISTO
    It pains me to give high secrets away.
    Goddesses rule in chilling loneliness,
    No place around them, time still less;
    To speak about them feels discourteous.
    They are the Mothers.
FAUST [*startled*]
             Mothers!
MEPHISTO
               Are you afraid?
FAUST
    The Mothers! It sounds so strange!
MEPHISTO
                   Indeed
    And strange it is. Goddesses whom
    Mortals don't know and we are loath to name.
6220   You'll tunnel deep to get where they reside
    And yours the fault that we have any need.
FAUST
    What way?
MEPHISTO
          There is no way. Into the untrodden,
    Not to be trodden, a way to the unbidden,
    The unbiddable. Are you prepared for that?
    There are no bolts to slide, no locks to undo
    But lonelinesses will bewilder you,
    Desolate loneliness, can you imagine it?
FAUST
    Spare me your speeches. There's something here
    Of the Witch's Kitchen atmosphere
6230   And long done years before all that.
    I dealt with the world, under duress

And learned and taught them emptiness.
When I said soundly what I thought was true
The opposite sounded doubly so.
Bad tricks were played me till I eschewed
Society for the wilderness and solitude
And life went by unlived, alone, until
Perforce I gave myself to the Devil.

MEPHISTO

And had you swum the length and breadth of the ocean
And seen the boundlessness out there   6240
Still you'd have seen the waves come on and on,
Even in the dread that you might disappear
You would see something. Doubtless you'd have seen
Patrolling dolphins in the quietened green,
Sun, moon and stars and drifting clouds no doubt –
But in that vacancy, eternally remote,
Nothing you'll see nor hear your taken step
Nor find a solid footing when you stop.

FAUST

You speak as primate of all mystagogues
Who lead true neophytes like lying rogues,   6250
Except you send me into vacancy
There to increase in art and potency,
Use me like a certain cat to claw you out
Chestnuts from the coals for you to eat.
No turning back! We'll fathom it! I shall
There in your Nothing hope to find the All.

MEPHISTO

Hats off to you before you leave!
You know the Devil well, as I perceive.
Here take this key.

FAUST

                  That little thing?

MEPHISTO

Take hold of it before belittling.   6260

FAUST

It's growing in my hand. It shines. It flashes.

MEPHISTO

Now do you see what gift you own in this?
The key will lead, it will divine and dowse,
Follow it down to where the Mothers house.

FAUST [*shuddering*]

The Mothers! Goes through me like a spear.
What is this word I cannot stand to hear?

MEPHISTO

So circumscribed? Troubled by a new word?
Will you only hear what you've already heard?
Nothing should trouble you, sound how it may,
6270   Of strangest things long since the habitué.

FAUST

I don't seek my salvation in a heart gone dead,
Best faculty in man's the thrill of dread;
Though this world makes us pay for it, we visit
The other deepest, being seized by it.

MEPHISTO

Sink then! Or climb, I might also say. It is
All one. Flee all that *has become*, enter
The zones of the undone images,
Delight in what has long ceased being there,
Like droves of clouds, and when it mills against you,
6280   Brandish the key, clear your way through.

FAUST [*full of enthusiasm*]

Holding it firm, I feel new energy,
Draw greater breath, for a large activity.

MEPHISTO

At last by a glowing tripod you will know
This is deep ground, the deepest you can go.
There you will see the Mothers in its light.
Some sit, some stand, others perambulate,
Just as may be. Shaping and transformation,
Eternal sense in eternal conversation.
Around them the imagery of all creation swarms,
6290   They will not see you, they see only forms.
Take courage then, the peril is very great,
Stride for the tripod, do not hesitate,

And touch it with the key.
[FAUST *makes a decisive and commanding gesture with the key.*]

MEPHISTO [*observing him*]
                          Exactly so.
It will attach itself and, as your servant, follow.
Climb then serenely, uplifted on your luck.
Before they notice, the two of you are back,
And having fetched it here you may invite
Hero and heroine out of the night,
The first who ever had the hubris to,
And then the deed is done, and done by you.   6300
Thereupon, by magic treatment, we shall make
Divinities appear in the incense smoke.

FAUST
And now?

MEPHISTO
              Now strive with your whole being down.
Sink by stamping, by stamping climb again.
[FAUST *stamps and sinks out of sight.*]

MEPHISTO
So long as he is well served by the key!
Will he come back? I'll be curious to see.

Brightly Lit Rooms

[EMPEROR, PRINCES *and* COURTIERS, *moving to and fro.*]

CHAMBERLAIN [*to* MEPHISTOPHELES]
We want your ghost-scene and we want it now.
The Emperor is impatient for the show.

MARSHAL
Asked after it only a moment since.
Bestir yourselves. Your failure gives offence.   6310

MEPHISTO
My colleague is absent for that very reason.
He has the thing in preparation

And labours quietly in a place apart
With quite exceptional assiduity.
For it needs wise magic and the highest art
To lift to light the treasure-trove of beauty.

MARSHAL

What arts it needs is your affair,
The Emperor only cares how slow you are.

BLONDE [*to* MEPHISTOPHELES]

Sir, a word. You see a clear face,
6320   In cursèd summer though that's not the case.
Then, to my grief, a hundred freckles spread
Over the white skin, a brownish red.
A cure!

MEPHISTO

                Alas, a sweetheart without spot
Marked in May like an ocelot!
Take frogspawn, tongues of toads and cohobate,
Further distil with care by fullest moonlight
And at the waning then paint cleanly on:
Come spring, the speckles are all gone.

BRUNETTE

The pushy crowd arrives to fawn and crawl.
6330   I beg you for a cure. A frozen foot
Hinders me walking out and at the ball,
Even in courtesies I'm hampered by it.

MEPHISTO

I'll strike it with my foot, if you permit.

BRUNETTE

Lovers allow some footwork, do they not?

MEPHISTO

My kick, my dear, is weightier than that.
Like cures like, whatever the malady.
As foot heals foot, so every part its mate.
Here then. But don't retaliate.

BRUNETTE [*screams*]

Oh! Oh! It burns! How hard you booted me,
Like a horse's hoof.

MEPHISTO

That's homoeopathy.   6340
Now you can dance until you drop
And footsy under the table while you sup.

LADY [*forcing her way forward*]

Oh let me through. My pains are hard to bear.
In the deep heart of me they squirm and sear.
My eyes were his salvation yesterday
But now he talks with her, and turns away.

MEPHISTO

A sorry plight. But give me your attention.
Put yourself close and quietly in his way
And with this charcoal make a mark upon
His sleeve, his cloak, his shoulder, where you can.   6350
In his heart he'll feel the stab of sweet contrition.
At once swallow the charcoal dry and neat,
No wine or water, and you'll have that man
Sighing at your bedroom door this very night.

LADY

Not poison is it?

MEPHISTO [*indignantly*]

Show due respect here, please!
You'll go a long way for a charcoal of that make.
Comes from a pyre, the sort we used to stoke
More diligently in the olden days.

PAGE

I am in love, they treat me like a ninny.

MEPHISTO [*aside*]

How I must turn and turn among so many!   6360
   [*To the* PAGE]
Don't put your money on the youngest one.
You'll be liked best by one who's getting on.
   [*Others press towards him.*]
Yet more. I am assailed on every side.
In the end I'll have to call truth to my aid,
Poor last resort. But they torment me so.
O Mothers, Mothers! Do let Faustus go!
   [*He looks around.*]

Towards the hall in gloomy luminance
There's movement of the courtiers all at once.
I see them process in their due series
6370   Through corridors and distant galleries.
Now in the ancient spacious ceremonial hall
They congregate, they fill it full,
The walls donate their hangings lavishly
And every niche is stiff with weaponry.
I doubt if any conjuror need say a word:
The ghosts would flock here of their own accord.

Twilit Ceremonial Hall

[*The* EMPEROR *and his* COURT *have entered.*]

HERALD
My old office, to herald a performance,
Is lessened in the case of phantom beings.
It would be contrary to common sense
6380   To dare to explicate their muddled doings.
The seats, the easy chairs are set for all,
The Emperor settled plumb before the wall.
There in the greatest comfort he may gaze
On woven battles of the heroic days.
The lord and all his court are seated round,
The crowded benches clutter close behind
And lovers for this dark and ghostly hour
Have cosied up together, pair by pair.
All seated as propriety would have them,
6390   Now we are ready, let the spirits come!
[*Trumpets.*]

ASTROLOGER
At once now let our spectacle begin!
The Emperor wishes it, walls you must open,
Nothing shall hinder us, we've magic here,
The tapestries vanish as though rolled up by fire,
The wall splits, it turns another face

And there arises a deep theatre set,
By strange illumination we are lit
And I ascend the stage to take my place.
MEPHISTO [*rising in the prompt-box*]
From here I hope to charm my audience:
The Devil prompts with honeyed eloquence.   6400
   [*To the* ASTROLOGER]
Knowing the starry rhythms as you do
You'll grasp with ease the lines I whisper you.
ASTROLOGER
The power of magic causes to appear
A massive ancient temple building here.
Like Atlas, once the upholder of the skies,
Plentiful columns stand in rows
Enough to bear a mountain. Two would suffice
To hold aloft any great edifice.
ARCHITECT
The antique style! That is no way to build.
Gross and ponderous, if the truth were told.   6410
Not noble: crude. No grandeur: clumsiness.
I love a slender striving into boundlessness,
A pointed arch's zenith lifts the mind,
We are most edified by buildings of that kind.
ASTROLOGER
Receive with awe the star-given moment now,
Bind reason up with magic but allow
The coming in of fantasy
Arriving from afar, bold, splendid, free.
View here the object of your brave desire,
A thing impossible – fit to believe, therefore.   6420
   [FAUST *ascends the far side of the stage.*]
In priest's robes, garlanded, this wonder man
Will now complete what he coolly began.
A tripod rises with him from the pit,
Already incense breathes from the bowl of it.
He makes to bless his lofty enterprise
So only good things will materialize.

FAUST [*in a grandiose manner*]
    In your name, Mothers, who regally inhabit
    Boundlessness, always alone and yet
    Having society. Around your heads the active
6430   Images of life hover, but do not live.
    All that once was is active there,
    All the bright appearances, wanting to live for ever,
    And these, you almighty powers, you distribute
    To the day's pavilion and the dome of night.
    Some will be taken up on sweet life's route,
    Others the intrepid magus will seek out.
    By faith then, in abundance, he presents
    The grave and wondrous things each human wants.
ASTROLOGER
    He touches the bowl with the glowing key,
6440   At once a vaporous fog is all we see:
    Comes creeping in, heaving in the manner of clouds,
    Stretches, clenches, crosses, couples, divides.
    Now see what a masterpiece the ghosts have made!
    They make a music as they promenade.
    And, who knows how, from airy chords they weave
    Melody in all and everywhere they move.
    Each column shaft, each triglyph rings,
    I do believe the whole temple sings.
    The haze sinks, out of the veil of light
6450   A beautiful youth steps to the music's beat.
    My part is silence now. So sweetly famed
    What need is there for Paris to be named?
        [PARIS *steps forward.*]
LADY
    Oh glorious bloom and potency of youth!
SECOND LADY
    Like a luscious peach, watering the mouth.
THIRD LADY
    Finely drawn lips, swelling in the sweetest way.
FOURTH LADY
    You'd like to sip and sup there, I daresay.

FIFTH LADY
  Pretty, but not what one would call refined.
SIXTH LADY
  He might be lighter in the limbs, do you not find?
KNIGHT
  I seem to sense a shepherd boy, no trace
  Of the prince in him nor any courtly grace.   6460
SECOND KNIGHT
  The boy looks well enough there half undressed
  But let's see him in armour. That's the test!
LADY
  Now he's sitting down, so soft and easily.
KNIGHT
  No doubt you'd like a session on his knee.
SECOND LADY
  The arm behind his head. Such a pretty pose!
CHAMBERLAIN
  From such uncouthness one averts one's gaze.
LADY
  You gentlemen, there's no contenting you.
CHAMBERLAIN
  To sprawl and loll like that in Emperor's view!
LADY
  He's acting. He supposes no one sees.
CHAMBERLAIN
  Even a play must mind its p's and q's.   6470
LADY
  Sleep takes him now. The sweet boy can't resist.
CHAMBERLAIN
  Next thing he'll snore. Your perfect naturalist!
YOUNG LADY [*beside herself*]
  What new scent infiltrates the incense fumes
  And floods the heart of me with freshening streams?
OLDER LADY
  Truly! A scent, the breath of him, inspires
  The deep soul.
OLDEST LADY
              So his being flowers.

It is the ambrosia of youth exhaling here
Like a heavenly body's atmosphere.
   [HELEN *steps forward.*]

MEPHISTO

So there she is. She would not trouble me.

6480   Pretty enough, but not my cup of tea.

ASTROLOGER

I cannot in all honesty pretend
To any further function. Here I end.
The lovely woman comes and had I tongues of fire . . .
Beauty was long the stuff of songs galore.
Whom she appears to, he feels ecstasy,
None she belonged to has she made happy.

FAUST

Can I still see? Oh beauty's wells are shown
Deep in my senses richly flowing forth!
My trek through terror has brought me blessed gain.

6490   The world, till now unopened, had no worth
But in my priesthood it becomes at last
Desirable, well grounded, fast.
May every breath of strength, if I grow used
Again to living without you, disappear!
That shapeliness that formerly
In the magic mirror delighted me
Was beauty's image only of foam and air –
It's *you* I owe as tribute every start
Of strength, my passion's innermost heart,

6500   My liking, love, devotion, lunacy.

MEPHISTO [*from the prompt-box*]

Control yourself. No more extempore!

OLDER LADY

Tall, shapely, but the head rather too small.

YOUNGER LADY

Her feet however are not small at all.

DIPLOMAT

But I have seen princesses of that cut.
I think her beautiful from head to foot.

COURTIER

Now she comes near the sleeper, slyly, softly.

LADY

Ugly beside his youth and purity.

POET

Her beauty's light is his illumination.

LADY

The image of Luna and Endymion!

POET

Indeed. The goddess seems to set   6510
And bow upon his mouth to drink at it.
I envy him. A kiss! Full measure there.

DUENNA

And people looking! She goes far too far.

FAUST

He'll rue her favouring him.

MEPHISTO

                              Be quiet, be still.
Allow the ghost to do what things it will.

COURTIER

She creeps away, light-footed. He awakes.

LADY

Just as I thought! She gives him backward looks.

COURTIER

He is amazed. He cannot comprehend.

LADY

She can. She knows exactly how things stand.

COURTIER

With true decorum she turns back to him.   6520

LADY

Ah, now she'll show him what it's all about.
In cases such as this the men are dim.
He thinks he is the first she's had, no doubt.

KNIGHT

Refined and queenly though, you must admit.

LADY

In my book she's a slut and nothing but.

PAGE

    I'd like to be where he is, I know that.

COURTIER

    Who would not be a prisoner in such bonds?

LADY

    The jewel has passed through many pairs of hands.

    They rubbed the gilding off the gingerbread.

ANOTHER LADY

6530   Already by the age of ten she was no good.

KNIGHT

    Each takes the best he can whenever he may.

    I'd take these lovely leavings any day.

SCHOLAR

    I see her plainly but in my opinion

    There is some doubt that she's the proper one.

    Presence inclines us to exaggerate.

    I chiefly hold to what the writers write

    And there I read that her effect on all

    Greybeards of Troy was quite exceptional.

    Now, as I think, that fits the case here. See,

6540   Though I'm not young, the effect she has on me.

ASTROLOGER

    No longer a boy! A man, a hero now

    He embraces her and how can she say no?

    Strength gathering in his arms, he lifts her up –

    To carry away?

FAUST

                You dare too much, fool. Stop!

    You overreach! Heed me! Unconscionable!

MEPHISTO

    You make your own ghost slapstick spectacle.

ASTROLOGER

    A word! After these events we call our play

    'The Rape of Helen', I should say.

FAUST

    The rape of her? You reckon without me.

6550   For I still hold the key here in my hand

    That guided me through the horrors of the sea

Of lonelinesses to this firm dryland.
Here I stand fast. And here realities reign.
The spirit can fight with ghosts on this terrain
And come into the mighty dual domain.
Far as she was, so near never again?
I rescue her and she is doubly mine.
Do it! O Mothers, allow me to. You must!
Once knowing her I can't let her be lost.

ASTROLOGER

Faustus, Faustus, what are you doing? He lays   6560
Violent hands on her, a darkness dyes
Her ghost. Against the youth he wields the key
And touches him. Alas! And instantly –

    [*Explosion,* FAUST *on the ground. The ghosts dissolve in
    a mist.*]

MEPHISTO [*taking* FAUST *over his shoulder*]

There you have it. Fools on his back
In the end even the Devil comes unstuck.

    [*Darkness, uproar.*]

ACT TWO

A Cramped and High-Vaulted Gothic Room

[*Formerly* FAUST's *study, unchanged.* MEPHISTOPHELES *appears from behind a curtain. As he lifts it and looks back,* FAUST *is seen stretched out on an antique bed.*]

MEPHISTO

Lie there, mischief, seduced into
Bonds of love hard to undo.
Stricken by Helen, any man
Has trouble seeing sense again.

[*He looks around.*]

6570 Look up or down or where I will
Nothing is altered or depleted.
The coloured panes are blacker still,
The cobwebs have proliferated,
The paper has yellowed, the ink solidified
But everything is where it was.
Even the quill with which Faust made
Himself the Devil's, there it is
And in it a droplet of the blood I tapped
Him for: sucked up and stopped.

6580 A collector of curiosities
Could find none curiouser than this!
The old fur hanging on the old hook
Reminds me of the liberties I took
Giving that boy instruction
The young man is perhaps still chewing on.
Indeed I feel a strong desire
Again to put on that smoke-warm clout
And with it the professorial air
Of knowing oneself to be completely right.

6590 Scholars can do it. The Devil though
Lost the knack of it long ago.

[*He takes down the fur and shakes it. Crickets, beetles and moths fly out.*]

CHORUS OF INSECTS

    Who's here? Look who's here
    Come visiting us!
    We flutter and buzz
    And know who you are.
    You planted us quietly
    One at a time,
    Now thousands of dancers
    Carry your name.
    Roguery hides   6600
    In the heart but a louse
    In a fur coat
    Soon shows his face.

MEPHISTO

  The sweet surprise of one's youthful creation!
  Scatter the seed, comes foison in due season.
  Another shake! Let's see what else will flit
  This shaggy pelt that had their lodgings in it.
  Up and away, my loves! We relocate you.
  A thousand novel hidey-holes await you.
  There in the stacks of ancient files,   6610
  Here in the darkened parchment scrolls,
  In dusty shards of earthenware,
  Or in that death's-head's empty stare.
  In all this junk and rotting life
  Nits and nitwittery are rife.
    [*He slips into the fur.*]
  Come, cover up my shoulders once again.
  Today, as once before, I am the Dean.
  But what's a name if only I confer it?
  Give me some people who will say, You are it.
    [*He tugs the bell. At its harsh, penetrating and resounding
    din the rooms shake and the doors fly open.*]

FAMULUS [*approaches with tottering steps down the long
    dark corridor*]

  Such a ringing, such a quaking,   6620

Stairs are lurching, walls are shaking,
Sheet on sheet of lightning shines
Coloured through the rattled panes.
Cracks attack the floor, down
Shifted dirt and plaster rain
And the locked and bolted door
Is unsealed by a magic power.
Horror! Horror! Standing there
A giant in Faustus' ancient fur!
6630   How he looks! He beckons me!
Under me my knees give way.
Shall I go or shall I stay?
Oh, what will become of me?

MEPHISTO [*beckoning*]
Enter, my friend. Your name is Nicodemus.

FAMULUS
Worshipful Eminence, it is – *Oremus*.

MEPHISTO
Let us not.

FAMULUS
                    What joy that you know me!

MEPHISTO
Indeed I do, under the verdigris
Of years still studying because
Studying is all the scholar ever does,
6640   Building himself a modest house of cards
And never finishes, for all his wit and words.
But oh, your Doctor Wagner! He's a brain
All knowing and by everybody known.
He has become the chief of the learned scene,
Holds it together, he alone
The daily increaser of wisdom.
Listeners, hearers, mill around him
Lusting after knowledge. Solo
He casts his luminance *ex cathedra*,
6650   He wields the keys like Saint Peter
And opens up the Above and the Below.
See him before the people flash and beam!

No fame, no reputation vies with his.
He even eclipses Faustus' name
And what he was now Doctor Wagner is.

FAMULUS

Forgive me if I contradict you,
Indeed, I wonder that I dare to:
Your Reverence, it is not so.
He thinks himself a very humble player.
The incomprehensible vanishing of that great man   6660
Undid him quite. And for his coming again
He prays as for the Comforter and Saviour.
Just as it was in Doctor Faustus' day,
Untouched since he went hence, the room
Waits for its master's coming home.
I dare no further than the doorway.
What rare conjunction must the stars have made?
The walls have a fearful look,
The doorposts shook, the locks broke –
How else would you have got inside?   6670

MEPHISTO

Where is he hiding? Lead me there,
Will you? Or you must fetch him here.

FAMULUS

His prohibition is too severe.
May I defy it? Do I dare?
Months on end, engaged on his great quest
He bides where quietness is quietest.
Least brawny man among the men of learning
He looks as though his job were charcoal-burning,
Blowing the fire reddens his eyes,
Blackens his face from ears to nose,   6680
He whets his lust on every moment,
The fire-tongs clattering in accompaniment.

MEPHISTO

And not see me? I am the one
To expedite his satisfaction.

[*Exit* FAMULUS. *Gravely* MEPHISTOPHELES *seats
himself.*]

Scarcely am I in my place
Appears a visitor, a familiar face
But now in the forefront of modernity.
How boundless his conceit will be!

BACCALAUREUS [*approaching fast and noisily down the
        corridor*]

All the doors are open wide!
6690   Can it be that those inside
Finally may hope to thrive
Who have mouldered in the grave
Nourished like the living dead
On the starving lives they led?

Walls and masonry incline
To a final falling down.
We shall lie, unless we run,
Under rubble, ton on ton.
I'm a bold man: even so
6700   Here's as far as I will go.

Wait though! Surely it was here
Years ago I came in fear
Bashful-tongue-tied to present
My fresher face, all innocent?
Trusted whiskered men and got
From their gab much benefit.

Told me from their crusted tomes
What they knew, lies in reams,
Not believing what they knew,
6710   Lost their lives and mine too.
But at the back, darkly lit
In his cell one sits there yet!

Amazingly still sitting there
As he was, in his brown fur!
Wrapped in that same shaggy fleece
Just as when I left the place!

True, he seemed a clever man:
I'd not understood him then.
He won't fool me any more.
Boldly now: I know the score.   6720
Unless, old Sir, dark Lethe has wiped clean
The memory in your slant-sunk hairless head
Here recognize the alumnus now outgrown
His Alma Mater's bench and rod.
I find you still as I found you before
But I am someone else returning here.

MEPHISTO

I am glad my bell brings you to me.
Back then I thought very well of you:
In the caterpillar and the chrysalis we see
The future butterfly, the bright imago.   6730
It pleased your boyish self to wear
Open collars and curly hair –
But not one for the pigtail, I'd have thought?
And now I see you Swedishly cropped short.
You look rock-solid and resolute, if not
Quite there, not *absolutely*, yet.

BACCALAUREUS

Old man, we may be where we were
But times have changed, we have new ways.
Spare us your ambiguities, we are
Quite different listeners nowadays.   6740
You duped the innocent lad I used to be,
Took little wit to do to me
What now the bravest man would not.

MEPHISTO

Tell the young the truth, they don't like it,
Green as they are, one little bit.
But let the years come over them, truth seize
And shake them by the throat and they suppose
All by themselves they saw the light
And say: My teacher was not very bright.

BACCALAUREUS

Not very honest perhaps: when will a teacher speak   6750

The truth before you with an open look?
All practise adding or subtracting, being grave
Or cleverly funny with the children who behave.

MEPHISTO

There is a time for learning but you seem
Yourself arrived now at the teaching-time.
Through many moonlight hours and some sunlight
You have amassed experience, no doubt.

BACCALAUREUS

Experience! All froth and dust
And a poor second to the spirit.
6760 Things we have known for long it would be best
We did not, as you must admit.

MEPHISTO [after a silence]

I was a fool. For some while now
I have thought myself soft in the head and shallow.

BACCALAUREUS

I'm pleased to hear it! You are talking sense.
The first old man who did in my experience.

MEPHISTO

I sought for treasure, the gold that lies hidden,
But frightful dross was all I carried home.

BACCALAUREUS

Your skull, admit it, your bald dome
Is worth no more than those – with nothing in.

MEPHISTO [amiably]

6770 Have you any idea, my friend, how rude you are?

BACCALAUREUS

In German the polite man is a liar.

MEPHISTO [wheeling in his chair closer and closer to the
        front of the stage, he addresses the audience in the
        stalls]

Up here I'm being starved of light and air.
Do you have any room for me down there?

BACCALAUREUS

It is conceit in has-beens to desire
To be something, who are nothing any more.
It's in his blood a man knows he's alive.

Who but the young man feels his life-blood move?
That living blood in fresh vigour will get
New life in the very act of living it.
All's on the move, and things get done,   6780
What's weak must fall, what's fit to live comes on.
We conquer half a world while you
Sit nodding, pondering the whole thing through,
Dreaming and planning yet another plan.
Old age, for sure, is a shivery
Cold state of need and tics and fads.
A man when he has gone past thirty
In truth he's dead, or as good as.
Best thing would be betimes to strike you dead.

MEPHISTO
Nothing the Devil can add to what you've said.   6790

BACCALAUREUS
No devil exists if I don't wish him to.

MEPHISTO [*aside*]
The Devil will trip you up soon even so.

BACCALAUREUS
And herein lies youth's noblest vocation:
The world that is, is by my sole creation.
I summoned up the sun out of the sea,
The moon began her changeful course with me,
The day adorned itself when I set forth
On the greening, blossoming and welcoming earth.
At a sign from me in that first night
The stars unfolded to their full estate.   6800
And what could free you from your philistine
Tight thought-bondage? No power but mine.
But I, as the spirit speaks to me,
Follow my inner light, joyful and free
And stride in an ecstasy of my own making
Forth from the dark into the new day breaking.

                                                        [*Exit.*]

MEPHISTO
Continue, idiot, loudly and gloriously!
How mortified you'd be to realize

No one thinks anything, dumb or wise,
6810   Their fathers have not thought already.
But even he is not much threat to us,
In a year or so things will be different.
The frothing juices make an awful fuss
But there will be a wine, after the ferment.
    [To the younger people in the pit, who have not applauded]
Never mind, my dears. I see my lines
And sentiments have left you cold.
Consider though: the Devil is old
And when you are, you will know what he means.

A Laboratory

[In medieval style, with extensive and cumbersome appar-
atus for fantastical purposes.]
WAGNER [at the fire]
The bell, the frightful bell, has rung
6820   Shuddering through the sooty walls.
Over our hopeful waiting now
The imminence of outcome falls.
Light in the dark begins to show,
Deep in the innermost phial
There's shining like a living coal.
As from a rare carbuncle-stone
Lightnings through the dark are strewn.
A brilliant white light appears!
Oh this time let me not lose it! –
6830   Oh God, a rattling at the doors!
MEPHISTO [entering]
Greetings! This is a friendly visit.
WAGNER [anxiously]
Greetings now the hour has come!
    [Softly]
But hold your breath and let your mouth be dumb.
A great work nears conclusion.

MEPHISTO [*more softly*]
   What is it?
WAGNER [*more softly still*]
        The making of a human.
MEPHISTO
   A human? Who's the loving pair
   You've bottled in that smokey cubicle?
WAGNER
   Oh God forbid! We think the ways that were
   In vogue for procreating risible.
   The delicate point from which life sprang,   6840
   The kindly force that from the centre flung
   And took and gave, following its own design,
   First making kindred stuff, then strange, its own,
   We have relieved that power of its high office.
   Beasts may continue happy in the practice
   But with their great capacities human beings
   Must have in future higher and higher beginnings.
     [*Turning to the fire*]
   Light flashes, see! – Now we may hope indeed
   That having in a measured fashion made
   By mixing (mixing is the key) from legion   6850
   Materials the material of man
   And sealed it in a flask (securely luted)
   And watched it well and truly cohobated
   Our secret work is consummated.
     [*Turning to the fire*]
   It comes to pass: the quick mass clarifies!
   Truer and truer our conviction grows:
   The mysteries in Nature we have praised
   We dare by reason now to anatomize
   And what till now Nature has organized
   Here we cause it to crystallize.   6860
MEPHISTO
   Live long enough, much comes around
   And then there's nothing new under the sun.
   In my first wanderings as a journeyman
   I saw a crystal form of humankind.

WAGNER [*who has been attentively observing the phial*]
  It rises, flashes, it is coming on,
  A moment more and it is done.
  Great projects at the outset seem insane.
  But we shall leave chance out of it in future
  And such an excellently thinking brain
6870 That too a thinker then will manufacture.
      [*In an ecstatic contemplation of the phial*]
  Such sweet and forceful ringing in the glass!
  It dims and clarifies – now it *becomes*!
  I see in tiny shapeliness
  A pretty manikin who moves his limbs.
  What more do we want, what can the world want more?
  In daylight now the secret is abroad.
  Listen to the sound of it and hear
  Sound become voice, become the spoken word.

HOMUNCULUS [*in the phial, to* WAGNER]
  How do we stand? So, Papa, you were serious!
6880 Come press me to your heart with proper tenderness
  But not too hard or the glass will break.
  That is indeed what things are like:
  What's natural seeks infinity of space,
  The artificial wants confining close.
      [*To* MEPHISTOPHELES]
  And you arriving very *à propos*,
  My timely cousin, rogue, I thank you.
  A happy fate conducts you here to us.
  Being, I must be industrious.
  I wish to gird myself for work immediately
6890 And you're the one can ease the ways for me.

WAGNER
  One further word! Till now I've been embarrassed
  By old and young perpetually harassed
  Who want to know. For example: none can tell
  How body and soul can fit together so well
  And cleave so tight as though they'd never split
  But live their life mutually spoiling it.
  And then –

MEPHISTO
                    Stop there! I'd rather ask the reason
    Why man and woman can't get on.
    You'll never get an answer, friend. But now
    There are things to do, to please this little fellow.   6900
HOMUNCULUS
    What things to do?
MEPHISTO [*pointing to a side door*]
                    Here show us what you can.
WAGNER [*still staring into the phial*]
    Indeed you are the sweetest little man.
        [*The side door opens.* FAUST *is seen stretched out on the
        bed.*]
HOMUNCULUS [*in astonishment*]
    My word!
        [*The phial escapes from* WAGNER'S *hands, hovers over*
        FAUST *and illuminates him.*]
                    Beautifully set! – Deep in a grove
    A clear pool. And women, the loveliest,
    Undressing! – And better still! Above
    And luminously different from the rest
    One of a high heroic or heavenly ancestry
    Who steps into the bright transparency
    And lets her body's lively fire chill
    In the cosying water's supple crystal.   6910
    But now what a din of rapidly beating wings
    And the smooth surface ploughed with a rush of splashings!
    The scared girls flee and leave alone
    And calmly watching all the queen
    Who with a proud and womanly pleasure allows
    The prince of swans to fawn between her knees
    Pressingly tame, becoming familiar.
    But now a mist lifts up and screens
    With a veil of close texture
    This sweetest of imaginable scenes.   6920
MEPHISTO
    The tales you tell! So small in size,
    So largely able to fantasize!

I see nothing.

HOMUNCULUS

How could you, given
The age of northern fog you grew up in?
In all that junk of priests and chivalry
How could you have the eyes to see?
In gloom you are at home and nowhere else.
[*Looking around*]
Browned stonework growing fungus, vile,
And pointy fancywork in wretched style.
6930   We are in trouble if he wakes up here:
One look at this, the poor man will expire.
Dreamer anticipating woodland springs
And swans and lovely women in the nude
How in this place shall he abide?
I scarcely could who can put up with most things.
Away with him!

MEPHISTO

I should welcome the chance.

HOMUNCULUS

Order the warrior where he can fight,
Conduct the girl where she can dance
And all resolves itself at once.
6940   And, now I come to think of it, tonight
Is Classical Walpurgis Night:
Happy conjunction! We are meant
To fetch him into his element.

MEPHISTO

I never heard of it.

HOMUNCULUS

I should
Be very surprised to hear you had.
Romantic ghosts are all that your sort know
But a real ghost must be classical too.

MEPHISTO

And what direction will this trip be taking?
My antique colleagues are not to my liking.

HOMUNCULUS

    The north-west, Satan, is your stamping ground   6950
    But south-east this time we are bound:
    A wide plain and Peneus flowing through
    Bushy and wooded, with quiet and watered dells,
    The flat land reaching to the ravined hills
    And up there lies Pharsalus, old and new.

MEPHISTO

    Oh dear. Leave off. And don't be bothering me
    With those old wars of tyranny and slavery.
    It bores me, for no sooner have they done
    At the beginning they begin again
    And no one notices that they are run   6960
    Around by Asmodeus, for his fun.
    Their 'fight for freedom' is a fight between
    Two lots of lackeys, if the truth be known.

HOMUNCULUS

    Leave human beings their cussed human nature.
    Each must defend himself the best he can
    From being a boy, till he becomes a man.
    The only question here is this one's cure.
    If you know how to do it, do it now.
    If not, then let me have a go.

MEPHISTO

    I know a little Brocken trick or two   6970
    But none the pagan folk will let me do.
    The race of Greeks were never up to much:
    All play and sensuous liberties and such.
    But they beguile the heart to cheerful sins
    While all we offer are the dismal ones.
    What's your idea?

HOMUNCULUS

                You are not backward usually
    And if I mention the witches of Thessaly
    That says something to you, I guess.

MEPHISTO [*lasciviously*]

    Thessalian witches! By Jove it does!

6980   I've long thought I should like to know those ladies.
        Cohabiting night after night
        I rather doubt if that would suit
        But a visit, an experiment . . .
HOMUNCULUS
                                    Your cloak, and here
        Wrap it around this gentleman.
        The rag has carried you before,
        The two of you, and will again.
        I'll light the way.
WAGNER [*anxiously*]
                                    And me?
HOMUNCULUS
                                    Why you
        Stay home with most important things to do.
        You must unroll the ancient parchments
6990   And, by the rules, collect life's elements
        And fit this one to that one with due care.
        Ponder the *what*, the *how* though even more.
        Myself meanwhile, touring about,
        Will dot an 'i' and cross a 't' no doubt.
        Thus the great work will take its final shape.
        Such a striving earns rewarding: wealth
        And fame and honour and long life in good health –
        And knowledge and virtue: these also, we hope.
        Farewell!
WAGNER [*unhappily*]
                                    Farewell! It gives me pain
7000   I fear I never will see you again.
MEPHISTO
        To the Peneus then! Full speed!
        Our little cousin gets things done!
        [*Ad spectatores*]
        In the end we are dependent on
        Creatures we ourselves have made.

Classical Walpurgis Night

Pharsalian Fields

[*Darkness.*]

ERICHTHO

On this night's grisly festival as often before
I make my entrance, I, the sombre Erichtho,
Not so abominable as our lying friends the poets
Who never know when to stop in eulogy and censure
Have said I am ... I see the valley, length and breadth
Gone pale already under the grey flood of tents,   7010
An after-image of the grief- and horror-night
So many times already come again and will
Into eternity ... None will allow the other
Rule of the land, none will who got by force and rules
By force allow it any man. For who cannot
Govern himself is all too eager to govern
His neighbour's wishes to suit his own proud thinking ...
But here, for a large example, it was fought out
How violence sets itself against a greater violence
And shreds sweet liberty's garland of a thousand flowers   7020
And bends the stiff laurel round a ruler's brow.
Here Pompey dreamed a flowering of early greatness
And Caesar there, unsleeping, watched the balance tremble.
They will go head to head. And the world knows who won.

Watchfires are shining, they dispense red flames,
The ground exhales a mirroring of spilled blood
And lured here by this night's phenomenal lustre
The legions of the myths of Hellas are foregathering.
Around each fire hovers unsteadily or sits
At ease some fabulous image of the ancient years ...   7030
The moon, misshapen but brilliantly bright,
Rises, donating mild light everywhere,
The illusory tents are vanishing, the fires burn blue.

But see in the sky above me, that strange meteor
Shining and lighting up a bodily sphere! I smell
The breath of a living thing. It is not right I should
Go near the living, for I can only do them harm,
Brings me into ill repute and does me no good.
And now the thing is descending. Best that I beat a retreat.
[ERICHTHO *withdraws. Enter the* AERONAUTS, *above.*]

HOMUNCULUS

7040 Over the zone of flames and fear
       One more tour before we land!
       Plain and valley, such a grand
       Spooky view we have up here.

MEPHISTO

       I see – as though I saw into
       Northern horrors there below –
       The foulest sort of ghost and ghoul.
       Quite at home it makes me feel.

HOMUNCULUS

       See that lanky figure making
       Hard away as we appear.

MEPHISTO

7050 As if afraid. She saw us streaking
       Hither through the upper air.

HOMUNCULUS

       Let her go. And now set down
       Your errant knight. And lo! Forthwith
       Life will enter him again.
       He seeks it in the land of myth.

FAUST [*touching the ground*]
       Where is she?

HOMUNCULUS

                     That I cannot say
       But here no doubt are some who may.
       Hurry now. Before daybreak
       Go snooping round from fire to fire.

7060 The man who had the nerve to seek
       The Mothers has nothing more to fear.

MEPHISTO

    I too have business here, people to see,
    And think our wisest course might be
    Among the fires each makes his quest
    For what adventure suits him best.
    Then when it's time to reunite
    Our little friend will sound and shine his light.

HOMUNCULUS

    See how it shines! Hear how it rings!
    [A powerful shining and resounding of the glass.]
    Away now after new and marvellous things!
          [Exit MEPHISTOPHELES and HOMUNCULUS.]

FAUST [alone]

    Where is she? – For now I set aside my question . . .   7070
    If not the very ground she trod
    And not the waves that tumbled where she stood
    Still it's the air she made her language on.
    Here, by a miracle, here in Greece!
    The instant I set foot I knew the place,
    In me, the sleeper, came new spirit like fire.
    I have the mettle of Antaeus standing here,
    And seeing so much around that's wondrous
    I'll thread this maze of flames with seriousness.
               [He withdraws.]

On the Upper Peneus

MEPHISTO [snooping around]

    Wandering my way among these dabs of flame   7080
    I find myself an alien through and through.
    Most naked; in their shirt-tails one or two;
    The sphinxes brazen, the gryphons without shame;
    And all, the curly or the winged kind,
    Ogling and ogled, frontal and behind . . .
    At heart, we are indecent as they are
    But the antique liveliness is hard to bear.

It wants controlling by the modern trick
Of slapping a motley make-up on it, thick . . .
7090   An odious race! But I must not spoil
My stranger's decent greeting with my bile . . .
Hail, lovely ladies! And you wise grey ones, hail!

GRYPHON [*growling*]

Not grey ones! Gryphons! No one wants you
Calling him grey. In every word echo
Its origins and show the way it grew:
Grey, graves and gruesome, grouchy, grim and grumbly,
All on a scale of likeness etymologically,
Mislike us.

MEPHISTO

                    Yet – on the subject we are on –
You like some 'Grr-s' in the title 'Gryphon'.

GRYPHON [*still growling*]

7100   Of course. The truth of them is proved
And gets us blamed, but more often approved.
We *gra*b at women, *gra*sp at crowns and gold,
And what we *gri*p Luck lets us have and hold.

ANTS [*of the colossal kind*]

You speak of gold, we had collected piles
And rammed it safe in caves and rocky holes.
The Arimaspians have sniffed out where
And carried it off – they laugh to think how far.

GRYPHONS

We shall oblige them to confess.

ARIMASPIANS

But not tonight – the free and joyous night.
7110   This time we shall enjoy success
And spend it all before daylight.

MEPHISTO [*who has sat down among the* SPHINXES]

How soon I feel at home and easy here.
I understand you, everyone.

SPHINX

We breathe our ghostly notes on the air,
You make their incarnation.
Now give your name, the better we may know you.

MEPHISTO

Men know me by many names, or think they do.
Are any British here? They travel a lot
In search of battlefields and waterfalls,
Classically heavy sites and fallen walls.   7120
This would be just their sort of spot.
Ask them. In their Morality
They brought me on as Old Iniquity.

SPHINX

Why so?

MEPHISTO

       It is a mystery to me.

SPHINX

Perhaps. Do you have any star-lore?
What can you say about the present hour?

MEPHISTO [*looking up*]

Star shoots at star, the docked moon shines bright
And in this comfy place I feel all right.
I warm myself against your lion's coat,
Presuming any higher would be a waste.   7130
Set me a riddle, do charades at least.

SPHINX

Utter yourself, that will be riddle enough.
Try it for once, and solve yourself all through.
'The good man needs me and the sinner too;
The first, to spar with in the ascetic fight;
The second, to riot with, as his best mate;
And for the fun of Zeus whatever we do.'

FIRST GRYPHON [*growling*]

I don't like him.

SECOND GRYPHON [*growling louder*]

       What does he want with us?

BOTH

He has no place here, ugly as he is.

MEPHISTO [*brutally*]

Don't think this stranger's nails less good   7140
At tickling than your sharp claws. That would
Be very unwise.

SPHINX [*mildly*]
          By all means stay.
  It is your own self will drive you away.
  You live the good life in your north countree
  But feel uneasy here, it seems to me.

MEPHISTO
  My mouth waters, viewing the top of you,
  But dries up at the beastly parts below.

SPHINX
  All wrong you are, you'll come to grief,
  Our paws are in a healthy state.
7150 You with your twisted horse's hoof
  Among us feel the odd one out.
    [*Prelude from the* SIRENS *above.*]

MEPHISTO
  What birds are they so sweetly rocked
  On the billows of the poplar trees?

SPHINX
  Beware, by songsters such as these
  The very best of men were wrecked.

SIRENS
  Why must you become attuned
  To the ugly-wondrous?
  Listen! Here are swarms of us
  Bringing you melodious
7160 Comforts of the siren kind.

SPHINXES [*to the same tune, mocking them*]
  Fetch them down here. No one sees
  While they're hidden in the trees
  The ugly talons they will rend
  Flesh from flesh with should you lend
  Their singing your ears.

SIRENS
  No more hatred, no more envy,
  Let us gather all the gaiety
  Strewn beneath the sun and stars
  On the water, on the land,
7170 All that clears the mind and cheers

To offer to our welcome friend.
MEPHISTO
  So this is all their novelty:
  The employment of their cords and throat
  To plait a text and melody.
  Their warbling is wasted here,
  It skitters at the outer ear
  But heartwards cannot penetrate.
SPHINXES
  Heart? What heart? A pouch more like.
  A shrunken leather purse would suit
  You better, the way you look.   7180
FAUST [arriving]
  Oh wonderful! This sight makes me content,
  Large robust traits in what appears repellent.
  I feel fate looking kindly on me here.
  Where am I sent to by that earnest stare?
      [Speaking of the SPHINXES]
  Oedipus stood confronting such as these.
      [Speaking of the SIRENS]
  These sang to the roped and writhing Ulysses.
      [Speaking of the ANTS]
  These laid up treasure beyond all price.
      [Speaking of the GRYPHONS]
  These guarded perfectly its hiding place.

  New spirits rush my blood through every vein,
  The shapes, the memories, what grandeur they own!   7190
MEPHISTO
  You used to pack that sort off with a curse
  But now you think them worth the time of day.
  A man seeking his love is not averse
  To asking even monsters the way.
FAUST [to the SPHINXES]
  I beg you, answer me. Has any one
  Among your womanly kind set eyes on Helen?
SPHINXES
  We do not reach in time to when she was,

Heracles killed the very last of us.
You might find out from Chiron where she is.

7200 He gallops among the other ghosts tonight.
Halt him, and your advantage will be great.

SIRENS

You might learn from us as well . . .
Odysseus, not hurrying by,
Lingering with us courteously,
He had many tales to tell:
We shall tell you all of them
If you follow us and come
Home to the green seas.

SPHINXES

Don't sink your noble wishes in their lies.

7210 Not like Odysseus who let himself be bound
Take our advice, our bond is tight and true.
Look out for Chiron. Being found
He will tell you what I promised you.

[FAUST *withdraws*.]

MEPHISTO [*peevishly*]

What is it screeching and flapping past?
It hurts to watch, they fly so fast
And always another after the last.
They'd bring a hunter to his knees.

SPHINX

Like things the winds of winter blow
Fast as bolts from Alcides' bow,

7220 These are the swift Stymphalides
With the feet of geese and the beaks of hawks
Who intimate by friendly squawks
They'd dearly love an entry in
Among us here as kith and kin.

MEPHISTO [*as though intimidated*]

And there's something else, all hiss and spit.

SPHINX

They will not do you any harm,
They are the heads of the Lernean worm
Bodiless now and proud of it.

But what in the world is wrong with you?
Why must you twitch and fidget so?   7230
Where is it you would like to be?
The chorus over there, I see,
Has turned your head. Go and say hello
To the pretty ones. Do what you want to do.
They are the Lamiae, lascivious chic,
With smiling mouths and a brazen cheek
That suits the Satyrs. Goat-foot
Whatever you want of them, you'll get.

MEPHISTO
But you'll stay here? I shall find you again?

SPHINX
Yes. Go with the airy company. Join in.   7240
We, from Egypt, fixed long since,
Expect to be so centuries hence.
Respect us for it. Thus we mind
The way the sun and moon go round.

Before us at the Pyramids pass
In review the doom of nations,
War and peace and inundations.
Nothing of it ruffles us.

On the Lower Peneus

[PENEUS *surrounded by waters and* NYMPHS.]
PENEUS
Let the reeds and rushes stir
Sibling whispers, breaths of air,   7250
Through the wavy willows soughing,
Through the tremulous aspens sighing,
Heal my interrupted dreams.
For a hint of horror wakes me,
Subterraneous moving shakes me
From the slumbers of my streams.

FAUST [*approaching the river*]
    There behind the plaited screen
    Of bush and branch and leafing green
    Surely I hear something like
7260   The sounds that human beings make:
    Water's idle colloquy,
    Breezes' mirthful gaiety.
NYMPHS [*to* FAUST]
      The happiest fate is
      You bide and you take here
      Reclining in coolness
      The rest that you ache for
      Enjoying some peace then
      As you never do
      While we purl and babble
7270   And whisper to you.
FAUST
    I am awake. Oh, let them last
    Those figures, like no others, cast
    There into vision by my stare.
    They thrill me through like mysteries.
    Are they my dreams? Or memories?
    I had this blessing once before.
    Through dense and softly troubled green
    The shaded waters sidle down
    Not rushingly, in trickles only,
7280   A hundred streams from all around
    Pool in a deepening of the ground
    Shaped to bathe, transparently.
    There young and healthy women pose
    Doubled to the excited gaze
    By watery mirroring. Gathered in
    One bowl: the bathers, some who keep
    Timidly shallow, some swim deep;
    Splashings, tussles, cheerful din.
    I should content myself with these,
7290   Make them the enjoyment of my eyes.
    But still my senses overshoot.

The sharp eye strikes at that green veil
Of copious leafings that conceal
The high queen from my striving sight.

Wonderful, now swans appear
From indents in the banks and steer
Majestically serene and sleek
Cosying into the company
With pride and with complacency
And supple thrust of head and beak.   7300
But one among them looks to ride
Highest in self-delighting pride,
Sails through them all, rapid, intent,
Puffing his plumage up, he seems
A wave that surfs a wave and homes
On the sanctum, hellbent.
The others meanwhile to and fro
With brilliant feathering on show
Cruise quietly, or by splendid strife
Distract the shy girls so they bend   7310
Away from duty and attend
Only to whether *they* are safe.

NYMPHS

Sisters, lay a feeling ear
Where the bank steps greenly forth.
Seems to me that I can hear
Horse-hoof-tremors through the earth.
Who's the messenger who fetches
Swift as this the night's dispatches?

FAUST

Feels to me a fast horse beats
The earth so it reverberates.   7320
See over there:
Fate coming near
With favours, the miracle
Arriving, without equal.
A horseman is coming licketty-split,
Gifted, I'd say, with mettle and spirit,

The horse he rides is blinding white . . .
Oh, beyond a doubt I am looking on
Philyra's celebrated son!
7330   Halt, Chiron, halt, I've things to say – oh, wait!
CHIRON
What is it you want?
FAUST
                        Rein yourself in!
CHIRON
I cannot rest.
FAUST
                        Oh, take me with you then!
CHIRON
Sit up. There I can ask you at my ease
Where to? You stand here on the banks.
I'll bear you through the river if you choose.
FAUST [*mounting*]
Wherever you will. You have my lasting thanks.
Great man and noble master of a school
Of heroes, of the Argonauts, the whole
Cast and adornment of the world of poetry
7340   For which your name will live eternally.
CHIRON
Enough of that. Not even Athene
Gets due credit for her mentoring.
After all they go their own sweet way
As if they never had an upbringing.
FAUST
Here I embrace in strength of body and mind
The physician to whom plants of every kind
And all the roots, into the depths, are known,
The healer of sickness, the easer of pain.
CHIRON
When near me heroes suffered hurts
7350   Then I was able to advise and mend
But I bequeathed my skills and arts
To priests and witches in the end.

FAUST

The greatness of a great man lies
In being deaf to praise. He shies
Away in modesty as though
What he does others also do.

CHIRON

You seem an excellent hypocrite, an equal
Flatterer of prince and people.

FAUST

But you were the fellow and the witness
Of the greatest of your age, you must confess.   7360
Strove with the noblest and with a hero's
Seriousness lived through your days.
But in that heroic circle was there one
You thought the nonpareil, the paragon?

CHIRON

Among the Argonauts, of high renown,
Each had a merit all his own
And by the power inspiring him he met
The need that his companions could not.
Wherever looks and youthfulness availed
The Dioscuri easily prevailed.   7370
As their sweet gift the Boreades had
Swift thought and deed for others' good.
Jason was forceful, thoughtful, foremost in
Shrewd counselling, and liked by women.
Then gentle Orpheus: reserved, but having power
Like no one else's when he touched the lyre.
Sharp-eyed Lynceus saw their good ship safe
By day and night through surf and reef ...
In common danger each must lend
His best effectiveness, that all commend.   7380

FAUST

You do not mention Hercules?

CHIRON

Don't wake my longing. Before my eyes
Looked on Phoebus Apollo or

Ares or Hermes or any of them
There present bodily I saw
What humans call divine, in him.
He was a natural king of men.
Young, a delight to look upon,
Bound in service to his older cousin
7390   And to the loveliest of women.
Gaia won't bear, nor Hebe lead
Heavenwards, his like again.
And many toil but none have made
The image of him in song or stone.

FAUST

They labour in vain and never so
Gloriously did he appear,
That most beautiful man. But now
The equal woman, speak of her.

CHIRON

Beauty in women is no great thing,
7400   A frozen image often. Only those
That have in them the wellspring
Of lust for living will I praise.
Beauty is its own paradise;
Wants nothing; what pulls us is grace,
Like Helena's when I carried her.

FAUST

You carried her?

CHIRON

                On this back of mine.

FAUST

More and more I'm bewildered here!
I ride where she rode!

CHIRON

                Into my mane
She thrust her hands, to hold me tight
7410   As you do now.

FAUST

             Oh, I am quite
Beside and beyond myself! Say how!

At her alone my desire runs.
Oh, you carried her! Where from? Where to?

CHIRON

Easy to answer your questions.
The Dioscuri having then set free
Their little sister from captivity
Her kidnappers, not liking this defeat,
Had roused themselves and were in hard pursuit.
And near Eleusis, in the marshes there, the three
Fleeing could not make swift headway.   7420
The brothers waded, I swam splashing through.
Then she jumped down and stroked my head
And sodden mane and petted me and said
Her thank-yous, knowingly sweetly bold.
Oh, how she charmed! So young, and me so old.

FAUST

She was only ten.

CHIRON

                  I see you are deceived
By scholars' lies that they themselves believed.
Peculiar, the woman in mythology . . .
The poet shows her as his needs dictate.
Never speaks for herself; is never elderly,   7430
Always in shape to whet the appetite;
Abducted young, and courted just the same
Years later. The poet is not bound by time.

FAUST

So let her not be bound by time either.
Achilles came to her at Pherae, there
Outside all time. Rare happiness
To wrest love out of fate's duress.
And shall not I by force of longing haul
Back into life that rarest shape of all,
That everlasting being, the gods' equal,   7440
So high in stature, tender, lovable?
You saw her once, but I saw her today,
Saw how my longing with her beauty lay.

She holds my thinking and my being captive,
Unless I have her, I cannot live.

CHIRON

Strange man, your human ecstasy
Among the ghosts looks like insanity.
But you're in luck. It is my habit
This night, each year, briefly to visit
7450 The daughter of Asclepius,
Manto. She prays to him in quietness
That he will rescue his good name and pour
Light into doctors' minds so they forswear
The ways of killing for the ways of cure.
She is my favourite in the Sibyls' guild,
Not nervy, not grotesque, but kindly mild.
With potent roots, I have no doubt, she'd heal
You thoroughly, if you would stay a while.

FAUST

I don't want healing, I stand tall.
7460 Healed, I'd be like the others, paltry, small.

CHIRON

Don't let good springs of healing go to waste.
Get down now. Here we are. Make haste.

FAUST

In this night of terrors to what other side
Through gravelly waters have I been conveyed?

CHIRON

Left, Olympus; Peneus on the right,
Here Greek and Roman power fought it out.
The greatest empire vanishes in the sands,
Over the King, the Citizen ascends.
See! On this close auspicious site
7470 The temple stands for ever in moonlight.

MANTO [*inwardly dreaming*]

 With hoofbeats
 The sacred step reverberates:
 Demigods are visiting me.

CHIRON

 Indeed!

Unlid your eyes and see.

MANTO [*waking*]

Welcome. As ever, you appear.

CHIRON

Your temple house still standing here!

MANTO

Still tirelessly you rove and roam?

CHIRON

In quietness still you keep at home.
I circle, that is my delight.   7480

MANTO

I bide. Time circles me. I wait.
And him?

CHIRON

          Flotsam from
This notorious night's maelstrom.
Helen has crazed his brains and now
All he wants is Helen but how
And where to start he does not know.
He needs, none more, Asclepius for his ill.

MANTO

I like a man who wants the impossible.
   [CHIRON *is already a long way off.*]
Enter, rejoice in your temerity!
This dark way leads to Persephone.   7490
Under Olympus, deep down,
She listens in secret for a forbidden sign.
I smuggled Orpheus in here.
Use it better. Come without fear.

                        [*They descend.*]

On the Upper Peneus, as before

SIRENS

Plunge into Peneus' flood!
That's the place to swim and frolic,
Make a lusty water music,

Do the unhappy people good.
Water is our sole salvation.
7500   Flit in our bright company
Fast to the Aegean Sea,
Savour every sweet sensation.
[*Earthquake.*]

Back the river froths and now
Will not keep its course below.
Bedrock quaking, waters choking,
Bank and gravel bursting, smoking,
All must flee from it, no one
Thrives on this phenomenon.

Revellers, come to the sea's
7510   Spirited festivities!
Murmurous waters lift and bear,
Wave on wave, their lights ashore;
Holy dew comes sprinkling down
Softly from the mirrored moon;
Freely moving life is there,
Here the quaking earth and fear.
None with any sense will stay
Here in horrors. Come away.

SEISMOS [*growling and poltering in the depths*]
One more time with muscle shove,
7520   Shoulders under it and heave
Through into the world above.
Nothing there will hinder us.

SPHINXES
Such a gross and nasty trembling,
Horrid, gruesome, ugly rumbling!
Such a shaking, such a teetering,
Rocking-this-and-that-way tottering!
So annoying! So obnoxious!
But we shall not quit this place
Ever, though all hell break loose.

Rises now a hump, a dome,   7530
Wondrously. It is the same
Ancient greybeard engineer
Who caused Delos to appear,
For a woman giving birth
Kindly brought the island forth.
He by striving, thrust and strain,
Sinew, muscle, backbone,
Working much as Atlas did
Lifts the earthy clod and sod,
Gravel, shingle, sands and clays   7540
And the bedded riverways,
Rips diagonally down
The valley's quiet counterpane,
Vastly straining, never tiring,
Mighty caryatid rearing
Half out of the earth, his neck
Weighted terribly with rock.
Enough's enough now. Let him not
Trespass where the Sphinxes squat.

SEISMOS

All my own work. You'll give me credit   7550
One fine day. Except for me
Rattling, banging, shaking it
How much less beautiful the world would be.
How should the mountains stand in pure
Splendour on the ethereal blue
Had I not raised them up to your
Painterly delighted view?
In Night and Chaos, of whose brood
I am, in the ancient days, when I came on
Big and with a gang of Titans played   7560
Ballgames with Ossa and Pelion
In youthful heat we kept the rampage up
Till we were sick of it and set
Insolently on Parnassus' top
Twin mountains, for a bicorn hat . . .
Now in the singing company of the Nine

Apollo has his charmed existence there,
And it was me who raised the throne
Of Zeus the Thunderer in the upper air.
7570 And now by a monstrous striving I
Have burst on daylight from the abyss
And shout for people fit to try
A new life here in cheerfulness.

SPHINXES
True enough, we should suppose
Ancient what is heaped up here
Had we not with our own eyes
Watched it murderously appear.
Scrub woodland spreads already while
Rock makes on rock a still unsteady pile.
7580 Sphinxes though are unperturbed,
We will not have our holy seat disturbed.

GRYPHONS
Gold-leaf, glitter-gold: we see quick
Flickerings through cracks in rock.
Such a treasure! Emmets, let
None but you go filching it.

CHORUS OF THE ANTS
Giants may pile it
Whatever height
Still you must scale it
On fidgety feet
7590 Quick as you can now
Search every crack
Again and again now
Every last speck
Little and littlest
Have it and hold
Through nook and cranny quest
After the gold
Every last ant of you
Rootle and pry
7600 Gold's all we want of you
Let the gangue lie.

GRYPHONS

    Bring the gold in. Make a pile.
    We will circle it with steel.
    A treasure with our claws around
    Is locked and bolted, safe and sound.

PYGMIES

    Here we are now. This is home.
    How it happened we don't know.
    Do not ask us where we came
    From to here. We are here now.
    For a merry seat of life   7610
    Every land is good and fit;
    Any rock-crack it's a safe
    Bet you'll find the dwarves in it,
    Male and female, busy as bees
    Every pair a model pair,
    Who knows if in Paradise
    That's already how things were.
    But we like it here the best,
    Bless with thanks this star of ours,
    Equally on East and West   7620
    Mother Earth's abundance pours.

DACTYLS

    She who in one night bore
    These little people here
    She will not fail to swell
    The tribe of the smallest of all.

PYGMY ELDERS

    Seize a position,
    Take quick possession,
    Busily bustle,
    Speed against muscle!
    Before hostilities   7630
    Build yourselves smithies
    Forge us the necessary
    Armour and weaponry.

Emmets so numerous
Busy yourselves for us,
Get us the metals!
Numberless Dactyls
Smallest of minuscules
Do as you're told,
7640 Fetch wood and build
The pyre that will hide
The fire that will yield
The charcoal we need.

COMMANDER-IN-CHIEF
With bow and arrow
Smartly to battle now
Out to the lakeside
Where in unseemly pride
Herons reside
A myriad brood.
7650 Massacre the lot,
Then we can strut,
Each of us pull
Plumes for his poll.

EMMETS AND DACTYLS
Who will save us?
We make the iron,
They chain us, enslave us.
But now's not the occasion
To tear ourselves free,
So: bend and obey.

THE CRANES OF IBYCUS
7660 Cries of murder, lamentation,
Wings in panic and commotion!
Agonies past telling cry
To the heights we occupy.
All are slaughtered, see the dead
Colour in the water red.
Ugly appetite assumes
The herons' noble plumes.
So adorned these paunchy thugs

Parade themselves on bowly legs.
Comrades of our army whose   7670
Swift formations cross the seas
We summon you to vengeance in
An affair of kith and kin.
Give your strength and blood, be sworn
Enemies of this foul spawn.

                  [They disperse in the air with harsh cries.]

MEPHISTO *[on the plain]*
I boss the northern witches, but with these
Foreigner ghosts I'm very ill at ease.
The Blocksberg is a cosy place. Up there
Wherever you are you soon know where you are.
Frau Ilse watches for us on her stone,   7680
And Heinrich on his heights is all serene,
The Snorers bawl at doleful Elend, true,
But in a thousand years there's nothing new.
Here, however, still or on the move,
Who can be sure the earth beneath won't heave?
I'm toddling gaily down a smooth valley
And then lifts up behind me suddenly
A mountain, not one worth the name
Of mountain but one high enough all the same
To hide my Sphinxes. Fires still jump   7690
Downstream and frock that monstrous tump . . .
Meanwhile my prettily lascivious troupe
Dawdle and jig and offer, and escape.
Gently does it. The self-indulgent man
Seizes his chances when and where he can.

LAMIAE *[drawing* MEPHISTOPHELES *after them]*
Quick, be quick!
Move on, move on!
Then slow, slow
And chatty. Oh
It is such fun   7700
Pulling Old Nick
Our way, astray
To his discomfit

With his stiff foot
Poor Awky Duck
Old Cripple-Crock
On his dicky pin
We run away
And he comes on.

MEPHISTO [*halting*]

7710   Oh be damned to this! Since Adam
Every manjack of us runs after them.
Older yes, wiser no.
Have they not made a big enough fool of you?
A thoroughly worthless tribe, I know:
Painted faces, everything on show
And no good flesh, no matter where you press
There's no resistance, like a rottenness.
We know it, see it, feel it but we still
Dance to whatever tune the trollops will.

LAMIAE [*pausing*]

7720   Stop, he's debating, hesitating. Pay
Him attention or he'll get away.

MEPHISTO [*continuing*]

Onward! Do not fall into
The foolish web of doubt and cavil.
For if there were no witches who
The devil would want to be a devil?

LAMIAE [*very winningly*]

Encircle this hero, hear
His consulted heart declare
He loves one of us, for sure.

MEPHISTO

True enough, you have the seeming

7730   Of pretty women in this gloaming.
Not a thing to scold you for.

EMPUSA [*butting in*]

Nor me either. Let me join
The train of pretty women, being one.

LAMIAE

Her now we can do without.

It spoils our fun when she's about.

EMPUSA [*to* MEPHISTOPHELES]

A warm welcome from your old chum,
Cousin Empusa with the ass's foot!
A horse's hoof is all you've got,
Cousin, but nonetheless: welcome.

MEPHISTO

I thought they were all strangers here   7740
And now, alas, close relatives appear.
But that's the way with genealogy:
From Harz to Hellas you meet the family.

EMPUSA

I do as I will and in a twinkling
Might turn myself into many a thing.
But to honour you on this occasion
It is the ass-head I've put on.

MEPHISTO

I see these people like to demonstrate
Affinity with what is great
But whatever happens I decline   7750
To acknowledge this thing in an ass-head mine.

LAMIAE

Ignore the foul creature, she will scare
Away what looks like love and beauty:
Wherever beauty and love might be
They die at once when she comes near.

MEPHISTO

These darlings too, so langorously slim,
I don't trust any one of them.
I fear behind such cheeks' roses
There also metamorphoses.

LAMIAE

We are many. Take your pick.   7760
Try it, chance it. If you're in luck
You'll pot the black and kiss the jack.
You lick your lips, you hum and hah,
Oh, what a sad punter you are!
Airs and graces, strutting up . . .

But now he's in among our crowd,
One by one let the masks slip,
Show him the thing itself, nude.

MEPHISTO

I hook myself the prettiest one . . .
    [*Embracing her*]
7770   Oh horror! A broomstick! Skin and bone!
    [*Seizing another*]
And her? An abominable face!

LAMIAE

You get the face that suits your case.

MEPHISTO

I'll take the little one: I feel
An escaping slippy lizard's tail,
A headpiece sleek and serpentine.
I'll take the tall one: I fondle
Instead of flesh a thyrsus handle,
The head on her a pine cone.
Where now? A fat one. She might provide
7780   Refreshment of the kind I need.
One last time! For best or worst!
Squashy, bowsy: charms like these
Pashas pay for through the nose –
Oh dear, the giant puffball's burst.

LAMIAE

Flutter asunder, gather and like
Jags of blackest lightning break
Around the intruder, the witch's brat,
Dizzy him in the fear that clings
Quiet on the face with a bat's wings.
7790   He owes us more than he's paid us yet.

MEPHISTO [*shaking himself*]

I seem no wiser than I ever was.
Here and the north: absurdities!
Ghosts mad in this and in the other place
And bad the poets and the populace.
Mummery here and mummery there,
Dance of the senses everywhere.

I snatch at pretty masks and hold
Creatures that make my blood run cold.
I'd gladly fool myself, at least
I should if only it would last.   7800
　　[*Getting lost among the rocks*]
Where am I? Where is it taking me?
My path's become my purgatory.
I started well on smooth ways
And finish among scarps and screes.
I scramble up and down in vain –
Will I ever see my Sphinxes again?
What bedlam is it that can raise
Overnight a hill this size!
And what a sabbath where they bring
A Brocken of their own along!   7810

OREAD [*from the natural rock*]
Up here! Mine is an ancient hill.
The shape I had, I have it still.
Honour the abrupt and rocky climbs,
The farthest flung of Pindus' limbs.
Thus unshakenly I stood
While over me Pompey fled.
But that illusion over there
At cock-crow will disappear.
I watch the rising up of these
Fictions and their swift demise.   7820

MEPHISTO
All honour to you! Tall oak trees
Wreathe with strength your noble brows
And are so dark, the clearest bright
Moonlight cannot penetrate.
But there along the bushes goes
A thing emitting very modest rays.
What strange turn of events is this?
Upon my soul: Homunculus!
Where have you been my little fellow?

HOMUNCULUS
Gliding from place to place to know   7830

How best to come to life and keen
To shatter my globe of glass. But what
I've seen of it – of life – so far I'm not
Inclined to take the plunge. However
If I may whisper in your ear:
I'm shadowing a philosophical pair.
I listened in and heard 'Nature! Nature!'
Surely they know the truth of life on earth.
I'll cleave to them for all I'm worth
7840   And doubtless in the end I'll learn
From them where I'll do best to turn.

MEPHISTO

Do it yourself! Do it your own way!
Wherever phantoms set up shop
Friendly philosophers too turn up,
Invent you further phantoms by the dozen
And make you grateful for such clever men.
You'll never learn unless you go astray.
To come to life, the best way is *your* way.

HOMUNCULUS

But good advice might help as well.

MEPHISTO

7850   Try it. We'll watch you. Time will tell.

[*They part company.*]

ANAXAGORAS [*to* THALES]

Your stubborn mind will not be swayed?
What more persuasion do you need?

THALES

The wave gives to every wind but backs
Off cool from the brusque rocks.

ANAXAGORAS

By force of gaseous fire those rocks were got.

THALES

Things that live are engendered in the wet.

HOMUNCULUS [*between them*]

Let me go side by side with you.
To come to life is my desire too.

ANAXAGORAS

    Tell me, o Thales, whether you ever did

    In one night bring such a mountain forth from mud?   7860

THALES

    The living flux of Nature was never bound

    To days and nights and the hourly round.

    She shapes all things after her ordinance

    And even in large there is no violence.

ANAXAGORAS

    But here there was! Fierce Plutonic fire,

    Aeolian gasses' vast explosive power

    Broke through the old crust of the level earth

    And forced a new mountain into instant birth.

THALES

    What next? What furthering has it made?

    But there it is, and good so, we concede.   7870

    Quarrelling thus we waste our time and troop

    Our followers around like sheep.

ANAXAGORAS

    The mountain swarms with Myrmidons. In a trice

    Of cracks in the rock they make a dwelling place.

    Pygmies and emmets, dwarves and every

    Kind of small creature eager to be busy.

      [To HOMUNCULUS]

    You've never striven for greatness but have spent

    Your days hermetically pent.

    Apply your mind to power and I'll give

    You creatures to be sovereign of.   7880

HOMUNCULUS

    Do you advise it, Thales?

THALES

                Not at all.

    With small creatures the deeds are small.

    With large the doer himself's enlarged.

    See there, the cranes in a black cloud

    Threatening the agitated crowd

    And would threaten the king likewise.

With sharp beaks and taloned feet
They skewer the little folk. So fate
Falls like lightning from the skies.
7890   Crime killed the herons who had made
The round pond their quiet abode
But cruelly on that rain of arrows
Revenge's bloody blessing follows,
Rage is quickened in near kin
Against the pygmies' criminal clan.
What use to the dwarves are spear and shield,
Helmet and heron-finery?
Emmets and dactyls hide. The army
Falters, flees, and heaps the field.

ANAXAGORAS [*after a pause, in ceremonious tones*]
7900   Always before praising the ones below,
Things falling thus, I appeal to heaven now . . .
You up above untouched by time,
Triple in shape, triple in name,
You I invoke in my people's misery
Diana, Luna, Hecate!
Widener of the heart, deepener of the mind's abyss,
Calm face of light, wreaker of grief and bliss,
Open your shadowy throat and let appear
In horror, without magic, the ancient power!
        [*Pause.*]
7910   Am I heard too soon
By her on high?
Praying, have I
Turned Nature's order upside down?
Ever larger now the enthroned
Goddess approaches, ringed round
With vast light, with red fire
And now the darkness at the core –
No nearer, orb of menace, or you lay
Waste our lives and all the land and sea!

7920   So is it true that women of Thessaly
By magic coaxing criminally

From your right path once sang you down
And forced you to deliver blight and bane?
The disc of light is in a ring of dark,
Cracks run through it, lightnings streak and spark!
Such a hissing, such a clanging!
Din of winds and thunder banging!
All the crime of it is mine.
I beg forgiveness at your throne.
   [*He prostrates himself.*]

THALES

The things this man has seen and heard!   7930
Myself, I do not quite know what occurred
Nor did I feel it as he did. Agreed
It was an aberrant episode.
Now Luna rocks in comfort where
She belongs, as heretofore.

HOMUNCULUS

But see, the Pygmies' house and home
Is now a peak, that was a dome.
I felt the impact of a massive stone
Fallen upon it from the moon
Without a by-your-leave or how-d'you-do   7940
Squashing and slaying friend and foe.
Still I admire the arts that so
Creatively within a single night
Working at once from above and from below
Have built a mountain on this site.

THALES

All in the mind. Nothing to fret about.
Good riddance to the nasty brood. Good thing
You never did become their king.
Come now to the cheerful festival of the sea
Where guests are welcomed for their oddity.   7950
   [*They depart.*]

MEPHISTO [*climbing up the opposite side*]

Here I must drag myself up dizzy flights
Of rock and through the old oaks' stiff roots.
In my Harz mountains the resinous scent

Reminds the nose of pitch – as pleasant
To me as sulphur is. But here among
These Greeks, no whiff of such a thing.
I wonder what they have that serves as well
To fry their sinners hot enough in hell.

DRYAD

Your lore will do at home. Abroad however
7960   Among the locals you are not so clever.
Don't turn your thoughts to your country but show
These sacred oaks due honour here and now.

MEPHISTO

We think of what we've left. The place
We're used to is our paradise.
But tell me, in that cavern there
What thing squats in the dim light, threefold?

DRYAD

The Phorcides! Address them if you dare
And you can bear to feel your blood run cold.

MEPHISTO

Why not! I see them: they amaze my eyes!
7970   Proud as I am, I must concede
I never did see things like these –
Worse than mandrakes, they are indeed.
Once having looked upon this triple beast
Who could think ugly in the least
Any of the old abominated sins?
No hell of ours, however grim,
Is grim enough to employ them.
And they root here in the Land of Beauty,
In famous Greek Antiquity . . .
7980   They seem to have my scent, they stir, and like
Bats, vampires, they twitter and squeak.

PHORCYAS

Give the eye to me, sisters. It will enquire
Who dares approach our temple. Who comes here?

MEPHISTO

Your reverences, allow me near you. Set
Your blessing on my head in triplicate.

You do not know me but, so I believe,
I am your kinsman, if at some remove.
Venerable deities I have already seen,
Humblest respect to Ops and Rhea shown,
And yesterday – was it? – or the day before   7990
The Fates, your sisters, sisters of Chaos, I saw.
But such as you I never looked upon.
I stand in silent rapture at the vision.

PHORCIDES

This seems a sensible ghost.

MEPHISTO

                                        I am amazed
That by the poets you have gone unpraised.
How came it? And I never saw you three
Imaged, though worthiest of all to be.
Let sculptors chisel stone and give us you!
Not Juno, Pallas, Venus and their crew.

PHORCIDES

No such thought ever came to us who bide   8000
Triply in silence, night and solitude.

MEPHISTO

How should it? Far from the world, no one
Seeing you ever and being seen by none,
You ought to inhabit places where
Art and magnificence share the seats of power,
Where daily from the marble block
A hero issues at the double-quick.
Where –

PHORCIDES

                Be silent. Do not make us crave.
What good is knowing better than we have?
Born in night, night's kindred, we are barely   8010
Known to ourselves, to the world unknown entirely.

MEPHISTO

That being the case, the obvious solution
Is to employ others for your self-translation.
One eye, one tooth, suffices for you three.
It would be proper, even mythologically,

To press the three essentials into two
And lend me the image of a third of you
A while.

ONE OF THE PHORCIDES
                    What do you say to that? We try?

THE OTHERS
We might – but not the tooth and not the eye.

MEPHISTO

8020   You take away the best! How shall we hit
The living-likeness of you without it?

ONE OF THE PHORCIDES
Easy: shut one eye and allow
One of your canine teeth to show.
At once in profile you will make
A perfect sister look-alike.

MEPHISTO
An honour! Agreed.

PHORCIDES
                    Agreed.

MEPHISTO [*as* PHORCYAS *in profile*]
                              Behold in me
The beloved Son of Chaos.

PHORCIDES
                    That we
Are the daughters of Chaos is beyond dispute.

MEPHISTO
Now I'm a damnable hermaphrodite!

PHORCIDES

8030   In this new sisterly triad, what a belle!
Two eyes we have now and two teeth as well.

MEPHISTO
I must remove myself from public view,
Go frightening devils in Hell's foulest stew.

                                                    [*Exit.*]

Rocky Coves on the Aegean Sea

[*The moon holding steady at the zenith.*]
SIRENS [*couched here and there on the rocks, making music
      and singing*]

Though by magic criminally
By the women of Thessaly
Once upon a night of horror
Luna you were lured down here
Quietly now from on the bright
Summit of your bow of light
Illuminate the quickly shifting   8040
Sparkling riotously lifting
Waves and bless us who abide
Your direction, tide by tide.

NEREIDS AND TRITONS [*as prodigies of the sea*]

Pitch your music higher, wind
Through the wide sea shocks of sound,
Let the deep creatures be called!
From the tempest's hideous throats
Here to these quiet retreats
By your songlines we were hauled.

Riding high in golden chains,   8050
Hanks of pearls and starry crowns,
Bangles, buckles: look on these
Insignia of our ecstasies.
All your produce! Wrecks the waves
Swallowed, treasures, sinking, sinking
You delivered us by singing,
You the daimons of our coves.

SIRENS

Though we know in the cool seas
Slippy fishes live at ease
Their supple lives and never sorrow   8060
We should like to know for sure,
Quick and festive as you are,

You are more than fish. Are you?

NEREIDS AND TRITONS

    Travelling hither we supposed
    This very question would be posed!
    Proof that we are more than fish
    Sisters, brothers, will appear
    Only a little way from here
    Soon and ample as you wish.

[They depart.]

SIRENS

8070   In a twinkle, in a trice
    Straight to Samothrace
    On a favourable wind they disappear.
    What thing could they bring to an end
    In the great Cabiri's land?
    Gods like none but themselves
    And they forever beget themselves
    And never know who they are.

    Sweet Luna, hold your height,
    Let it continue night,
8080   Be kind, do not let the day
    Drive us away.

THALES [*on the shore, to* HOMUNCULUS]

I'd lead you to old Nereus with pleasure,
Indeed, his cavern is not far from here.
But he's a difficult old cuss,
So contrary, the sourpuss,
The human race, the lot of them,
Can't do right for doing wrong by him.
But he can foresee what will happen
And that impresses everyone,
8090 It's something they respect him for.
Besides, he has been helpful, many a time.

HOMUNCULUS

Worth a try. Let us knock at his door.
That can't cost me my glass and flame.

NEREUS

Are those the voices of humans I can hear?
Grates me at once, even to the heart's core.
Strivers to equal the gods but damned to be
Themselves on their own level eternally.
For aeons I've had a god's leisure but must
Use it trying to further mankind's best.
Then in their deeds I could discern no trace   8100
At all that I had given them advice.

THALES

And yet, Old Man of the Sea, we trust in you.
You are the wise man, don't chase us away.
Behold this flame, a human shape, it's true,
But not one inch from your advice he'll stray.

NEREUS

What difference did advising ever make?
A wise word dies the death in stony ears.
So often the deed was its own grim rebuke!
But humans stick in that self-will of theirs.
How I warned Paris, as a father would a son,   8110
Before his lust ensnared a foreign woman!
He stood there boldly on the Greek shore.
I told him what my seeing spirit saw:
Red spate, the very air choking for breath,
The rafters incandescent, below them murderous death:
Troy's day of reckoning, fixed in metre, down
The millennia, as terrible as well known.
The old man's word, the bold youth thought it null,
He followed his desires, and Ilium fell –
A vast cadaver stiffening after long torment,   8120
To Pindus' hungry eagles heaven-sent.
Likewise Odysseus! Did I not foretell
Him Circe's wiles and the Cyclopean hell?
His dallying, his comrades' want of sense,
And all the rest? All made no difference.
Until, much-tossed, he flung up luckily
At last where there was hospitality.

THALES

    Behaviour like that gives the wise man pain
    But the good man tries and tries again.
8130   An ounce of thanks gives him such happiness
    It quite outweighs the ton of thanklessness.
    We ask you no small thing. In brief:
    This boy desires wisely to come to life.

NEREUS

    Don't spoil my humour, good for once. Today
    Will bring quite other things my way.
    I have summoned all my daughters here, the sea's
    Graces, the fifty Nereides.
    No shape of beauty on Olympus or
    Upon your earth in moving pleases more.
8140   They fling themselves, in the loveliest attitudes,
    From waterspouts astride Poseidon's steeds,
    So wedded to the element they seem
    Lifted still higher by the very foam.
    In a play of colours, riding Venus' shell,
    Comes Galatea, the most beautiful,
    Who, Cypris having turned away from us,
    As goddess herself now is worshipped at Paphos,
    Inheriting therewith the town
    Of temples and the chariot-throne.

8150   Now go. A father's pleasures sort
    Ill with a scolding mouth or a hating heart.
    Go and ask the wondrous Proteus what is
    The way to come to life and metamorphosis.

                          [He departs towards the sea.]

THALES

    We are no further forward. Suppose we chance
    On Proteus, he will dissolve at once.
    And even if he listens, all he'll do
    By answering is amaze and muddle you.
    Yet counsel such as his is what you need.
    We'll make the test of it. Let us proceed.

                              [They depart.]

SIRENS [*above, on the rocks*]

    What is it we can spy there   8160
    Sliding through the world of water?
    Like an approach of sails
    Whose slant the wind rules
    So bright they are on the eyes,
    Clear women of the seas,
    And voices are coming in,
    Let us climb down and listen.

NEREIDS AND TRITONS

    Our cradling arms are full
    Of good for one and all.
    The giant shell of Chelone shines   8170
    Bright with strong designs:
    It is gods we bring.
    What song of songs will you sing?

SIRENS

    Small in stature
    Great in power
    Gods worshipped by shipmen
    For help since wrecks began.

NEREIDS AND TRITONS

    We bring the Cabiri
    To this peaceful festivity.
    Their holy workings incline   8180
    Neptune to be benign.

SIRENS

    We are less than you.
    When a ship breaks up
    Nothing will stop
    Your will to save the crew.

NEREIDS AND TRITONS

    We have brought three of them,
    The fourth would not come,
    And he was the best of them all, he said,
    The cleverest head.

SIRENS

8190
A god may mock a god
But you had best be glad
And grateful for the good
They do and fear the bad.

NEREIDS AND TRITONS

They are seven – or should be.

SIRENS

Where are the other three?

NEREIDS AND TRITONS

That is not known to us.
Ask on Olympus.
The eighth is there too, no doubt,
That nobody thought about.

8200
Their help is very present
Who are themselves still fluent.

Nothing and no one
Is like them, their hunger
Is longing made stronger
By what it feeds on.

SIRENS

Prayers and praise to
The impossibly far.
The moon and the daystar:
Adore them. It pays to.

NEREIDS AND TRITONS

8210
And it shall be our highest fame
To lead in this festivity.

SIRENS

It dims the name
Of the heroes of antiquity
However bright, in whatever place.
They won the Golden Fleece,
You the Cabiri.
[*They repeat this,* SIRENS *and* CABIRI *singing together.*]
They won the Golden fleece,

We ⎫
You ⎭ the Cabiri.

[NEREIDS *and* TRITONS *pass over.*]

HOMUNCULUS

They look to me like common pots,
Earthen and misshapen.   8220
And these the scholars test their wits
And dash their brains out on?

THALES

They care for such things keenly. Rust's
What most excites numismatists.

PROTEUS [*whom they have not noticed*]

Hats off to them. The oddballs are the best.
Take it from me, your ancient fabulist.

THALES

Where are you, Proteus?

PROTEUS [*in ventriloquist fashion, now close, now far away*]
                        Here. And here.

THALES

The old joke. I forgive you. I am sure
You will lend a friend a serious ear.
I know that where you speak's not where you are.   8230

PROTEUS [*as though at a distance*]

Farewell.

THALES [*softly to* HOMUNCULUS]

            He's close. Now shine afresh.
He is as quizzy as a fish.
Wherever his present lodging is
By flames he'll be enticed to us.

HOMUNCULUS

The body of my light I will express,
But moderately, not to smash the glass.

PROTEUS [*in the form of a giant turtle*]

What pretty thing is it shining so?

THALES [*covering* HOMUNCULUS]

You can see it close if you have mind to
And all we ask – no sweat, no harm –

8240   You appear in biped human form.
       By our favour, by our deciding,
       Who wishes to view what we are hiding.
       PROTEUS [*in a noble shape*]
           You still know a wordly trick or two.
       THALES
           And shifting shape still amuses you.
               [*He has uncovered* HOMUNCULUS.]
       PROTEUS [*astonished*]
           A shining manikin! It beggars belief!
       THALES
           He seeks advice. He wants to come to life.
           He came into the world, so he tells me,
           Scarce half made up, most curiously.
           He does not want for mental qualities
8250   But does for useful tangibilities.
           Thus far only his glass has given him weight
           But now he thinks it's time to be incarnate.
       PROTEUS
           You are a virgin birth! Before
           You ought to be, already there.
       THALES [*softly*]
           And otherwise too he seems to me not right:
           I think he's a hermaphrodite.
       PROTEUS
           All the easier a happy end to it.
           Wherever he lands up, he'll fit.
           But this is not a matter for much thought:
8260   In the wide sea you must make a start!
           There you begin in a small way
           Devouring the smallest, which is fun,
           And growing little by little, day by day,
           You shape towards a higher consummation.
       HOMUNCULUS
           How soft the air is here. The scents of brewing
           Greenery fill me with wellbeing.
       PROTEUS
           I'm sure they do, dear boy! And over there

It is far more agreeable
Out on that spit of sand, the atmosphere
Around yet more ineffable   8270
And in the foreground floats
And ever closer undulates
The masque. Come with me!

THALES

We will indeed.

HOMUNCULUS

A triply wondrous ghost parade!

[*Enter the* TELCHINES OF RHODES, *riding on hippocamps
and sea-dragons and brandishing Neptune's trident.*]

CHORUS

We fashioned with fire the trident for Neptune,
Rough as the waves are, it quietens them down.
The Thunderer may open the water clouds full
But Neptune opposes the hideous swell;
Though lightning-jags fall from above, blow on blow,
He fizzes the rollers with stabs from below   8280
And all of the thrashing, the throes and the suds
Sink down the throat of the deepest of gods.
For which he has passed us the sceptre today:
Festively, quietly and lightly we sway.

SIRENS

Helios' votaries whom the joyous
Hours of sunny daylight bless
We salute you as we raise
Luna's worship to the skies.

TELCHINES

Sweet goddess aloft on the iris of night
Praising your brother, we give you delight.   8290
Listen to Rhodes, from that fortunate island
Praise and thanksgiving ascend without end.
Daybreak, he rises, he opens, he sees
Us in the fire of the beams of his eyes.
The mountains, the townships, the shore and the sea
They please him, the god, their brightness, their beauty.
Fog never shrouds us, breezes and sun

Cleanse from the island whatever creeps in.
The god sees himself then a hundredfold shown:
8300   Youthful, colossal, tremendous, benign.
For we were the first to set up the divine
Power in man's likenesses fit to be seen.

PROTEUS
   Leave them to self-congratulation!
   In the holy life-beams of the sun
   Dead work like theirs is risible.
   They smelt and shape it tirelessly
   And cast in bronze it looks to be,
   To them at least, remarkable.
   But what does all their pride come to?
8310   The images of the gods stood tall
   Till the earth shoved at them and they fell
   Back in the melting-pot long long ago.

   Doings on the earth, it does not matter what,
   Are toil and trouble and nothing but.
   The waves are better for life. And now
   Proteus-Dolphin will carry you
   Into the eternal waters.
   [*He transforms himself.*]
                                    Done!
   Climb up and I will ride you home
   Into the happiest possible outcome.
8320   I'll wed you to the ocean.
THALES
   Go with the estimable longing
   To begin creation at the beginning.
   Be ready for quick work. You'll fashion
   Yourself along eternal norms
   Through a thousand thousand forms
   And need not hurry to be human.
   [HOMUNCULUS *mounts the* PROTEUS-DOLPHIN.]
PROTEUS
   Come, spirit, into the roomy wet
   And live at once without limit

And move however you like best
Only don't strive to join the higher echelons   8330
For once you're in the race of humans
Then well and truly you are lost.

THALES

Depends. A good man in his day
Is a fine thing to become, I'd say.

PROTEUS [to THALES]

A man like you, no doubt. Such stuff
Lasts a while, true enough.
Through all the many hundred years
In the white swarm of ghosts I still see yours.

SIRENS [on the rocks]

Look, a cloudy halo rings
The moon. Ah no, it is the light   8340
Of doves, it is a wealth of wings
Of circled love there, burning white.
All this swarming of desire
Paphos sends our festival
So we are completed. Clear
Joyous lightness fills us full.

NEREUS [approaching THALES]

Night travellers would think this lunar
Ring an atmospheric show
But we spirits hold another
And the only proper view: 8350
Doves they are, in convoy round
My scallop-riding child, they zoom
Here on magic of a kind
Learned in the early years of time.

THALES

I too hold the best to be
This, that all good humans love:
Close and warm at home to have
Something holy, livingly.

PSYLLI AND MARSI [riding on sea-bulls, sea-calves and
        sea-rams]

In the harsh cave-vaults of Cyprus

8360   The Sea God not ransacking them
        Yet, nor Seismos wrecking them,
        Among eternal breezes
        As in the ancient of days
        Body and soul at ease
        That is where we house
        Cypris' shell and on murmurous
        Nights through the weaving waters,
        The modern race oblivious,
        We usher the loveliest daughter in.
8370   At our quiet work we wait on
        Neither eagle nor winged lion
        Nor cross nor crescent moon
        Their high dwelling and throne
        Their hectic side-to-side
        Cleansing and homicide
        Flattening city and seed
        But we bring in the Sovereign,
        The loveliest, again and again.

SIRENS

        Moving light, a measured hastening,
8380   Ring on ring around the shell,
        Line in line, an interfastening
        Snakelike, coming on like swell,
        Close, come closer, strong Nereides,
        Larky women, easy-wild,
        Usher hither, fond Dorides,
        Galatea, her mother's child:
        Seriousness in her look
        Such as all the immortals have
        But humanly womanlike,
8390   Graced, alluring us to love.

DORIDES [*in a choir passing by* NEREUS *and all riding on dolphins*]

        Lend us, Luna, light and shadow!
        Clearly let our father see
        Flowering youth. We come to show
        Him our spouses, with a plea.

[*To* NEREUS]
These are lads whose lives we freed
From the surf's desolate throat,
Bedded them on moss and reed,
Warmed them back towards the light.
Look benignly on them now,
They must pay us what they owe: 8400
Kiss for kiss and heat for heat.

NEREUS

Truly a happy double when a deed
Of mercy and enjoyment coincide!

DORIDES

So approving, Father, grant
Pleasure for our pains: we want
Boys between our breasts, to hold
Never dying, never old.

NEREUS

Enjoy your pretty catches, make
Yourselves of every boy a man.
However, the benefit you seek   8410
I cannot give. Only Zeus can.
The waters rock you to and fro:
What footing shall a love find there?
So play while it amuses you
Then gently set your mates ashore.

DORIDES

Sweet lads, we like you. We are loath
To say goodbye to you.
We did desire eternal troth
But the gods say no.

YOUTHS

The solace we have had from you   8420
Only let it last.
No better thing can happen to
Poor lads before the mast.
[GALATEA *approaches, riding on the scallop shell.*]

NEREUS
    My darling!
GALATEA
                    My father! How happy I am!
    Linger here, dolphins, don't take me from him.
NEREUS
    Already gone, already passing over.
    The circling! Oh the leaping and the zest!
    What do they know of the secret heart's unrest?
    Could I go with them in their crossing over!
8430   And yet one glance delights me so
    It lasts the sad year through.
THALES
    Praise and praise be, I relish
    My life anew, I flourish!
    The truth and beauty of it enter me again:
    In water all lives began
    And water upholds them. Go on
    Giving and governing, ocean,
    Sending your clouds and spending
    Freely on streams and tending
8440   Rivers their ways and ending
    Them deep and wide. For what would they do,
    The mountains, the plains, the world, without you?
    You are the element quick life can thrive in.
ECHO [*a chorus of all the company*]
    You are the element life came alive in.
NEREUS
    They turn away in the unsteady distance,
    Glance no longer meets with glance,
    Their countless company
    Displayed for the festivity
    Extends in chaining loops, they wind and veer.
8450   But Galatea's scallop throne
    I see, I see it shine
    Starlike. So through

All the crowding
And medley beams a beloved thing!
However far
It shimmers bright and clear
And always near and true.

HOMUNCULUS

In this kind wateriness
All I illuminate
With beauty works on me.   8460

PROTEUS

In this life-wateriness
Now at last your light
Sounds forth splendidly.

NEREUS

What novel mystery wishes its presence made
Live on our eyesight in that multitude?
Round Galatea's shell, flames licking round her feet
Flaring up mightily, smooching down sweet,
Love seems the motor and mover, it pulses.

THALES

That is Homunculus, seduced by Proteus . . .
Symptoms those are of imperious striving,   8470
Those are the groans of a thing close to riving,
He'll smash into pieces against the bright throne:
A flaring, a flashing, he spills, it is done!

SIRENS

What fiery wonder transfigures the waves?
They smash one another in sparkling shives.
A lightning, a teetering coming on bright
Of bodies effulgently sailing the night
And fire around all things, fires are running.
Eros is sovereign! Of all, the beginning!
See the holy fire that weaves   8480
On the waters in the waves!
Praise the seas and praise the fire,
Praise their wondrous meeting here!

ALL

> Praise the mildly leaning breezes!
> Praise the caves of mysteries!
> Higher, higher, let all four
> Elements be worshipped here!

ACT THREE

Outside the Palace of Menelaus in Sparta

[*Enter* HELEN, *and a* CHORUS *of captive Trojan women led by* PANTHALIS.]

HELEN

Greatly admired and censured greatly Helena
I come from the sea, this minute set ashore and from
The rocking to and fro of lively waves still reeling   8490
That on their high and bucking backs by the favour of
Poseidon and by Euros' strength have carried us
Home to these bays from the killing fields of Phrygia.
Down there now King Menelaus is rejoicing with
His bravest fighting men that they have made it home.
But you, o lofty house my father Tyndareus
Homecoming from the hill of Pallas Athene
Built by the rising ground and through my sisterly
Childhood with Clytemnestra and all my careless play
With Castor and Pollux adorned more splendidly   8500
Then any house in Sparta, oh welcome me home!
Wings of the doors of bronze, I greet you! It was through
Your wider and wider opening once, at your friendly
Inviting me in, that towards me, chosen from many,
Menelaus shone forth with the light of marriage.
Open again now that I may faithfully accomplish
The urgent bidding of the King, as befits his wife.
Allow me in, and let be put behind me and there remain
All that till now has stormed around me, fateful.
For since the day I left this threshold without a care   8510
To attend the temple of Cythera in my sacred duty
And there the marauder, the Phrygian, seized hold of me
Much has happened that it amuses people far
And wide to tell but that the subject of the story
Is not amused to hear spun into fairytale.

CHORUS

      O Lady, do not think it a poor thing
      To honour in yourself the highest of gifts
      And have, you alone, the luckiest lot,
      The fame of beauty, so none is like you.
8520   The noise of the hero's name precedes him
      And he walks proud
      But the stubbornest man bows down at once
      His neck before beauty, the tamer of all.

HELEN

      Enough. With my husband I am shipped home here
      And sent ahead by him into his city now
      But what intention he nurtures I cannot guess.
      Do I come here as a wife? Do I come as a queen?
      Come as a sacrifice to the Prince's bitter pain
      And to the longsuffering Greeks, for their misfortunes?
8530   I am the captured prize, but am I a prisoner?
      Indeed the immortals determined equivocally
      For me my name and fate, the dubious escorts
      Who stand either side of me and my beauty even here
      On the threshold, they are my shadows, threatening.
      For in the hollow ship itself only rarely would
      My husband look at me nor spoke any heartening word
      But faced me as though he were brooding some bad thing.
      But scarcely had the beaks of the foremost ships
      Drawn into the shore and the deep mouth of the Eurotas
8540   And greeted the land, than he, as if the god prompted,
          spoke.
      'Here my warriors will disembark in proper order
      And I shall muster them ranged along the shore of the sea
      But you continue your way. Follow the fruit-endowed
      Banks of the sacred Eurotas, higher and higher, heading
      The horses through the glories of the wetted meadows
      Until you come into the beauty of the levels
      Where Lacedaemon settled a wide and fertile field
      Closely surrounded by solemn mountains. Then
      Enter the towering dwelling place of the kings
8550   And muster for me the serving women whom I

Left there together with the shrewd old housekeeper.
Let her show you the rich store of the treasures that
Your father bequeathed and that in war and peace I have
Myself heaped ever higher, forever increasing them.
You will find all things in their proper order because
It is the ruler's right that when he returns he finds
All true in his house and every single thing
There in its rightful place still the way he left it.
For the servant has no authority to alter a thing.'

CHORUS

    Delight your eyes, delight your breast   8560
    On treasures ever more plentiful!
    For crowns and necklets, all the adornments,
    They lie there proudly, they pride themselves,
    But you go in and challenge them,
    They will arm at once.
    I shall love to see beauty in combat with
    Gold and pearls and the precious stones.

HELEN

There followed then my commander's further commands.
'When you have looked through all things in their proper
    order,
Take then such tripods as you think will be needed   8570
And all such vessels as the sacrificer wants
To hand for the ceremony according to holy custom:
The cauldrons, bowls, also the flat round dishes;
And in the tall pitchers let there be the purest water
From the sacred spring; wood also have ready, dry
And rapidly eager to receive the flames; lastly
Let there not be lacking a very well sharpened knife.
All else I commend to your own anxious attention.'
Those were his words, he hurried me to leave, but nothing,
Ordering all, of living breath did he indicate   8580
That he, to honour the Olympians, intends to butcher.
This troubles me. But I will not dwell on my fears
And all things will let rest in the hands of the high gods
Who accomplish whatever they have a mind to accomplish
Whether humans account it good or whether they account

It bad. Mortal, we suffer it. Times before now
A man has lifted for sacrifice the heavy weight of an axe
Over the neck of the beast bowed down to earth
And could not accomplish the offering. There intervened
8590   A closing enemy or God, and prevented it.

CHORUS

The coming events are unfathomable
Queen, by you, so stride
Forward with courage.
Good and ill arrive
Unlooked for on humans;
Even foretold us, we disbelieve.
Troy was in flames, we were looking
Death in the face, a shameful death,
And are we not here
8600   Gladly attending on you
And see the blinding sun of the skies
And the loveliest of the earth
You, our good fortune, kind to us?

HELEN

So be it, however it is. Whatever awaits me, my duty
Is now to ascend without delay the steps of the palace
Long done without, much missed and almost forfeited,
That stands before my eyes again, I know not how.
But today my feet will not go forward so boldly
To climb the high steps I overleaped as a child.

[*Exit* HELEN.]

CHORUS

8610   Throw, sisters, you
Sad captives, all of your
Sufferings into the winds.
Share in the lady's luck
Share in Helena's luck
Who to the hearth of her father's house
Late, it is true, but with
Stride all the surer
Joyously nearer returns.

Praise to the holy
Happily restoring and   8620
Homebringing gods!
For the unchained, as though
Now given wings, surmount
Harshest fate while the chained
Yearningly, vainly
Over the spikes of their jail
Widen their arms, and pine.

But a god took her up
Far away
In the rubble of Ilium   8630
And carried her hither
Home to the old newly brightened
Fatherly house
After unspeakable
Pleasures and pains
Freshly to think of
Years of her girlhood.

PANTHALIS [*as leader of the* CHORUS]
  This path of choral song that leads you among pleasures
  Leave it and turn your eyes to the open wings of the doors.
  Sisters, what do I see there? Some violent consternation   8640
  Hurrying her steps, the Queen is returning to us.
  What is it, Lady? What in the rooms of your house
  Instead of your people's welcome could you have met with
  That has shaken you so beyond your concealing it?
  For I see the mark of revulsion on your brows,
  I see there a noble anger contending with surprise.

HELEN [*leaving the doors open, speaks in some agitation*]
  A common fear does not become the daughter of Zeus,
  A fleeting touch of the hand of fright will not affect her.
  But horror that rises from the womb of ancient night,
  From the first beginnings, still undecided in its shapes,   8650
  Like reddening clouds from the fiery choke of a mountain
  Piling up and out, shakes even the hero's heart.
  Thus here and now the Stygians have prescribed for me

An entry into my house so full of dread that I
From this threshold often crossed and greatly yearned for
Like a visitor dismissed might take myself far away.
But no. I fall back here into the light and further,
Powers whoever you are, you will not drive me.
I will think of cleansing rites then, purified, the flames
8660   Of the hearth will welcome home their lady and their lord.

PANTHALIS

What is it, Lady? Tell us, your serving women who
Revere you and stand by you, what the occurrence is.

HELEN

What I have seen, you also must with your own eyes
If ancient Night has not gulped back the thing she made
At once into the deep womb of her prodigies.
But so you will know it I will tell it you in words.
Entering the palace's solemn interior with all
Ceremoniousness and thinking of my first duties
I was amazed by the silence of the deserted corridors.
8670   I heard no noise of people hurrying about their tasks,
No bustle and busyness were anywhere in sight,
No maid appeared before me, no housekeeper,
Kind welcomers of every stranger in the past.
But when I drew near the lap and hearth of the house
There by the pale remainders of the ash I saw
A bulky woman cloaked, sitting on the floor, who seemed
Not to be sleeping but to be thinking rather.
With a mistress's words I roused her up to her work,
Supposing her to be the housekeeper appointed
8680   By my forethoughtful husband in the meantime;
But she still sat unmoving, wrapped in among her folds,
And only under my threats at last with her right arm
She gestured as though to banish me from hearth and
        home.
I was turning away in anger and hurrying at once
Towards the steps on which the thalamos in all
Its adornment rises and close by it the treasury
But thereupon the wondrous creature started up,
Stood in my path commandingly and showed itself

Gaunt and tall with cavernous bloodily troubled eyes,
A weird appearance, bewildering sight and mind. 8690
But I waste my breath, words struggle piece by piece
And fail to build and bring to life the shapes of things.
See it for yourselves! It dares come into the daylight!
But until our lord and king arrives we are the masters
  here
And the friend of beauty, Phoebus Apollo, will drive
The night's foul births back into their caves, or tame
  them.

[PHORCYAS *appears in the open doorway.*]

CHORUS

Much I have lived through, youthfully though still
Flounces and curls the hair at my temples.
Many and terrible things I have witnessed,
War and its misery, Ilium's night 8700
When it fell.

Through the enshrouding dust of the bawling
Battering fighters, I heard the chilling
Yells of our deities, I heard the brazen
Shouting of Discord clang through the field
At our walls.

Oh, a while stood Ilium's
Walls still. But flames were already
Calling from neighbour to neighbour.
Wider, further, from here, from there, 8710
Riding its own waves, the firestorm
Traversed the night of the city.

Fleeing then through the furnace smoke,
Through the flarings of tongues of flame
Nearer I saw the atrocious gods
Angry, fabulous, vastly
Striding through black clouds lit by
Lightning reds, coming closer.

Did I see it or did the
8720   Mind in its coils of terror shape
Such confusion? I cannot say
Ever, but this now with eyes
This I have seen and this now I
Swear to, sure of, this horror,
Grasp it even, with hands, I might –
Did not fear of the harm it
Would do me hold me in check.

Which of Phorcys'
Daughters then are you?
8730   For I perceive that
Family likeness.
Have you come as one of the
Greyborn, the one eye, one tooth
Swapping between them,
The Graeae, have you?

Foulness, how dare you
Show yourself here
Next to Beauty and in
Phoebus the connoisseur's view?
8740   Step forward nevertheless:
The eyes of the god do not see
What is ugly and have
Never looked into shadows.

On us however, who die and love
Beauty, a sad misfigured fate
Inflicts the sight of things for ever
Unfit to be seen, ill-favoured things,
Hurting our eyes unspeakably.

Hear then, if you impudently
8750   Counter us, maledictions, hear
Scoldings, threats – all manner of –
Out of the cursing mouths of the blessed
Whom the hands of the gods have shaped.

PHORCYAS

    The saying is old but true and sovereign nonetheless
    That Shame and Beauty will never go walking hand in
        hand
    Together on the earth's green paths. Deep-rooted
    In each against the other is an ancient hatred
    Such that whenever they meet in whatever place
    They meet as opponents, each from the other averts her
        face
    And with a harder tread they hurry on their ways,   8760
    Shame saddened but Beauty all the bolder until
    At the last the hollow night of Orcus embraces both
    Unless before that time old age has broken them.
    You now I find here, brazen, from a foreign land,
    Apparelled in arrogance, and like a squadron
    Of loudly hoarsely skriking cranes that pass over
    Our heads in a long cloud croaking down on us
    Such din that the quiet traveller is induced
    To look above him, but they continue on their course
    And he continues his, and so it will be with us.   8770

    Who are you then that feel yourselves free to riot
    Maenad-wild, like drunks, through the King's palace?
    Who are you then that you howl at the housekeeper
    Like a pack of bitches howling up at the moon?
    Do you suppose what race you are is unknown to me,
    You spawn of war, raised on battle, young women
    Set on men, seduced, seducing, sucking out
    The nerve of strength from the warrior and the citizen.
    Seeing the mass of you I seem to see a swarm
    Of locusts dropped like a blanket on the greening fields,   8780
    Devourers of somebody else's labour, nibblers
    At the sprouted seed of wealth, annulling it all,
    Booty you are, traded, goods that have gone the rounds.

HELEN

    Who scolds the servants in the presence of their mistress
    Encroaches rudely on her rights in her own house.
    For it is hers, nobody else's place, to praise
    Whatever merits praise and punish all misconduct.

Moreover I am well contented with the services
They rendered me when Ilium's high mettle
8790   Stood beleaguered, fell and lay; and likewise
In the ever-changing tribulations we endured
In our hard wanderings, when most care most for self.
Here too from their bright company I expect the same.
Not what they are who serve, the master asks, but how.
Therefore be silent, you. Cease grimacing at them.
If you so far in the place of the mistress of the house
Have kept house well, that will be to your credit.
But now she is here herself withdraw yourself so that
Punishment does not replace deserved reward.

PHORCYAS

8800   Threatening the household is a large prerogative
That by long years of managing things wisely
The wife of a heaven-blessed ruler earns herself.
Since you I now acknowledge have returned into
The place of queen and mistress of the house, seize hold
Again of the reins that have too long been slack
And rule and repossess the treasure store and us;
But most extend to me, the elder, your protection
Against this gaggle who next to you, the beautiful
Swan, are squawking geese of very poor plumage.

PANTHALIS

8810   How ugly next to beauty ugliness appears.

PHORCYAS

How foolish next to good sense foolishness appears.
   [*Henceforth one member of the* CHORUS *after another
   steps forward to reply.*]

FIRST MEMBER OF THE CHORUS

Give us news of Father Erebus and Mother Night.

PHORCYAS

Speak to me then of Scylla, your sister flesh and blood.

SECOND

Some monstrous creatures clamber up your family-tree.

PHORCYAS

Go visiting in Orcus. Your kith and kin are there.

THIRD

All dwellers in that place are far too young for you.

PHORCYAS

Try old Tiresias. Suggest yourself to him.

FOURTH

Orion's wet nurse was your great-great-granddaughter.

PHORCYAS

The Harpies, I should say, fattened you up on filth.

FIFTH

Such soigné scrawniness! What diet are you on? 8820

PHORCYAS

No diet of blood, at least, that whets the sex in you.

SIXTH

But you whet yours on corpses, stinking corpse yourself.

PHORCYAS

I see white vampire teeth shining in your rude gob.

PANTHALIS

I'd stop yours soon enough by saying who you are.

PHORCYAS

First say what your name is. Two riddles solved in one.

HELEN

I step between you not in anger but in sadness
Forbidding the quarrel's turbulent to and fro.
No thing more harmful meets the man who rules than such
A festering of discord in the serving body.
For then he gives commands and no melodious 8830
Echo answers him in quickly accomplished deeds.
But only for itself an uproar breaks around him
So he is lost and scolds into a nothingness.
But that's not all. By your ill-mannered ragings you
Have conjured my calamities and terrors hither
So that they press about me and I feel the pull
Of Orcus, the meadows of my homeland unavailing.
Is it my memories? Was it delusion taking me?
Was I all that? Am still? And will be in the future
The nightmare image of the woman who wasted cities? 8840
The girls shudder. But you the oldest of us all
You stand unperturbed. Speak some sense to me.

PHORCYAS

    Whoever thinks of many years of mixed fortune
    Will think in the end the favours of the gods a dream.
    But you, favoured beyond all measure – and for what? –
    In the serial of life saw only the hungry lovers
    Who flamed up fast for every sort of reckless act.
    Theseus, the appetite excited, seized you early
    With the strength of Heracles, a man of splendid beauty.

HELEN

8850   Kidnapped me, ten years old, a leggy fawn, and shut
    Me up in Attica, in the castle of Aphidnus.

PHORCYAS

    But soon by Castor and Pollux freed from there you stood
    Surrounded by suitors, the elite of the host of heroes.

HELEN

    But my quiet favour, I confess, before them all
    Patroclus had, who was Achilles' very image.

PHORCYAS

    Your father's will however bound you to Menelaus,
    The bold sea wayfarer and house-upholder too.

HELEN

    Gave him the daughter, gave him the kingdom's
        governance.
    And from the married union came Hermione.

PHORCYAS

8860   But when he went contesting the inheritance of Crete,
    To you, left solitary, came a pretty guest.

HELEN

    Why bring our minds to that half-widowhood and what
    Ruin for me was hideously born of it?

PHORCYAS

    That same voyage on me, in Crete a freeborn woman,
    Fetched my captivity and my long slavery.

HELEN

    He appointed you at once to here as housekeeper
    Much overseeing, the castle, the bravely won treasures.

PHORCYAS

    Which you deserted, turning your face towards the towers
    Encircling Troy and love's not yet exhausted pleasures.

HELEN

    Don't speak of pleasures. An all-too-bitter sorrow   8870
    Poured unendingly over my head and breasts.

PHORCYAS

    But, it is said, there were two images of you
    Appearing in Ilium and in Egypt also.

HELEN

    Don't muddle my bewildered head's remaining wits.
    For even now which one I am I do not know.

PHORCYAS

    Then people say up from the cavernous realm of shades
    Achilles, so desirous, rose and joined with you,
    Loving you earlier, against Fate's prohibitions.

HELEN

    I as an idol coupled with him, the idol.
    It was a dream. Do not the words themselves say so?   8880
    I faint and fade, becoming an idol to myself.

    [*She faints and is supported by women in the* CHORUS.]

CHORUS

    Silence! Be silent
    Evil-eying, evil-speaking, you!
    One tooth in your grisly head
    What foulness reeks
    From the lips of your gullet of horrors!

    For evil seeming kind, wolf-
    Savagery under a sheep-woolly fleece,
    Terrifies me more by far than the three-
    Headed dog's wide mouths.   8890
    We stand here anxiously hearkening.
    When? How? Where next of her guile
    Will the deep
    Ambushing monsters fall?

Now when you might with mild and friendly words
Freighted with copious comfort have lent us Lethe
Why must you quicken of the past
Not the good but the worst
And darken at once not only
8900 The shine of the present
But also the future's
Glimmer of a dawning hope?

Silence! Be silent,
So the soul of the Queen
Near taking flight
Will hold and her human form
Hold fast that is like
None other the light of the sun ever saw.
[HELEN *has recovered and stands again in their midst.*]

PHORCYAS
From the clouds that briefly hid you, glorious daystar
      reappear!
8910 Even veiled you thrilled the heart – now your sovereign
      bareness blinds.
As the world opens before you, so you face it, open too.
Ugly though they say I am, still I know what beauty is.

HELEN
Stumbling swaying from the wastelands all around me in
      my swoon
Peace is what I wish for, quiet, such fatigue is in my limbs.
Queens however, all however, humans all are duty-bound
Not to founder but whatever ills assail us still to stand.

PHORCYAS
Standing in your greatness now, in your beauty standing
      there,
By your looks you issue orders. What then? Utter your
      commands.

HELEN
Make good quickly what by rudely quarrelling you left
      undone.

Make ready for sacrificing, as the King commanded me. 8920

PHORCYAS

All is ready in the house, the dishes, tripod, sharpened
    axe,
For the asperging, for the censing. Say what shall be
    sacrificed.

HELEN

There the King gave no instruction.

PHORCYAS

                    Told you nothing? Sorrow! Sorrow!

HELEN

Why has sorrow stricken you?

PHORCYAS

                    Queen, you are the intended thing.

HELEN

I am?

PHORCYAS

    These too.

CHORUS

           Sorrow! Sorrow!

PHORCYAS

                    You will fall under the axe.

HELEN

Horror, but suspected. Piteous.

PHORCYAS

                    Inescapable it seems.

CHORUS

Oh, and us? What happens to us?

PHORCYAS

                    She will die the noble death,
You however from the house's gable-bearing beam indoors
High like fastened thrushes swinging in a row you'll dance
    and kick.

    [HELEN *and the* CHORUS *stand astounded and terrified in
    an expressive and carefully arranged tableau.*]

PHORCYAS

Ghosts! You stand there like petrified images 8930

Frightened to quit the daylight that does not belong to you.
For human beings and ghosts, all of them, like you
Never willingly relinquish the lovely light of the sun
But no one can beg them free or rescue them from the end
As they all know but very few does it please.
Enough! You are lost. And now there is work to be done.
[*She claps her hands, whereupon dwarfish muffled figures
appear at the doors and speedily carry out her orders as
she utters them.*]
You dismal breed of globular monstrosities
Roll up, roll up, here's every mischief you could wish!
Make room for the portable altar, golden-horned, and lay
8940   The axe along the silver edge of it, catching the light,
And fill the water pitchers, there'll be a sluicing clean
To do of the black blood's horrible pollution.
Spread out here over the dust a costly covering
So that the sacrifice royally may kneel and with
The head cut off be wrapped up at once and so
Fitly, with all due honour, go to her burial.

PANTHALIS
The Queen stands to one side, thinking her own thoughts,
The girls are faint, like the mown grass of the meadow,
But I, the eldest among them, think it my sacred duty
8950   To have some words with you who are the oldest of the
        old.
You are experienced, wise, seem kindly disposed to us
Although this brainless gaggle met you with ignorance.
Say therefore what you know of possible rescue still.

PHORCYAS
Easily said. It lies with the Queen herself alone
To save herself and you, her appendages, with her.
Resolve, of the swiftest kind, will be necessary.

CHORUS
Most revered of all the Parcae, wisest of the Sibyls, hold
Shut the golden scissors, promise safe and sunny days for
us.
For we feel our feet already tread on nothing, kick and
dangle

Joylessly who first would rather joyfully be dancing then   8960
Rest upon a sweetheart's breast.

HELEN

Let these be fearful. I feel sorrowful not fearful.
But if you know an escape, we shall be glad and thank you.
For to the wise, the widely circumspect, indeed
Often the impossible looks possible. Tell us.

CHORUS

Speak and tell us, tell us quickly, how shall we elude the
    cruel
Ugly nooses fastening like the shoddiest jewellery round our
    necks
Tighter, tighter? Pity us already feeling what it feels like
Being throttled, wanting breath. Mother of all the gods,
    have mercy
Ancient Rhea, pity us.   8970

PHORCYAS

Have you patience to listen in silence while I lay
A long account before you? Many and various stories.

CHORUS

Patience in plenty! While we listen we are alive.

PHORCYAS

The man who stays at home and safeguards his good
    wealth
And cannily clads the walls of his tall dwelling place,
Secures the roof also against the indriving rain,
He will do well throughout the long years of his life.
But who with itchy feet steps over and lightly
Leaves the sacred level of his threshold for ill deeds
When he comes home no doubt he finds the place again   8980
But altered everything if not wholly destroyed.

HELEN

What use are such well-known old wisdoms here?
You had a story. Do not rake at unhappy things.

PHORCYAS

Facts of the story. I intended no reproaches.
The pirate Menelaus sailed from bay to bay,
Touched every shore and island as a predator,

Returning laden, cramming the house with booty.
Ten long years he spent outside the walls of Troy
And how many years homecoming I do not know.

8990 And now I ask you in this place how do things stand
With the noble house of Tyndareus and all the realm?

HELEN

Is scolding in your blood so thoroughly that you
Can't move your lips except for finding fault?

PHORCYAS

So many years the mountain valley lay abandoned
That climbs behind Sparta northwards higher and higher,
Taygetus backing it, from where as a cheerful stream
Eurotas tumbles down and through our lowland, reeds
On either side, widens and gives your swans a home.
Back there by stealth high in that mountain valley,
      thrusting

9000 Down from the Cimmerian night, a tribe has settled
And raised up unassailable forts from where
They tribulate the land and people as they please.

HELEN

And they could do it? It seems wholly impossible.

PHORCYAS

They had the time. It must be almost twenty years.

HELEN

Is one their lord? And many robbers, all in league?

PHORCYAS

They are not robbers. One, however, is their lord
And though he raided here I don't think ill of him.
He might have taken everything but was content
With a few gifts, as he called them, not tribute.

HELEN

9010 His looks?

PHORCYAS

                    By no means bad. I thought him pleasing.
He is a cheerful man, bold, strapping and handsome
Like few among the Greeks, a man of understanding.
They call his race barbarians but I'd say
Not one of them's as barbarous as some heroes

Who at the walls of Ilium turned cannibal.
I marked his greatness, I should trust myself to him.
And then his castle! That is indeed a sight to see,
A thing very unlike the ponderous work of walls
Your fathers piled up higgledy-piggledy,
Cyclopean like Cyclops, one shapeless stone   9020
Abruptly dumping on another. There the vertical
And horizontal lines are true and regular.
See from outside! How it strives up into the heavens
Erectly, so well fitted and mirror-smooth like steel.
The very thought slips off and falls from scaling it.
Within those walls are spacious courtyards, having
Buildings around of every sort and purpose. Pillars
You see there, tall and small, and arches, high and low,
Balconies and galleries, to peer into and out of,
And coats of arms.

CHORUS

And what are coats of arms?

PHORCYAS

Ajax   9030
Bore twined snakes on his shield, you must have seen them.
The Seven against Thebes each carried on his shield
Designs and images, all richly meaningful.
Moon and stars were there on the nightly space of heaven,
Heroes and goddesses, swords, ladders, torches also
And cruel and violent things that threaten the good cities.
Likewise our hero's troops bear such devices
In brilliant colours come down from his far ancestors.
There you see lions, eagles, talons and beaks as well.
The horns of oxen, wings and roses, peacock tails   9040
And bands of gold and sable, azure, silver, gules.
Row upon row such things are hung in halls, in rows
Down never-ending halls wide as the world.
There you could dance!

CHORUS

And are there dancers? Tell us that.

PHORCYAS

The best! Young men with golden curls, a host of them,

All in the bloom and scent of youthfulness, like Paris
When he approached too near the Queen.

HELEN

You say far more
Than it's your part to say. Enough. Your last words now.

PHORCYAS

You speak the last. Say aloud and so you mean it: yes
9050   And I'll at once surround you with that castle.

CHORUS

Oh, say
That little word and save yourself and us with you.

HELEN

Am I to fear that King Menelaus would so
Evilly transgress that he would do me harm?

PHORCYAS

Have you forgotten how he spoiled the looks of your
Deiphobus who got you, widow, for his concubine,
The fool, glad of his luck, after his brother Paris
Was fought to death? Unheard-of thing, he lopped him
Ears and nose and more. All sickened at it, watching.

HELEN

He did those things to him, he did them because of me.

PHORCYAS

9060   Because of him he'll do those things to you. Beauty
Is not to be shared out, whoever had it whole
Wants that, damns anything less, destroys all rather.

[*Trumpets at a distance, they send a shudder through the*
CHORUS.]

How sharp the blast of trumpets rips at the ears
And guts, so likewise do the claws of jealousy
Fasten on the heart of a man who never will forget
What he owned once and lost and now no longer owns.

CHORUS

Horns are blaring, can't you hear them? Weapons flashing,
can't you see them?

PHORCYAS

Lord and King, I bid you welcome, gladly render my
account.

CHORUS
   What of us?
PHORCYAS
           You know the answer. Death is coming into view,
   Hers out here, yours indoors there. No, you are all beyond
       help now.								9070
   [*Pause.*]
HELEN
   I have thought out my nearest move and will risk it.
   You are a counter-spirit, I am very sure of that
   And fear what things are good you will turn them to bad.
   But first of all I will go with you to the fortress.
   What else, I know. For what the Queen may choose to
       hide
   Deep in the secret places of her heart, let no one
   Have entry into it. Old woman, lead.
CHORUS
       Oh on hurrying feet
       Glad to be gone from here
       Death at our backs
       And before us again						9080
       The unscalable walls
       Of a towering fastness.
       May it protect as well
       Even as the fort of Troy
       Which finally fell
       Only to treacherous slyness.
   [*Mists roll over enveloping the background and the fore-
   ground also, as desired.*]
       Now, oh what now?
       Sisters look around you!
       Was it not bright daylight?						9090
       Fogs wobble up in waves
       From Eurotas' sacred waters.
       Already the lovely reed-
       Garlanded banks have vanished,
       Also the freely softly-gliding
       The finely proud swans

In the sociable pleasures of swimming
Alas, I can see them no more.

But I hear them
9100   Yet and still
Their hoarse tones at a distance
Which are, it is said, an announcement of death.
Let them not for us also
Instead of a promised rescue and safety
Announce our final perdition,
Us who resemble the swans
Our necks, the stretch of white beauty, and oh
Our swan-got queen
Alas, oh alas!

9110   All already has gone
Under fogs all around.
Each loses the sight of the next.
What is this event? Are we walking
Or trailing on tripping feet a little above the ground?
What can you see? Is that Hermes
Hovering ahead? And his golden staff flashing
Commanding, ordering us back
Into unhappy Hades full
Of shapes not able to be embraced
9120   Into the over-full and for ever empty Hades
Where days break grey.

Suddenly the light has thickened, lifting mist, but nothing
     brightens,
Greys and darkens, drab as walls. And the eyes in search of
     freedom
Hit on sullen ungiving walls. Is it a courtyard? Or the deep
     pit?
Either way a horror. Sisters, oh alas now we are captives
Bad as ever we were before.

The Inner Courtyard of a Castle

[*Surrounded by richly fantastical buildings of the Middle Ages.*]

PANTHALIS

Hasty and foolish, true women all of you, on
The moment depending, playthings of changing weather,
Of chance, good and ill, and neither do you know how
To bear with an even spirit. But one of you with a passion   9130
Must contradict the others, and her words the others
    cross.
You have one tone in joy or pain, howling or laughing.
Be silent and bide now listening to what the sovereign
    lady
From her high mind may decide that concerns herself and
    us.

HELEN

Where are you Pythonissa? Whatever name you go by
Appear now from the vaults of this sombre castle.
If you went ahead to announce us to the place's
Marvellous lord and hero, preparing me a welcome,
I thank you. But lead me to him at once for I
Want an end of wandering. It is some peace I want.   9140

PANTHALIS

Queen, you look around you on every side in vain,
The unlovely sight has vanished, remained behind
    perhaps
Back there in the fog out of whose bosom we to here,
I cannot say how, have come without step and swiftly,
Or strays perhaps in doubts in the labyrinth of this
Fastness of many parts become a wondrous whole
Asking for its lord that he will make a princely greeting.
But see up there in multitudes along the galleries
And at the windows, in the doorways, to and fro
Servants are hurrying which I think announces   9150
A richly courteous welcoming of us strangers.

CHORUS
        Leaping up of my heart! Oh, see over there
        How with decorum down, all with a lingering step,
        Moves in a measured fashion strictly processing
        Youth at its sweetest. Why? Who has ordered
        Such an appearance, such rows, such a race
        Of boys shaping so beautifully into men?
        What to admire on them most? Grace of their walk,
        Curls of their heads of hair on the clear brow?
9160   Cheeks like peaches, the blush on them and the bloom,
        Downed, so it looks, just lately and soft to stroke,
        Tempting to bite in, but I shudder to do so
        For in the past, so tempted, the mouth – a
        Horror to say it – was stopped with ash.

           Now though approach us
           All of their loveliest:
           What are they carrying?
           Steps to a throne,
           Carpets, a seat,
9170   Drapes for a tent's
           Opulent show
           That lifts and in garlands
           Of cloud billows over
           The head of our queen
           Climbing as bidden
           To sit in splendour.
           Step on step now
           Row upon row
           Solemnly we stand.
9180   So fitly you receive us, we
           Equal you with thanks and blessings.

        [*All is performed in order as the* CHORUS *describes it.*
        Once the pageboys and squires in a long procession have
        descended, FAUST *appears at the head of the stairs in the*
        court dress of a knight of the Middle Ages, and in slow
        and stately fashion he too descends.]

PANTHALIS [*watching him closely*]
   Unless the gods, as they quite often do, have lent
   Only a while this man his admirable form,
   His poise and dignity and amiable presence
   And none of it will last, he will in everything
   Succeed he ever begins, be that the wars of men
   Or in the smaller war with the loveliest of women.
   He is indeed to be preferred above a host
   Of others I have looked on who were well regarded.
   I see the prince, stepping with slow solemnity,   9190
   Reserved in reverence. Turn to him, Queen.
FAUST [*approaching, a man in chains at his side*]
   There should be greeting with all ceremony
   And reverential welcoming. Instead
   I bring you him, hard bound in chains, the serf
   Who failing in his duty lost me mine.
   Go on your knees, at this high lady's feet
   Depose the full confession of your guilt.
   Sovereign, this is the man of rare brightness
   Of sight commanded from the high tower
   To look around him, sharply to scrutinize   9200
   The spaces of heaven and the whole wide earth
   For what might show a presence here or there
   And might from the ring of hills into the valley
   Be heading towards the fort, flocks in waves,
   An army on the move: we shield the first,
   Confront the second. Oh, what a lapse today!
   You approach, he does not signal it, the duest
   Honouring welcome of so high a visitor
   Is missed. His crime has forfeited him
   His life, he'd lie already in the blood   9210
   Of death deserved – but you alone shall give him
   Punishment or pardon, as it pleases you.
HELEN
   Such high authority you grant me here
   As judge, as sovereign, even though it be
   To tempt me, as I think I must suppose –

So I will exercise a judge's first duty
Which is to hear the accused. Speak then.

LYNCEUS, THE WATCHER IN THE TOWER

    Let me kneel and let me see,
    Let me live or let me die,
9220   I am given up already
    All to this god-given lady.

    Waiting for the joy of daylight,
    Spying for coming easterly,
    Suddenly and southerly
    Came a strange sun on my sight.

    All my vision fastened there,
    Nothing else in the earth's or sky's
    Vast geography but her
    Interested my spying eyes.

9230   Like the treetop lynx I beam
    Light and sight from gifted eyes
    But I struggled in the throes
    Of a deep and darkening dream.

    All my whereabouts were lost,
    Bolted portals, turret, tower.
    Then the unsteady shifting mist
    Opened on this goddess, clear.

    Eyes and breast turning towards her
    In I sucked the kindly light.
9240   Beauty blinds: this poor beholder
    Looking lost all power of sight.

    I forgot my watchman's duty,
    Horn of office quite forgot.
    I will die if you will not
    Soften anger under beauty.

HELEN

  The wrong that I brought with me I may not
  Punish. How hard a destiny, alas,
  Rides after me that everywhere I so
  Bewilder men they spare neither themselves
  Nor any worthy thing. Stealing, seducing,   9250
  Carrying away in violence here and there,
  Demigods, heroes, gods, and spirits even,
  They led me in errancy there and here.
  My one self mithered the world, my doubled more,
  Triple and fourfold I pile grief on grief.
  Take this good man away and set him free,
  No shame fall on a man the gods have fooled.

FAUST

  Astounded, Queen, I see together here
  The woman aiming true and him she hit.
  I see the bow the arrow was dispatched from,   9260
  Wounding him. Now arrows follow arrows
  Hitting me. On all sides crisscrossing I feel
  Their feathered hushings through the courts and halls.
  Where am I now? Suddenly you have made
  My loyalest men rebellious and my walls
  Unsafe. Indeed, I fear my troops belong
  Already to the unconquered woman conquering.
  What is there left for me to do but render
  Myself and all I thought was mine to you?
  Allow me then, freely and loyally, kneeling   9270
  To call you sovereign who on entering
  At once ascends the throne of all I own.

LYNCEUS [carrying a box, and more are carried in after
      him]

  Lady, you see a rich man who
  Returns to beg a look of you.
  He looks at you and feels at once
  Poor as a beggar, rich as a prince.

What was I then? What am I now?
What shall I want? What shall I do?
The lightning of my eyes goes forth
9280   And striking you it falls to earth.

We came out of the East, we were
The end the West was waiting for.
A heavy tribe, so long, so vast,
The first knew nothing of the last.

The first would fall, the second stand,
A third man's spear was there to hand.
Each fortified a hundredfold,
Slaughtered in thousands, untold.

We came in force, we came apace,
9290   We lorded it from place to place.
The word was mine! But come next day
Some other robber had his say.

We looked – the looking was always fast.
One took the woman who looked best,
Another the steadiest treading bull,
And as for horses: we took them all.

But I loved spying for what has been
By very few men ever seen,
And dross was anything I found
9300   Not only I but others owned.

I was a treasure-seeker whose
Foragers were his sharp eyes,
Purse and pocket spied into,
Walls of shrine and tomb saw through.

Gold I had but jewels I gave
The first place in my treasure-trove:
Only this emerald's greening light
Is fit to pulse on your heartbeat.

The blushing of your beauty shames
The ruby's too apparent flames   9310
But let this sea-bed pearly drop
Dangle between lobe and lip.

And so I set before you here
Treasure past counting or compare.
Let bloody warfare's profit come
Here to your feet, like harvest home.

I bring you boxes by the score,
Iron boxes, more and more.
Let me follow you. I will
Cram your treasure-houses full.   9320

No sooner you ascend the throne
Than wit and wealth and power incline
And bow to you for they have no
Shape of worship now but you.

All this I held tightly for mine
That quits me now and mine is thine.
I thought it rare and true. I know
That it was null and nothing now.

Vanished is everything I had
Like something scythed, dying, dead.   9330
With one unclouded look quicken
All of its virtue again.

FAUST

Quickly remove these boldly got burdens
And though not scolded go without reward.
All that this castle harbours in its womb
Is hers already. To offer her parts of it's
Superfluous. Heap treasure now on treasure
In good order. Erect the idol of our
Unseen magnificence. Let the vaults
Sparkle like heavens freshened, make   9340
From lifeless life a suite of paradises.

Hurry before her feet with an unrolling,
A flowering, of carpet upon carpet, meet
Her step with softness, and with highest brilliance
Her gaze – goddess, it will not dazzle her.

LYNCEUS

This is little, when we obey,
Sir, we stage a paltry play.
All our goods and blood are laid
Low under this beauty's pride.
9350   All our troops are tame already,
All their swords blunt and unready.
Stance and stature of her stun
Cold and pale the astounded sun,
And her face, its plenteous
Gifts of beauty empty us.

                                                          [*Exits.*]

HELEN [*to* FAUST]

I wish to talk with you, but come up here,
Sit by my side. The empty place
Calls for its lord, who will secure me mine.

FAUST

Lady, accept first from me on my knees
9360   The dedication of myself and let
Me kiss the hand that lifts me to your side.
Strengthen me regent with you over your
Empire that knows no frontiers, acquire
The admirer, watchman, servant, all in one.

HELEN

Manifold wonders I am seeing and listening to,
I am astonished, much I should like to ask.
But I wish you to teach me why that man's
Speech rang strange to me – rang strange and friendly.
It seemed that one sound settled with another
9370   And when a word had made friends with the ear
There came another to caress the first.

FAUST

If you already like our peoples' speaking
Surely our poetry also will delight you
By sound and sense contenting to the depths.

But safest is, we practise it at once:
Speech to and fro entices, calls it forth.

HELEN

In such sweet speaking how shall I take part?

FAUST

Easy enough. It must come from the heart
And when from there the feelings overflow
I look and ask . . .

HELEN

                              from whose glad heart also?   9380

FAUST

We let go past and future then and press
All in the here and now . . .

HELEN

                              our happiness.

FAUST

Our wealth, high winnings, pledged possession – and
Where is the proof of it?

HELEN

                              Here in my hand.

CHORUS

Who will mind that our mistress
Grants the castle's master
This friendly demeanour?
For – are we not? – we are all
Prisoners as so often
Since the disgraceful ending   9390
Of Ilium and our fearful
Wanderings through a maze of sorrow.

Women used to the love of men
Choosers they are not
But connoisseurs
And to the shepherd boys with golden curls
Or the black-bristly fauns
As chance will have it, over
Their bodies' hills and declivities
They extend the same full rights.   9400

Close and closer their sitting
And their leaning together
Shoulder to shoulder, knee to knee
And cradling hand in hand
Over the throne's
Pillowed-up splendour.
So Majesty permits itself
Before the eyes of the people
A very bold openness
9410   Of private pleasures.

HELEN

I feel myself so far and yet so near
And say – how happily! – here I am, here!

FAUST

I scarcely breathe, it shakes and stops my voice,
It is a dream, erasing time and place.

HELEN

I seem to have lived, and yet to be so new,
Woven into you, the stranger, true to you.

FAUST

Don't puzzle at this the unlikeliest event.
Being here's our duty, though it last one moment.

PHORCYAS [*entering abruptly and noisily*]

Finger through Love's ABC,
9420   Play with love's sweet puzzles only,
Puzzle on for love's sake idly,
But there is not time enough.
Can't you feel the thunder lowering?
Listen: those are trumpets blaring.
Now your ruin is not far off.
Menelaus' multitude
Rises on you like the tide.
Bitter strife is coming: prepare!
Swamped by them victorious,
9430   Cut up like Deiphobus,
Your chivalry will cost you dear.
First these light commodities

Will swing. But on an altar lies
A newly whetted axe for her.

FAUST

This rude intrusion! She forces in disgustingly.
Even when there's danger I hate senseless rushings.
The comeliest messenger, bad tidings make him ugly,
And you, the ugliest possible, like no tidings but bad.
But you'll have no joy this time, you agitate the air
With empty breaths. There is no danger here and even   9440
Were there danger, its threatening would be vain.

[*Signals, explosions from the towers, trumpets and cornets,
martial music, a tremendous army marches through.*]

No – in a moment you'll review
Heroes ranked in solid stance.
He earns the love of women who
Marshals strength in their defence.

[*To the captains, who step forward from among their men*]
With bated quiet fury you are
Set on certain victory,
You, the northern youthful flower,
You, the bright eastern energy.

In steel, and lightning-haloed-round,   9450
Kingdom breaking after kingdom,
Our armies entering shake the ground
And exit, thunder following them.

We beached our ships on Pylos' shore,
Venerable Nestor's dead and gone,
All petty royal bonds were there
Smashed by our armies who had none.

Forthwith now from these walls drive
Menelaus back into the sea.
There let him lurk and rob and rove   9460
Which always was his fate and fancy.

The Queen of Sparta bids me greet
You all as dukes of a terrain.
Lay hills and valleys at her feet
And make her empire's gains your own.

We charge you, Germans, to defend
The Lap of Corinth's harbour towns.
Goths, to your keeping we commend
Achaia's hundred deep ravines.

9470   The Franks will settle on Elis,
Messenia is the Saxons' deal,
The Normans raise up Argolis
And cleanse the seas for us to sail.

Then each will have his domicile
And turn abroad his brazen face
But bow beneath the Queen's rule
In Sparta, her ancient dwelling place.

She'll watch you in the enjoying of
Land kind enough for any man
9480   And at her feet you'll seek and have
Her blessing on your place in the sun.
[FAUST *steps down, the princes form a circle around him
to be given more precise orders and arrangements.*]

CHORUS
Who desires the loveliest for himself
Above all let him be forceful
And smart in looking around for weapons.
True, he'll have won by cajoling
The highest there is on earth
But the ownership is uneasy:
Smooth men by cunning will cajole her from him,
Brigands by boldness will tear her from him.
9490   He should give thought to prevention.

I commend our prince for this,
Rate him higher than others
That he cleverly bravely allied himself
With strong men who obey him and stand
Tuned to his beck and call
And loyally do as he bids
Each for his own advantage and for
His lord's who thanks and requites him and both
Earn large winnings in fame.

For who now will tear her away   9500
From him, her powerful possessor?
Him she belongs to, let her be allowed him
And doubly by us whom he,
With her, ringed innerly with the safest of walls
And with the mightiest of armies out there.

FAUST

The gifts here portioned out to these –
To each of them a wealth of land –
Are splendid. Let them go their ways.
Here at the centre we take our stand.

While they protect with all their might   9510
There in the close and leaping sea
The almost-island, the farthest-reaching light
Branch of a limb of Europe's mountain-tree.

Blessed more than any other land's
People be those under the sun
Of this land given into the hands
Of her, my Sovereign Queen, who when

In reeds, Eurotas whispering by,
The light of her broke from the shell
Leda and the Dioscuri,
The bright-eyed, saw hers brighter still.   9520

This land, turning to you alone,
Offers you now its finest bloom.
Though all the globe is yours, incline
Chiefly to this, your native home.

And though upon the mountains' back
The spiked head feels the sun's cold steel
There is a greening over cliff and rock
And goats with relish make a meagre meal.

9530   The spring springs up, brooks into union race;
Green are the meadows, slopes and rocky cracks;
Across a hundred hills' unbroken space
You see a spreading out of woolly flocks.

Fewer together, warily, step by step,
The horned beasts ambulate along the edge.
A hundred vaulted caves below that drop
Lend each and every one a place to lodge.

Pan guards them there and there the life-nymphs house
In rooms in damply freshened bushy clefts
9540   And yearningly towards a height of skies
Twig by twig a pent-up thicket lifts.

Ancient woods! The oak hardens in power
And branches jag from branches as they please;
The mild plane, sweetly juicing, in a pure
Uprising buoys its weight with playful ease.

And motherly in a peaceful ring of shade
For child or lamb warm milk spurts readily;
Fruit is to hand, the plains' ripe food,
And honey trickles from the hollow tree.

9550   Wellbeing here is handed on at birth,
It brightens over faces in a smile.
Each is immortal on his patch of earth:
All are contented, whole and hale.

To manhood then in the clear light of day,
To womanhood the blessed children grow.
They excite astonishment. Still whether they
Are gods or humans, we do not know.

So like the shepherds did Apollo appear
Their best in looks resembled him.
Where Nature works in one pure sphere   9560
All worlds have ways connecting them.
[*He takes his seat by her.*]

So you and I have proved. And now we bid
The past get it behind us. You began
As seed and springing of the highest god:
Inhabit wholly that first world again!

No castle cabin you! There waits
For us, still young, still strong, still good,
The old abiding garden of delights,
Arcadia, in Sparta's neighbourhood.

Beckoned to live on blessed ground,   9570
Fled to the cheerfulest destiny!
These thrones becoming bowers, we'll find
Our happiness in Arcadian liberty.

[*The scene changes utterly. Caves in the rock and against
them bowers, with closed entrances. A shady grove which
extends to the surrounding rock-face.* FAUST *and* HELEN
are nowhere to be seen. The CHORUS *lie dispersed and
asleep.*]

PHORCYAS

How long they have been sleeping I do not know
Nor whether the things that I have seen with my own eyes
Bright and clear have appeared to them in their dreams.
So I will wake them. Youth shall be astonished. So
Shall you, the bearded, sitting down there and waiting
To watch our credible wonders find an outcome.

9580   Wake up! Wake up! Shake back the hair from your eyes,
        Rub out the sleep. You sit there blinking. Listen.
    CHORUS
        Speak then, tell us, say what marvels happened here while
            we were sleeping.
        Best we'd like to hear of things so wonderful we can't
            believe them.
        Time hangs heavy having only walls of rock to
            contemplate.
    PHORCYAS
        Scarcely have you knuckled your eyes free of sleep and you
            are bored.
        Hear then, children, in these caverns, grottoes, bowers,
            there was given,
        As to any pair of lovers in an idyll, care and cover
        To our lord and to our lady.
    CHORUS
                                There, you say, in there?
    PHORCYAS
                                                    Cut off
        From the world, for their quiet service me they summoned,
            only me.
9590   Honoured so highly, I stood ready, but, as any trusted
            servant
        Should, I busied myself elsewhere. Foraged here and there
            and found them
        Roots and mosses, tree-barks, wise to all the virtue, all the
            workings,
        Left them to their solitude.
    CHORUS
        To hear you tell it is as though in there whole universes
            lived,
        Woods and meadows, streams and lakes – you spin us webs
            of fairytale.
    PHORCYAS
        You know nothing. Those indeed are depths no one has
            burrowed into:

Room on room and court on courtyard, these I mused the
    presence of.
Suddenly there came a laughter, echoing in the cavern
    spaces,
When I looked a boy was leaping from the woman to the
    man, from
Lap to lap, the father's, mother's, such a petting, such a
    dangling,   9600
Teasing frets of silly loving, cries of jesting, joy's hurrahing
Turn and turn they mobbed my ears.

Naked, wingless spirit, faunlike – like without the
    brutishness –
Springs to the solid ground but working back at him the
    solid ground then
Rockets him to an airy height till twice or thrice thus
    leaping bouncing
Higher he tigs the vaulted roof.

Anxiously the mother: Leap and leap up to your heart's
    content but
Flying, no: beware of flying. Flying free is forbidden you.
So the loving father warns him: In the earth resides the rush
    that
Powers you upwards, touch on the earth and touch it even
    with a tiptoe   9610
Like that son of the earth Antaeus, there and then it
    strengthens you.
So he grasshoppers upon the rocky mass and from its drop
    he
Springs to the next and every which way springs much like
    a struck ball bouncing.

Suddenly though down a ragged fissuring crack he
    disappears
And we think him lost to us. Mother grieves and father
    comforts,

Fearfully I stand by, shrugging. Then: astounding
  reappearance!
Treasures must have lain down there. For in flower-banded
  robes he
Stands attired and dignified.

Tassels dangle from his sleeves, ribbons flutter on his
  breast,
In his hands the golden lyre, a true Apollo in miniature,
Stepping blithely to the cliff-edge, where it overhangs: we
  marvel.
Father, mother, each, ecstatic, falls into the other's arms.
Such a radiance haloes him! But the shining, who shall
  name it?
Gold adorning, or the flame of overruling force of spirit?
So he moves already acting, as a boy already announcing
Future mastery of beauty when the eternal melodies will
Ride his veins. So you will hear him, so, the dancer, you
  will see him
In a never was before nor will again be wonderment.

CHORUS

You call this a marvel
You, Crete-begotten?
Never listened and let
The poets teach you?
Never heard Ionia's
Nor Hellas' either
Abundant ancestral
Songs of the gods and heroes?

Whatever happens
These days now
Only sadly echoes
The splendour of the ancient days.
Your telling of tales is nothing beside
The lies, lovely lies
More believable than truth
That were sung of the son of Maia.

9620

9630

9640

That pretty infant
Newborn but strong
A gaggle of gossiping nurses
Dumbly deluded
Swaddled in pure down
Swathed tight in soft finery   9650
But strong as he was
This pretty villain
Soon wriggled his smooth
And elastic limbs
Cunningly free and left lying the crimson
Suffocating shell
Like the ready butterfly
Slipping off quickly and wings unfolding
The pupa's stiff jacket
And boldly going his own way flitting   9660
Through the ether's sunbeams.

So too did he, the quickest,
To be for all thieves and rogues
And seekers after advantage
Always a helpful angel.
As he proved at once
With the niftiest tricks:
Filching in a trice the Sea Lord's
Trident and from Ares himself
Slyly the sword from the scabbard,   9670
From Apollo the bow and arrow,
From Hephaestus the tongs
And even from Zeus, his father, he'd have had
The lightning but for his fear of fire.
But Eros he tripped
And forced to submission in wrestling
And Cypris while she was fondling him
Lost to his thieving fingers her cestus.
[A *charming music of stringed instruments, purely
melodious, is heard from the cave. All hearken to it and
soon appear to be deeply moved. From this point until*

*the stage direction at 9938 there is a full musical accom-
paniment.*]

PHORCYAS

    Hear these luscious melodies,
9680   Free yourselves from fables fast.
    All your hotchpotch deities
    Are dead and done now. Let them rest.

    None now understand your speech.
    We have better speaking parts.
    Only heartfelt things will reach
    Out to other human hearts.
    [*She withdraws to the rocks.*]

CHORUS

    Frightful hag, if even you
    Lend these flattering tones your ears,
    Us they heal and soften to
9690   The pleasurable point of tears.

    Let our days of sunlight end.
    If there's daybreak in the soul
    We in our own hearts amend
    All the things of earth that fail.
    [HELEN, FAUST *and* EUPHORION *in the costume described
    above.*]

EUPHORION

    Follows on this childish singing
    Fun for you now. Watch me keep
    Time in jigging, prancing, springing:
    Your parental hearts will leap!

HELEN

    Love adds one and one. The two
9700   Make human felicity.
    Adds one more: the sweet trio
    Makes for heavenly ecstasy.

FAUST

    Therewith everything is found:
    I am yours and you are mine.

    So we stand, so we are bound,
    Were and are and will remain.

CHORUS

    Now upon this happy pair
    Pleasure in the child will grow
    Like a radiance, year on year.
    Oh, their union moves me so!   9710

EUPHORION

    Let me go leaping!
    Let me go skipping!
    For my desire
    Is higher and higher,
    To enter the airstreams,
    They seek me, they take me!

FAUST

    Softly though, softly!
    No overweening
    Or it will end in
    Stalling and tailspin,   9720
    Downfall for us,
    With our dear son.

EUPHORION

    I won't be stranded
    Longer down here.
    Let go my hands,
    Let go my hair,
    Let go my clothes!
    They are all mine.

HELEN

    Remember, remember
    Who you belong to,   9730
    How you distress us,
    How you undo
    The beautifully won
    By me, you and him.

CHORUS

    The union, I fear,
    Begins to dislimn.

HELEN AND FAUST

  Quieten, oh quieten
  For love of us
  Lessen your more than
9740 Mad liveliness.
  Settle in idyll,
  Adorn the plain.

EUPHORION

  Only for you I'll
  Rein myself in.
  [*He winds among the* CHORUS, *dragging them away into
  the dance.*]
  This cheery tribe I
  Court on light feet.
  Movement and melody
  Equally right?

HELEN

  Here I approve of you
9750 Leading these beauties through
  The intricate dance.

FAUST

  Would it were done with
  Soon as begun with.
  Frivolous nonsense!
  [EUPHORION *and the* CHORUS, *dancing and singing, move
  together through the figures of the dance.*]

CHORUS

  Offering your arms so
  Knowingly sweet,
  Shaking your curls to
  Catch in the light,
  Slinking with steps like
9760 The slide of a snake,
  Slipping your shape into
  Ours in our moving, you
  Have what you wished to have,
  Beautiful boy,
  None of us coy

All of us leaning to love.
[*Pause.*]

EUPHORION

You are so many
Light-footed deer
Sportingly ready
Scented and near.   9770
I am the hunter,
You are the prey.

CHORUS

Leisurely hunt!
Amateur sport!
For all we want
Is to be caught.
You are a game
We like to play.

EUPHORION

Heltering through greenery,
Skeltering cross-country,   9780
Things got too easily
Excite my disgust,
Things that resist me
Excite my lust.

HELEN AND FAUST

Such a raving headstrong folly!
Not a hope of moderation!
Through the woodland, down the valley
Like a winding hunting horn –
Such behaviour! What a yelling!

CHORUS [*entering singly and fast*]

He ran past us all, ignoring   9790
Us or doling us his scorn.
Of the lot of us comes hauling
One, the wildest one, this way.

EUPHORION [*carrying in a young girl*]

This unbashful little thing I
Fetch to forcibly enjoy.
It excites me, it delights me

Doing to lips and breasts some things she
Has no wish that I should do,
Show my will and mettle so.

GIRL

9800
Let me go. Under this skin there's
Just as mettlesome a spirit.
Our will is, no less than yours,
Proof against assaults on it.
Think you have me where you want me?
Hold me tight, you muscle-powered
Fool, and soon you'll feel I won't be
Hot the way that you desired.
[*She bursts into flames that leap into the air.*]
Tight in the earth, loose on the air,
Seek me here and seek me there,
9810
Snatch for what has disappeared.

EUPHORION [*shaking off the last of the flames*]
Huddles of rock press
In on me, tree and bush
Cramp me in narrowness,
Me who am young and fresh,
Winds meanwhile rushing,
Waves meanwhile crashing,
Both sounding far.
I want them near.
[*He leaps higher and higher up the rocks.*]

HELEN, FAUST, CHORUS
Must you play the chamois game?
9820
And tumble down? Our blood runs cold.

EUPHORION
Higher and higher I must climb,
More and more I must behold.
Now I know where I stand
At the heart of Pelops' land,
The island's centre, earth and sea
Are kith and kin to me.

CHORUS
Will you not bide in

Peace among hills and trees?
Come and we'll feed on
Grapes on the terraces
Lined along, figs and   9830
Apple-gold, oh
Here in this gentle land
Be gentle too.

EUPHORION

Dreaming of peaceful days?
Dream if you please.
War is our slogan,
Victory, on and on.

CHORUS

Whoever in peace
Wishes for war
Saddens his house,   9840
Shows Hope the door.

EUPHORION

Those this land bore
In danger to more
Danger, who brave and free
Gave their blood prodigally
Now in their struggle
Let their unquenchable
Sacredly whole
Spirit prevail.   9850

CHORUS

Look up, see how high he is
Yet no smaller, as it seems.
Clad as if in Victory's
Suit of bronze and steel he gleams.

EUPHORION

Neither walls nor ramparts. Best
Is the self's own citadel.
Hold within the armoured breast
The assailed heart impregnable.
Live in freedom in your land by
Arming lightly, swiftly striking;   9860

Amazons, the women; every
Child a hero in the making.

CHORUS

Even though Poetry
Highly and holily
Climbs, like the loveliest star
Shines far and from afar
Still she is visible,
Audible yet and still
Touches us here.

EUPHORION

9870   No, I did not come as a child
But bearing arms, as a young man
Friends with the strong, the free, the bold
And in the spirit deeds already done.
Go now,
Follow
An opening fame, it leads me on and on.

HELEN AND FAUST

Scarcely summoned to enjoy
Life in daylight's cheerful home
From a dizzying perch you eye
9880   Open lands where sorrows teem.
Are we so
Little to you?
And our lovely bond a dream?

EUPHORION

Do you hear the thundering on the sea?
And echoing from every valley?
Fleet and army, dust and spray,
Head to head, in hurts, in agony . . .
I must go.
Death says so.
9890   I understand him perfectly.

HELEN, FAUST, CHORUS

Horrors swarm in what you say.
You do what Death bids you do?

EUPHORION

    Must I watch from far away?
    What they suffer, I will too.

HELEN, FAUST, CHORUS

    Rushing at deadly things,
    Fatally bold.

EUPHORION

    Yes, and a pair of wings
    On me unfold.
    Where I must fly now
    Carry me! Thus!

    9900

    [*He flings himself into the air, his clothes bear him up for
    a moment, there is a radiance around his head, light trails
    after him.*]

CHORUS

    Icarus! Icarus!
    Sorrow on sorrow.

    [*A beautiful youth falls dead at the parents' feet. We seem
    to recognize in him a well-known figure. But the physical
    remains disappear at once, the aureole rises like a comet
    towards heaven, leaving the clothing and the lyre behind.*]

HELEN AND FAUST

    On joy at once follows
    Ferocious pain.

EUPHORION'S VOICE [*out of the depths*]

    Oh, here among shadows
    Mother don't leave me alone.

    [*Pause.*]

CHORUS [*a threnody*]

    Not alone! Wherever you may
    Bide you are familiar.
    Though you speed from the light of day
    All will be with you for ever.

    9910

    Scarcely know why we should grieve,
    Envyingly we celebrate
    One who made a large and brave
    Beauty of black days and bright.

Born for earthly happiness,
High ancestry and strength and zest,
Soon lost to yourself, alas,
Youth torn off like blossom, fast.
Viewed the world without illusion,
9920   Tested all things on the pulses,
Women, the best, loved you with passion,
Poetry like no one else's.

Headlong of your own free will
Netted in complexity
You entered into violent quarrel
With Law and Morality
Till at last high aspiration
Lent your airy courage weight,
Wished to make the best things happen,
9930   Saw your hopes disintegrate.

Who does not? A dismal question.
Shrouded fate declines to speak
When on the day of wrack and ruin
Nations on their bloodshed choke.
But there come returns of green,
The living lift from among the dead,
Earth brings verses forth again,
Bears and gives as she always did.
        [*A complete pause. The music ceases.*]
HELEN [*to* FAUST]
    I too confirm, alas, what is always said: that beauty
9940   Can't join with happiness in a lasting union.
    The bond of love is torn and the bond of life and
    Grieving over both in pain I say farewell to you
    And one last time will hold you in my arms.
    Persephoneia, receive the boy and me.
        [*She embraces* FAUST. *Her body vanishes, he is left holding
        her dress and veil.*]
PHORCYAS [*to* FAUST]
    Hold tight to what of all of it is left you.

The dress, don't let it go. Demons already
Are tugging at the ends, would dearly like
To haul it away to the underworld. Hold tight.
It is no longer the goddess – you have lost her –
But is divine. Make good use of this high   9950
Inestimable favour, lift yourself up,
And it will speed you over the commonplace
Through the upper air, so long as you can last.
We shall meet again, far, very far, from here.
    [HELEN's *clothes become clouds, envelop* FAUST, *lift him
    up high and carry him away.*]
PHORCYAS [*taking up* EUPHORION's *clothes and the lyre
        from the ground, coming to the front of the stage and
        holding these* exuviae *aloft*]
    A lucky thing to get my hands on!
    The flame itself, of course, has gone,
    The world though's none the worse for that.
    These few remains are quite sufficient
    To swear in poets and to set
    Them backbiting. I can't give talent   9960
    But can at least lend out the kit.
    [*She sits down at the front of the stage against a pillar.*]
PANTHALIS
    Hurry, girls, now we are unbewitched and our minds
    Are freed from the hag of old Thessaly's evil coercion
    And all the delirium of vilely muddled jingling
    That confuses the ear and, worse, the inner sense.
    Down now to Hades. The Queen with solemn strides
    Has hurried ahead of us, down. In her footsteps
    Should be fitted at once the steps of her faithful maids.
    We shall find her at the throne of the unknowable goddess.
CHORUS
    Queens, of course, like being wherever they are;   9970
    Even in Hades theirs is the higher place,
    Consorting proudly with their own kind,
    The close familiars of Persephone.
    We meanwhile in the background,
    Deep in the meadows of asphodel,

Given for companions only
Lofty poplars and fruitless willows,
What pastimes will be ours?
To squeak and twitter like bats
9980   Displeasing, ghostly.

PANTHALIS
Who never won a name and want nothing that is noble
Belong to the elements. Go. I have the passionate wish
To be with my queen. Not only by achievements
Also by loyalty a person is made who will last.

[*Exits.*]

ALL THE CHORUS
So we are given back to the light of day,
Persons no longer, that is true,
We know it, we feel it, but
Never shall we return to Hades.
Nature living for ever
9990   Lays on us ghosts and we
On her a vested claim.

A PART OF THE CHORUS
We within these thousand branches' whispering trembling,
    lifting soughing
Tease and play and softly beckon from the roots into the
    twigs the
Living waters; first by leafing then by blossoming more on
    more we
Dress their heads of lifing hair in freedom for an airy
    thriving.
When the fruit falls then at once come live and lusty beasts
    and people
Crowding fast and busily for the seizing and the feasting,
All, as though before the first gods, all around us bowing
    down.

ANOTHER PART OF THE CHORUS
Up against the smooth far-shining mirrorings of these walls
    of rock we
10000   Press and fit our lithely moving undulating bodyselves,

Hark and listen to every sound, the singing birds, the
    fluting reeds,
Even the fearful voice of Pan, we never tarry with our
    answers.
Any soughing, so we answer, soughing; any thunder, our
    own
Thunders doubly, triply, tenfold roll reverberating after.

A THIRD PART OF THE CHORUS

Sisters, we with livelier senses hurry onwards with the
    streams, those
Distant beautifully apparelled troupes of hills are tempting
    us.
Down and down and deeper, deeper, we, meanderingly
    travelling,
Water pastures, then the meadows, then the gardens round
    the houses.
There the cypress marks them, rising slimly on the
    landscape over
Riverline and rippling surface, fingertip to the upper air.   10010

A FOURTH PART OF THE CHORUS

Trek wherever you like. But we shall with a murmuring
    encircle
This the thoroughly planted hill where vines are leafing
    round their stakes and
Hour by hour of every day the grower, in his passion, lets us
Watch how lovingly he labours through the risks towards
    reward.
Mattockwork and spadework, pruning, earthing up and
    binding are the
Prayers he prays to all the gods, the sun god first and
    foremostly.
Bacchus, softly idle, pays his faithful servant no attention,
Sleeps in arbours, slumps in caves and twaddles with the
    youngest faun.
All he has a need of for his half-inebriated dreamings
He has skins and jugs and jorums full of, handy by, in
    cooling   10020

Caverns, left and right, enough to last him through eternity.
When however all the gods, and chief among them Helios,
    have by
Airing, wetting, warming, basking heaped up clustered
    horns of plenty,
Where the quiet grower laboured suddenly there's
    animation
Rushing through the leaves and rustling in and out among
    the stocks.
Basket-creak and bucket-clatter, groaning panniers humped
    away
All towards the giant vat for treading by the strapping
    dancers.
There the sacred copiousness of juicy berries, born so pure,
    gets
Rudely trampled, squashed to mush and seething, spitting,
    sparkling, mixes.
10030 Now the brassy clang of cymbals hurts the hearing,
    Dionysus
Out of mysteries arises, shows himself, the god, and strides
Out accompanied by goatfoots, billies rollicking their she's.
Old Silenus' eary beast meanwhile releases shrieking
    hee-haws.
Nothing's spared, all good behaviour's trampled under
    cloven hooves,
All the senses whirling stupid, hearing battered into
    deafness;
Heads and bellies full to bursting, still the sozzled grope for
    more.
Foresightful some may be, but they only aggravate the
    tumult
Since to lay the new wine down they swill the old fast as
    they can.

[*The curtain falls.* PHORCYAS, *front stage, rises up gigantically, but then steps down from the buskins, removes the mask and veil and shows herself as* MEPHISTOPHELES, *to comment on the play in an epilogue, in so far as that might be necessary.*]

ACT FOUR

High Mountains

[*Stark, jagged, rocky summits. A cloud approaches, dips, settles on a projecting slab, and parts.* FAUST *steps out.*]

FAUST

Seeing below me the deepest lonelinesses
I set foot on the hem of these high peaks with caution,   10040
Dismissing my cloudy carriage that has conveyed me
Smoothly over land and sea through clear daylights.
It does not dissipate, but looses from me slowly,
The mass, with a clenched intent, strives off eastwards
And the eyes in awe and wonderment strive after it
That moves away like waves, never the same, undoing.
But taking shape now – oh, my eyes do not deceive me!
Stretched out magnificently on pillows in the sunlight
A woman's image, huge, like a goddess, there
Visible – resembling Juno, Leda, Helena,   10050
In a lovely majesty wavering in my eyes.
But oh! it shifts already, widens out of shape, and holds
Piled in the east like far ice hills reflecting
The vast sense of the hastened days in blinding glimpses.

But a waif of mist, an airy light, still coolly
Caresses my brow and breast and I am brightened,
And lifts now, lightly, higher and higher, and lingers
And makes a shape that charms me to believe in it:
The youthful primal highest good, long lived without,
The earliest treasures welling from the heart's deep core,   10060
Aurora's love, the easy lilt and verve, the first
And barely understood but quickly infelt look
That, held on to, outshone all other treasures.
The dear appearance heightens like the soul's beauty,
Does not dissolve, lifts into the upper air
And takes my innermost best being away with it.

[*A seven-league boot steps into view. A second follows at once.* MEPHISTOPHELES *climbs down. The boots stride off at speed.*]

MEPHISTO

So finally we made some progess!
But what possessed you to come down
In the midst of such an awfulness
10070 Of grisly riven-open stone?
I know it well, though not in this place here,
For, truth to tell, it used to be Hell's floor.

FAUST

You never want for silly tales. No doubt
You are about to trot another out.

MEPHISTO [*in a serious voice*]

When the Lord God – and I know why – flung us
Down from the air as deep as you can go,
There at the centre where continuous
Fire by fire was whitened through and through,
Squashed in there overheated, overlighted,
10080 We were most inconveniently situated.
The devils all fell to coughing then and wind
Broke out of them from either end
So bloating Hell with sulphur's foul acidity.
Gasses galore! A monstrous quantity.
And very soon, thick though it was, the flat
Crust of the countries stretched and cracked and split.
We take a look at things now the other way up,
What was the bottom once become the top,
On which the excellent teaching may be based:
10090 The lowest shall be made the uppermost.
For we escaped the hot pit of servitude
To rule the free air's super-plenitude.
It is an open secret, from the people
Guarded well as long as possible (Ephesians 6:12).

FAUST

The mountain-mass keeps nobly quiet with me.
I don't ask how or why it came to be.
When Nature in herself laid down her own

Grounds and rounded the orb of the earth off clean
She took delight in peaks and in ravines,
Joined rocks to rocks, mountains to mountains,   10100
In easy stages then shaped the hills down
Quietening into the valleys in a gentle line.
And there it greens and grows, she needs no mad
Upheaval-tumblings to be glad.

MEPHISTO

You say so and you think it sunshine-clear.
But hear it truer from one who was there
As I was when the abysmal hole below,
Still boiling up, in fires overflowed
And from rock-smithying Moloch's hammer flew
The shatterings of mountains far and wide.   10110
The land's still littered with erratic blocks.
Who can explain such catapulting power?
Not the philosopher: he sees the rocks
Beyond a doubt are there but why they are
And how they got there he has no idea.
Only the honest common people know
And won't be moved from what they know is true,
They reached wise understanding long ago:
It is a miracle. They give Satan his due
And hobble on the crutch of faith   10120
From Devil's Bridge to Devil's Mouth.

FAUST

It is indeed remarkable to see
How Nature looks viewed devilishly.

MEPHISTO

What do I care? Be Nature what she will!
It's a matter of honour. She worked with the Devil.
We are the lads to get things done. See there:
Force, riot, chaos, the signs of it everywhere.
But let me speak now to be understood.
On all our surface did you find nothing good?
For you were shown the immeasurable sum   10130
Of the kingdoms of the world and the glory of them
        (Matthew 4).

But being as you are very hard to please
No item took your fancy, I suppose?

FAUST

Wrong. Something great drew my attention.
Guess what it was.

MEPHISTO

                          That's easily done.
Myself, I'd settle in some capital
Of grisly burgher-vittals, all
Pokey streets, gables and garrets,
Cramped market, onions, cabbages, carrots
And butchers' blocks where the red meat crawls
Feastingly with bluebottles.
There every hour would offer you
Much stink and many things to do.
There are wide streets and spacious squares
To show yourself and put on airs,
And more amenities extend
Beyond the walls without an end.
Watching the traffic would be fun,
The shunting to and fro, the din
The eternal comings and goings, the hill
Of ants, distracted, never still.
And when I rode and when I drove
I'd seem the centre and receive
Their reverence a hundred-thousandfold.

FAUST

That would not satisfy me. One
Is glad the people breed and thrive
After their fashion and improve
Even their minds but all the yield
One has of it's rebellion.

MEPHISTO

Then grandiosely, knowing my own worth,
I'd build for fun on some nice patch of the earth.
Field, meadow, woodland, hill and vale
I'd make a garden of, in splendid style:
Green walling, velvet lawns, dead-straight

Allées, the shadows drawn just right,
And cascades mating round the rocks
And fountains playing all manner of tricks,
A high and noble jet – that sideways hisses
And pisses out a thousand pettinesses.
But then I'd build some nice and intimate   10170
Petites maisons and there accommodate
The prettiest women and spend aeons
Hermiting with sweet companions.
Note I said women: once and for all
I think of beauties in the plural.

FAUST

Sardanapalus! Modish and trivial!

MEPHISTO

The thing that you are striving for is rare
And difficult, no doubt. You flew
Closer to the moon and like the lunatic you are
You ask for her now. Only the moon will do.   10180

FAUST

Not at all. For great deeds there is still
Room enough on this earthly round.
I will do things that will astound.
I have the strength to set to with a will.

MEPHISTO

So it's fame you're after? Obvious
You've been with demigoddesses.

FAUST

I dominate, I make things mine.
And not for fame, for the deed alone.

MEPHISTO

But there'll be poets, sure to be,
Who'll speak your glory to posterity   10190
And so with folly excite further folly.

FAUST

None of this is vouchsafed to you.
Of man's desires, what can you know
Or of his needs, you who oppose
All with a biting bitterness always?

MEPHISTO

    Be it as you wish. And now make known
    How large the fancies are you entertain.

FAUST

    My eye was drawn to the seas. They swell,
    They climb, they tower, they overreach

10200   And topple and their breakers spill
    In a long and broad assault up the flat beach.
    And that annoys me. Any man
    Who values freedom and his rights would feel
    By such an insolent presumption
    Flung into discontent and turmoil.
    I thought this need not be. I watched and saw
    The tide stand still and then withdraw
    From the proud-won goal. But came
    The hour again and it replayed the game.

MEPHISTO [ad spectatores]

10210   He tells me nothing I don't know.
    For a hundred thousand years I've seen it so.

FAUST [continuing passionately]

    Creeps in here, there and everywhere and gives,
    Lifeless itself, nothing that lives
    But swells and waxes, rolls and yet again
    Overruns the waste and horrid zone.
    Strength and spirit, wave on wave, arrive,
    Nothing accomplishing, and leave.
    This brings me through disquiet to despair.
    The unruly elements in their pointless power!

10220   My spirit outbids itself and I desire
    To fight and conquer nowhere else but there.

    And that is possible. Beginning to fill,
    The tide must ease and fit round every hill.
    Busily overbold it may be, yet
    Every slight eminence stands up to it,
    Every slight hollow sucks it powerfully in.
    Rapidly then I fashioned plan on plan
    To enjoy a sweet achievement. I will bar

The masterful sea from coming near the shore,
Set limits on its stretch of wet   10230
And cram it deep back down its own gullet.
Step by step I thought the project clear
And wish to act now. Help me if you dare.
   [*Drums and martial music behind the audience, in the
   distance from the right.*]

MEPHISTO

Easy. – But hark! Drums in the distance.

FAUST

More war. Bad sound to any man of sense.

MEPHISTO

In peace or war the man of sense will seek
Hard for whatever advantage he may take.
Spy for your chances. Come the most
Promising offer, seize it, Faust!

FAUST

Spare me your riddle-rot. Be plain   10240
And brief. What is it? What do you mean?

MEPHISTO

I could not help but notice on my progress
Our friend the Emperor suffers much duress.
You know how he is. When we were his support
And played him phoney wealth, he thought
The whole world could be bought and sold.
Still young, he got the throne to have and hold
And graciously he formed the wrong judgement
It would be very desirable and fine
And surely not too difficult to combine   10250
Ruling the country with his own enjoyment.

FAUST

A grave error. The man made to command
Must find his highest bliss in doing so.
Volition fills his heart, but the end
He wishes, nobody must know
Except his trusted few, until, astonished,
The wide world sees his whisperings accomplished.
Highest and fittest he is and will remain

      Above the enjoyment in which others join.

MEPHISTO

10260   Not fit nor high, he enjoyed himself in style,
      The Empire sliding into anarchy the while.
      Strife among great and small on every side,
      Much brotherly expulsion and homicide,
      Burgh against burgh, city against city,
      Guilds feuding with the nobility,
      The bishop with his chapter and his see,
      Eyes never meeting but in enmity,
      Murder in the churches, and on the road
      No mercy shown to travellers or trade.

10270   And everyone grew bold because no one
      Survived who didn't. So the show went on.

FAUST

      Went on! It limped, it tumbled, rose again,
      Fell roly-poly in a heap, lay upside down.

MEPHISTO

      Who could complain? Such free-for-all
      Suits the pushy. The very small
      Get big ideas about themselves till in the end
      It's more than the proper top people can stand,
      The great and good rise up in force and say:
      Who restores us order here, him we'll obey.

10280   The Emperor can't or won't so let us have
      A new Emperor and let him give
      The Empire its soul and us our place again
      Secure and Peace and Justice live
      Happily married in a world made sane.

FAUST

      Priest twaddle.

MEPHISTO

                 You may be sure of that –
      Priests keeping their bellies safe and fat,
      They had more fingers in the pie than anyone,
      Rebellion swelled, they blessed Rebellion,
      And our Emperor, whom we left sitting pretty,

10290   Falls back to fight his last fight very likely.

FAUST

I'm sorry for him. He was good and guileless.

MEPHISTO

Let's see. For where there's life there's hope.
We'll liberate him from this narrow pass
And multiply his chances. With more scope
More luck may move his pieces on the board.
And vassals throng around a winning lord.

[*They climb over the intervening hills and observe the
disposition of the army in the valley. Drums and martial
music audible from below.*]

MEPHISTO

They are well placed, I see. We contribute
A little and their victory's complete.

FAUST

What good is there in such performance?
Deceit, illusion, magic, hollow appearance.   10300

MEPHISTO

A stratagem. So battles are won.
Abiding firm in your intention,
Keeping your own noble end in view,
If we secure the Emperor throne and country
You kneel and take from him as due
Reward the boundless shore in feudal fee.

FAUST

You've done so much already, go
And win yourself a battle too.

MEPHISTO

No, you win it. For you shall be
On this occasion C.-in-C.   10310

FAUST

A fine thing. I who understand
Nothing of war am in command.

MEPHISTO

Leave it to the general staff. We shall
Do very well as field marshal.
Knowing how poor their counsels are
I've made my own council of war

From the ancient mountains' ancient stock.
Happy the man that such men back!

FAUST

Who are these bearing arms? Have you

10320 Levied a mountain folk commando?

MEPHISTO

No, but like friend Peter Squenz
Of all the gang they're the quintessence.

[*Enter the* THREE MIGHTY MEN (2 *Samuel* 23:8).]

Here come my lads. In age they are
In their apparel and their gear
All very different. I am sure
You will do well with these three here.

[*Ad spectatores*]

Every schoolboy nowadays
Loves men dressed up as knights and these
Scoundrels, being allegories,

10330 Costumed thus are bound to please.

THUG [*young, lightly armed, gaily dressed*]

No one looks at me without
I smack his front teeth down his throat
And no wet-leg who runs away
From me will live to fight another day.

GRABBER [*a grown man, well armed, richly dressed*]

Seems to me a waste of time
And the occupation of a fool.
Taking is the only game,
Do it hard, that's worth your while.

TIGHTFIST [*elderly, heavily armed, without robes*]

All that venture, little gain,

10340 All you got you lose again
Down life's river, very soon.
Taking is good, but keeping's better still.
Suffer the Old Man to guide you and you will
Be robbed of nothing you got for your own.

[*Together they go further down the mountain.*]

On the Foothills

[*Drums and martial music from below. The* EMPEROR's *tent is being put up.* EMPEROR, COMMANDER-IN-CHIEF, BODYGUARD.]

COMMANDER-IN-CHIEF

It seems our well-considered plan was right
To pull the whole army back
Into this handy valley, closing tight.
I have good hope the place will bring us luck.

EMPEROR

Events will tell. But how I hate
This giving ground, this half-retreat.   10350

COMMANDER-IN-CHIEF

But, Sir, look on our right flank: just
The terrain to please the strategist.
The hills not steep, but not an easy access –
For us helpful, for the enemy treacherous.
Up here the undulations half conceal our presence,
So that their cavalry will not dare advance.

EMPEROR

I find you have done all things for the best.
Here we'll put strength and courage to the test.

COMMANDER-IN-CHIEF

There on the roomy levels of the middle ground
You see our phalanx, fightingly inclined.   10360
Sun glancing on their pikes, it throws
Gleamings of steel through the early morning haze.
The vast square heaves blackly, it breeds
In thousands the makings of great deeds.
You see the strength of mass. On this
I trust we'll split the strength of our enemies.

EMPEROR

Now having this fine sight before my eyes
I see an army worth one twice its size.

COMMANDER-IN-CHIEF

Our left I need not speak of. Good men occupy

10370   The ungiving rocks, the stony cliffs that spy
      On the important passage through the tight defile
      Sparkle with weapons. Here will fail
      And founder the enemy's force in blood, outcome
      Foreseen by us but not by them.

EMPEROR

      So they arrive, my false kith and kin,
      Who called me brother, uncle, cousin,
      Took liberties and took and took again
      Strength from the sceptre, respect from the throne,
      Fell out, laid waste the Empire and rise
10380   Rebelling against me now in common cause.
      The mob wavers, unsure, then goes
      With the current, wherever the current flows.

COMMANDER-IN-CHIEF

      A faithful man, sent out for news, we hope
      Successfully, hurries down the rock-slope.

FIRST SCOUT

      Bravely, cunningly, the art
      That we practise saw us through
      There and back – but we report
      Little to encourage you.
      Many swear you fealty,
10390   Loyal forces too, but send
      None and make apology:
      Unrest, peril in the land.

EMPEROR

      Self is the one thing the selfish heed
      Not honour, duty, affection, gratitude.
      Do you never think that, when the bill falls due,
      Your neighbour's house, burning, will burn yours too?

COMMANDER-IN-CHIEF

      The second scout: how slowly he climbs down.
      His limbs are trembling with fatigue and strain.

SECOND SCOUT

      First we saw with satisfaction
10400   Only wildness, folly, error.
      Suddenly, unthought of, then

Enters a new Emperor!
Now proceeding as they're told
Through the land the people troop
Following en masse the unrolled
Lying banners – like sheep.

EMPEROR

An anti-emperor is a blessing. He
Awakes at last the Emperor in me.
I armed only as a soldier. Now I lend
My armoured self to a higher end.   10410
Our brilliant entertainments were short
Of nothing, except I had no dangerous sport.
I longed for joustings but by your tame
Advice must make do with the ring game.
Had you not counselled me away from wars
My deeds by now would shine among the stars.
Once in the realm of fire, viewing my part,
I felt the seal of self stamped on my heart.
Fearful the element, coming on and on!
All an illusion, but a powerful one.   10420
Victory and fame have been my muddled dream.
Now I make good, where I was much to blame.

[*The heralds are dispatched to challenge the* ANTI-
EMPEROR. *Enter* FAUST *in armour, his visor half down,
and the* THREE MIGHTY MEN, *armed and dressed as
above.*]

FAUST

We trust our entrance won't be frowned upon.
Even without need, there's wisdom in precaution.
You know the mountain folk are deep, adept
At seemings, versed in Nature's stony script.
Spirits, long since retreated from the plains,
Are all the kinder to the stony mountains.
They work through quiet labyrinths of tunnels
In the noble gas of vapours rich in metals.   10430
They sunder, test and fuse, they quest
Solely for the New, they never rest.
With the light touch of spirit-powers they grow

Shapes that the light of the eyes shines through
And in the crystal's sealed code they have
Sight of the happenings in the world above.

EMPEROR

I've heard it and believe you but am unclear,
Friend, what good your telling it does here.

FAUST

Norcia's necromancer, the Sabine,
10440   Is your good loyal servant. He had seen
A bad end hideously near:
The kindling crackling, licks of fire,
Dry billets stacked up in a tight clutch
And sulphur sticks mixed in with them and pitch.
Not man, nor God, nor the Devil could intercede
But Majesty threw the flame-doors open wide.
That was in Rome. He lives since in your debt
And bends his care wherever you set foot.
From that hour on he forgot himself. The stars
10450   And depths he consults in no concern but yours.
He bade us hasten here and wait
On you with help. The mountains' powers are great,
Unstoppable, when Nature is set free,
Which priests, the fools, condemn as sorcery.

EMPEROR

Welcoming guests on a holiday
Arriving gaily for more gaiety
Each pleases us, elbowing in until
Space by space the roomy halls are full.
But most welcome of all is a good man
10460   Who sides with us in strength upon
The opening of a day that lies in doubt
Under the balance and the tilt of fate.
But now, the crisis come, I ask that you
Hold back your swords from what they long to do.
Honour this hour as many thousands stride
Forward to settle it for one or the other side.
I am the man. I must be shown
In proper person fit for crown and throne.

And the figment risen up against us
That calls himself Emperor, prince of our territories,   10470
Our vassals' lord, our army's chief, I'll thrust
Him down among the dead with my own fist.

FAUST

Fine though it be to achieve a greatness, still
Risking your head for it you do not do well.
The helmet with its crest and plume keeps safe
The head that lends our courage the light of life.
What can the limbs do on their own?
Head nods in sleep, the limbs lie down.
The head being hurt, the limbs are wounded too;
Quickly recovering, it makes them good as new.   10480
The arm, deploying its strong self to the full,
Lifts the shield, quickly protects the skull.
The sword, knowing its duty, there and then
Parries the blows, and gives them back again.
And the brave foot has its part in this good luck:
It steps hard on the dead man's neck.

EMPEROR

My rage wants this. I want his proud head put
To use as stool and step beneath my foot.

HERALDS [returning]

Scant and slight consideration
They accorded us. At our   10490
Strong and noble proclamation
How they laughed: 'You jokers, your
Emperor's lost, he has become
An echo in the valley. As
A fairytale we'll think of him:
Once upon a time he was.'

FAUST

This suits the wishes of the best
Side by side with you, steadfast.
The enemy nears, your men are hot to fight.
Order the attack now, the time is right.   10500

EMPEROR

I shall not be the one who gives commands.

[*To the* COMMANDER-IN-CHIEF]
So let your duty, Prince, be in your hands.

COMMANDER-IN-CHIEF
Let our right wing go forward now so that
The enemy's left, begun the climb already,
Will be thrown back before they finish it
By our youthful strength and tested loyalty.

FAUST
Allow this cheerful stalwart here
To join your ranks forthwith – to join
Deep in the body of you all and there,
10510   Your comrade, give his strength free rein.
        [*He points to the right.*]
THUG [*stepping forward*]
The man who looks at me, before he can
Look anywhere else I pulp his face and bash
The back of the head of any man
Who turns away into a bloody mush,
And if your men will cleave and brain
Like me, amok, the way they should,
Our enemies will all fall down
And drown in their own blood.
                                              [*Exit.*]

COMMANDER-IN-CHIEF
The phalanx of our centre softly coming forward
10520   Engages the enemy cleverly and hard,
A little to the right, enraged, our men
Having already undermined their plan.

FAUST [*pointing to the second of the* THREE]
Command him too. He is not slow
And where he ventures, all will follow.

GRABBER [*stepping forward*]
The imperial troops' heroic courage
Must couple with their love of pillage
And all upon one goal be bent:
The Anti-Emperor's precious tent.
He shan't sit there much longer proud.
10530   I'll join the phalanx – I will lead.

LOOTFAST [*a camp-follower, snuggling up to* GRABBER]
  Him and me are noways wed
  But he's the best lover I've had.
  We will ripen! We will fatten!
  Nothing like a grabbing woman,
  And when she robs, she's hard, hard.
  To victory! And no holds barred.

  [*Exit both.*]

COMMANDER-IN-CHIEF
  Upon our left, as was foreseeable,
  Their right wing hurls its strength. We shall,
  Man for man, withstand their first fierceness
  And hold the rock way through the tight pass.   10540

FAUST [*gesturing towards the left*]
  Consider him too, Sir. An extra arm
  Of strength will do the strong no harm.

TIGHTFIST [*stepping forward*]
  For the left wing you need have no fear.
  Where I am, possession is secure.
  The old man does what he does best,
  Lightning won't part what I hold fast.

  [*Exit.*]

MEPHISTO [*coming down from above*]
  Look how every jagged throat
  Of rock behind us there spews out
  Men and their weapons pell-mell
  Who make the narrow paths narrower still,   10550
  Armoured, armed with shield and sword
  They wall our backs and on a word
  From us will lend their strength to ours.
    [*Softly to those in the know*]
  But where we got them's no business of yours.
  True, I've cleared the lumber-rooms
  Hereabouts of martial heirlooms.
  On foot and horse they stood as though
  They ruled the world as long ago
  When they were emperors, kings and knights who are
  Empty snail-shells now and nothing more.   10560

Many a ghost has squatted them and stages
His own vain version of the Middle Ages.
But whatever devils are in them for today
They make a pretty show, wouldn't you say?
    [*Aloud*]
But hark already to their angry pother
And clanking of tin on one another!
And see the rags of flags on poles that so
Long have wished a breath of fresh air would blow.
Take note, these men of old are here
10570   And would be glad to join in your new war.
        [*A terrible trumpet blast from above, a noticeable faltering
        in the enemy ranks.*]

FAUST
Along the horizon all is dark
Except for here and there a spark
Of direly red prognostication.
And now the weapons glint with blood,
The rocks are reddened and the wood,
The atmosphere and all of heaven.

MEPHISTO
The right wing holds up mightily
And tall among them all I see
Friend Thug, the nifty giant, he
10580   Has his own way of keeping busy.

EMPEROR
At first I saw one arm and now
A dozen dealing blow on blow.
This is no natural event.

FAUST
Have you not heard of skeins of haze
That haunt Sicilia's capes and bays?
In daylight clear and hesitant
Raised up into the middle air
Fata Morgana appear
Mirrored in a vaporous element:
10590   Cities quiver up and fade,
Gardens climb, gardens cascade,

On blue, the images, surgent.

EMPEROR

And yet how troubling. Each tall spear
Flickers with lightnings, on the bare
Lances of our phalanx little flames
Are dancing nervously. It seems
A spectral, weird affair.

FAUST

Forgive me, Sir, those are the last
Marks of essences now past,
Haloes of the Dioscuri   10600
Whom all who sailed the seas swore by,
Their lingering virtue is collecting here.

EMPEROR

But say, whom must we thank for this
That Nature, thus inclined to us,
Gathers up a thing so rare?

MEPHISTO

None but that eminent master who
Follows your fortune with his every thought.
Your enemies' strongly threatening you
Alarmed him in his innermost heart.
His thanks will be to see you safe   10610
Though saving you cost him his life.

EMPEROR

How gleefully they paraded me around!
But I was boss, I wished to prove it, found
It fit, without much thought, to send
His white whiskers a little cooling wind.
I spoiled the priesthood's sport for once and got,
Of course, no thanks from them for that.
And have I now, years later, won
Advantage from a thing I did for fun?

FAUST

The yield of a generous deed is rich.   10620
Look up. I think he will send a sign
There above and very soon
The meaning will be evident. Watch.

EMPEROR

    An eagle soars high in the heavens,
    A savage gryphon nears and threatens.

FAUST

    But watch. This seems to me auspicious.
    The gryphon is only fabulous.
    And how should such a beast prevail
    Against an eagle, who is real?

EMPEROR

10630   Now widely wheeling they gyrate
    Each round the other – but see now
    Suddenly they both fall to
    And claw and hack at breast and throat.

FAUST

    But note the gryphon-pest endures
    Hacking, mauling, till he lowers
    His lion-tail and from the skies
    Plummets among the summit-trees.

EMPEROR

    So understood, let it come true.
    Amazed, I will believe it of you.

MEPHISTO [*looking towards the right*]

10640   Battering, battering, we drive
    The enemy so hard they give
    And in the confusion of the fight
    Crowd themselves towards the right,
    Disarraying thus their main
    Force along its left. Our own
    Stiff and sturdy phalanx-spike
    Moves right and like a lightning strike
    Hits that weak spot. Now the way
    Driven breakers dash and spray
10650   Equal forces, large as those,
    Rage in double battle throes.
    Finer thing than this there's none.
    The fight is over. We have won.

EMPEROR [*on the left, to* FAUST]

    There things don't look good for us.

Our position's perilous.
Unopposed by us they scale
The lower rocks and we meanwhile
Leave the higher free for them,
The enemy, and on they come,
Hustle up at us en masse.   10660
Soon they will have seized the pass.
So unholy strivings yield
Nothing. All your arts have failed.
    [*Pause.*]

MEPHISTO

Ah, now my raven-pair are here.
What kind of tidings do they bear?
None good, I fear, about our plight.

EMPEROR

Why have these birds come? They have flown
On black sails from the field of stone
To us, alas, from the heat of the fight.

MEPHISTO [*to the ravens*]

Perch close on me, one by each ear.   10670
Whom you protect, there's still hope for.
Your advice is good. You reason right.

FAUST [*to the* EMPEROR]

You've heard no doubt of the birds that home
From however far away, they come
Back to the nest and their brood and food.
But fit your bird to the time and place:
The dove will courier well for peace,
In war it's raven-post you need.

MEPHISTO

Grim news they bring, around the rim
Of rock our men no longer stem   10680
The terrible assault. See there:
The nearest heights are lost and should
We lose the pass as well, how could
We hold a footing any more?

EMPEROR

So after all I am your fool.

You netted me and now I feel
Horror in the entanglement.

MEPHISTO

All's not lost. Be brave, patient
And canny for the final twist.
10690   It's always tense towards the end
But I have messengers I can trust.
Command – that I be given command.

COMMANDER-IN-CHIEF [who has entered in the meantime]

You have bound yourself to these.
I have watched with a cruel unease.
Conjured luck is treacherous stuff.
The battle's lost, I cannot mend it.
As they began it, let them end it.
So I give you back your staff.

EMPEROR

Keep it for the happier hour
10700   That luck, perhaps, will vouchsafe us.
My flesh creeps at this dealer here
Thick with ravens as he is.
   [To MEPHISTOPHELES]
I cannot give the staff to you.
You do not seem the proper man.
But take command, effect our rescue
And let happen whatever can.
      [Exit into the tent with the COMMANDER-IN-CHIEF.]

MEPHISTO

Let the idiot staff be his protector.
Us it can do little for.
There was a touch of the Cross about it.

FAUST

10710   What's to be done?

MEPHISTO

                    I'll see to it.
Go, my black mates, swift servants, give
The undines in the mountain lake my love
And ask them for an appearance of their water.
By secret female arts they can set free

Appearance from reality
And make believe the former is the latter.
  [*Pause.*]

FAUST
  Our ravens must have pleasing ways.
  The watery girls could not refuse.
  Already a trickling has begun.
  In many dry and bare places of rock   10720
  Springs are developing, full and quick.
  The victory's lost the enemy thought won.

MEPHISTO
  Strange greeting this that has dismayed
  The boldest in their escalade.

FAUST
  Streams fall on other rushing streams and rise
  Again from gullies twice the size,
  And now a river dives through its own rainbow,
  Then lies out where the rocks are flat and wide
  And topples foaming over every side,
  Pitch by pitch going headlong for below.   10730
  Heroic stemming does no good
  But all are washed to glory in a mighty flood.
  The spate that takes them shakes my heart also.

MEPHISTO
  I can see nothing of these watery lies,
  They only impose on human eyes.
  This wondrous fall of things delights me though.
  Men tumble down in heaps and droves and shoals
  Drowning, as they do believe, the fools,
  And puff and pant on dry land all the while,
  Career about in silly swimming-style.   10740
  Confusion reigns, confusion is total now.
    [*The ravens have returned.*]
  Well done. The Master shall hear of this. Now try
  The master-role yourselves and fly
  Fast to the white-hot smithy where
  The race of gnomes, who never tire,
  Beat stones and metals into sparks

And spinning whatever tales you please
Ask for a fire that shines and winks and sprays,
Ask for the royal fireworks.

10750   True, very distant sheets and flares
And the rapid chutes of dizzy stars
Occur on every summer night;
But flarings through the tanglewood
And stars that hiss and slither on the mud
Are not at all a common sight.
Don't overtax yourselves. Request
It kindly first, and then insist.

       [*Exit the ravens. The effects already described occur.*]

MEPHISTO
    Thick darkness on the enemy!
    Quick march into obscurity!
10760   Will-o'-the-wisps, to lure and lose;
    Lightnings, to blind the eyes;
    It is a very pretty show
    But we need the din of terror too.

FAUST
    The fresh air has done wonders for
    Our noble excavated suits of armour.
    Up there already, hark how they
    Clatter and rattle, wonderfully off-key.

MEPHISTO
    Indeed. No stopping them. The air
    Resounds with chivalrous thwacks as though we were
10770   Back in the sweet days of yore.
    Brassard and vambrace, cuisse and greave
    Like Guelphs and Ghibellines revive
    Apace the squabbles of yesteryear.
    Set in their ways and comfortable
    They prove themselves implacable,
    Their rumpus thunders everywhere.
    After all, the sectarian sort
    Of hatred's best for the devil's sport.
    With stop-at-nothing cruelties
10780   And hither-thither mortal panic,

Ugly, lurid, hot-satanic,
It feeds its terror down the valleys.
  [*Tumult of war in the orchestra pit, finally going over into
  cheerful military tunes.*]

The Anti-Emperor's Tent

[*Throne, an opulent setting.* GRABBER *and* LOOTFAST.]

LOOTFAST

First on the scene is me and you.

GRABBER

Ravens fly slower than we do.

LOOTFAST

Look how they've heaped their treasure up!
Where shall I start? Where shall I stop?

GRABBER

The place is full. There's so much stuff
One pair of hands is not enough.

LOOTFAST

That rug would do me. I should be
Softer with that thing under me.

GRABBER

Just such a morning-star of steel
I've wanted for a good long while.

LOOTFAST

That red cloak hemmed with gold, it seems
The sort of cloak you wear in dreams.

GRABBER [*taking the weapon*]

This in your fist, the job's soon done:
Knock him dead and carry on.
You're loaded with all manner of swag
But nothing proper's in the bag.
Leave lying all the rubbishy stuff
And carry one of those coffers off.
They're the chests the army keeps
The red gold in to pay the troops.

10790

10800

LOOTFAST

   It weighs a ton, I'll never lift it.

   Heavy as hell, I'll never shift it.

GRABBER

   Stoop, will you. Bend down quick.

   I'll hump it on you piggyback.

LOOTFAST

   Oh dear, oh dear, that's the end of that!

   The weight of it has squashed me flat.

    [*The chest falls and bursts open.*]

GRABBER

   The red gold tumbles down like grain,

10810   Be quick and pick it up again.

LOOTFAST [*crouching down*]

   Here's my lap. You load me, then

   We'll have enough when I say when.

GRABBER

   Enough now. Hurry, let's be gone.

    [LOOTFAST *stands up.*]

   Bad scrat, there's a hole in your apron

   And where you walk and where you stand

   Prodigally you seed the land.

BODYGUARDS [*of our* EMPEROR]

   You trespass here. How dare you pry

   And poke where the Emperor's treasures lie?

GRABBER

   We hired life and limb. This is

10820   Payment for our services.

   Soldiers loot. They always do.

   Since we are soldiers we will too.

BODYGUARDS

   Soldiers, are you? Or thieving scum?

   The two together are not welcome.

   You must be honest soldiers or

   You cannot serve our Emperor.

GRABBER

   We know the honest soldiers' game.

   'Contributions' is its name.

You're all alike, whoever, wherever.
Your motto is: Stand and deliver.   10830
  [*To* LOOTFAST]
Keep what you've got and disappear.
It seems that we're not wanted here.

                    [*Exit* GRABBER *and* LOOTFAST.]

FIRST BODYGUARD

  Why didn't you clout his head at once
  To punish him for his impudence?

SECOND BODYGUARD

  I don't well know. I didn't dare.
  There was something spooky about the pair.

THIRD BODYGUARD

  And something wrong with my eyesight –
  A flickering, I couldn't see right.

FOURTH BODYGUARD

  And nor can I say what was wrong,
  So hot it was, all the day long,   10840
  So stifling close, so fearful,
  One man stood, another fell,
  Your sword was like a blindman's stick
  But killed with every stroke you struck;
  Mist in the eyes and all around
  A buzzing, whistling, hissing sound.
  And so on. Now we're here, but how
  It came about we do not know.

    [*Enter the* EMPEROR *and four* PRINCES. *The* BODY-
      GUARDS *leave.*]

EMPEROR

  Be all that as it may, for us the battle's won,
  The enemy over the plains runs to oblivion.   10850
  Here stands the empty throne and all around it see
  The richly draped encumbering pelf of treachery.
  Guarded by our own men and honoured we are here
  To receive the peoples' envoys, we, their Emperor.
  Tidings from every quarter, and none we hear is bad:
  The Empire quiet now, disposed to us and glad.
  If there ran through our fighting a strain of hocus-pocus

Still in the end we fought the fight only for us.
Accidents may do the combatant some good,
10860   Heaven served the enemy a stone, a rain of blood,
Mouths of rock spoke out in vast and wondrous voices
That lifted our spirits up, and sank the enemy's.
He fell, he lay beneath our mockery and pride
And we, the winners, praise God, who is on our side.
And all join in, they want no telling by me to raise
To the Lord God a million-throated song of praise.
But, as my highest praise, I'll hold communion
Again with my own heart, a thing too rarely done.
A young and sprightly prince may choose to waste his days
10870   But the years teach him their lesson, till every moment
          weighs.
So at once I bind myself to you four worthy men,
Good of my house and court and realm resides therein.
    [*To the first*]
Prince, you had shrewd charge of the army's hierarchy
And bold and brave command of the moment's strategy.
In peace, as the time requires, now take your work forward.
I name you High Marshal. I present you with this sword.

HIGH MARSHAL
When your loyal troops, till now busy at home, have gone
Out to the frontiers to strengthen you and the throne
Allow me then in our spacious ancestral halls
10880   To lay the feast for you at thronging festivals
And carry unsheathed before and stand with at your side,
Constant escort of Highest Majesty, this blade.

EMPEROR [*to the second*]
You, a courageous man, conciliatory too,
Be our High Chamberlain. A hard task I give you.
Be first and foremost in my household. Some quarrel
Among themselves and do not serve me well.
I set you up as fine example from now on
Of how to please the Lord, the court and everyone.

HIGH CHAMBERLAIN
A man who serves his Lord's great purposes is glad.
10890   He will assist the best, not harm even the bad,

Candour without guile, calm with no deceit,
Contented, Sir, if I am open to your sight.
May I project my thoughts to that ceremonial meal?
When you proceed to table, I offer the golden bowl,
I hold your rings for you, among so many joys
As you refresh your hands, so you gladden my eyes.

EMPEROR

I feel too earnest yet to wish to celebrate.
Still, we shall go well if cheerfully we set out.
   [*To the third*]
We make you our High Seneschal. From this day on
Over the hunt, the poultry, the estates let your writ run.   10900
Have all my favourite dishes, the choice, throughout the
     year,
In the fullness of each month prepared for me with care.

HIGH SENESCHAL

My happiest duty now shall be to strictly fast
Until we set before you a gladdening repast.
The kitchen will unite behind its Seneschal
To call in far away and speed the seasonal.
And yet a simple nourishing goodness suits your taste,
Not foreign, forced on early, such as the banquets boast.

EMPEROR [*to the fourth*]

Festivities perforce being here our one affair
We change you, brave soldier, into our cup-bearer.   10910
So, my Lord Cupbearer, your care must be to fill
All my cellars with wine, plenteously and well.
Be moderate yourself, do not allow the way
Of junketing temptation to beckon you astray.

IMPERIAL CUPBEARER

My Prince, the youth you put your trust and faith in grows
To solid manhood faster than any would suppose.
I too will labour for that great festivity
And ornament the imperial buffet splendidly
With vessels of gold and silver, glorious, but the best
I set aside for you: it is the loveliest   10920
Clear Venetian glass in which wellbeing waits,
The wine's taste fortifies, never inebriates.

Some trust too much too often in such a precious power:
Sir, in your moderation you are safer by far.

EMPEROR

Now at this earnest juncture you have heard the true
Close utterance of what I had in mind for you.
By the Emperor's saying so the given gift's assured.
Still, for a strengthening, it needs the written word,
A noble signature. To see that properly done
10930   Here comes at the very moment indeed the very man.

[*Enter the* ARCHBISHOP *(*LORD CHANCELLOR*).*]

A vault that meets and trusts the keystone and fits fast
Henceforth for evermore securely it will last.
You see four princes here. We first have given thought
To things conducing to the good of house and court.
But now let what concerns the realm's entire estate
Be laid upon the *five*, a power and a weight.
More than all others' lands I wish your lands to shine
And here at once enlarge the extent of what you own
With portions that had been theirs who turned from me.
10940   Now many a lovely land is yours, for loyalty,
And with it too the right, whenever comes the chance,
To spread yourselves by purchase, exchange, inheritance.
Likewise the right to enjoy, and no man interfere,
What may belong to you, as liege lords, by the law.
All final sentencing is yours. You overrule
The highest courts throughout your lands without appeal.
Then taxes, coin and kind, fief, escort, excise, all
To you with dues of salt and mines and mint shall fall.
For I have lifted you into the very sphere
10950   Of Majesty, to pay my grateful debt entire.

ARCHBISHOP

In the name of all of us: our deepest thanks! As you
Fasten and strengthen us you strengthen your power too.

EMPEROR

I lay yet greater honour and onus on you five.
I live still for my Empire and wish to stay alive,
But my long ancestry reminds me I must heed
In present busy haste, the future – and provide.

The day will come when I must join those gone before.
Your duty then will be to name my successor.
Crown him and raise him up on God's altar and may
Things end in peace that were so stormy in my day.   10960

ARCHBISHOP [*as* LORD CHANCELLOR]

Proud in their innermost hearts, showing a meek
    submission,
These princes bow to you, and otherwise to no one.
And while the loyal blood still moves through our full veins
Your wishes have in us their body and their means.

EMPEROR

So to conclude for now. Let us set down and sign
For all the years to come what we have put in train.
The lands are yours in free and total ownership
On this condition: you never divide them up.
However you increase what you receive from us
The eldest son must have the whole of it, no less.   10970

ARCHBISHOP [*as* LORD CHANCELLOR]

Glad at heart I shall entrust these weighty laws
At once to parchment now, for the Empire's good and
    ours.
Faircopying and seals are the Chancellory's affair
But you, Lord, are its force, your holy signature.

EMPEROR

So I dismiss you now that each man of you may
Collectedly reflect on this momentous day.

[*The* TEMPORAL PRINCES *leave, the* SPIRITUAL PRINCE
(the ARCHBISHOP*) remains.*]

ARCHBISHOP [*with pathos*]

The Chancellor has left, the Bishop stays behind.
The spirit of solemn warning bids him speak his mind.
He feels on your account a father's anxious care.

EMPEROR

What anxious care, tell me, at such a joyful hour?   10980

ARCHBISHOP

How sorely at this hour it grieves me that I find
Your most sacred person and Satan so conjoined.
Safe on the throne you may be – so it appears – but as

A thing offending God and the Holy See, alas.
The Pope, hearing, at once will excommunicate
Your sinful empire – judge, punish, annihilate.
For he has not forgotten that you intervened
To save the necromancer the day that you were crowned.
When that first beam of mercy, flung from your diadem,
10990   Touched the accursèd head, it harmed all Christendom.
But beat your breast and from your criminal fortune pay
Back to the Holy Father a mite without delay.
That broad space of hills where your pavilion stood
And spirits fought for you, an evil brotherhood,
And you were the acquiescent listener to the Prince of Lies,
Now pious, give that land for a holy enterprise,
Its mountains and thick forests as far as they extend,
High slopes that wear the green of lushest pastureland,
And limpid fishy lakes and streams that countlessly
11000   Topple and snake at speed down, down into the valley,
And that wide valley itself, the deep moist meadow ground!
Where you express remorse, there mercy will be found.

EMPEROR
My grievous trespass now so deeply frightens me,
You set the boundaries where you think they should be.

ARCHBISHOP
Announce first that the place your sinning desecrated
Now to the service of God on high is dedicated.
The mind's eye sees the speedy uprising of strong walls,
Already on the chancel bright morning sunlight falls,
The growing building shapes a cross, the faithful have
11010   Much joy in the lengthening and high aspiring nave,
Already they force in fervour through the great west door,
The first bells having summoned them from near and far,
Clanging from the high towers that strive hard at heaven.
The penitent approaches, to make his life again.
On consecration day – let that high day come soon –
Your presence will be the highest ornament and crown.

EMPEROR
Let this noble work proclaim a pious will

To praise the Lord our God, and cleanse my soul as well.
Enough. My spirit feels already elevated.

ARCHBISHOP

As Chancellor, I will have the formal act completed.   11020

EMPEROR

The lands go to the Church. Set the transaction down
In a formal document that I will gladly sign.

ARCHBISHOP [*having taken his leave and exiting he turns
back again*]

Allocate to the work from the outset as it grows
The tithes, the coin, the kind, all of the land's dues
In perpetuity. An adequate upkeep
And close and careful management are never cheap.
And to expedite construction on so wild a site
Let us have gold from your accumulated loot.
Moreover, I cannot but advise you we must fetch
Timber from far away, and lime and slate and such.   11030
The people will load and cart. The pulpit will make clear:
The Church will pay with blessings all who drudge for her.

[*Exit.*]

EMPEROR

It is a heavy weight of grievous sin I bear.
The wretched magic folk have cost me very dear.

ARCHBISHOP [*returning again, bowing very low*]

Forgive me, Sir. You made that very wicked man
Lord of the Empire's shore, which land the Papal ban
Will also fall upon unless from there likewise
In penance you grant the Church tithes and all other dues.

EMPEROR [*crossly*]

The land is not there yet. It lies beneath the tide.

ARCHBISHOP

Give us the rights. We are patient. Time is on our side.   11040
Your word remain in force for us until that day.

[*Exit.*]

EMPEROR [*alone*]

So in no time at all I'd sign the Empire away.

ACT FIVE

Open Country

TRAVELLER
> There they are, the linden trees,
> Dusky, ancient and still strong!
> So my sight comes back to these
> After journeying so long.
> Here's the place and there indeed
> Is the house that sheltered me
> When into the dunes the tide

11050
> Flung me in the storm-fury.
> Now I wish to bless the pair,
> So quick to help, who took me in
> If they still live here who were
> Old enough even then.
> They were good people. Should I
> Shout or knock? – Good day to you,
> Kind ones, if you still enjoy
> The happiness good deeds bestow.

BAUCIS [*an amiable and very old woman*]
> Dear arrival! Quiet! Quiet!

11060
> Let my husband take his rest.
> Sleeping long the old may yet,
> Briefly waking, work with zest.

TRAVELLER
> Still alive to hear me say
> Thanks to you and him again
> For what you and he, Lady,
> Did for my young life back then?
> Baucis who when I had no
> Breath gave me the kiss that saves!
>   [*Enter the husband.*]
> Vigorous Philemon, who

11070
> Hauled my treasures from the waves!

Then the flames of your swift fire,
The silver tinkling of your bell,
You were in my grim adventure
Given me, to end it well.

Let me now complete the way
And look upon the boundless sea,
Let me kneel and let me pray
Or the soul will choke in me.
   [*He strides forward on the dunes.*]
PHILEMON [*to* BAUCIS]
Go and set the table, quick,
Where the cheerful garden grows.   11080
Let him run and look in shock.
He will not believe his eyes.
   [*Standing next to the* TRAVELLER]
Where you took a beating from
Savage breakers, blow by blow,
All's made over now, become
A paradisal garden show.
I had aged and could not be
Helpful as I would have been,
Felt the strength go out of me,
Watched the salty waters wane.   11090
Clever masters set their men
Ditching, damming, everywhere
The sea had rights they muscled in
Till they were the masters there.
See the meadowland, so verdant,
Woodland, garden, village green.
Come now, though, take some refreshment
For the sun will leave us soon.
Sails, passing far away,
Want safe haven for the night.   11100
Birds are roosting, so will they:
That's the harbour now. Eyesight
Hardly reaches to the sea's
Blue hem, but far and wide

All is settled, people house
Packed in tight on every side.
    [*The three of them at table in the little garden.*]

BAUCIS

Speechless? And you cannot bring
A morsel to your hungry mouth?

PHILEMON

Dumb because he's wondering.
11110   Talker, you tell him the truth.

BAUCIS

A wondrous thing it was indeed,
Even today it troubles me,
For the means that were employed
Were not as they ought to be.

PHILEMON

Can the Emperor commit a sin
Who made him the seashore's lord?
Did not a herald with trumpet din
Come riding by and speak the word?
Near our dunes, just beyond,
11120   There they made the first forays;
Tents and huts. But soon on land
Already green a palace rose.

BAUCIS

Days in vain the navvies battered,
Pick and shovel, thud, thud.
Nights the little flames fluttered:
There next day a dam stood.
It cost human blood. At night
We heard the killing being done.
Fires ran seawards. At first light
11130   Down their route a canal ran.
He is godless. He desires
Our little house and grove of trees.
This puffed-up neighbour of ours
Says we must do what he says.

PHILEMON

But did he not offer us

Good land on the land he gained?
BAUCIS
Don't trust where the water was,
Stand firm on your higher ground.
PHILEMON
Step to the chapel. The light of day
Is leaving us, let's look our last,   11140
Toll the bell and kneel and pray
To the old God – in him we trust.

A Palace

[*A spacious ornamental garden, a large, dead-straight
canal.* FAUST *in extreme old age, pacing and thinking.*]
LYNCEUS THE TOWERMAN [*through a speaking-trumpet*]
Sunset and the last ships bear
Cheerfully into harbour. Down
The length of the canal from there
A heavy barge will berth here soon.
Gaily pennanted, each mast
Stands stiffly to attention.
Your boatmen reckon themselves blessed,
Luck greets you at your culmination.   11150
[*The little bell rings on the dunes.*]
FAUST [*startled*]
Damned tinkling! The shame of it!
I suffer ambush and attack!
Looking before I have no limit
But this annoyance at my back
Tolls me the envious advice
That there are things I do not own:
The brown dwelling, the linden close,
The crumbling church, they are not mine.
Suppose I strolled in there? The shade,
Not being mine, would not be peace   11160
But pricks in the eyes, thorn in my side.

If only I could leave this place!

TOWERMAN [*as above*]

How joyfully the bright barge plies
Towards us on the evening breeze,
Crates, sacks and boxes mounded high
Enlarging fast upon the eye.

[*A magnificent barge, richly and brightly laden with
goods from foreign lands.* MEPHISTOPHELES. *The* THREE
MIGHTY MEN.]

CHORUS

So here we are
Ashore again.
We greet our master
11170   The patron.

[*They disembark, the cargo is landed.*]

MEPHISTO

We have been busy and shall be
Happy if our patron's happy.
With just two ships we sailed from here
And now we anchor with a score.
The nature of our deeds is seen
There in the freight that weighed us down.
The open ocean frees the spirit.
No shilly-shallying: you do it.
Grab when you can, let nothing slip,
11180   You catch a fish, you catch a ship
And once you're lord of three be sure
Soon you'll hook your number four,
And five will come without a fight,
You have the might and might is right.
It's ends that matter, not the means.
What happens in the shipping lanes?
War and trade and piracy,
The indivisible trinity.

THE THREE MIGHTY MEN

No thanks, no smile!
11190   No smile, no thanks!

        So what we brought
        His Lordship stinks?
        He pulls a sour
        Face at us
        Though we've made him
        Rich as Croesus.
MEPHISTO
        Don't expect more
        Reward than that.
        You have already
        Taken your cut.   11200
THE THREE
        That was only
        Tippling money.
        We want fair shares,
        Every penny.
MEPHISTO
        First lay out
        All together
        Room on room
        The whole treasure
        And when he sees
        What's in the shop   11210
        And more exactly
        Tots it up
        You won't find him
        Tight-fisted then,
        He'll treat the fleet
        Again and again.
        The tarts arrive tomorrow. I
        Can promise you a good supply.
        [*The cargo is carried away.*]
MEPHISTO [*to* FAUST]
    With black looks and a gloomy frown
    You apprehend your noble fortune.   11220
    A lofty wisdom has prevailed,
    Shore and sea are reconciled.

Ships put out from shore, they ride
Fast away on the willing tide.
Admit it now: from this palace
You take the world in your embrace.
This was the starting point, here stood
The first house of planks of wood.
We scratched a ditch in here. They row
11230   Busily splashing down it now.
Your vision, your people's industry
Have won the prizes of land and sea.
From here –

FAUST
                    I say be damned to here!
Here's the ill I cannot bear.
Much travelled you, must you be told
It stabs me through and through, I'm maimed
By it, oppressed, travailed
And speaking of it I'm ashamed.
The old people over there must move,
11240   I want their limes for my demesne.
Though I own the world, that little grove
Cankers the lot, not being mine.
There I would lay from bough to bough
A platform, open up the view
All around for me to see
All that has been done by me,
And so survey entire at once
This masterpiece of man's intelligence:
The clever making active use
11250   Of the people's wide new living space.

So mine is the harshest torment,
Feeling in wealth what we still want.
The tinkling bell, the scent of limes
Beset me as would church and tombs.
The all-powerful will, the choice it makes,
Hits on that patch of sand, and breaks.

How can I evict this from my spirit?
The bell tolls and I rage at it.

MEPHISTO

Of course such an annoyance would
Turn your life to gall and wormwood.   11260
Goes without saying: the tinkling's more
Than any sensitive ear can bear.
And that damned ting-a-ling-a-linging
Fogging the fine skies each evening
It interferes on every occasion
From your first bath to your inhumation
As though between the ding and the dong
You dreamed a life not lasting long.

FAUST

Their resistance and self-will
Blight my splendid gains and still,   11270
Tormented to the heart, I must
Fatigue myself in being just.

MEPHISTO

Why all the fuss? What's stopping you?
Colonization's overdue.

FAUST

Then get them out of my way!
I chose the old people, as you know,
A pretty place for them to go.

MEPHISTO

We carry them off and set them down
And very soon they're right as rain.
And once they're through the violence   11280
A nice home will be recompense.

    [*He whistles piercingly. Enter the* THREE MIGHTY MEN.]
The Master calls. There's work to do.
Tomorrow he will feast his crew.

THE THREE MIGHTY MEN

The tight old Master fasted us
But must by rights be generous.

                                                        [*Exit.*]

MEPHISTO [*ad spectatores*]
    The old, old story, usual game,
    Naboth's vineyard was much the same (1 Kings 21).

Deep in the Night

LYNCEUS THE TOWERMAN [*on the watchtower, singing*]
    Born to see,
    Appointed to be
11290   The tower's looker-out,
    All pleases me.
    I can spy far
    And I see near
    The moon and the stars,
    The woods and the deer
    And seeing in all things
    The eternal show
    Of beauty I like it
    And like myself too.
11300   These lucky eyes
    Whatever they have seen
    Whatever its nature
    How lovely it has been!
    [*Pause.*]
    But not only for my pleasure
    Am I set so high up here.
    What atrocity and horror
    Threaten me from the dark world there?
    I see sprays of sparklight lifting
    Through the lime trees' double night
11310   And the wind comes working, wafting
    At an incandescent heat.
    Oh, the mossy house is blazing
    In the moistness where it stood!
    Rescue's needed, no time losing,
    No one's there to help who would.

Oh, the good old people, ever
Very careful with their fire,
Now they choke on smoke and suffer
Terror in this adventure.
Flames are flaming, throbbing red   11320
Stands the blackened cottage shell.
Pray the honest pair have fled
This savagery of fires of hell!
Leaves and twigs are ravelled by
Climbing lightnings and the dry
Branches crackle up and flare,
Briefly brilliant, and fall.
Oh, the pain of seeing far,
Seeing all and knowing all!
The little chapel's back breaks   11330
Under the falling branches' weight.
Points of flame, like tongues of snakes,
Set the tops of the trees alight.
Through the hollow trunks and down
To the roots is molten crimson.
[*Long pause, singing*]
What for centuries was shown
Kindly to the eyes, is gone.

FAUST [*on the balcony, looking out towards the dunes*]
Singing whimpering from above,
His words and melody both too late.
He grieves. I have the annoyance of   11340
A deed that was precipitate.
Still, if the linden trees are done for,
Their trunks a coaled atrocity,
I'll soon erect a look-out there
To gaze into infinity.
I see also the new abode
Enclosing the old pair allowed
By me to have an eventide
Of life in happy gratitude.

MEPHISTO AND THE THREE [*below*]
We come at a gallop. Very sorry: 11350

The affair did not end amicably.
We knocked, we hammered at the door,
No one opened. More and more
We rattled and we banged at it
Until the rotten thing fell flat.
We shouted loud and threatened hard,
No one answered, no one heard,
And, as is usual, they could not
Hear us – because they would not.

11360 We, though, without more ado
We smartly cleared them out for you.
The pair had less pain than they might
For on the spot they died of fright.
A stranger hiding there and who
Offered fight, we topped him too.
And in the struggle, brief but sore,
Coals, being strewn around, set fire
To straw and lo! it has become
A blazing pyre for the three of them.

FAUST

11370 So you were deaf to what I said?
My word was *swap* not rob. You did
A wild and heedless thing. I lay
My curse on it: share that for pay.

CHORUS

It is the old commandment! Do
What violent power tells you to.
For if you're bold and answer back
You risk your house and home – and neck.

[*They exit.*]

FAUST [*on the balcony*]

The stars will neither watch nor shine,
The fire sinks, the flames die down;
11380 Comes a cold draught and fans it higher,
Wafts smoke and haze over here.
Soon said and too soon done! – What are
These shapes of shadows floating near?

Midnight

[*Enter* FOUR GREY WOMEN.]

FIRST WOMAN
My name is Want.

SECOND
My name is Debt.

THIRD
My name is Care.

FOURTH
My name is Need.

THREE OF THEM
The door is closed and we cannot go in.
A rich man's in there, we don't like to go in.

WANT
There I become shadow.

DEBT
There I cease to be.

NEED
Rich men avert their spoiled faces from me.

CARE
Sisters, you cannot and may not go in.
But Care through the keyhole, she can slip in.   11390

[CARE *vanishes.*]

WANT
Grey sisters, come, this is no place to bide.

DEBT
I keep with you, fasten close by your side.

NEED
Need follows you closely. We tread the same path.

THE THREE OF THEM
The clouds pass away, the stars disappear.
Behind them! Behind, in the distance, see where
He is coming, our brother is coming – Death!

[*They exit.*]

FAUST [*in the palace*]
I saw four come, only three go.

And what their speaking meant I do not know.

11400 Words hanging in the air like breath:

Need. And a dire companion: Death.

Empty they sounded, hushed and ghostly.

I've not fought free yet. Oh, if only

I could clear necromancy from my way,

Wholly unlearn the magic formulae

And face you, Nature, as a man alone

Then being human would be worth the pain.

I was that man before I searched in darkness

And cursed the world and cursed myself, lawless.

11410 But now the air's so full of spectral trade

Some truck with it's impossible to avoid.

Perhaps clear reason smiles at us in daylight

But we are caught in webs of dreams by night.

We come in from the youthful meadows glad.

A bird croaks. Croaks what? Something bad.

Snared early and late in superstitions,

Signs and warnings and premonitions

Intimidate us. We are all alone.

The door creaks. Who enters? No one.

   [*In great alarm*]

11420 Is someone there?

CARE

                        The answer must be yes.

FAUST

   And who are you?

CARE

                        Am here, no more, no less.

FAUST

   Remove yourself.

CARE

                        I am where I should be.

FAUST [*at first angry, then calming himself,* sotto voce]

   Beware. No magic formulae.

CARE

        Should the ears not hear me, still

The echoing heart-chambers will.
Ever changing shape, I use
Any violence I choose.
Travel with me by land or sea
You travel with Anxiety.
No one seeks me but they find,   11430
Curse me cruel and wish me kind.
Have you and Care not ever met?

FAUST

I have run through the world, grabbed at
My lusts and dragged them by the hair
And left them lying when I wanted more,
And what escaped I let them go.
All I have done is lust and do
And want again and so stormed through
My life with power; at first mightily great
But wisely now, now I deliberate.   11440
I know the round earth well enough
And what's beyond, the view of it's blocked off.
The man's a fool who ogles over there
And dreams his kind inhabit the upper air.
Let him stand still and look around him here,
This world speaks to the man who stands four-square.
Why wander off into eternity?
He makes the things he *knows* his property.
So let him journey through his earthly day;
However haunted, still go on his way,   11450
Onwards, to happiness and torment,
And never satisfied by any moment.

CARE

Whom I ever once possess
To him all the world is useless;
Lasting gloom falls from the skies,
Sun will never set nor rise,
Though his outer senses thrive
In him shades of darkness live,
None of any good fortune
Can he ever make his own.   11460

Sad or glad on any whim,
Starves in plenty all around him;
Till the next day he postpones
Any pleasures, any pains;
Waiting on the future can
Here and now get nothing done.

FAUST

Enough! That will not work with me.
I will not listen to such stuff. Have done!
All your miserable litany
11470   Would turn the cleverest to a simpleton.

CARE

Shall he go or shall he stay?
All his will is taken away;
Plumb on easy roads he gropes
Like the blind, he totters, creeps.
Deep and deeper goes below,
Sees things more and more askew,
Burdening himself and others,
Drawing breath but still he smothers;
Doesn't smother, doesn't live;
11480   Won't give up, nothing to give.
So a ceaseless to and fro,
Hates leaving be, hates having to do;
Never freed but swiftly crushed;
Sleeping badly, ill refreshed;
Bound to where he is until
He is well enough for Hell.

FAUST

Wretched spectres, so you will abuse
The human race again and again and again
And convert even ordinary days
11490   Into foul muddles, toils, trammels of pain.
Hard to be rid of daemons, their severe
Bonds on the mind, I know, cannot be cut.
But your insidious empire, Care,
I never will acknowledge it.

CARE

    Then feel it as I turn from you
    Quickly with a curse and vanish.
    Humans are blind their whole lives through,
    Be blind now, Faustus, as you finish.

                              [*She breathes on him. Exits.*]

FAUST [*blinded*]

    Night forces deep and deeper in but light
    Starts up within me, a blazing light.   11500
    I rush to carry my intentions out.
    Only the ruler's word has any weight.
    Diggers, get up, every man of you, and on
    The glad gaze of the world cast my bold vision.
    Seize tools, get busy with shovel and spade!
    After the marking out now comes the deed!
    By order, discipline, swift enterprise
    We shall achieve the very highest prize.
    One mind sufficiently commands
    To that great end a thousand hands.   11510

In the Palace's Great Forecourt

[*Torches.*]

MEPHISTO [*as overseer, leading*]

    This way! This way! Come along! Come along!
    You trembling wambling lemurs,
    Of bones and sinews and ligaments
    Cobbled-up half-creatures.

LEMURS [*as a chorus*]

    Double quick we're at your side
    For we've been hearing rumours
    About a far and spacious land
    Intended all for us.

And we have poles to stick the ground
11520   And miles of measuring chain.
We knew once why you summoned us
But now it's gone again.

MEPHISTO
Nothing fancy here. Your own
Measurements are all we need.
The longest of you, you lie down,
The rest go round him with a spade.
The same as for our forefathers: a shape
Six foot long and six foot deep,
So passing from the palace to the pit
11530   And that's the stupid end of it.

LEMURS [*clowning as they dig*]
When I was young and lived and loved
Then life was very sweet.
Where there was fun and a jolly din
There I had dancing feet.

But now I go on cripple sticks
Across the dancing floor
And trip over the threshold of
Death's ever open door.

FAUST [*emerging from the palace, groping for the doorposts*]
Oh, how I love the clang of spades!
11540   My navvies, slaving for all they're worth,
Returning earth to earth,
Curbing the proud waves and the tides
And shutting up the sea with doors.

MEPHISTO [*aside*]
You labour in our behalf not yours.
Dam by dam and groyne by groyne
You're laying up for Father Neptune,
The water devil, a fine repast.
This way or that you lose, we and
The elements are in league, we bend
11550   All to nothing at the last.

FAUST

  Gangmaster!

MEPHISTO

        Here!

FAUST

             Get me workmen,
  Thousands, by any means, with cash,
  And whores and drink and with the lash
  Encourage, tempt, pressgang them in.
  I want news every day how far
  Along with digging at that trench you are.

MEPHISTO [sotto voce]

  The news I hear is that the trench begun
  Will not be long – just long enough for one.

FAUST

  The mountain has a skirt of bog
  That poisons all I have already done.   11560
  Draining the wet from that foul quag
  Shall be my last work and the best work done.
  I open room for many millions to live
  Lives – it is true – not safe, but free and active.
  The fields greening and fertile; humankind
  At home with their livestock on the newest ground;
  A people settling close around the hill
  Of strength flung up by their energetic will.
  In here a paradisal land; out there,
  Rising to the brim, let the waves tear   11570
  With their teeth and batter at the wall.
  The people stop the breach, all aiding all.
  This sense of things wholly takes hold of me.
  This is the highest pitch of wisdom:
  He alone deserves his life and liberty
  Who every day must fight for them.
  So here, in danger, human life will have
  Zest through all its ages till the grave.
  Such a swarming I should like to see,
  Stand on a free ground with a people who are free.   11580

Then to the moment I'd be allowed to say
Bide here, you are so beautiful!
Aeons will pass but the marks made by my stay
On the earth will be indelible.
I enjoy the highest moment now in this,
My forefeeling of such a happiness.
    [FAUST *falls back, the* LEMURS *catch him and lay him on
the ground.*]

MEPHISTO

Lusts cannot fill him nor happiness content,
He whores after changing shapes and cannot rest,
And the last miserable empty moment
11590   The poor wretch seeks to hold it fast.
He held out hard against me but Time commands:
Now the old man lies here in Time's sands.
The clock stands still –

CHORUS

                Stands still! Like midnight, the clock is hushed.
Now the hand falls.

MEPHISTO

                    It falls and it is finished.

CHORUS

It is over.

MEPHISTO

             Over! A stupid thing to say!
Why say it's over?
Over and never was, either or neither way.
All this eternal bringing into being!
And being brought from being back to nothing!
11600   'Now it is over.' What might that mean?
That it might just as well never have been
And still goes round and round as though it were.
Eternal emptiness would suit me much better.

Entombment

LEMUR [*solo*]
> Who bodged a house as bad as this
> With shovels and with spades?

LEMURS [*chorus*]
> Dumb guest, for you in your hempen shift
> It's fine beyond your needs.

LEMUR [*solo*]
> Who furnished the room so wretchedly?
> Where are the tables and chairs?

LEMURS [*chorus*]
> It's rented for only a little while.
> So many creditors!   11610

MEPHISTO
> The corpse is prone and when the spirit flies
> I show her my entitlement, blood-signed.
> But alas by so many methods nowadays
> The Devil sees his souls purloined.
> The old procedures give offence
> And nobody commends us in the new.
> I managed on my own once
> But have to fetch in extras now.
>
> We are not doing well wherever you care to look!   11620
> Traditional practices, the old book . . .
> In nothing and in no one can you trust.
> On the last breath the soul would leave her house,
> I'd be there waiting, however quick the mouse
> Snap! I shut my claws around her fast.
> But now she dawdles, she is loath to quit
> The horrid corpse, that dismal tenancy,
> Until the elements, longing to split,
> Evict her ignominiously.
> Day after day I worry, hour after hour,   11630
> But can't be sure of when and how and where.
> Death's lost his old quick strength. There's even a doubt

Sometimes whether the light of life has quite gone out.
I've licked my lips at many a stiff and then –
All show! – it moved, it stirred again.
   [*He makes gestures of conjuration, like some fantastical*
   fugleman.]
Step up now at the double, one-two, one-two,
Lads of the straight horn, lads of the bent,
All of the good old stuff of devilment,
And bring the mouth of Hell along with you.
11640   True, Hell has many many mouths and throats
And swallows according to class and quality;
But how this entertainment terminates
In future we shall not be quite so fussy.
   [*The frightful mouth of Hell opens up left.*]
Canines gape; firestorms spew
From under the great gob's hollow dome.
There at the back, in the steaming brew,
I see the City of Everlasting Flame.
A red surf tumbles to the teeth,
On it the damned, hoping for rescue, ride;
11650   But the vast hyena mauls them in its mouth
And their hot travels are renewed.
In nooks and crannies there's still much to note.
Such horrors, so many and such a squeeze!
You do very well to give sinners a fright.
They think it's all a dream or a pack of lies.
   [*To the fat devils with short straight horns*]
Now, paunchy villains with the fiery cheeks,
You, fat on sulphur, hotly luminescent,
My stiff-necked, red-necked, short-arsed oiks,
Keep watch down here for something phosphorescent.
11660   It will be the little soul, Psyche, the butterfly,
And when you pluck her she's an ugly worm.
I stamp her with my seal and then good-bye
To her in the whirling fire-storm.

Keep a particular watch low down,
As is your duty, fat bellies.

That was perhaps her favoured zone,
None knows precisely where the soul's seat is.
She likes the navel for a home. Be sure
She doesn't give you the slip from there.
   [*To the scrawny devils with long bent horns*]
Flibbertigibbets, my bean-pole fuglemen,   11670
Scratch at the air, keep a ceaseless watch,
Arms out, claws showing sharp, and when
She flutters up and flees, you snatch.
She can't be comfy in the old lair,
And genius – it seeks the upper air.
   [*Heaven opens in glory, above right.*]

HEAVENLY HOST
   Heaven's kith and kin,
   Angels, fly in
   On leisurely wings
   To sinners: forgive;
   To the dust: let it live.   11680
   Hovering above
   Lingeringly give
   All living things
   Their kindness again.

MEPHISTO
I hear a hideous discordant jangling
Fall from above with the unwelcome daylight,
A little-boyish-girlish music-bungling,
A simpering soppy pious heart's delight.
When in the baddest of our wicked sessions
We plotted the extermination of humanity   11690
We dreamed up nothing that would be
Half so frightful as their orisons.

This sneaky creepy pansy crew
Will lift a soul from underneath your nose.
They fight dirty, the way we do.
They're devils too, but in disguise.
If we lose here we'll never live it down.
Surround the grave now, hold the line!

CHORUS OF ANGELS [*strewing roses*]

11700
    Roses on roses, a sweet
    Perfume, a dazzling light,
    Floating and fluttering,
    Secretly quickening,
    Sprigged-out and sailing,
    Budding, unsealing,
    Hurry to flower!

    Let the spring loose,
    Red and green, over
    His sleeping face
    Carry a paradise.

MEPHISTO [*to the satans*]

11710
    Ducking and diving? Poor sort of hellish host!
    Stand firm and let them strew!
    Every damn fool of you stand to his post!
    They think they'll bury us hot lads in snow
    With all their floral fol-de-rols but blow
    On them, they'll melt and waste.
    So blow, my putti, blow! And now lay off.
    You've bleached the whole swarm with your fiery puff.
    Gently! Shut your mouth- and nose-holes up!
    You've blown too hard. Never know when to stop,

11720
    But always running to extremes.
    See, not just shrivelled: browned, crisped, in flames!
    They strafe us now with clear and toxic fire.
    Resist it! Stand four square!
    But the virtue leaves them, all their fight has gone,
    The devils feel a strange warmth coming on.

CHORUS OF ANGELS

    Flowers and blessings,
    Fires and rejoicings,
    The glad heart receives
    Widening waves

11730
    Of incoming love.
    Words that are truthful
    From the eternal

        Hosts in the ethereal
        Daylight above.

MEPHISTO

    Shame on the cursed ninnies evermore!
    Satans with their legs in the air,
    The fat fools cartwheel round and round
    And into Hell they go arse over tit.
    Enjoy your hot bath! You deserve it.
    I however stand my ground.   11740
        [*Flailing at the floating roses*]
    Daft jack o' lanterns, however bright you shine,
    When I catch you you're sloppy gelatine.
    Fluttering, fluttering, will you leave me alone?
    Sticks on my neck like fire and brimstone.

CHORUS OF ANGELS

        All that is strange to you
        You will avoid;
        Troubling change in you
        You can't abide.
        Such hard invasion
        Answer who can,   11750
        Only the loving will
        Love usher in.

MEPHISTO

    My head's on fire, my heart, my liver,
    The devil's element only devilisher,
    Far more pricking than the flames of Hell!
    I see why lovers when things don't go well
    Yammer so loud and turn their necks and gaze
    After the beloved whom they do not please.

    And me! What drags my head that side?
    Are love and I not sworn always to feud?   11760
    Till now we faced in sharp hostility.
    Now something strange transfixes me so that
    I find the sweet boys lovely to look at.
    Why can't I curse? What is it stopping me?
    If they bend me, henceforth all bent and straight

Sheep and goats may copulate.
Oh, these effulgent youngsters, whom I hate,
Now seem to me exceptionally sweet.

My pets, my beauties, answer me this:
11770 Are you not also Lucifer's progeny?
So pretty you are, so fit to kiss,
I feel you have timed your coming perfectly,
So right I feel, it feels so natural,
As though I'd seen you a thousand times before,
So slyly-kittenish desirable,
More lovely at every look, oh more and more!
Come close, give me one look, just one.

ANGELS

Why do you back away when we come on?
We near you, stand to meet us if you can.

  [*The* ANGELS, *never still, occupy all the space.*]

MEPHISTO [*forced into the proscenium*]

11780 You call us devils and you damn us
But you are the real necromancers,
For you seduce woman and man.
Curse the adventure! And is this
The element of love? The whole
Body of me so in flames I feel
The searing of my neck much less.
Lower yourselves from hovering, display
Your beauties moving in a worldlier way.
Solemnity is of course your proper style,
11790 But if for once I could see you smile
I'd dwell in the joy of it till kingdom come.
I mean how lovers look, oh some
Tremor of a hint around the mouth – just so.
I like you, friend, the best – how tall
You are! The churchy look's not you at all,
Eye me a mite lasciviously, can't you?
And you might go decently a bit more nude,
That long nightgown is far too much the prude.
They turn, we view the other – the back – side!

    Mouthwatering little rogues they are indeed!   11800
CHORUS OF ANGELS
    Let them be clarified
    By fires of love!
    Truth heal them of
    The hells they have made;
    Set themselves free
    Of wrong joyously,
    Glad in the espousal
    Of all within all.
MEPHISTO [*coming to his senses*]
    What is this? Boil on boil, like Job,
    All of him become a horror to himself,   11810
    He triumphs when he wholly knows himself
    And puts his trust in himself and all his tribe.
    The devil's noble parts are saved. It was a touch
    Of the hex of love, skin-deep, a scratch.
    The accursèd flames have already burned out,
    I curse the lot of you, as is meet and right.
CHORUS OF ANGELS
    Those around whom
    Wings of light flame
    They live with the good
    Their lives and are glad.
    All as one rise,   11820
    All of you praise,
    The air is made clear,
    Let the spirit respire!
    [*They rise, carrying off that which is immortal of* FAUST.]
MEPHISTO [*looking around him*]
    Now what? Where have they gone?
    The under-age pack have had me for their fool
    And carried off the swag to heaven.
    Explains their nibblings at the charnel hole!
    I have been robbed of a very great treasure.
    This eminent soul, pawned mine by signature,   11830
    They have filched from me by tricks and guile.

Where is the court that will hear my plea?
Who will get me what I am owed?
In my old age they have hoodwinked me.
It serves me right. All's hideously screwed.
Disgraceful failure, a vast
Investment scandalously blown,
Absurd lovey-dovey, a common lust
Infects the Devil, supposed to be immune!
11840 So he, the wise and worldly guy,
Letting himself into this silly business,
Ends it and exits defeated by
An almighty foolishness.

Peaks and Ravines

[*Trees, rocks, wilderness. Holy anchorites on the peaks at various heights and in the clefts between.*]

CHORUS AND ECHO
　　　　Forest comes swaying in;
　　　　Boulders, they weigh upon;
　　　　Roots fasten tight upon;
　　　　Boles, they crowd on and on.
　　　　Torrents collide and fly,
　　　　Deep in the caves is dry.
11850　　Round us the friendly
　　　　Lions pad silently,
　　　　Honour the place where love
　　　　Stacks like a treasure-trove.

PATER ECSTATICUS [*rising and sinking in the air*]
　　　　Burning eternal bliss,
　　　　White heat of love's duress,
　　　　Scalding and hurt
　　　　Of God in the heart.
　　　　Arrows, strike through me!
　　　　Lances, subdue me!
11860　　Batter me, rive me,

Lightnings, come cleave me
Till all the nothingness
Vapours and vanishes!
Let the bright seed-stone
Of lasting love shine.

PATER PROFUNDUS [*in a deep region*]

Here at my feet the toppled stone
Piles on the brink of further fall
And streams in thousands hurtle down
Through foam and rainbows, fearful,
And tree boles by their own will shove   11870
Themselves erect into the air:
So all-powerful is the love
That makes and mothers all things here.

A savage roaring all around me
Heaves through the rock-floor and the trees,
But down the gullet lovingly
Sighing abundant water follows
Her vocation to wet the plains;
And lightning, striking in with fire,
Falling upon, unclouds and cleans   11880
The fouled heart of the atmosphere –

They are love's messengers, they show
What moves and makes around us always.
Oh, fire the life in me also!
I feel my muddled spirits freeze,
My trammelled senses cannot speak,
Shut-up, they are, self-chained, self-hurt.
O God, leaven my thinking, make
Light come upon my needy heart.

PATER SERAPHICUS [*in a middle region*]

Through the fir-trees' waving hair   11890
Creeps a swarm of morning mist.
What lives in its heart? Those are
Lives no sooner come than lost.

CHORUS OF BLESSED INFANT BOYS
  Father, tell us where we are going.
  Good man, tell us who we are.
  All of us are happy. Our being
  Is an easy thing to bear.

PATER SERAPHICUS
  Little born-at-midnight children,
  Soul and senses half open,
11900 Lost to parents there and then,
  What they lost the angels won.
  Can you feel one full of love
  Is present? If you can, come near.
  In you there's no inkling of
  Earth's hard paths. How lucky you are!
  Climb down in my eyes, into
  The organ earth and world require,
  Use them as your own and view
  All that's circumambient here.
  [He takes them into him.]
11910 Those are boulders, those are trees,
  That's a river of water bent
  With huge impetus on ways
  Of hastening a sheer descent.

BLESSED INFANT BOYS [from within him]
  Such a powerful thing to see!
  But how dreary-dark the place is!
  Shakes and terrifies us. Be
  Good and generous and release us.

PATER SERAPHICUS
  Ascend into the higher sphere
  And in the quiet manner there
11920 Grow with God as more and more
  Purely you and He grow near.
  For such food the spirits feed on
  In the ether's untroubledness:
  Eternal loving's revelation,
  The opening on blessedness.

CHORUS OF BLESSED INFANT BOYS [*circling the highest
     peaks*]
       Take hands and spin
       Happiness, sing
       Holiness in
       This feeling ring.
       Trust the instruction   11930
       Of heaven. Never fear:
       You will soon look on
       Him you revere.
ANGELS [*hovering in the upper atmosphere and carrying what
     is immortal of* FAUST]
       We bring from evil this noble limb
       Of the spirit world safe home.
       The striver, the endeavourer, him
       We are able to redeem.
       And if, besides that, from above
       Love had a part in him
       He'll meet the blessed host and have   11940
       Among them warm welcome.
THE YOUNGER ANGELS
       Roses from the penitent hands
       Of women, holy-lovingly
       Helped us win our victory
       And accomplish our great ends.
       So this soul-booty was lifted.
       Strewing, we dispersed the wicked;
       When we hit, the devils fled;
       Used to the pains of Hell, instead
       The spirits learned that Love can hurt;   11950
       Even the old Satan-Master's heart
       Suffered a cruel transfixion.
       Alleluya! It is done!
THE MORE PERFECTED ANGELS
       All earthly remnant
       It pains us to bear.
       Were he of amiant
       Still he's impure.

When force of the spirit
Seizes and bonds
11960   The elements into it
Even an angel's hands
Can't split the closely
Passionate two-in-one
Cross-between. Only
Eternal love can.

THE YOUNGER ANGELS
Pinnacle-wreathing
I feel there moves
Closer a seething
Of spirit lives.
11970   The nebula clarifies,
I see the infant boys
Freed from the earth's heaviness
In the upper world, clothing
Newly in spring
Quickening in blessedness,
They dance in a ring.
So let him join
Them outsetting here,
Join in and gain
11980   The increase entire.

BLESSED INFANT BOYS
We receive joyously
Him in the chrysalis,
With him is given us
Angelic surety.
Undo the cocoon
See how in beauty
Already the holy
Life in him's grown.

DOCTOR MARIANUS [*in the highest and purest of the cells*]
The outlook is open here,
11990   The spirit lifts clear.
Women are passing there,

Hovering higher.
Among them, so sovereign,
Haloed with stars,
Regina of heaven,
What radiance she wears!
[*Ecstatic*]
Highest in the firmament,
Lady, let me see
In the blue wide-opened tent
Of sky your mystery.   12000
Be gentle on the things that move
A man towards you, all his freight
Of serious and tender love,
His sacred sharp delight.

Nothing daunts the heart's courage
Under your domain;
Comes upon our fire and rage
Your peace, your small rain.
Girl of beauty shining pure,
Mother of our reverence,   12010
Our elected queen, before
You no god has precedence.

    Round her a wreathing
    Of penitents wispily
    Coiling and clinging,
    A delicate colony
    Climbing her knees,
    Thirsting and lapping
    The ether for grace.

You become untouchable   12020
Nonetheless it's you
The easily seduceable
Trustingly come to.

Into weakness carried off
They are all but lost.
Who alone has strength enough
To stop what they want most?
On a slant and smooth path
Slipping's easy done.

12030   Glancing, greeting, swapping breath
Will soften anyone.

[MATER GLORIOSA *floats into view.*]

CHORUS OF THE PENITENT WOMEN
High in the eternal
You rise to your place.
You without equal
Hear us, o bountiful
Giver of grace.

MAGNA PECCATRIX (Luke 7:36)
By the love the Pharisees
Scolded when it wept upon
Feet whose ache she wished to ease,

12040   The feet of your God-lighted son;
By the hair and hands with which
Those white feet were wiped and dried;
By the box whose scents in such
Spilling richness she applied –

MULIER SAMARITANA (John 4)
By the well where long ago
Abraham watered flock and herd;
By the lifted bucket so
Grateful to the parching Lord;
By the clear abundant water

12050   Starting there and setting forth,
Forever bright, down every quarter
Through the countries of the earth –

MARIA AEGYPTIACA (*Acta Sanctorum*)
By the holy sanctum where
The body of the Saviour lay;
By the arm that barred the door
Against me, warning me away.

By the forty years I kept
Penitent in barren lands;
By the blessed final script
I set in the desert sands –   12060

THE THREE OF THEM TOGETHER

Lady who will not refuse
Even bad sinners your presence
But to eternities will raise
The profit of their penitence,
Let in this good woman who,
Self-forgetting only once,
Never guessed the wrong she'd do
Her and your forgiveness balance.

UNA POENITENTIUM [*formerly called* GRETCHEN, *pressing close*]

You without equal,
Lady of Light, incline   12070
Your countenance mercifully
Over this joy of mine.
The one I loved early
Now without trouble
Is coming back to me.

BLESSED INFANT BOYS [*approaching in a circling motion*]

How he outgrew us!
How big his limbs are!
He will repay us,
With interest, our care.
We were soon lost to   12080
The living chorus,
But he has learned, now
He will instruct us.

THE PENITENT [*formerly called* GRETCHEN]

Full in the spirits' holy choir
The newcomer is still unclear,
He scarcely feels life freshen, nor
His likeness to the company here.
See how he struggles from the old
Bonds that encased him on the earth

12090 And in the upper air, unveiled,
   The first strength of youth steps forth.
   The new day blinds him. Oh, let me,
   Lady, be his teacher now.

MATER GLORIOSA
   Come! Rise to higher zones. When he
   Senses you there, he will follow.

DOCTOR MARIANUS [*face down, in adoration*]
    All softly penitent raise your eyes
    To hers that save, and be
    For a blessed enterprise
    Altered gratefully.
12100   Let the good in body and mind
    Do you faithful service.
    Maiden, mother, queen, be kind,
    Be merciful, goddess.

CHORUS MYSTICUS
    Time-dying things are
    A likeness, a hint;
    Falling short there,
    Here the event;
    Things past description
    Here they are done;
12110   Eternal woman
    Hithers us on.

        FINIS

Notes

ACT ONE

A Pleasant Place

4613 *A Pleasant Place*: The *locus amoenus* of classical idyll and pastoral.

4613 ARIEL: The name of Prospero's helping spirit in *The Tempest*. In the 'Walpurgis Night's Dream' in *Part I*, he appears with Puck, from *A Midsummer Night's Dream*, and closes that intermezzo. Now he opens *Part II*.

4626 *four watches*: The traditional three-hour divisions of the night, from 6pm to 6am. The Chorus sings a strophe for each.

4666 *the ... Hours*: The Horae, daughters of Zeus, described by Homer (*Iliad* V) as keepers of the gates of heaven. They marked not just the hours but other fixed phases and seasons.

4671 *Phoebus*: Here as the sun god, the Hours being his attendants.

4679–4727 These lines are in *terza rima* (aba bcb cdc, etc.), the form used by Dante in his *Divine Comedy*. The poem 'Im ernsten Bein-haus' (In the Solemn Charnel-House), a meditation on Schiller's skull, written in 1826, not long after this passage, is the only other instance of *terza rima* in Goethe's work.

Throne-Room in the Imperial Palace

4732 JUNKER: A young German nobleman.

4743–50 *What's always cursed ... sight?*: Mephistopheles, usurping the place of the regular Fool, asks a riddle, the answer to which may be Fool or Devil.

4845 *Ghibelline or Guelph*: Anachronistic allusion to two warring factions, the first supporting the Emperor, the second the Pope, in the Holy Roman Empire of the twelfth and thirteenth centuries. But here and at 10772 the sense of the allusion is not specific but generic.

4892   *Will root the deepest up*: Alluding to the Devil's ability, of some
           importance in *Part I* (2675–7 and 3664–73), to detect and recover
           buried treasure.

4955–70   *The Sun is gold ... our number can*: The Astrologer,
           prompted by Mephistopheles, rehearses the traditional associ-
           ations of the planets with their metals and particular functions or
           areas of influence. Thus Sun with gold, Moon with silver, Saturn
           with lead, Venus with love, Mars with war, etc. Sun and Moon,
           coming into conjunction, will be very favourable to the Emperor's
           wishes. The crowd are right to be sceptical.

4979–80   *mandrake root ... Black Hound*: The root, human in shape,
           grows under the gallows-tree from the emission of a hanged man
           and can only be dug up by a black dog. It has magical powers and
           is especially useful in searching for buried treasure.

5011   *saltpetre bloom*: The salts forming on the cob walls of sheds and
           stables were useful for pickling and in folk medicine.

5025–6   *the staves have rotted through ... tartar now*: The tartaric
           acid deposited on the inside of the wine barrels encases the wine
           after the wood itself has rotted.

5041   *golden calves*: False gods, as in Exodus 32 and 1 Kings 12:28.
           Mephistopheles idly indicates the true nature of what he is offering.

5057–60   *jollity ... Ash Wednesday ... carnival*: The traditional feast-
           ing and merrymaking before Lent, the period of fasting which
           begins on Ash Wednesday.

Spacious Hall with Adjoining Rooms

5065   *the masque*: Goethe organized such things for the Weimar court.
           He had seen the Roman Carnival in 1788 and describes it in his
           Italian Journey. Other sources for the figures and details here are
           Mantegna's *Triumphs of Caesar*, Dürer's *Triumph of the Emperor
           Maximilian* and a collection by Antonio Francesco Grazzini of
           masques and parades held in Florence under the Medicis.

5065 ff.   The Herald, as master of ceremonies, promises a masque in
           the Italian Renaissance style, not the German medieval, and credits
           the Emperor with importing it from Rome. Goethe's Emperor is a
           composite figure. Here he is less Maximilian I (1493–1519) than
           Charles IV (1346–78), who travelled to Rome to be confirmed in
           office, kissing the Pope's slipper (5072–3), and was notably open
           to Italian culture.

5072   *Peter's Stool*: The papal throne.

5128   *Ceres*: Roman goddess of the crops.

5136 *Theophrastus*: A philosopher from Lesbos (*c*. 372–*c*. 287 BC), student of Aristotle. Among his surviving works are two substantial treatises on plants.

5144 *a challenge*: It was customary in Renaissance masques for one figure to challenge another to a duel of words.

5156 *Flora*: Roman goddess of growth and flowering.

5158 *theorbos*: Archaic bass lutes. In the next stage direction the 'guitars' are presumably the flower girls' mandolins.

5215 *PUNCHINELLOS*: Clowns, a stock figure in *commedia dell'arte*. 'Punch' is an abbreviated English version of their name.

5237 *PARASITES*: From Greek παράσιτος, 'fellow-diner', a man who flatters the rich to get a meal. Again a popular comic figure.

5265 *OBJ!*: Oh Be Joyful!, a real ale.

5298 *Poets of the Night and the Graveyard*: Goethe here satirizes the 'Gothic' strain in contemporary Romanticism, which, though he had himself contributed to it with his poem 'Die Braut von Korinth' (The Bride of Corinth, 1797), he thought morbid, preferring a 'wholesome' classicism. In this stage direction, as also in those following 5198 and 5294, there is a suggestion of dialogue Goethe never got round to writing.

5299 *THE GRACES*: Greek goddesses, daughters of Zeus, they give charm and beauty to social intercourse. They are usually three in number, Thalia most often appearing in the place of Goethe's Hegemone.

5305 *THE FATES*: Greek goddesses, usually seen as old women, they oversee human destiny and are implacable. Traditionally, Clotho spins the thread of life, Lachesis measures it and Atropos cuts it. Clotho and Atropos swap roles for this masque.

5349 *the Furies*: Graeco-Roman goddesses of vengeance, their names are suggestive: Alecto (unceasing in anger), Megaera (jealous), Tisiphone (avenger of murder). They bring pestilence, war, famine and death. Here they work in relations between the sexes.

5378 *Asmodeus*: A Hebrew demon. In the apocryphal book of Tobit, in love with Sarah, Asmodeus kills her seven successive husbands on their wedding nights. Here and at 6961 he is a general stirrer-up of strife.

5395–5403 *A mountain shoulders forward … woman either side*: This allegorical group derives, in part at least, from Mantegna's *Triumphs of Caesar*.

5457 *ZOILO-THERSITES*: Here, in the traditional anti-masque, Mephistopheles enters as a composite epitome of scurrilous mockery. Zoilus was a Cynic philosopher of the fourth century BC,

famous for his rancorous criticism of great poets, Homer especially.
Thersites is an ugly and foul-mouthed mocker of heroics in the
Iliad II (also in Shakespeare's *Troilus and Cressida*).

5511   *splendid chariot*: After Mephistopheles (who metamorphoses
out of Zoilo-Thersites into an egg out of which spring an adder
and a bat) comes Faust himself as Plutus, god of wealth, riding on
a chariot driven by a boy who characterizes himself as Poetry and
as such prefigures Faust's child, Euphorion, in Act Three. Goethe
interpreted this episode to a bemused Eckermann in December
1829 (see The Writing of *Faust*).

5613   *wind-bride*: German *Windesbraut*, usually translated as whirl-
wind.

5623   *spirit of my spirit*: Perhaps echoes of Adam's view of Eve in
Genesis 2:23: 'This is now bone of my bones, and flesh of my
flesh.'

5627   *sprig of green*: The laurel.

5629   *Beloved Son*: See Mark 1:11, at Christ's baptism: 'Thou art my
beloved Son, in whom I am well pleased.' This allusion affirms the
kinship between Plutus/Faust and the Charioteer/Euphorion.

5632   *My little spray of flame alights*: Like Pentecost, Acts 2:3: 'And
there appeared unto them cloven tongues like as of fire, and it sat
upon each of them.' It should be noted that these biblical references
sort very uneasily with the context into which Goethe introduces
them.

5640   *Him up there*: Another metamorphosis of Mephistopheles, as
Goethe told Eckermann, this time into Avaritia (miserliness, greed),
the opposite of the prodigal Plutus and his charioteer Poetry. He
appears first as Skin-and-Bone then, at 5767, as Skinflint.

5666   *his dragons*: These allegorical creatures draw the chariot driven
by the Boy Charioteer and carrying Plutus and Skin-and-Bone/
Skinflint.

5698   *the closest kith and kin I have*: The uneasy relationship,
embodied in Goethe himself, of poetry and patronage.

5781   *I'll mould the gold there like wet clay*: Skinflint/Mephistopheles
kneads the gold into a phallus.

5804   *Great God Pan*: The Emperor in disguise (Plutus/Faust knows
him, 5807). In the role of the Greek god of wild nature, fertility,
sexual potency he enters with fauns and a satyr, gnomes, giants
and nymphs.

5819   *FAUNS*: After Faunus, a Roman god of nature. Fauns are a hybrid
of goat and youth; they have short horns, pointed ears and are
sexually voracious.

5829 *SATYR*: Greek counterparts of fauns, traditionally the companions of Dionysus, human and beastly, bald, bearded, ithyphallic.

5840 *GNOMES*: In European folklore, dwarfish, subterranean goblins or earth spirits. The sixteenth-century Swiss alchemist Paracelsus describes them as capable of moving through solid earth as fish move through water. Here, as miners, they resume the promise of treasure from the earth, knowing very well what bad things men will do with it.

5872 *NYMPHS*: Usually at risk from fauns, satyrs and Pan, the nymphs here surround Pan and praise him as the God of All Things, alluding to the eerie stillness when he sleeps at noon and to the panic – the all-pervading fear – he may cause.

5896 *honour be paid where honour is owed*: Another allusion to Romans 13:7. In the 'Walpurgis Night' scene in *Part I* (3964) honour was to be paid to Mother Baubo, the lewd nurse of Demeter; here it is to the Great God Pan. Would St Paul be amused?

5934–66 *And now a very great mishap . . . we can bear*: Goethe adapts an incident described in Johann Ludwig Gottfried's *Historische Chronica* (1642), an illustrated book he had read as a child. At a masked ball at the court of Charles VI of France in 1394, the king appeared with six of his lords as wild men and satyrs. His costume of hemp and pitch caught fire when the Duke of Orleans approached too close with a lighted torch. There followed a general conflagration which burned four lords to death and tipped the already unbalanced king into insanity.

A Pleasure-Garden

5990 *And I was Pluto*: Pluto (or Hades) is in Greek mythology god of the underworld. The Emperor, having looked into the well of treasure, significantly associates Plutus (wealth) with the demonic zone from which Mephistopheles and Faust will fetch him wealth.

6022 *Curious Nereids*: Sea-nymphs, daughters of the ancient sea god Nereus. Father and daughters figure prominently in Act Two.

6025–6 *Thetis . . . second Peleus*: Thetis, one of the Nereids, married the mortal Peleus. Their son was Achilles. Mephistopheles flatteringly suggests that she would be pleased to marry the Emperor now. Having imagined a watery extension of the Empire (after the fiery) he is moving into the air (Olympus, 6027) when the Emperor halts him, preferring to bide on earth as long as possible.

6031, 6033 *Arabian Nights . . . Scheherazade*: In the book of that name (also known as *The Thousand and One Nights*) Scheherazade keeps her husband from killing her, as he has done his previous wives, by telling him such beguiling stories that he always wants to hear more. The work, translated into French in 1704–17 and into German in 1823, was of considerable importance to Goethe in the composition of *Faust, Part II*. See David Luke, pp. xx, xxvi and xxix.

6055   *the fateful paper*: Faust and Mephistopheles have solved the Emperor's problems with paper money. This strategy had been developed in Europe during the eighteenth century. In France, the banker John Law set up a scheme whose collapse in 1720 had a profoundly unsettling effect at home and abroad. In Goethe's own lifetime, the *assignats* issued by the French during the Revolution and other notes by the Austrians around 1800 further debased the reputation of paper money.

6149   *BANNERET*: A knight ranking next to a baron and above other knights.

Dark Gallery

6185   *Paris and Helena*: See Introduction, pp. xlvi–xlvii, and further notes on Act Three.

6216   *They are the Mothers*: See Preface, p. xv and Introduction, p. xliv.

6229   *the Witch's Kitchen*: Referring to the scene in *Part I*, 2337 ff.

6253   *a certain cat*: See La Fontaine's fable (Book 9, 17) 'Le singe et le chat'.

Brightly Lit Rooms

6325   *cohobate*: In alchemy, to distil repeatedly. Goethe uses the word again in his last letter to Humboldt. See The Writing of *Faust*.

6357   *Comes from a pyre*: That is, from the burning alive of a witch or heretic.

Twilit Ceremonial Hall

6400   *The Devil prompts*: As at 4955 ff., Mephistopheles signals his involvement in the proceedings by acting as the Astrologer's prompter.

6405   *Atlas*: The Titan forced by Zeus to support the heavens on his shoulders.

6409   *That is no way to build*: Ancient Greek and European medieval
        architectures are here opposed. Goethe himself, when he encoun-
        tered the former in the early Doric temples at Paestum, was at first
        shocked by its massiveness. In the *Italian Journey*, describing that
        encounter, he uses terms very like those used by the architect here.

6420   *A thing impossible – fit to believe, therefore*: Mephistopheles
        (prompting the Astrologer) alludes to the theological opposition
        of faith and reason contained most famously in the statement
        'credo quia absurdum' (I believe because it is absurd).

6447   *triglyph*: A part of the frieze in buildings using the classical Doric
        order, they are projecting rectangular blocks, each ornamented
        with three vertical channels on the face.

6459   *shepherd boy*: Paris, though the son of King Priam of Troy, was
        herding sheep on Mount Ida when Aphrodite, Hera and Athene
        appeared to him and asked him to say which of them was the most
        beautiful.

6483   *had I tongues of fire*: Pentecost again, Acts 2:3–4, as at 5632 ff.

6496   *magic mirror*: In which Faust was shown a vision of female
        beauty in the 'Witch's Kitchen'. See *Part I*, 2429 ff.

6509   *Luna and Endymion*: Luna (or Selene) the moon goddess fell in
        love with the shepherd Endymion while he slept, and descended to
        him.

6530   *by the age of ten she was no good*: See also 7426 and 8850.
        Helen was abducted by Theseus at a very early age – thirteen, ten
        or seven, scholars cannot agree.

6537–8 *her effect on all ... was quite exceptional*: In the *Iliad*
        (III.154–8) this effect of Helen on the old men of Troy is described.

6563   *Explosion*: Two sources have been suggested for this violent
        finale. One is a poem by the sixteenth-century German poet Hans
        Sachs about the Emperor Maximilian, who conjures up the spirit
        of his dead wife. When he tries to embrace her she vanishes in
        noise, smoke and tumult. Secondly, a story by Anthony Hamilton
        (1646–1720), *Faustus, the Enchanter* (translated into German
        1778), in which Faust conjures up Helen, Cleopatra and the Fair
        Rosamund before Elizabeth I, but when the Queen tries to embrace
        Rosamund there is a thunderclap and Faust is knocked uncon-
        scious.

ACT TWO

A Cramped and High-Vaulted Gothic Room

6571   *Nothing is altered or depleted*: Much in the following lines recalls
       Faust's opening monologue (354 ff.), the wager (1530 ff.) and
       Mephistopheles advising the student (1868 ff.) in *Part I*.

6619   *He tugs the bell*: This apocalyptic ringing must be heard by
       the Famulus, the Baccalaureus and Wagner simultaneously, but it
       brings the first two on stage one after the other and Wagner hears
       it only at 6819, a moment before Mephistopheles enters. As David
       Luke notes (p. 273), the same strategy – a sequencing of simultan-
       eity – is employed in 'Classical Walpurgis Night' in the responses
       to the earthquake.

6634   *Your name is Nicodemus*: The Famulus in *Part I* was Wagner;
       he attended on Faust. Wagner, who in Faust's absence has grown
       in stature, now has a famulus of his own. The name Nicodemus
       associates him ironically with the Pharisee in John 3:1–3 who visits
       Jesus by night and is told that only the born-again can see the
       kingdom of God.

6635   *Oremus*: (Latin) let us pray.

6650   *He wields the keys like Saint Peter*: Alluding to Matthew 16:18–
       19, when Christ tells Peter he will found his church on him: 'And
       I will give unto thee the keys of the kingdom of heaven.'

6683–4 *I am the one ... satisfaction*: Here and at 6831 Mephisto-
       pheles indicates his involvement in the success of Wagner's 'great
       work'. And Homunculus himself seems to acknowledge it. See
       6885–6: 'And you arriving very *à propos,*/ My timely cousin,
       rogue, I thank you.'

6689   *BACCALAUREUS*: This is the freshman who came to Mephisto-
       pheles (taking him to be Faust) for advice in *Part I*, 1868. He is
       now a Bachelor of Arts. In him Goethe satirizes 'the kind of
       presumption that is especially characteristic of youth' (in conver-
       sation with Eckermann, 6 December 1829) and perhaps also,
       though he denied this, certain egocentric tendencies in the Idealist
       philosophy of Fichte and Schopenhauer ('*absolutely*', 6736, may
       allude to Fichte's *absolutes Ich*).

6733–4 *pigtail ... Swedishly cropped short*: The graduate student
       wears his own hair modishly short 'in Swedish style' and was never,
       Mephistopheles ironically supposes, one for the Rococo powdered
       wig and pigtail. But since Goethe's Duke Karl August wore his

hair 'Swedish' as early as 1780, the student is perhaps not so very avant garde after all.

A Laboratory

6835   *The making of a human*: Wagner, perhaps with a little help from Mephistopheles, imitates God's act of creation (Genesis 1:26–7).

6852   *luted*: Lute is the clay or cement used to seal a flask or retort.

6864   *a crystal form of humankind*: Mephistopheles might mean Lot's wife, who was turned into a pillar of salt (Genesis 19:26).

6879   HOMUNCULUS *[in the phial, to* WAGNER*]*: Engendered in the phial, Homunculus will remain in it, shining and resounding, until he smashes himself against Galatea's shell (8473).

6903   *My word!*: Homunculus can see, and he describes, what Faust is dreaming. The images derive from Correggio's *Leda and the Swan*, of which Goethe had an engraving in his collection of works of art.

6941   *Classical Walpurgis Night*: Goethe's invention, as a counterpart to the northern Walpurgis Night (30 April–1 May) celebrated in *Part I*.

6952   *Peneus*: A river in Thessaly, northern Greece, rising in the Pindus Mountains, flowing through the Vale of Tempe between Mount Olympus and Ossa, entering the Aegean on the north-east coast.

6955   *Pharsalus*: Town on the Apidanus in Thessaly, near which on 9 August 48 BC Julius Caesar defeated his chief rival Pompey, effectively ending the Roman Republic and ushering in the Empire.

6970   *I know a little Brocken trick or two*: The Brocken is the mountain in the Harz where the northern Walpurgis Night is celebrated and where Mephistopheles feels at home.

6977   *the witches of Thessaly*: Thessaly was renowned for its witches. The Latin poet Lucan (AD 39–65) speaks of them in Book VI, and describes the Battle of Pharsalus in Book VII, of his *Pharsalia*. Apuleius (second century AD) has much to say about the power and the lasciviousness of Thessalian witches in the first three books of *The Golden Ass*.

6985   *The rag has carried you before*: A cloak served Faust and Mephistopheles for their first flight together (2065). In fact, with Homunculus, they will fly to Greece in what seems to be a hot-air balloon (7035). Faust returns in a cloud, Mephistopheles in or on a seven-league boot (10039 ff. and 10067). They left Auerbach's Cellar on a barrel (*Part I*, 2330).

7002   *Ad spectatores*: Goethe's own stage direction; Latin, meaning 'To the audience'.

Classical Walpurgis Night
Pharsalian Fields

7005 *ERICHTHO*: The notably abominable witch whom Pompey's son Sextus consults before the Battle of Pharsalus. Lucan describes her in Book VI. She has a horror of daylight. Here she speaks in classical trimeters, six-feet unrhyming iambic lines. Helen takes up the measure again when she opens Act Three. *On this night's grisly festival*: On the anniversary of the battle, 9 August.

7022 *Pompey*: Gnaeus Pompeius Magnus (106–48 BC), Roman general. After his defeat by Caesar at Pharsalus he fled to Egypt but was stabbed to death as he landed.

7023 *Caesar*: Gaius Julius Caesar (100–44 BC), Roman general whose many victories brought him autocratic power as consul and dictator. He was assassinated in the conspiracy led by Brutus and Cassius.

7077 *Antaeus*: A giant, the son of Poseidon, god of the sea, and Gaia, goddess of the earth, his strength was renewed every time he touched the earth. Heracles defeated him by holding him aloft and cracking his ribs.

On the Upper Peneus

7092–7103 *And you wise grey ones ... Luck lets us have and hold*: There is here a good deal of punning, wordplay and false etymology, impossible to translate closely. Mephistopheles addresses the Gryphons (in German, *Greifen*) as *kluge Greise*, which means 'wise old ones'. They object to being called old. They acknowledge in their name a (false) etymological connection with the German words *grau*, *grämlich*, *griesgram*, *greulich*, *Gräber*, *grimmig* (my line 7096, not in that order), but add that even if that is so (*stimmig*) it annoys them (*verstimmen uns*). Laboriously, Mephistopheles says that at least they like the first four letters of their name *Greifen*, which they concede because that word means not only 'gryphon' but also 'to grab' or 'to grip' (they are notable grabbers of, especially, gold). Gryphons have the body of a lion and the head and wings of an eagle.

7106 *Arimaspians*: According to Herodotus (III.116), they were a one-eyed Scythian tribe who sought to steal the Gryphons' gold.

7114 *SPHINX*: First in Egyptian mythology, a creature having the winged body of a lion and a human, usually female, head. Famous for riddling, see 7132–7.

7118 *Are any British here?*: Britons predominated among the early modern explorers of the Ancient World.

7123   *Old Iniquity*: A name – written so in Goethe's text – for the Devil in the late medieval English morality plays.

7134–7   *The good man needs me ... whatever we do*: The answer to the riddle is the Devil himself.

7151   SIRENS: Half woman, half bird, their usual habitat is rocky islands where by their singing they cause the wreck of ships.

7185   *Oedipus stood confronting such as these*: By answering the riddle posed by the Sphinx at Thebes, Oedipus destroyed her and won Jocasta (his own mother) as a prize.

7186   *These sang to the roped and writhing Ulysses*: Passing their island, Ulysses (Odysseus) had himself bound to the mast so that he could listen to the Sirens' song and not be lost to it. See the *Odyssey* XII.39–54 and 154–200.

7197–8   *We do not reach ... very last of us*: The Sphinxes belong in pre-Hellenic mythology (the Sphinx of Thebes is an isolated survival), but there is no story that Heracles killed the last of them.

7199   *Chiron*: A centaur, a wise healer and the educator of many heroes. See 7337 ff.

7219   *Alcides*: Heracles, grandson of Alcaeus.

7220   *Stymphalides*: Monstrous birds with beaks, claws and wings of bronze. They fired off feathers like arrows and excreted poison. Their home was the Stymphalian Marsh in Arcadia until Heracles, as his Sixth Labour, killed a good number of them and drove the rest away.

7227   *They are the heads of the Lernean worm*: This was the many-headed Hydra, killed by Heracles as the second of his Labours. It lived in a marsh near Argos and its heads, as he severed them, multiplied.

7235   *Lamiae*: Sexually voracious spirits embodying themselves as young women. Keats wrote of one such in his narrative poem 'Lamia'.

On the Lower Peneus

7249   PENEUS: He speaks as the river god with his tributaries and nymphs around him.

7294   *high queen*: Leda, Queen of Sparta. Zeus approached her in the form of a swan. She gave birth to Helen and Castor and Pollux. In this passage Faust recalls his dream put into words by Homunculus (6903 ff.).

7329   *Philyra's celebrated son*: Chiron was the son of Cronus and Philyra.

7338   *the Argonauts*: Fifty heroes, led by Jason, who sailed in the *Argo* to find the Golden Fleece.

7341–2   *Athene . . . for her mentoring*: Daughter of Zeus, she appeared to Telemachus in the form of Mentor, his tutor, to advise him how to find his father, Odysseus. See the *Odyssey* II and III.

7370   *The Dioscuri*: Castor and Pollux, twin brothers of Helen.

7371   *the Boreades*: Calais and Zetes, twin sons of Oreithyia and Boreas, the North Wind. As they grew to manhood, they sprouted wings.

7373   *Jason*: Leader of the Argonauts. His uncle Pelias deprived him of the kingdom of Iolcus but undertook to restore it to him if he would fetch the Golden Fleece from Colchis. He brought Medea, daughter of the King of Colchis, back with him also, unhappily for both of them.

7375   *Orpheus*: Son of the Thracian king Oeagrus and the Muse Calliope, his poetry and singing had a legendary power. He could charm the animals, the trees, even the rocks. When his wife, Eurydice, died of a snake bite, he went down to Hades after her and she was allowed to follow him up into the world again – on condition that he would not look back. He did look back, and lost her.

7377   *Lynceus*: A lynx-eyed hero from Messene. He could see in the dark and divine the whereabouts of buried treasure. He was lookout man for the Argonauts. Goethe gives his name to the watchman in Act Three and Act Five.

7381   *Hercules*: Or Heracles, son of Alcmene and Zeus (who seduced her in the form of her husband Amphitryon). Hercules' powers were colossal. He needed them in his Twelve Labours.

7383   *Phoebus Apollo*: Son of Zeus and Leto, the god of light and poetry.

7384   *Ares*: God of war. *Hermes*: Son of Zeus and Maia, the messenger god, the conductor of souls into the underworld, he has a reputation for cleverness, trickery and thieving.

7389   *his older cousin*: Eurystheus, whom Goethe calls – incorrectly – Heracles' older brother. They were cousins, both of the House of Perseus, and by the intervention of Hera Heracles was born after Eurystheus and obliged to serve him.

7390   *loveliest of women*: For three years Heracles was the slave of Omphale, Queen of Lydia.

7391   *Gaia*: The earth herself. *Hebe*: Daughter of Zeus and Hera, she serves the gods their nectar on Olympus and was given to Heracles as his wife when he became one of them.

7415–26   *The Dioscuri . . . I see you are deceived*: Theseus and his

friend Peirithous abducted Helen, aged only ten or less, from the
Temple of Artemis in Sparta, and drew lots for who should have
her. She fell to Theseus, who hid her at Aphidnae in Attica. Some
time later, when Peirithous and Theseus on a further adventure
were confined in Tartarus, the Dioscuri, Helen's brothers, rescued
her. Chiron's part in this is Goethe's invention.

7419   *Eleusis*: West of Athens and famous for the Mysteries. It was
marshy still in Roman times.

7435   *Achilles came to her at Pherae*: After his death Achilles was
allowed to live with the shade of Helen (whom he already loved)
on the island of Leuce, in the Black Sea. According to one tradition,
they had a winged son called Euphorion. Faust locates their union
at Pherae, in Thessaly, so associating this story with another: that
of Admetus whose wife, Alcestis, agreeing to die in place of him,
was fetched back from the underworld by Heracles.

7450   *daughter of Asclepius*: Manto, a prophetess, was actually the
daughter of the seer Tiresias. Goethe makes her the child of
Asclepius, god of medicine, to substantiate her function as a healer.

7455   *Sibyls' guild*: The Sibyls were a varying number (usually nine or
ten) of women of the Ancient World possessing powers of prophecy
and divination.

7466   *Here Greek and Roman power fought it out*: Chiron has brought
Faust to the battlefield of Pydna where in 168 BC the Roman
consul Aemilius Paullus defeated King Perseus of Macedonia and
thereby subjugated the rest of the empire of Alexander the Great
to the Roman Republic. But Pydna is well to the north of Olympus;
Goethe mislocates it.

7490   *Persephone*: Daughter of the earth goddess Demeter, she was
carried off by Hades and obliged to spend half of the year in the
underworld with him.

7493   *I smuggled Orpheus in here*: Goethe invents for Manto a part in
Orpheus' unsuccessful attempt to bring his wife, Eurydice, back
from the dead. Faust descends here, as he did to the Mothers in
Act One, and will not surface in the play again until he receives
and marries Helen in Act Three.

On the Upper Peneus, as before

7519   SEISMOS: The word in Greek means earthquake. It was one of
the epithets of Poseidon, who, as god of the sea, also caused such
movements. Goethe here makes Seismos a force or deity in his own
right, the volcanic principle.

7530   *Rises now a hump, a dome*: Seismos has heaved up an entire new mountain. Such appearances (and also disappearances) are common enough in volcanic zones. Near Naples, in the so-called Campi Phlegraei (visited by Goethe in 1787), the Monte Nuovo was thrown up in 1538; and a new island, Great Kaimeni, surfaced off Thera in 1712.

7533-4   *caused Delos to appear . . . a woman giving birth*: Leto, pregnant by Zeus and in flight from his jealous wife Hera, gave birth to Apollo and Artemis on the island of Delos. The name 'Delos' derives from the Greek word meaning 'to show', 'to make manifest'. And doubtless it was revealed out of the sea by volcanic eruption; but another story is that Delos was a drifting island until Poseidon transfixed it with his trident, as a safe haven for Leto.

7545   *caryatid*: A female figure used as a supporting column in classical architecture.

7558-61   *In Night and Chaos . . . Ossa and Pelion*: Seismos claims to be one of the Titans, descendants of Night and Chaos, who in their struggle against the new gods piled Ossa on Pelion, to assault Olympus.

7564-7   *on Parnassus' top . . . Apollo has his charmed existence there*: Parnassus, above Delphi, has twin peaks. The whole mountain is sacred to Apollo, god of poetry, and to the Nine Muses.

7568-9   *And it was me . . . in the upper air*: So Olympus, Zeus' throne, is another of Seismos' works.

7601   *gangue*: 'The earthy or stony matter in a mineral deposit; the matrix in which an ore is found' (*Oxford English Dictionary*, henceforth OED).

7606   PYGMIES: The battle of the Pygmies with the cranes (7884-99) has a source in the extended simile employed by Homer in the *Iliad* III.3-8.

7622   DACTYLS: From a Greek word meaning 'fingers'. In ancient myth they are ten small and very dexterous creatures, five male, five female. Here, with the ants (Emmets), they are slave-labourers for the Pygmies.

7660   CRANES OF IBYCUS: Ibycus, a lyric poet of *c*. the sixth century BC, was murdered by robbers, who were then denounced by cranes, birds sacred to Apollo, and brought to justice. Schiller wrote a ballad on the subject, 'Die Kraniche des Ibykus', in 1797. Cranes have a similar function in Aeschylus' *Eumenides*. Here they call on more of their kind to avenge the Pygmies' slaughter of the herons. This duly happens at 7884 ff.

7678-82   *Blocksberg . . . Frau Ilse . . . Heinrich . . . Snorers . . . Elend*: Features of the Blocksberg (the Brocken) in the Harz, Mephisto's

home ground. See 'Walpurgis Night' in *Part I*, the setting, and the
notes to 3879–80 and 3968. The word 'Elend', the name of a
village there, means 'misery'.

7732 *EMPUSA*: The Empusae are the demon-daughters of Hecate.
They have the haunches of an ass and, metamorphosing into attractive young women, seduce men and suck the life out of them.
The Empusa here appears with an ass's head and feet to match
Mephisto's hoof.

7777 *thyrsus*: 'A staff or spear tipped with an ornament like a pine-cone, and sometimes wreathed with ivy or vine branches; borne
by Dionysus (Bacchus) and his votaries' (*OED*).

7797 *I snatch at pretty masks*: Mephistopheles has no more luck with
the Lamiae than he does in Act Five with the angel boys.

7811 *OREAD*: A mountain nymph; here, rather, the voice of the mountain itself.

7814 *The farthest flung of Pindus' limbs*: The Pindus mountains
border Thessaly on the west. Mephistopheles seems to have wandered as far as their foothills.

7816 *Pompey*: See 6955 and 7020–24 and notes. After the Battle of
Pharsalus Pompey fled, though not, according to Plutarch, over
Pindus. He went north to the sea via Larissa and through the Vale
of Tempe.

7836 *I'm shadowing a philosophical pair*: They are Anaxagoras and
Thales, two pre-Socratic philosophers. Anaxagoras (*c.* 500–430 BC), an Athenian, taught that the heavenly bodies were not
gods but masses of burning stone; Thales of Miletus (*c.* 620–546)
taught that the material world and life originated in water. Goethe
presents in them a contemporary cosmological debate, between
the Vulcanists and the Neptunists. Himself a confirmed Neptunist,
in Naples in 1787 he met a very eminent Vulcanist, Sir William
Hamilton. See Introduction, p. xxxv.

7865–6 *Fierce Plutonic fire ... vast explosive power*: The fire wells
up from under the earth, zone of the god Pluto (see 5990). Aeolus
was god of the winds and kept them pent up in a cave.

7873 *Myrmidons*: Particularly, the tribe Achilles led from Thessaly to
the siege of Troy. But their name was derived (and supported with
myths) from a word meaning 'ants', and it is in the sense of 'busy
little creatures' that Anaxagoras uses it here.

7905 *Diana, Luna, Hecate*: Diana (Greek Artemis), sister of Apollo,
god of the sun, is closely associated with the moon, chastity and
hunting. Luna is the moon goddess (who loved and came down
to the shepherd Endymion) and the moon herself ('moon' is a

masculine noun in German, 'Luna' is a way of addressing her
as female). Hecate is a very ancient goddess who inhabits the
underworld and is in charge of witches (as in *Macbeth*, III.5 and
IV.1). So Anaxagoras, invoking the moon as a trinity, suggests
many of her aspects.

7920–23 *So is it true . . . blight and bane?*: Lucan describes this power
of the Thessalian witches over the moon in his *Pharsalia* VI.

7959 DRYAD: A tree nymph.

7967 *The Phorcides*: Also known as the Graeae, the three daughters
of the ancient sea god Phorcys, they are sisters of the three Gorgons
and live out of sight of the moon and the sun. Haggish in appear-
ance, they have only one eye and one tooth between them.

7982 PHORCYAS: One of the Phorcides. Conflated with Mephisto-
pheles – he borrows her appearance at 8026 – she has an important
part in Act Three.

7989 *Ops and Rhea*: In Greek mythology, Rhea is the wife of Cronus;
the equivalent Roman pair are Ops and Saturn. They are the older
generation of goddesses, their son being Zeus/Jupiter.

7991 *The Fates, your sisters, sisters of Chaos*: On the Fates see 5305
and note. They were the granddaughters of Chaos, from whom all
the generations sprang. Mephistopheles gives the Phorcides a very
ancient lineage, but they don't in fact go quite so far back. Their
father Phorcys was a great-grandson of Chaos.

7999 *Juno, Pallas, Venus*: Or Hera, Athene (Minerva), Aphrodite.
They are the recent Olympian generation of goddesses.

8027–8 *beloved Son of Chaos . . . daughters of Chaos*: At 7987,
Mephistopheles claimed to be a distant relative of the Phorcides.
The brother-and-sister kinship here is symbolic, not mythological.
The title 'beloved Son' makes Mephistopheles sound like Christ
(or God like Chaos). Faust called him 'strange son of chaos' at
their first meeting (*Part I*, 1383).

Rocky Coves on the Aegean Sea

8044 NEREIDS AND TRITONS: The Nereids are the fifty daughters of
the ancient sea god Nereus (see 8082) and the nymph Doris. Triton
began as an individual son of Poseidon and the nereid Amphitrite.
He became pluralized as creatures human above the waist and fish
below.

8071 *Samothrace*: An island in the north-east Aegean on which were
worshipped the so-called Great Gods, pre-Hellenic deities, among
whom were the Cabiri.

8074 *Cabiri*: Mysterious, probably Phrygian, deities who promoted fertility and were kind to sailors. Their number varies. Sometimes they were worshipped as earthenware pots (see 8219) with human heads. They were much discussed in Goethe's day – by, for example, the classical scholar G. F. Creuzer (1771–1858) and the Idealist philosopher F. W. J. von Schelling (1775–1854). For the purposes of *Faust*, Goethe seems to have been attracted by their association with such other figures as the Dioscuri, the Dactyls and the Telchines (see 7370, 7622, 8274 and notes); also by something protean and unfinished in their nature and appearances. See also 8172–8220.

8110   *How I warned Paris*: According to Horace, *Odes* I.15, Nereus told Paris in detail what would happen as a consequence of his abducting Helen from Menelaus.

8119   *Ilium*: Troy.

8121   *Pindus*: See 7814 and note. The birds of Pindus might have fed on the dead at Pharsalus or Pydna, but scarcely on the 'vast cadaver' of Troy on the other side of the Aegean. Perhaps Goethe or Nereus meant the near mountains to stand for any.

8122   *Likewise Odysseus*: It seems to be Goethe's invention that Nereus also advised Odysseus.

8123   *Circe's wiles and the Cyclopean hell*: Odysseus' adventures with the enchantress Circe and with the one-eyed, man-eating Cyclops are related in the *Odyssey* X and IX respectively.

8126–7   *Until ... there was hospitality*: In the *Odyssey* V the ship-wrecked Odysseus washes up on Scheria, the island of the hospitable King Alcinous.

8144–9   *riding Venus' shell ... chariot-throne*: The fond father Nereus makes up a myth of his own: his favourite daughter Galatea has assumed the role of Aphrodite (Venus), that goddess herself having withdrawn. Paphos is the place on Cyprus where Aphrodite (sometimes called Cypris for that reason) came ashore, riding a shell, after her birth in the foam. The statue that Pygmalion (its sculptor) fell in love with was given the name Galatea when Aphrodite, pitying him and recognizing herself in the work, brought it to life.

8152   *wondrous Proteus*: Another Old Man of the Sea, a son of Poseidon, he had the gift of prophecy but disliked being asked to prophesy or give advice. He would flee all enquirers by rapidly changing his shape, but if caught and held firmly then he would resume his true shape and speak.

8170   *The giant shell of Chelone*: Chelone was a nymph transformed into a tortoise by Hermes. Here the sense is that the Nereids and Tritons come bearing the Cabiri on a giant tortoise shell.

8215–16 *They won the Golden Fleece ... Cabiri*: Fetching the Cabiri
from Samothrace, say the Sirens, is a greater feat even than the
Argonauts' fetching the Golden Fleece from Colchis.

8275 *TELCHINES OF RHODES ... hippocamps*: The Telchines (there
were nine of them) originated on the island of Rhodes. They had
flippers for hands and the heads of dogs. They were notably good
metal-workers – they made Poseidon's trident, for example – and
were the first to carve images of the gods. A hippocamp is a
seahorse. It has two fore-feet and a body ending in a dolphin's or
fish's tail.

8285 *Helios*: The sun personified as a god.

8289–90 *Sweet goddess aloft ... Praising your brother*: The Telchines
here address Artemis (as goddess of the moon) in their praise of
her brother Apollo (as god of the sun), to whom the island of
Rhodes was sacred.

8300 *Youthful, colossal ... benign*: Referring to the Colossus of
Rhodes, one of the Seven Wonders of the Ancient World, a vast
bronze statue of the sun god, erected 292–280 BC, which, as
Proteus points out (8310–12), was toppled by an earthquake (in
224 BC) and little by little pillaged and melted down.

8347–8 *this lunar/ Ring*: The ring – sometimes called the corona –
seen round the moon in certain atmospheric conditions.

8359 *PSYLLI AND MARSI*: Two ancient tribes, the first from North
Africa, the second from the Apennines. But the elder Pliny, in his
Natural History XXVIII, says they both originated in Cyprus,
which perhaps encouraged Goethe to make them the guardians of
Cyprian Aphrodite's chariot.

8371–2 *Neither eagle nor ... crescent moon*: The worship of Aphro-
dite/Galatea has continued in Cyprus as invaders have come and
gone. The eagle may stand for both Rome and Byzantium; the
winged lion (of St Mark) is Venice; the cross is the nations of
Christian Europe; the crescent is Muslim Turkey.

8385 *Dorides*: The daughters of Nereus and Doris, usually synony-
mous with the Nereids but here perhaps to be thought of as their
sisters.

8424 *GALATEA approaches, riding on the scallop shell*: Goethe owned
an engraving of Raphael's fresco *The Triumph of Galatea* (1512),
in which she, nymph or goddess, rides the shell drawn by dolphins
and accompanied by Tritons and Cupids.

8479 *Eros is sovereign!*: This triumph of Eros prefigures much in the
finale of Act Five.

ACT THREE

Outside the Palace of Menelaus in Sparta

8488   *Greatly admired and censured greatly Helena*: Here Goethe
resumes the classical trimeters of lines 7005 ff. (see note). Later there
will be other such metrical imitations and adaptations. Altogether,
this opening scene is classical in tone. Many allusions to classical
tragedy connect it with the Ancient Greek tradition. Euripides, for
example, has a similar chorus of women captured by the Greeks at
the fall of Troy in his *Hecuba* and *The Trojan Women*.

8492   *Euros*: The east wind.

8493   *Phrygia*: Troy was in western Phrygia, on the Hellespont.

8496   *Tyndareus*: The husband of Helen's mother, Leda, although
Helen's father was very likely Zeus.

8497   *Homecoming ... Pallas Athene*: This suggests Tyndareus
returned from Athens, whose acropolis was Athene's principal
place of worship.

8499–5000   *Clytemnestra ... Castor and Pollux*: Leda had four chil-
dren: these three and Helen. But who was whose father – Tyndareus
or Zeus – is a vexed question.

8505   *Menelaus*: Helen was courted by all the princes of Greece. She,
or Tyndareus, chose Menelaus, who became King of Sparta after
the latter's death.

8511–12   *temple of Cythera ... the Phrygian*: In one version of the
story Helen was seized by the Phrygian Paris on Cythera, Aphro-
dite's island. But usually she is said to have eloped with him from
Sparta, of her own free will, when he came visiting. In the famous
beauty competition on Mount Ida, Aphrodite had induced Paris
to prefer her to Hera and Athene, his reward being Helen,
Menelaus' wife.

8516   *O Lady ...*: For the speeches of the Chorus Goethe adapts the
distinctive metres and patterns employed in such passages by the
classical tragedians.

8524   *Enough. With my husband I am shipped home here ...*: Much
in this long speech of Helen's (and in the Chorus's interpolations)
recalls Euripides' *Hecuba* and *The Trojan Women*.

8539   *Eurotas*: Sparta's river, flowing into the Gulf of Laconia, where
Menelaus and Helen land on their return from Troy. In the myth
Helen was conceived and born by the Eurotas. See 6903 ff. and
7294 ff. and notes.

8547   *Lacedaemon*: A son of Zeus, he founded Sparta, his name becoming synonymous with the place itself.

8649–52   *But horror that rises . . . hero's heart*: Recalling a passage in Aeschylus' *Eumenides*. A priestess there enters the temple and at once returns to tell what she has seen: the Furies sleeping around the altar.

8653   *Stygians*: Gods of the underworld, named after the Styx, which is one of the four rivers there.

8685   *thalamos*: The inner or secret room of the house, the women's quarters, or here most likely the marriage bedroom.

8697–8721   *Much I have lived through . . . such confusion*: There are such descriptions of the fall of Troy at the conclusion of *The Trojan Women* and, fuller, in Virgil's *Aeneid* II.

8735   *Graeae*: See 7967 and note.

8755–6   *That Shame and Beauty . . . green paths*: See Ovid, *Epistulae* XVI.288, and Juvenal, *Satires* X.297–8, for a similar saying.

8762   *Orcus*: The underworld.

8772   *Maenad-wild*: The Maenads were the ecstatically wild and violent female followers of Dionysus. They tore Orpheus and King Pentheus to pieces, for example.

8810–25   *How ugly . . . solved in one*: The Chorus and Phorcyas trade insults in one-liners, the stichomythia (line-speech) of classical drama.

8812   *Father Erebus . . . Mother Night*: Two of the primal deities, born of Chaos. Erebus means 'darkness'.

8813   *Scylla*: A female monster with six heads. She lived in a sea-cave opposite the maelstrom Charybdis. Odysseus lost six of his men to her (*Odyssey* XII). Since she was a daughter of Phorcys, she is actually a sibling of Phorcyas.

8817   *Tiresias*: The blind seer of Thebes whom Oedipus has to deal with in Sophocles' *Oedipus* and *Antigone*. He spent seven years of his very long life as a woman.

8818   *Orion's wet nurse*: Orion, a hunter, son of Poseidon, was killed by Artemis and set among the stars as a constellation. But the point of the reference here is to insult Phorcyas by claiming she is five generations older than the mythically ancient Orion.

8819   *The Harpies*: Winged female creatures, loathsome in appearance and in deed. They fall on human food, gobble it, vomit it, befoul it.

8840   *the woman who wasted cities*: 'Waster of cities' is a typically Homeric epithet, applied to Ares, Odysseus, Heracles, Achilles . . . Here Helen applies it to herself, as 'cause' of the Trojan War and the sacking of the city. See W. B. Yeats, 'No Second Troy': 'Was there another Troy for her to burn?'

8848–51 *Theseus ... Aphidnus*: See 7415–26 and note. Aphidnus was Theseus' friend at whose 'castle' Helen had been left.

8855 *Patroclus*: Achilles' comrade, killed by Hector. The *Iliad* XXII recounts Achilles' terrible revenge.

8859 *Hermione*: Helen abandoned her, aged nine, eloping with Paris, the 'pretty guest' (8861).

8872 *there were two images of you*: Some say that the real Helen was spirited away to Egypt by Hermes at Zeus' command. The Helen Paris brought back to Troy, and who spent the war there, was a phantom fashioned from clouds by Hera (or possibly Proteus).

8876–8 *Then people say ... Loving you earlier*: See 7435 and note.

8879 *I as ... the idol*: The same word (*Idol* in German) is used of the vision of Gretchen in the 'Walpurgis Night' scene in *Part I* (4190).

8889–90 *the three-/ Headed dog's wide mouths*: This is Cerberus, who guards the entrance to the underworld.

8896 *Lethe*: A river in the underworld. Whoever drinks from it, forgets.

8909–29 Here (and in 8957–61, 8966–70, 9067–70, 9122–6) Goethe, imitating Euripides, writes trochaic tetrameters.

8928–9 *You however ... dance and kick*: Phorcyas promises them the death the servant girls suffered when Odysseus came home and exacted revenge. See the *Odyssey* XXII.462–73.

8957 *Parcae ... Sibyls*: The Parcae are the Fates, see 5305 and note. For Sibyls, see 7455 and note.

8996 *Taygetus*: The high mountain range running north–south to the west of Sparta.

9000 *Cimmerian night*: The Cimmerians, according to Homer (*Odyssey* XI.14–19), lived at the limits of the known world, close to an entrance into Hades, in cloud and fog, never seeing the sun. Herodotus knew of Cimmerians living north of the Caucasus. On Goethe's location for the meeting of Helen and Faust, see Introduction, p. xxxiii.

9020 *Cyclopean*: The Cyclopes were one-eyed giants with whom Odysseus had to contend (see the *Odyssey* IX). 'Cyclopean' suggests work done by fabulous builders of immense strength and no taste. It is used as a technical term to describe the massive polygonal walling at, for example, Tiryns or Mycenae, very clever and pleasing work in fact. The medieval castle Phorcyas describes might be one built by the Crusaders at Mistra, just north of ancient Sparta. See Introduction, p. xxxiii.

9030   *Ajax*: One of the Greeks at Troy. He carried a 'sevenfold shield', with a device of snakes and a panther.

9032   *The Seven against Thebes*: The seven fighters whom Polynices brought with him to attack Thebes, his native city. In Aeschylus' play of that name a messenger describes the devices on each of their shields.

9054–8   *Have you forgotten how . . . nose and more*: Menelaus' mutilation of Deiphobus is described in Virgil's *Aeneid* VI.494 ff.

9087   *treacherous slyness*: The stratagem of the Trojan Horse.

9115   *Hermes*: This is Hermes Psychopompus ('conductor of souls'), who with his staff marshals the dead into the underworld.

The Inner Courtyard of a Castle

9135   *Pythonissa*: Strictly, a title of the priestess at Delphi (after the serpent Python killed there by Apollo). More generally, as here, addressing Phorcyas–Mephisto, any wise woman and soothsayer.

9164   *was stopped with ash*: Rather as though they had bitten into Apples of Sodom (which grew where Sodom and Gomorrah were destroyed). Milton (*Paradise Lost*, X.564–6) describes the experience thus: 'they fondly thinking to allay/ Their appetite with gust, instead of fruit/ Chewed bitter ashes'.

9192   *There should be greeting with all ceremony*: Faust, speaking in blank verse (the five-feet iambic pentameter of Shakespeare and of classical German drama), effects the move from ancient to modern forms. Helen replies (9213) in the same verse, so at once accommodating herself to him.

9218   LYNCEUS, THE WATCHER IN THE TOWER: See 7377 and note. He speaks in rhyming stanzas, employing an imagery reminiscent of German *Minnesang* (courtly love poetry) and European Petrarchism.

9254–5   *My one self . . . my doubled . . . Triple and fourfold*: Helen in her own person; doubled as a phantom in Troy and Egypt; triple by her appearance in such classical plays as Euripides' *Helena*; and now, fourth appearance, in a classical-romantic play with Faust.

9281   *We came out of the East*: Lynceus numbers himself among the many thousands of barbarians invading the Graeco-Roman zone during the great period of the migration of peoples (*c.* AD 300–700) and thereafter. See also Faust's speech at 9446 ff.

9369   *It seemed that one sound settled with another*: Helen is intrigued and pleased by Lynceus' rhyming speech. Faust then inducts her into the art of it. There is a good deal of this mingling of the arts of poetry and love in the poems Goethe addressed to Marianne von Willemer (and in her responses) in his *West-Eastern Divan*, the loveliest being 'Behramgur, sagt man, hat den Reim erfunden' (They say that Bahram Gur invented rhyme) in which the invention of rhyming by two lovers is celebrated.

9454–5 *Pylos ... Nestor*: Nestor, an old and garrulous Greek at Troy (see the *Iliad* II.336 ff., for example), was King of Pylos, on the west coast of the Peloponnese.

9466–81 *We charge you, Germans ... in the sun*: With small historical basis Faust, moving anticlockwise round the Peloponnese, assigns particular areas to particular northern tribes: Corinth to the Germans (the name might include any of the Germanic tribes described by Tacitus); Achaia (behind Patras) to the Goths; Elis (west coast) to the Franks; Messenia (extreme south-west) to the Saxons; Argolis (north-east, below Corinth) to the Normans. For Helen and himself he reserves the central segment, Sparta, to which, in his next speech (beginning 9506), he annexes its northern neighbour, Arcadia.

9512–13 *The almost-island ... mountain-tree*: Faust imagines the mountains of Europe as a vast tree, one of whose branches reaches down into the Peloponnese – which is an island attached to the mainland at the isthmus of Corinth (only since 1893 cut by the canal).

9526–73 *And though upon the mountains' back ... Arcadian liberty*: Faust evokes the landscape and blessings of mythical Arcadia, the real site of which borders Sparta.

9558 *So like the shepherds did Apollo appear*: Apollo, as punishment for killing the Cyclopes, served a year in the sheepfolds of King Admetus.

9574 *The scene changes utterly*: Some editors start a new scene here, lasting until the end of Act Three, and called either 'Arcadia' or 'Shady Grove'.

9578 *you, the bearded*: Phorcyas addresses the audience, who in Ancient Greek times would all have been men.

9611 *Antaeus*: See 7077 and note. Faust's advice to his ebullient son, Euphorion, recalls his own association of himself with Antaeus when he first set foot on Greek soil (7077).

9616 *astounding reappearance*: Euphorion reappears in the costume of the Spirit of Poetry.

9630 *Crete-begotten*: Phorcyas–Mephistopheles invented this biography at 8864–5.

9633   *Ionia*: Ancient Greece in Asia Minor, birthplace of many poets (among them, probably, Homer) and location of many myths.

9644   *son of Maia*: This is the god Hermes, born in Arcadia, full of tricks and the inventor of the lyre.

9672   *Hephaestus*: The lame god of fire and of smithying.

9678   *cestus*: A belt or girdle. The cestus of Cypris (Aphrodite) has particular power.

9679–9906   The text of this whole section, until the death of Euphorion, is best understood as a libretto, the music of which was never written. The mode is largely burlesque and the tone frivolous or ironic – difficult, like much else in *Faust, Part II*, to integrate into any unity of purpose.

9810   *Snatch for what has disappeared*: Like Mephistopheles, disappointed by the Lamiae and, in Act Five, by the pretty angel boys.

9824   *At the heart of Pelops' land*: In the centre of the Peloponnese – of which Pelops, a son of Tantalus, was the legendary ruler.

9901   *Icarus! Icarus!*: Icarus flew too close to the sun on wings made for him by his craftsman father, Daedalus. When the wax in them melted, he fell to his death.

9902   *We seem to recognize in him a well-known figure*: The figure is Byron, who died in the Greek War of Independence in 1824. On Goethe and Byron, see Introduction, p. xxxiv. Byron is the subject of the threnody (lament) sung by the Chorus at 9907–38.

9939   *I too confirm, alas, what is always said*: Signalling that the episode with Faust is over, Helen and after her the Chorus revert to classical verse-forms.

9944   *Persephoneia*: Another name for Persephone, forced consort of Hades, god of the underworld.

9955   *exuviae*: Goethe uses this Latin word, which means the 'cast skins, shells, or coverings of animals; any parts of animals which are shed or cast off' (*OED*).

9975–80   *meadows of asphodel . . . Displeasing, ghostly*: All details to be found in Homer's *Odyssey*: the asphodels at XI.539; willows and poplars in Persephone's grove at X.510; the bat-like twittering and squeaking of the dead at XXIV.6.

9992 ff.   They become Dryads, nymphs of the trees.

9999 ff.   They become echoes; or perhaps Oreads, nymphs of the rocks and mountains.

10005 ff.   They become Naiads, water-nymphs.

10011 ff.   They enter into the cultivation of the vine and the celebrations of the vintage.

10033   *Old Silenus' eary beast*: Silenus, the Satyr, the goat-man, companion and teacher of Dionysus, riding on a donkey. The scene ends in drunken riot and noise, like the satyr-play performed in classical theatre after the tragedy. In the stage directions Mephistopheles puts off the role of Phorcyas. He has had a directing part in the whole of Faust's episode with Helen and would be well able to comment sardonically on it. Classical tragedians wore buskins (thick-soled boots), a mask and a veil between the mask and the face.

ACT FOUR

High Mountains

10039   *A cloud approaches*: This 'cloudy carriage' (10041), formed of Helen's discarded clothing (see stage direction at 9954), has conveyed Faust through time and space out of the classical zone into the northern modernity of Act One. His soliloquy is in iambic tetrameters, as though he were still lingeringly connected to the world of Act Three.

10044–66   *The mass, with a clenched intent ... being away with it*: Two forms of cloud are described. The first, like cumulus, drifts away eastwards, back towards Greece, in a shape resembling the classical beauty of Juno, Leda or Helen. The second (at 10055), like cirrus, reminds Faust of his first love, the young girl Gretchen, and prefigures her appearance in the final scene of the play. Goethe was much interested in clouds. He read the English meteorologist Luke Howard (who gave the clouds their names in 1803) and wrote a good deal on the subject himself, in prose and in verse.

10061   *Aurora's love*: The sense is that Gretchen was Faust's first love, the 'dawn' of his new life.

10067   *A seven-league boot*: As in Perrault's fairy story *Hop o' my Thumb*, this is a boot which enables the wearer to stride seven leagues at every step.

10094   *Ephesians 6:12*: Here and elsewhere in Acts Four and Five Goethe himself added biblical references in more or less ironic commentary on his text. The verse reads, 'For we wrestle not against flesh and blood, but against principalities, against powers, against the rulers of the darkness of this world, against spiritual wickedness in high places.'

10109   *rock-smithying Moloch's hammer*: Moloch appears in Milton's *Paradise Lost* (I.392–405 and II.43 ff.) as a particularly violent ally of Satan in the revolt against God. In Klopstock's *Messiah* (II.352 ff.), the epic poem closely modelled on Milton's, he has his home among mountains, as here.

10131 *Matthew 4*: More precisely, verses 8–11, where Satan takes Jesus 'up into an exceeding high mountain', and shows him 'all the kingdoms of the world, and the glory of them', to tempt him.

10176 *Sardanapalus*: Babylonian king, famous for luxury and debauch. Byron dedicated his play of that name (1821) to Goethe.

10321 *Peter Squenz*: Alluding to *Absurda Comica oder Herr Peter Squenz* by Andreas Gryphius (1657 or 1658), which itself derives from the Bottom–Peter Quince scenes in Shakespeare's *A Midsummer Night's Dream*. Here Peter seems intended to represent in his one person a whole amateur hotch-potch.

10322 *THREE MIGHTY MEN (2 Samuel 23:8)*: By the reference we are directed to King David's three champions in his war against the Philistines. Mephistopheles enlists their colossal violence for the Emperor. In 2 Samuel they have Hebrew names; Goethe gives them German 'speaking names': Raufebold, Habebald and Haltefest, which have been variously translated, their essences being 'fighting', 'grabbing' and 'holding tight to what you have grabbed'. They are allegorical figures in the manner of Baroque drama.

On the Foothills

10417 *Once in the realm of fire . . .*: The Emperor recalls his fiery experience in Act One (see 5989 ff.).

10439 *Norcia's necromancer, the Sabine*: Goethe knew from his translation of Benvenuto Cellini's *Autobiography* (Book II, chapter 1) that Norcia, in the Sibilline Hills, was famous for necromancy; and in his note XII on Cellini's book he mentions Cecco d'Ascoli, who was burned in Florence in 1327, accused of that art. He invents the story of the Sabine necromancer, the first half of which is, so to speak (the Emperor confirms it), true; the latter part – that one good turn deserves another – being Faust's fiction.

10531 *LOOTFAST*: See Isaiah 8:3. In Luther's Bible the name of the prophetess's child – left in Hebrew in the Authorized Version – is translated as Raubebald/Eilebeute. The first Goethe adapted for one of his Three Mighty Men (see 10323), the second, meaning 'hurry to loot', he gives to the camp-follower here.

10588 *Fata Morgana*: 'A kind of mirage most frequently seen in the Strait of Messina, attributed in early times to fairy agency' (*OED*). The etymology is interesting: Italian *fata*, a fairy, and *Morgana*,

sister of the British legendary hero Arthur, apparently located in
Calabria by the Norman settlers.

10593–600   *Each tall spear ... Dioscuri*: Like St Elmo's fire, 'the ball
of light which is sometimes seen on a ship (especially about the
masts or yard-arms) during a storm' (*OED*). For the Dioscuri, see
7370 and note. During a storm on the *Argo*, stars hovered over
their heads. As gods, they looked after sailors in distress.

10606   *that eminent master*: The necromancer of Norcia. He is also
the owner of the white whiskers at 10615 and the Archbishop
alludes to him at 10988–90. The Emperor (10612–17) recalls how
he intervened to save him.

10712   *undines*: Female water-spirits. See also *Part I*, 1274.

10772   *Guelphs and Ghibellines*: See 4845 and note.

The Anti-Emperor's Tent

10791   *morning-star of steel*: 'A weapon consisting of a heavy ball set
with spikes and either attached to the head of a club or connected
to a handle by a length of chain' (*OED*).

10849   *Be all that as it may ...*: The verse until the end of the act is
rhyming alexandrine couplets, which is the form used in French
classical and German Baroque drama, long out of fashion in Ger-
man when Goethe composed this scene. On the investiture itself,
see Introduction, pp. xxxv–xxxvi.

10930   *ARCHBISHOP (LORD CHANCELLOR)*: Two offices, one spir-
itual, one temporal.

11035   *that very wicked man*: Faust. The Emperor has rewarded
him with the coastal lands, as Mephistopheles said he would at
10304–6.

ACT FIVE

Open Country

11051–2   *Now I wish to bless the pair ... who took me in*: Goethe
adopts the story of Philemon and Baucis, who, unlike all others
in the neighbourhood, gave hospitality to Jupiter and Mercury,
travelling in disguise, and were rewarded for it by being allowed
to die, when their time came, at the same moment and being then
transformed into a pair of trees. Goethe's reworking of Ovid's
version (*Metamorphoses* VIII) is of great interest. In Ovid the

angry gods flood the land, for example, saving only Philemon and
Baucis: Faust drains it, and murders them.

11143   *LYNCEUS*: See 7377 and note.

11170   *The patron*: Here in the sense of the ships' owner.

11196   *Croesus*: The last king of Lydia (reigned *c.* 560–546 BC),
renowned for his very great wealth.

11287   *Naboth's vineyard . . . (1 Kings 21)*: Goethe supplies the refer-
ence for the biblical story of Naboth, whose vineyard King Ahab
coveted. Ahab's wife, Jezebel, then plotted against Naboth and
had him killed.

Midnight

11384   *My name is Debt*: The German word is *Schuld*, which can mean
either 'debt' or 'guilt', and that latter sense, in reading and in
translating, has sometimes been preferred here. But 'debt' is much
more likely. Of the four grey visitants only Care enters; the other
three, Want, Debt and Need, cannot enter because Faust is rich.
True, he is also guilty, but only briefly and very inadequately does
he feel himself to be. Care – the German word is *Sorge* – might
also be thought of as 'anxiety', especially in her speeches 11453–
66 and 11471–86.

In the Palace's Great Forecourt

11512   *lemurs*: Spirits of the dead in Roman mythology – not the
wide-eyed nocturnal mammals of Madagascar, though when Lin-
naeus named these he doubtless had the spirits in mind. Goethe
uses the word of the skeletal and decomposing corpses still able to
move and dance that are depicted in a painting on a tomb near
Cumae (see his essay 'Griechisches Grabmal bei Cumae' (A Greek
Tomb near Cumae)), and that is how they should be imagined in
this scene.

11531–8, 11604–7   *When I was young . . . beyond your needs*: Goethe
reworks the gravedigger's song in *Hamlet* (V.1.61–4, 71–4, 94–
7), using the version of it printed by Bishop Percy in his *Reliques
of Ancient English Poetry* (1765; I.161).

11542–3   *Curbing the proud waves . . . with doors*: Faust arrogates
to himself powers that in Job 38:8–11 God, in similar words,
calls his.

11556–8   In these lines Faust speaks of digging a ditch or trench;
Mephistopheles replies *sotto voce* that they are digging his grave.

There is a pun in German on *Graben* (ditch) and *Grab* (grave) which translators have to manage the best they can.

11582 *Bide here, you are so beautiful!*: So Faust utters the words he wagered he never would utter (see *Part I*, 1700) but in so conditional a fashion – looking to a future satisfaction – that it is not clear whether Mephistopheles has won or not. On this and the whole question of damnation and salvation, see Introduction, pp. xxxviii–xli.

11594 *It falls and it is finished*: Alluding to *Part I*, 1705 and to Christ's words on the cross (John 19:30): 'It is finished.'

Entombment

11608–11 *Who furnished the room ... creditors*: See 11531–8, 11604–7 and note. Here Goethe adds lines of his own to the Shakespeare/Bishop Percy song.

11613 *my entitlement, blood-signed*: See *Part I*, 1736–7.

11635 *fugleman*: 'A soldier especially expert and well drilled, formerly placed in front of a regiment or company as an example or model to the others in their exercises' (*OED*).

11742 *When I catch you you're sloppy gelatine*: The roses become disgusting to his touch as did the Lamiae at 7770 ff.

11770 *Lucifer's progeny*: See also 11696 ('They're devils too, but in disguise'). The devils, Lucifer their chief, were angels before they fell from heaven. In that sense Mephistopheles, a devil, and the alluring Chorus of Angels are related. And it may be said of these angels that their tactics towards Mephistopheles are devilish.

11809 *Boil on boil, like Job*: See Job 2:7. Boils were among the many afflictions visited on Job by God and Satan in their wager. Mephisto's comparison is of course ironic since the Job-figure in the story, beginning with the 'Prologue in Heaven' in *Part I*, is Faust.

Peaks and Ravines

11844 *Trees ... anchorites ... clefts between*: The setting and some of the figures of this scene derive from engravings, which Goethe knew well, of frescoes in the Campo Santo at Pisa. They depict early Christian anchorites (hermits) disposed at various levels in a landscape – supposedly the Theban wilderness – of rocks, forest and rushing waters.

11854 *PATER ECSTATICUS* ... : The three Fathers and the Doctor are
presented in order of ascending knowledge and sanctity, the first,
'Ecstaticus', marked by his ability to levitate.

11866 *PATER PROFUNDUS*: An epithet traditionally given to
St Bernard of Clairvaux (1090–1153), who, in Dante's *Paradiso*,
is the poet's final conductor into the vision of God.

11890 *PATER SERAPHICUS*: An epithet given to St Francis of Assisi
(1182–1226).

11936–7 *The striver, the endeavourer, him/ We are able to redeem*:
In his manuscript Goethe set quotation marks around these lines to
emphasize them. On their significance, see Introduction, p. xxxix.

11956 *amiant*: (Or amianthus) a kind of asbestos. This substance was
believed in legend to be either incombustible or, if lit, inextinguish-
able. The sense here seems to be that however pure (having passed
through the fires) an earthly remnant might be, still it is not pure
enough for the angels.

11989 *DOCTOR MARIANUS*: The epithet indicates his particular
devotion to the Virgin Mary. Being at the highest and purest
level, he is a part of the celebration of Eternal Woman which
is the climax of this scene and of the play. In the final canto of
Dante's *Paradiso*, St Bernard supplicates Mary on the poet's
behalf.

12032 *MATER GLORIOSA*: That is, the Virgin Mary in Glory, in con-
trast to the Mater Dolorosa, Our Lady of Sorrows, to whom
Gretchen prayed in *Part I* (3587 ff.). See also note to 12069–72.

12037 *MAGNA PECCATRIX (Luke 7:36)*: This is the 'woman, which
was sinner', generally thought to be Mary Magdalene, whom
Christ forgives. The episode is related in Luke 7:36–50.

12045 *MULIER SAMARITANA (John 4)*: The Samaritan woman, whom
Christ meets at Jacob's Well and says to her: 'Give me to drink.'
She is a sinner, perhaps, in that she has had five husbands and is
now living with a man who is not her husband. The encounter is
related in John 4:5–42.

12053 *MARIA AEGYPTIACA (Acta Sanctorum)*: The Egyptian Mary,
whose story is told, under 2 April, in the *Acta Sanctorum* (Acts of
the Saints), a calendar of the lives of the saints and martyrs put
together in the seventeenth–nineteenth centuries, and before that
in the thirteenth-century *Golden Legend* by Jacobus de Voragine.
This Mary was a prostitute for seventeen years who repented when
she found herself barred by a mysterious force from entering the
Temple in Jerusalem. She did penance then in the desert for forty-
seven years. At the end of her life she was given the sacrament by

the monk Zosimus, and, when she died, left a message in the sand
for him, that he should bury her.

12069–72   *You without equal ... mine*: The lines echo and change
Gretchen's prayer to the Mater Dolorosa in *Part I*, 3587 ff. She
appears here as Una Poenitentium, one of the penitent women.

PENGUIN CLASSICS

MOZART'S JOURNEY TO PRAGUE AND SELECTED POEMS
EDUARD MÖRIKE

'In his creative work, as in his pleasures,
Mozart exceeded any limit he could set himself'

Mozart and his charming young wife Constanza are en route to Prague for the opening of *Don Giovanni* when the composer absent-mindedly wanders into the garden of a noble Bohemian family and finds himself the unwitting guest of honour at their daughter's wedding. This delightfully high-spirited novella paints an unforgettable picture of Mozart's creative genius – its playful heights and its terrible depths. Mörike's own lyrical powers are displayed in an extensive collection of his poetry, which includes his most popular romantic and classical folk and fairy tale poems, among them the comic idyll 'The Auld Weathercock'.

The only dual-language version of the poetry available in paperback, this volume also includes an appendix on Mörike and Hugo Wolf, who set Mörike's poems to music.

'Annotated with scholarly tact, finely rendered into English ... this selection from Mörike is a joy, in just harmony with its content' George Steiner, *Observer*

Translated with an introduction and notes by David Luke

PENGUIN CLASSICS

BEYOND GOOD AND EVIL
FRIEDRICH NIETZSCHE

'That which is done out of love always takes place beyond good and evil'

Beyond Good and Evil confirmed Nietzsche's position as the towering European philosopher of his age. The work dramatically rejects the tradition of Western thought with its notions of truth and God, good and evil. Nietzsche demonstrates that the Christian world is steeped in a false piety and infected with a 'slave morality'. With wit and energy, he turns from this critique to a philosophy that celebrates the present and demands that the individual imposes their own 'will to power' upon the world.

This edition includes a commentary on the text by the translator and an introduction by Michael Tanner, which explains some of the more abstract passages in *Beyond Good and Evil*.

'One of the greatest books of a very great thinker' Michael Tanner

Translated by R. J. Hollingdale with an introduction by Michael Tanner

THE STORY OF PENGUIN CLASSICS

Before 1946 ... 'Classics' are mainly the domain of academics and students; readable editions for everyone else are almost unheard of. This all changes when a little-known classicist, E. V. Rieu, presents Penguin founder Allen Lane with the translation of Homer's *Odyssey* that he has been working on in his spare time.

1946 Penguin Classics debuts with *The Odyssey*, which promptly sells three million copies. Suddenly, classics are no longer for the privileged few.

1950s Rieu, now series editor, turns to professional writers for the best modern, readable translations, including Dorothy L. Sayers's *Inferno* and Robert Graves's unexpurgated *Twelve Caesars*.

1960s The Classics are given the distinctive black covers that have remained a constant throughout the life of the series. Rieu retires in 1964, hailing the Penguin Classics list as 'the greatest educative force of the twentieth century.'

1970s A new generation of translators swells the Penguin Classics ranks, introducing readers of English to classics of world literature from more than twenty languages. The list grows to encompass more history, philosophy, science, religion and politics.

1980s The Penguin American Library launches with titles such as *Uncle Tom's Cabin*, and joins forces with Penguin Classics to provide the most comprehensive library of world literature available from any paperback publisher.

1990s The launch of Penguin Audiobooks brings the classics to a listening audience for the first time, and in 1999 the worldwide launch of the Penguin Classics website extends their reach to the global online community.

The 21st Century Penguin Classics are completely redesigned for the first time in nearly twenty years. This world-famous series now consists of more than 1300 titles, making the widest range of the best books ever written available to millions – and constantly redefining what makes a 'classic'.

The Odyssey continues ...

The best books ever written

PENGUIN (🐧) CLASSICS

SINCE 1946